The Elemental Guardians

By George London

© 2024 by [George London]

All rights reserved. No part of this publication may be reproduced, distributed, or transmitted in any form or by any means, including photocopying, recording, or other electronic or mechanical methods, without the prior written permission of the publisher, except in the case of brief quotations embodied in critical reviews and certain other noncommercial uses permitted by copyright law.

This book is a work of fiction. Names, characters, businesses, organizations, places, events, and incidents either are the product of the author's imagination or are used fictitiously. Any resemblance to actual persons, living or dead, events, or locales is entirely coincidental.

Introduction

Under the celestial tapestry of the night, the forest was alive with the whispers of ancient trees and the soft murmur of nocturnal creatures. In a small clearing, surrounded by the towering sentinels of nature, our four adventurers lay in slumber, their breaths gentle in the cool air. The campfire had dwindled to a bed of glowing embers, casting a faint, protective light over the group.

Nathan, with his mechanic's hands folded across his chest, dreamed of martial arts mastery, his spirit restless even in sleep. Lucy, her archaeologist's mind ever curious, twitched slightly as she delved into dreams of undiscovered ruins and hidden treasures. Ayden, the young priest, lay serene, a soft smile gracing his lips as he communed with the divine in his dreams. And Hadley, the aspiring singer, her chest rising and falling rhythmically, hummed a faint melody that seemed to harmonize with the forest's nocturne.

Beside them, their loyal canine companions were also at rest, each curled up close to their respective owners. Gizmo, the tiny warrior in a teacup Chihuahua's body; Ellie, the small but fierce protector; and Jack, the doodle hound with a heart as big as his bark, all lay in peaceful repose.

But as the night deepened, a change began to stir. The fragments of the mysterious stone they had found earlier that day started to emit a soft, pulsating glow. It was a silent call that beckoned the sleepers to awaken. And as the light grew stronger, it promised to unveil powers beyond their wildest imaginations, heralding the dawn of a new chapter in their lives. The adventure was about to take an extraordinary turn, and the awakening of their true
potential was imminent.

Chapter 1: The Mysterious Bayou

Nathan, a young man with a fervent passion for martial arts and combat fighting, hailed from the picturesque city of Albany. Since his childhood, he found solace and fascination in the art of combat, surrounded by the breathtaking landscapes of his hometown. His days were a blend of honing his skills at the local gym and delving into the intricate mechanisms of cars as a mechanic.

In Albany, Nathan's elder sister Lucy shared his ardor for combat sports. A formidable archaeologist by profession, Lucy was renowned for her prowess in cage fighting and boxing. Despite her tough exterior, she held a soft spot for K-Pop music and indulged in leisurely TV shows during her downtime.

Across the neighboring town of DeRidder, their cousins Ayden and Hadley led lives marked by spiritual and artistic pursuits. Ayden, a devout young priest, had traversed the globe in pursuit of profound insights into the teachings of the Holy Bible. His journey bestowed upon him a deep understanding of diverse religious doctrines.

Meanwhile, Hadley, the youngest of the quartet, harbored dreams of becoming a renowned singer. Her artistic endeavors manifested in daily vocal exercises, fueled by aspirations to share her melodious talents with the world.

United by familial bonds and shared adventures, the group embarked on a fateful camping expedition into the heart of the woods. Accompanied by their cherished canine companions—Nathan's diminutive Chihuahua, Gizmo, Lucy's loyal Ellie, and Ayden and Hadley's affectionate doodle hound, Jack—they ventured forth, unaware of the transformative journey awaiting them amidst the wilderness.

The family arrived at the edge of the Bayou, their excitement palpable. Nathan, Lucy, Hadley, and Ayden stepped out of the car and took in the sight before them. The dense foliage loomed over them, creating an enchanting canopy that seemed to whisper secrets.

The family continued to set up their campsite near the Mysterious Bayou, the excitement of the unknown swirling around them like the mystic whispers that hung in the air.

Nathan carefully placed a small dog bed next to their tent, gently settling Gizmo, the tiny teacup Chihuahua, into it. Lucy, with Ellie the white Chihuahua, in her arms, chuckled at Gizmo's curious sniffing of the unfamiliar surroundings.

"Hadley, be sure Jack is comfortable too," Nathan called out, looking over his shoulder at his cousin. Hadley crouched down, patting the light brown doodle hound's head affectionately. Jack wagged his tail, seemingly captivated by the mysterious vibes of the Bayou.

As the family settled in, the four-legged companions seemed to sense the otherworldly energy. Gizmo's ears perked up, and Ellie's eyes widened as if she, too, could hear the ancient whispers. Jack's keen senses picked up on the subtle vibrations, and he let out a low, curious woof.

Nathan gathered the family together near the flickering campfire, the warmth contrasting with the cool Bayou breeze. "I know it might sound crazy, but I feel like this trip is more than just a vacation," he began, his eyes gleaming with excitement.

"There's something in the air, something magical." Lucy nodded in agreement, gently cradling Ellie in her arms. "I think our furry friends sense it too," she said, glancing down at the Chihuahuas, who seemed to be gazing into the depths of the Bayou with a mix of curiosity and enchantment.

Hadley looked at Jack, her eyes reflecting the flickering firelight. "There's a connection here, a bond between us and this mystical place," she mused, her voice filled with wonder.

Ayden, who had been silently observing, spoke up. "It's as if the Bayou is calling to us, beckoning us to uncover its secrets," he said, his gaze fixed on the dark expanse before them.

Nathan nodded, a sense of determination in his eyes. "Well then, let's embrace this adventure. Tomorrow, we explore the heart of the Bayou and see what mysteries it holds for us."

As the family settled in for the night, the Bayou echoed with the whispers of a thousand untold stories, promising a journey into the supernatural that would forever change their lives.

Nathan turned to his family with a mischievous grin. "All right, folks, let's set up camp and get ready for an adventure we'll never forget!"

Lucy nodded eagerly, her fiery red hair reflecting the sunlight. "I can't wait to explore this mysterious place. I have a feeling there's something extraordinary waiting for us.

" As they began pitching their tents and arranging their belongings near the water's edge, a gentle breeze swept through the Bayou, carrying whispers that danced in the air. The family exchanged curious glances, their senses tingling with anticipation.

As dusk settled over the Bayou, a gentle breeze rustled through the trees, carrying with it whispers that seemed to emanate from the heart of the mystical realm. The family huddled closer together near their campsite, their senses heightened and curiosity piqued.

Nathan's sharp eyes scanned the surrounding trees, his instincts on high alert. He turned to his family, a furrow forming on his brow. "Do you hear that?" he asked quietly, his voice barely above a whisper. "It's like the wind is carrying secrets."

Lucy nodded, her fierce gaze narrowing as she listened intently. "I hear it too," she confirmed, a shiver running down her spine. "The air feels charged with something...otherworldly."

Hadley's midnight black hair swayed gently in the breeze as she gazed into the depths of the Bayou. The whispers seemed to call out to her, enticing her with promises of hidden knowledge. "There's more to this place than meets the eye," she murmured, her voice filled with awe.

"I can't help but feel drawn to it." Ayden closed his eyes and focused on the subtle vibrations that danced through the air. The divine forces seemed to grow stronger as darkness fell upon them. "There's a harmony here," he said softly, his voice carrying a sense of reverence. "A sacred energy that beckons us to embrace our destinies."

The family exchanged knowing glances, their hearts pounding with excitement and trepidation. Their fingertips tingle with anticipation as they stood at the threshold of a hidden world that awaited them.

As night descended upon the Bayou, shadows lengthened and the whispers grew louder, weaving an enchanting tapestry of ancient prophecies and forgotten tales. Nathan looked at his family, determination shining in his eyes.

"We can't ignore this," he said firmly. "We were chosen for a reason." Lucy nodded in agreement, her fiery spirit only intensified by the mysterious whispers. "We have to embrace whatever lies before us," she declared. "We're protectors now, and we won't back down from whatever challenges may come our way."

Hadley's green eyes sparkled with curiosity and a thirst for knowledge. "We're on the verge of uncovering secrets and unraveling mysteries that have been concealed for centuries," she whispered. Ayden placed a reassuring hand on each of his siblings' shoulders, his voice filled with calm and wisdom.

"Together, we will navigate this mystical realm," he said softly. "And bring hope and light to those who need it most." Their resolve solidified in that moment as they stood amidst the whispers in the wind, ready to face the unknown and fulfill their roles as guardians of Ember Bay.

As they ventured forth, with their pets with their footsteps mingling with the rustling leaves beneath them, they couldn't help but feel a sense of unity. They were bound together not only by blood but also by destiny.

The night air grew thicker with magic as they ventured further into the heart of the Bayou. Each step brought them closer to unlocking the secrets that awaited them, and they knew that their lives would never be the same again.

But for now, they embraced the exhilarating unknown, following the whispers in the wind that guided their way. Together, they stepped into a new world—one where their destinies would unfold amidst the enchantment of Ember Bay and where their courage would be tested in ways they couldn't yet fathom.

And so, with hearts full of hope and determination, they vanished into the depths of the Bayou, ready to discover what awaited them beyond its mysterious veil. As the family delved deeper into the heart of the Bayou, the air grew thick with mystery and anticipation. The whispers that had beckoned them now surrounded them, swirling in an ethereal dance that drew them further into the unknown.

Nathan's agile movements allowed him to effortlessly navigate through the dense undergrowth. His senses were heightened, attuned to every rustle and every subtle shift in the air. He glanced back at his family, his eyes filled with determination. "We must follow this call," he said softly, his voice steady and resolute.

"Something extraordinary awaits us." Lucy followed closely behind, her fiery red hair shining like a beacon of courage in the moonlight darkness. She felt a surge of adrenaline
coursing through her veins, urging her onward. "I can't explain it," she admitted, her voice alive with excitement. "But I feel a connection to this place—a connection that demands action.

" Hadley's slender frame moved with grace and purpose as she kept pace with the others. Her piercing green eyes scanned their surroundings, taking in every detail with an observant gaze. She could feel the energy in the air, growing stronger with each step. "There's an ancient power here," she murmured, her voice barely above a whisper.

"And it's calling us to uncover its secrets." Ayden's calm and gentle presence provided a steadfast anchor for the group. He moved with an air of serenity, his steps guided by intuition and divine vibrations. As they ventured deeper into the mystical realm, he closed his eyes briefly, drawing upon his inner strength.

"We are destined to bring harmony and healing to this place," he said softly, his voice filled with compassion. "And I believe our journey begins here." The whispers in the wind seemed to guide their path, leading them further into the heart of Ember Bay.

The trees loomed larger and more otherworldly, their branches intertwining like ancient guardians watching their progress. Suddenly, a clearing appeared before them—a sacred space bathed in moonlight. The atmosphere was charged with an undeniable energy that pricked their skin and quickened their pulses.

Nathan looked around, a sense of awe washing over him. "This place feels...sacred," he whispered reverently. Lucy nodded in agreement, her vibrant heart pulsating with anticipation. "It's like stepping into another realm entirely," she marveled. Hadley's eyes widened as she took in the mythical creatures carved into the surrounding trees—an homage to the protectors who came before them.

"These carvings tell a story," she mused aloud. "A story we are meant to discover." Ayden stepped forward slowly, his hands reaching out to touch one of the carvings gently. As soon as his fingertips made contact, a surge of celestial energy coursed through him, reverberating throughout his entire being. He turned to face his family, his eyes sparkling with newfound clarity and purpose.

"Our journey has only just begun," he declared, his voice infused with certainty. "In this sacred place, we will unlock our true potential and unveil the hidden truths that lie within us." The family stood together within the moonlit clearing, their hearts aligned with a shared mission—to protect Ember Bay from supernatural threats and fulfill their destinies as elemental guardians.

The whispers in the wind echoed around them, now clearer than ever before. They were no longer distant murmurs but guiding voices that urged them forward. With renewed determination and unwavering resolve, Nathan, Lucy, Hadley, and Ayden took one last deep breath before stepping further into the sacred space.

Their journey had only just begun, but they were ready to embrace whatever challenges lay ahead. Together, they would uncover the ancient prophecies that bound them to this mystical realm and face the darkness that threatened Ember Bay.

As they disappeared into the depths of the clearing, following the whispers in the wind, they left behind their previous lives and embarked on an extraordinary adventure—one that would test their strength, forge unbreakable bonds between them, and determine the fate of not only themselves but also all those who called Ember Bay home.

Little did they know that their legendary journey would soon propel them into battles against formidable foes and lead them to encounter mythical creatures beyond their wildest imaginations. But for now, in this sacred space where time seemed to stand still, they embraced their role as protectors and guardians of Ember Bay—ready to face their destiny head-on and forever change the course of history.

With hearts ablaze and minds alight with curiosity, Nathan, Lucy, Hadley, and Ayden pressed deeper into the heart of the Bayou. "Let's camp here for the night," Nathan suggested in anticipation of the unknown sparking in their eyes.

As the morning sun cast its golden rays over their campsite, the family eagerly continued their journey into the depths of the mysterious Bayou. "Look, Hadley!" shouted with her finger outstretched toward a hidden cave entrance.

Without hesitation, they entered the cavern, where a dim light revealed a makeshift table surrounded by ancient stones. In the soft illumination, each stone pulsed with a unique essence, filling the air with an electrifying energy. The cave held a silent invitation, and the family gathered around the table.

Four stones, each with its distinct glow, beckoned them. Nathan, drawn to a deep shade of black, reached out and grasped his stone. Its surface shimmered with a shadowy aura, sending a chill down his spine as he held it tightly. The coolness against his palm was a conduit for a surge of power, coursing through his veins like an electric current. Lucy's eyes gleamed with excitement as she took hold of her stone.

It was a vibrant shade of red, emanating a fierce force that seemed to dance across her fingertips. She felt a surge of strength and determination, knowing that this stone held the power she needed to protect her loved ones. Hadley marveled at her stone's beauty as she gently cradled it in her hands. Its color shifted from shades of green to blue, casting an ethereal glow upon her skin.

As she focused on its radiant energy, she could feel a sense of enchantment stirring within her, beckoning her toward her destiny. Ayden's fingers curled around his cross pendant, feeling its warmth permeate throughout his being.

The cross glowed with a celestial light, illuminating his surroundings and filling him with inner peace. As he closed his eyes, he could feel a divine presence guiding his every step.

The family looked at one another with awe and wonder, their hearts filled with gratitude for the powers bestowed upon them by the enchanted stones.

They knew that these artifacts held the key to unlocking their true potential and fulfilling their destinies as guardians. Nathan's voice broke the silence as he lifted his gaze from the stone to meet the eyes of his siblings. "We have been chosen," he said, his voice steady and filled with conviction.

"These stones are not mere objects—they are our guides, our sources of power." Lucy nodded in agreement, her fiery red hair catching the sunlight. "With these stones," she said, her voice brimming with determination, "we will become unstoppable.

" Hadley's eyes sparkled with curiosity as she studied her stone intently. "I can't help but wonder," she mused aloud, "what secrets lie within these stones? What hidden truths will they reveal?" Ayden's gentle smile reassured his family as he clasped his pendant tightly.

"These stones are vessels of immense power," he said softly. "But they also carry the weight of responsibility—the responsibility to protect Ember Bay from darkness and restore balance to this sacred place.

" Nathan tightened his grip on his stone, his eyes shining bright with resolve. "Our journey begins here," he declared, his voice echoing with authority. "We will learn to harness the powers within us and channel them towards protecting those who cannot protect themselves.

" Lucy's fierce gaze met her brother's, her voice filled with unwavering determination. "We won't let anything stand in our way," she vowed. "No matter what trials we face or enemies we encounter, we will stand strong together.

" Hadley nodded in agreement, her midnight black hair framing her face like a cloak of shadows. "We're not alone in this," she stated firmly.

"These stones have united us—bound us together for a shared purpose." Ayden's calming presence enveloped the group as he gazed at each member with compassion in his eyes. "We will support one another," he said softly.

"Through darkness and light, our bond will remain unbreakable." With renewed determination and unity, Nathan, Lucy, Hadley, and Ayden stood shoulder to shoulder—their hands clutching their respective stones tightly.

They were ready to embrace their destinies and face whatever challenges lay ahead. As they looked towards the horizon, their hearts filled with hope and anticipation—a new chapter in their lives had begun.

With their enchanted stones in hand, they would embark on an extraordinary journey—one that would test their limits but also reveal the strength that resided within them. Little did they know that their path would lead them into encounters with mythical creatures, battles against formidable foes, and the unraveling of ancient prophecies that held the fate of Ember Bay.

But for now, in this moment of unity and empowerment, they knew that they were more than just individuals—they were elemental guardians entrusted with protecting the Bayou from supernatural threats. And so, as the sun continued its ascent into the sky, Nathan, Lucy, Hadley, and Ayden exchanged determined glances—one step closer to embracing their roles as Elemental Guardians and ushering in a new era for Ember Bay.

The family stood in awe as they looked at each other, the weight of their newfound powers sinking in. The enchanted stones pulsated with energy, their colorful hues reflecting the uniqueness of each individual.

Nathan's usually aloof expression was replaced with a steely resolve. He tightened his grip on his stone, feeling the darkness within him align with its shadowy essence. "I've always been a ninja at heart," he said confidently.

"But now, I have the power to match." Lucy's fiery determination intensified as she stared at her stone. Its vibrant force seemed to seep into every fiber of her being, igniting a flame that burned brighter than ever before.

"I am an Amazonian guardian," she declared. "And no one will dare threaten the ones I love." Hadley's eyes shone with curiosity and excitement as she marveled at her stone's soft glow. She could feel the pull of the ancient civilization beckoning her, urging her to uncover its hidden truths. "I am the Night Owl," she whispered to herself.

"A keeper of secrets and a seeker of knowledge." Ayden's face softened with compassion and wisdom as he held his cross pendant close to his heart. The celestial light radiating from it filled him with a profound sense of peace and purpose.

"I am a healer," he said softly. "With the power to soothe and restore balance." In this moment of realization, the family exchanged determined glances, understanding that their lives would never be the same again. They were chosen not only to protect Ember Bay but also to embrace their true selves and unlock the potential within. Nathan stepped forward, his voice resolute.

"We are no longer ordinary individuals," he proclaimed. "We are guardians, destined to defend this sacred place from supernatural threats." His eyes met each family member, conveying both strength and unity. Lucy nodded in agreement, her fiery spirit burning bright in her emerald gaze.

"Together, we will be unstoppable," she declared. "With our combined powers, we will bring light to the darkest corners of Ember Bay." Hadley's eyes danced with anticipation, eager to explore the mysteries that awaited them. "We are bound together on this journey," she said, her voice filled with conviction.

"And nothing will stand in our way." Ayden smiled warmly at his family, his voice carrying a soothing reassurance. "We must remember that our powers come with great responsibility," he reminded them gently.

"We have been entrusted with safeguarding not only Ember Bay but also the harmony of all existence." With their goals set and their roles defined, the family knew that they had a long road ahead. They needed to master their powers, strengthen their bond as a team, and face the formidable enemy that awaited them.

But for now, they stood together in unwavering determination. "We will train endlessly," Nathan stated firmly. "To become masters of our craft." Lucy clenched her fist, fueling her determination further.

"We will push ourselves beyond our limits," she said fiercely. "To protect those who cannot protect themselves." Hadley's eyes sparkled with eagerness to learn and grow.

"We will unlock the hidden secrets of our enchantments," she vowed passionately. Ayden's calming presence infused them with hope and unity.

"And we will support one another every step of the way," he said softly, his voice filled with wisdom. "For we are stronger together than we could ever be alone." As they basked in the shared understanding of their mission, Jack, Gizmo, and Ellie joined them - transformed into their new majestic forms: a mighty light brown bear, a sleek black wolf, and a regal white lioness.

The family looked upon their animal companions with awe, recognizing the bond between them and their own elemental powers. They knew that together they formed an unbreakable alliance - united by destiny and an unyielding commitment to protect Ember Bay. With hearts full of purpose and minds focused on their goals, the Elemental Guardians departed from their campsite - ready to embark on a journey filled with adventure, danger, and self-discovery.

They would face battles unlike any they had encountered before as they sought to master their abilities and vanquish darkness forever. But deep within their souls burned a fire that could not be extinguished - a fire sparked by their unwavering belief in themselves and their shared destiny. And so, as they ventured forth into the unknown, surrounded by the enchantment of Ember Bay and guided by the whispers in the wind, they embraced the challenges ahead with courage and determination.

Their destinies were entwined with each other and with the very fabric of Ember Bay itself. Little did they know that their journey would test them in unimaginable ways, forcing them to confront not only external threats but also their own fears and doubts.

But in this moment - standing on the cusp of greatness - they were ready to face whatever lay ahead as they embodied The Elemental Guardians.

As the family ventured deeper into the Bayou, the whispers in the wind grew louder and more distinct. Each step they took brought them closer to their destiny, and an air of anticipation filled their hearts.

Nathan led the way, his movements stealthy and precise, embodying the essence of a true ninja. His eyes gleamed with determination as he scanned the surroundings, alert for any signs of danger. He turned to his family, a smirk playing on his lips.

"We're getting closer," he said, his voice full of confidence. "I can feel it." Lucy followed closely behind Nathan, her fiery hair reflecting the sunlight like a crown of flames. Her fierce gaze never wavered as she surveyed their path ahead. "We've come so far," she remarked, her voice filled with admiration.

"And we won't let anything or anyone stand in our way." Hadley moved gracefully through the shadows, her steps light and silent. Her piercing green eyes darted from tree to tree, taking in every detail of their surroundings. "There's a power here that can't be denied," she whispered to herself, her voice holding a sense of wonder.

"And I'm ready to unlock its secrets." Ayden brought up the rear, his calm presence emanating from him like a protective aura. He observed his surroundings with a serene expression, attuned to the subtle energies flowing through the Bayou.

"We are guardians," he reminded his family gently, his voice filled with wisdom and reassurance. "And together, we have the power to bring balance and healing to this sacred place." The path before them twisted and turned, leading them deeper into the heart of Ember Bay.

The sounds of nature surrounded them - the chirping of birds, the whisper of leaves rustling in the wind - creating an enchanting symphony that echoed their journey.

Suddenly, they came upon a clearing bathed in dappled sunlight. In the center stood a mythical creature, its ethereal form shimmering with all the colors of the rainbow. Nathan's eyes widened with awe as he recognized the creature before them. "It's a Guardian Spirit," he exclaimed, his voice filled with reverence.

Lucy approached cautiously, her hand reaching out to touch the creature's translucent form. As her fingertips made contact, an electric surge passed through her body, igniting a connection that pulsed with strength and guidance.

Hadley stepped forward next, her gaze fixed on the Guardian Spirit's radiant presence. She closed her eyes and allowed herself to be enveloped by its energy, feeling a profound sense of belonging and purpose wash over her.

Ayden approached last, his gentle smile illuminating his features as he basked in the spiritual aura that surrounded them. He held out his hand, and the Guardian Spirit extended one of its shimmering appendages in response, forming an unbreakable bond between them.

Their touch completed a circuit of energy that reverberated through the clearing. The atmosphere was charged with an otherworldly glow as visions filled their minds - glimpses of battles yet to be fought, challenges yet to be overcome, and victories yet to be won.

Nathan's voice broke through their shared connection, bringing them back to their present reality. "This is a sign," he declared with conviction. "We are meant to be here - protectors chosen by the very essence of Ember Bay itself.

" Lucy nodded in agreement, her fierce determination burning brighter than ever before. "This is our destiny," she affirmed. "To stand against the darkness and illuminate this world with our strength and unity.

" Hadley's eyes shone with newfound clarity as she embraced her role among her fellow Guardians. "Together," she said softly but firmly. "We will unravel the mysteries that lie within this realm and confront danger with unwavering resolve.

" Ayden's voice carried the weight of wisdom as he spoke his truth. "Our powers are gifts," he said gently. "Gifts meant to heal and bring harmony to this sacred place. Let us use them wisely and protect what is most dear to us.

" As their words echoed through the clearing, a sense of purpose settled over them like a warm embrace. The Guardian Spirit basked in their resolve, absorbing their intentions and infusing them with divine guidance. With renewed determination burning in their hearts and souls entwined with ancient prophecies, Nathan, Lucy, Hadley, and Ayden left the clearing behind - stepping further into the mystical realm of Ember Bay.

Their journey was only just beginning, and there were trials and tribulations awaiting them - challenges that would test their limits and forces that sought to extinguish their light. But armed with their newfound powers and bound together by a shared mission, they knew that nothing could break their indomitable spirit.

Their destiny awaited them - a destiny entwined with elemental forces and entrusted with safeguarding Ember Bay from darkness. And so they pressed forward - united as Elemental Guardians - ready to embark on an adventure beyond imagination.

Chapter 2: The Whispers of the Bayou

As the family ventured deeper into the heart of the Bayou, following the echoes of mystical whispers, Nathan's ninja senses heightened. He moved stealthily through the dense undergrowth, his agile movements barely making a sound as he navigated the twisting path.

Lucy walked beside him with fierce determination, her fiery red hair matching the intensity in her eyes. "There's something powerful here," Nathan whispered, his voice carrying a hint of excitement.

"I can feel it in the air." Lucy nodded, her hand instinctively reaching for the hilt of her sword. "We're getting closer to the answers we seek," she replied. "I can sense it too." The towering cypress trees formed an enchanting canopy above them, casting dappled shadows on the moss-covered ground.

The air was thick with anticipation, as if every leaf and blade of grass held its breath, waiting for the family to uncover the secrets hidden within the Bayou. A hidden chamber beckoned them forward, concealed within a grove of ancient trees.

Its entrance was flanked by intricately carved symbols and inscriptions, their meaning shrouded in mystery yet undeniably powerful. Nathan and Lucy exchanged glances before stepping inside, their footsteps echoing in the stillness.

As they entered the chamber, its walls revealed themselves in all their mysterious glory. Vibrant murals adorned every inch, depicting scenes of supernatural battles and celestial forces at play. The colors seemed to glow with an ethereal light, reflecting off their faces as they gazed in awe. Hadley's piercing green eyes widened in wonder as she approached a mural that resonated deep within her soul. It depicted water cascading around her, embodying grace and fluidity.

"This is my destiny," she murmured, her voice barely above a whisper. "I am meant to harness the power of water and become the Aquatic Sentinel of Ember Bay." Ayden stood before a mural that showed celestial energy radiating from his outstretched palms. He closed his eyes and breathed deeply, feeling a profound sense of serenity wash over him.

"I am destined to be the Celestial Healer," he whispered, his voice filled with awe. "To channel divine energy and bring peace to this land.

" Nathan's gaze fell upon a mural that depicted him navigating treacherous underground tunnels with his ninja skills fully honed. A surge of determination ignited within him as he studied every detail. "I am the Shadow Warrior," he said with conviction.

"To protect Ember Bay from the shadows and keep our loved ones safe." Lucy's eyes alighted on a mural surrounded by flames, her hair mirroring the intensity of the inferno. She felt a deep connection to the image before her, recognizing her role as the Fiery Guardian of Ember Bay.

"I will fight with everything I have," she declared, her voice infused with fiery determination. "To protect those I hold dear and vanquish any threat that comes our way." Together, they shared their revelations, each piece of the puzzle falling into place as they wove together the fragments of their individual destinies.

Their voices trembled with excitement and determination as they discussed the implications of their newfound roles as protectors of Ember Bay. "We are stronger together," Nathan affirmed, his words resonating with unwavering resolve. "No matter what challenges lie ahead, we will face them united.

" Lucy nodded in agreement, her expression fierce yet determined. "Ember Bay will not fall under darkness while we stand together," she declared. Hadley looked at her fellow protectors with a sense of wonder and purpose shining in her eyes. "Our destinies are intertwined," she said softly. "And together, we will uncover the hidden truths of this ancient civilization.

" Ayden smiled gently at his companions, his presence calming and reassuring. "Let us embrace our roles fully," he suggested, his voice filled with wisdom. "And unlock our true potential as guardians of Ember Bay.

" As they exited the chamber, the whispers of the Bayou seemed to grow louder, congratulating them on embracing their destinies and solidifying their bond as guardians. With renewed purpose and determination, they continued their trek through the mystical landscape, ready to face whatever trials lay ahead.

The Elemental Guardians were now more than just individuals; they were a united force against the impending darkness that threatened their beloved Bayou.

The family's footsteps echoed through the chamber as they approached their respective murals, drawn to the depictions that resonated most with their own essence. Each protector stood before their mural, their eyes fixed on the vibrant imagery that represented their destiny.

Nathan focused his gaze on the underground tunnels depicted in his mural. Shadows danced across his face as he traced the intricate details with his finger. "This is my path," he said softly, his voice tinged with determination.

"I will navigate the treacherous darkness and protect Ember Bay as the Shadow Warrior." Lucy's eyes blazed with fiery intensity as she stood before her mural engulfed in flames. She reached out and touched the painting, feeling a surge of power within her.

"I will be the Fiery Guardian," she declared, her voice steady and strong. "I will wield the flames and shield our loved ones from harm." Hadley's slender fingers traced the water cascading around her in her mural.

She closed her eyes and let the image wash over her, feeling a deep connection to the element. "The Aquatic Sentinel," she whispered, her voice barely audible. "I will harness the waters' power and defend Ember Bay against any threat.

" Ayden's serene presence radiated as he stood before his mural, celestial energy emanating from his outstretched hands. His eyes sparkled with a sense of purpose as he embraced his role. "I am the Celestial Healer," he said softly, his voice filled with compassion. "I will bring balance and healing to Ember Bay.

" Their voices intertwined like a symphony, each protector voicing their destiny and igniting a newfound determination within themselves. The murmurs of the Bayou seemed to grow louder, encouraging them to step into their roles fully. "We are chosen for a reason," Nathan said, his voice carrying a quiet confidence.

"We must embrace our destinies and stand united against the darkness that threatens our home." Lucy nodded, her fiery gaze meeting each of her companions'. "We have been brought together for a purpose," she affirmed.

"Together, we are an unstoppable force." Hadley felt a surge of excitement course through her veins as she looked at her fellow protectors. "Our powers are stronger when we work together," she added, her voice filled with conviction. "We will face whatever challenges come our way as one.

" Ayden smiled warmly at his comrades, love and understanding shining in his gentle eyes. "Let us trust in ourselves and in each other," he suggested, his voice soothing yet resolute. "Our unity will guide us through even the darkest of times." With renewed purpose and unwavering determination, they exited the chamber, their bond solidified by their shared destinies.

The whispers of the Bayou seemed to applaud their resolve as they continued their journey through the mystical landscape. The Elemental Guardians had unveiled the ancient prophecy written within the walls of the hidden chamber.

Each step they took now was fueled by a deeper understanding of their roles as protectors of Ember Bay, their powers honed and ready to face whatever trials lay ahead. As they ventured further into the heart of the Bayou, they could sense that their path was leading them closer to the source of the impending darkness.

But with their newly discovered purpose and unyielding bond, they were prepared to confront any obstacle that dared to threaten their beloved home. The Elemental Guardians had come together, united in their mission to protect Ember Bay and preserve its magical essence for generations to come.

As each family member shared their revelations and embraced their destinies, a deep sense of unity enveloped them.

They looked at each other with a newfound understanding and respect, their individual roles now intertwined into a tapestry of shared purpose.

"We are guardians," Nathan affirmed, his eyes shining with determination. "Together, we will protect Ember Bay from any threat that comes our way." Lucy nodded, her fiery gaze mirroring her indomitable spirit.

"No darkness will prevail while we stand together," she declared, her voice filled with unwavering resolve. Hadley smiled, a mysterious glint in her green eyes. "Our journey has only just begun," she said, her tone brimming with anticipation. "We will uncover the hidden truths of this ancient civilization and defend Ember Bay with all that we have."

Ayden's calming presence grounded the group, his gentle smile offering reassurance. "Let us embrace our roles fully and unlock the true potential within ourselves," he suggested, his voice filled with wisdom.

"Together, we can bring peace and harmony to this land." With fortified resolve and unbreakable bonds, they exited the chamber of murals, feeling a surge of energy coursing through their veins.

The whispers of the Bayou grew louder, almost as if they were celebrating their acceptance and readiness for the challenges that lay ahead. As they continued their journey through the mystical landscape, the guardians felt a subtle shift in the air.

The Bayou seemed to respond to their newfound purpose, guiding them towards their next destination. Suddenly, a gust of wind rustled through the trees, carrying with it a faint melody that danced on their ears like an enchanting lullaby.

The family turned their heads towards the source of the sound and saw a pathway materialize out of thin air, leading them further into the heart of the Bayou. Nathan raised an eyebrow as he observed the ethereal trail before them.

"This seems like our next trial," he noted, his voice tinged with excitement. Lucy's eyes sparkled as she surveyed the path ahead. "It's time to test our connection to nature's elements," she mused, anticipation coursing through her veins.

Hadley nodded in agreement, her green eyes shining with intrigue. "Let us embrace these trials and prove ourselves worthy of our titles," she suggested, her voice full of determination.

Ayden smiled gently at his companions, his presence a calming force amidst the growing anticipation. "Remember to trust in your abilities and in each other," he reminded them, his voice soothing yet firm.

"Together, we are unstoppable." With renewed purpose and unwavering determination, they stepped onto the newly formed path, feeling nature's energy course through their bodies.

The whispers of the Bayou guided their every step as they embarked on their next set of trials.

As they ventured further into the mystical realm, they could feel the weight of responsibility resting upon their shoulders. But with their shared purpose and unwavering bond, they knew that no obstacle was insurmountable.

The Elemental Guardians had unveiled the ancient prophecy and accepted their destinies as protectors of Ember Bay. Their journey had only just begun, but they were ready to face whatever challenges awaited them. Together, they would harness nature's power and prove themselves worthy of their titles.

United by strength, courage, and an unyielding belief in their mission, the Elemental Guardians would rise above any darkness that threatened to engulf their beloved land. As they walked along the path bathed in dappled sunlight and accompanied by the whispers of the Bayou, a sense of camaraderie settled into their hearts.

They were ready to carry out their sacred duty and protect Ember Bay with every fiber of their being. The Elemental Guardians had finally fully embraced their destinies as protectors—and now it was time to face their next set of trials head-on. Trial by Elements - Harnessing Nature's Power The family found themselves at the edge of a vast clearing, surrounded by an array of natural wonders representing each element - earth, fire, water, and air.

The earth beneath their feet hummed with ancient power, urging them to heed its call. Towering rock formations dominated one side of the clearing, emanating strength and stability. Nathan stood before them, his ninja senses heightened as he prepared himself for the trials that lay ahead.

Gizmo, his faithful wolf companion, paced beside him, its keen senses attuned to the mystical realm. "We must navigate this labyrinth of stone," Nathan said, his voice steady. "It will test our agility and resourcefulness.

" Gizmo let out a low growl in agreement, its eyes glinting with anticipation. They ventured towards the rocky maze, ready to face whatever challenges awaited them in the depths below. On another side of the clearing, flames danced within an enclosure, crackling with intensity and whispering secrets to Lucy.

She approached the fiery obstacle with unwavering determination, her sword held firmly in her hand. "I must conquer this trial of fire," Lucy declared, her voice resolute. "It will test my endurance and inner strength.

" Ellie, her majestic white lion companion, padded beside her with regal authority. Its golden eyes matched the intensity in Lucy's gaze as they stepped into the ring of flames, ready to face the searing heat.

Cascading waterfalls greeted them on yet another side of the clearing, their gentle roar a soothing melody to Hadley's ears. She felt drawn to the shimmering pool at the base of the falls, its depths inviting her to immerse herself in its cool embrace.

"This trial of water will test my resilience and adaptability," Hadley mused, her voice filled with both excitement and trepidation.

Jack, now transformed into a mighty bear, lumbered alongside her with pride and strength. Its light brown fur blended harmoniously with the surrounding nature as they approached the cascading waters, prepared to conquer the aquatic challenge that awaited them.

A gust of wind rustled leaves overhead on the final side of the clearing, beckoning Ayden towards it. He closed his eyes and allowed the breeze to caress his face, embracing its gentle touch with serenity.

"This spiritual trial will test my connection to the unseen forces," Ayden murmured softly, his voice carried away by the wind. Ayden's cross glowed with celestial light as if acknowledging his words. It radiated warmth and tranquility as they made their way towards an ethereal path that led them deeper into the heart of the Bayou.

With their animal companions by their sides and determination pulsing through their veins, the Elemental Guardians stood together at these elemental challenges. They were ready to harness nature's power and unlock their true potential as protectors of Ember Bay. Nathan surveyed the underground tunnels that awaited him amidst the rock formations.

As he descended into their depths, shadows enveloped him like a cloak. He maneuvered through narrow passages and unexpected turns with silent grace, his ninja skills guiding every step. Gizmo padded silently at his heels, its keen senses alert for any hidden dangers that might lurk in the darkness.

The bond between them was forged not only through trust but also through a shared purpose - to protect Ember Bay from supernatural threats. Lucy faced the roaring flames head-on, its intense heat radiating across her defiant stance.

She raised her sword high in preparation for any fiery adversary that dared approach. Ellie prowled gracefully beside her as they moved swiftly through the searing inferno. With every stride they took together, their unity grew stronger and their determination burned brighter - a testament to their unbreakable bond.

Hadley submerged herself in the crystalline waters with ease and grace. Her body flowed effortlessly with each stroke as she navigated swirling currents and unexpected obstacles. Jack waded alongside her effortlessly, blending into the watery surroundings like a shadow. In tandem, they embraced their roles as guardians of Ember Bay's aquatic realm and let the water guide their every move.

Ayden closed his eyes and allowed celestial energy to flow through him like a gentle breeze. His mind ascended alongside wisps of wind carrying whispers from distant realms. His cross glowed brightly as he communed with higher planes, seeking guidance and enlightenment from unseen forces.

Together with his cross as his beacon and source of power, he harnessed divine energies like a conduit for healing and balance. As each family member faced their respective elemental trials head-on, they found themselves pushed beyond their limits while simultaneously unlocking deeper layers of their powers.

Their strengths were honed and refined through these challenges as they faced adversity together. With every tunnel conquered by Nathan's stealthy movements, every flame quelled by Lucy's fierce resolve, every obstacle overcome by Hadley's fluid adaptability, and every celestial force embraced by Ayden's calm wisdom, the Elemental Guardians grew more formidable with each trial surmounted.

In unity and newfound harmony with nature's elements, they solidified their bond as protectors of Ember Bay and emerged from these elemental trials stronger than ever before. The Elemental Guardians had harnessed nature's power, their connection to earth, fire, water, and air now infused with an unwavering resolve to safeguard their beloved Bayou against any impending darkness.

As they stood at the edge of the elemental challenges, a sense of triumph resonated within them. They knew that no matter what lay ahead, their united strength would carry them through. Together, Nathan, Lucy, Hadley, and Ayden, stood ready, their animal companions by their sides, to face whatever trials awaited them next in this mystical realm.

Nathan emerged from the underground tunnels, a satisfied smile crossing his face. The darkness had challenged him at every turn, but he had navigated the treacherous maze with his agility and stealth intact.

Gizmo, his loyal companion, padded alongside him, their connection stronger than ever. "We did it," Nathan said with a sense of accomplishment. "The shadows have become my ally." Gizmo let out a low growl of agreement, its piercing eyes gleaming in the dim light.

Together, they had conquered the underground labyrinth, proving that they were a force to be reckoned with. Lucy emerged from the ring of flames, her body unscathed despite the searing heat that surrounded her.

Her force fields had shielded her from the inferno, their strength matching her fiery determination. Ellie, her regal lion companion, roared triumphantly as they stepped out of the fiery enclosure. The bond between them had grown even stronger through their shared challenge, and their presence exuded an air of invincibility.

"We are unstoppable," Lucy declared, a fierce glint in her eyes. "The fire bows to our will." Hadley emerged from the cascading waters, her slender form dripping with the element she had conquered. She embodied grace and adaptability as she effortlessly navigated the swirling currents and conquered each water-based obstacle.

Jack, now in his large bear form, shook himself free from the water's embrace. His light brown fur glistened in the sunlight, harmonizing with the surrounding nature. Hadley and Jack stood side by side, a testament to their unity and resilience.

"We have tamed the waters," Hadley said confidently. "No aquatic challenge can daunt us." Ayden emerged from his communion with the unseen forces, his serenity unbroken even in the face of spiritual trials.

His cross glowed brightly, illuminating his path as he rejoined his companions. "The celestial energies flow through me," Ayden stated calmly.

"Harmony and healing are within our grasp." Together, the Elemental Guardians stood tall and united, their newfound powers honed and ready for any challenge that awaited them. Each trial had tested their connection to nature's elements and solidified their purpose as protectors of Ember Bay.

As they looked upon each other with pride and determination, a sense of invincibility washed over them. They had proven themselves worthy of their titles and were prepared to face whatever darkness threatened their beloved Bayou.

Nathan glanced at his three companions, a knowing smile on his face. "This is just the beginning," he said confidently. "We are destined for greatness." Lucy nodded in agreement, her fiery gaze meeting each of her comrades' eyes.

"Embarking on this journey together was no coincidence," she remarked. "We were meant to stand side by side." Hadley's green eyes twinkled with excitement as she surveyed her fellow guardians. "Our unique abilities complement one another," she observed. "We are stronger as a united front.

" Ayden's calming presence grounded the group, his voice filled with wisdom and tranquility. "Let us continue on this path with unwavering resolve," he suggested. "Ember Bay deserves nothing less than our best." With renewed purpose and unwavering determination, they ventured further into the mystical realm, guided by nature's energy and their unbreakable bond.

Their next set of trials awaited them on the horizon, but together they were ready to face anything. As they took their first steps towards the unknown, a symphony of whispers echoed through the Bayou—a chorus of encouragement and support from the very land they vowed to protect. The Elemental Guardians had harnessed nature's power and proven themselves worthy of their titles.

They stood ready for whatever challenges lay ahead—united as an unstoppable force against darkness. Their journey was far from over, but with their shared purpose and unwavering dedication, they would face the trials together—emerging victorious at every turn.

As the Elemental Guardians continued their journey through the Bayou, they felt a sense of anticipation building in the air. The whispers of the elemental forces seemed to grow louder, guiding them towards their next trial.

Nathan, with Gizmo faithfully by his side, approached a massive boulder that stood at the center of the clearing. Sweat dripped down his temples as he surveyed the challenge before him. This trial would test his strength and resilience, pushing him to his limits. "Time to prove my agility," Nathan declared, his voice filled with determination.

He took a deep breath, drawing upon the ninja skills he had honed over the years. With a swift leap, he launched himself onto the boulder, using every muscle in his body to maintain balance.

Gizmo watched from below, its keen eyes tracking Nathan's every move.

As Nathan navigated the treacherous surface of the boulder, Gizmo let out a low growl of encouragement. Their bond grew stronger with every step Nathan took, their movements becoming perfectly synchronized.

Meanwhile, Lucy and Ellie stood before a wall of roaring flames that blocked their path. The intensity of the heat was palpable, but Lucy refused to be intimidated.

She tightened her grip on her sword, her fiery determination matching the blaze before her. "I will bend this fire to my will," Lucy exclaimed, her voice infused with confidence.

With a swift motion, she swung her sword, directing powerful gusts of wind towards the flames. As the wind buffeted against the inferno, it began to wane, leaving an opening for Lucy and Ellie to pass.

Ellie let out a mighty roar as she followed Lucy through the dwindling flames. Her presence exuded regality and authority, and her lion form seemed to radiate power. Their synergy was undeniable as they faced each challenge head-on. Hadley and Jack approached a raging river that surged with untamed energy.

The rushing water threatened to sweep them away, but Hadley refused to be deterred. She closed her eyes and focused on the ebb and flow of the current, attuning herself to its rhythm. "I am one with the water," Hadley whispered, her voice barely audible over the roaring rapids.

With a leap of faith, she dove into the water and allowed its currents to carry her effortlessly downstream. Jack followed closely behind, his bear form gliding smoothly through the water alongside Hadley.

Together, they moved with grace and agility, expertly navigating through the swirling eddies and avoiding submerged obstacles. The water seemed to recognize their mastery over it, eventually guiding them to solid ground on the other side of the river. Ayden approached a serene meadow blanketed in wildflowers and watched as gentle breezes danced among the petals.

He closed his eyes and raised his hands towards the sky, allowing his connection to air to guide him through this trial. "I am one with nature's breath," Ayden breathed softly.

A gentle gust of wind embraced him, lifting him off his feet and carrying him above the meadow. His body seemed weightless as he soared gracefully across the sky.

With every twist and turn in the wind's embrace, Ayden channeled his celestial energy and felt an indescribable sense of freedom. His cross glowed brightly, illuminating his path as he flew higher and higher.

The Elemental Guardians moved through their respective challenges with unwavering determination, their connections to nature's elements growing stronger with each passing moment. They had forged unbreakable bonds not just with each other but also with the very forces they sought to harness.

As they completed their trials and reunited in the center of the clearing, they couldn't help but feel a surge of pride in their accomplishments. Together, they had overcome formidable obstacles that tested their strength, agility, and connection with nature itself.

Nathan extended a hand towards Lucy, Hadley, and Ayden, a smile playing at his lips. "We did it," he declared triumphantly. "Just as we are united in purpose, we must continue to stand together in this journey.

" Lucy clasped Nathan's hand with a firm grip. "Our strength lies not just in our powers but also in our unwavering support for one another," she said fiercely. Hadley nodded in agreement, her eyes shining with newfound confidence. "We have proven time and time again that we can conquer any challenge when we work together," she confirmed.

Ayden joined their circle, his gentle presence calming any lingering doubts or fears. "Let us never forget that our unity is our greatest strength," he added softly. As they stood united in the clearing, surrounded by nature's beauty and infused with its elemental power, they felt an overwhelming sense of gratitude for having found one another.

Their trials had not only strengthened their individual abilities but had also solidified their bond as guardians of Ember Bay. With renewed purpose and unwavering determination burning in their hearts, they set off deeper into the mystical realm of the Bayou.

More trials awaited them on their path—challenges that would test not just their physical abilities but also their emotional fortitude.

But no matter what lay ahead, the Elemental Guardians knew one thing for certain: their unity would guide them through any darkness that threatened Ember Bay.

Chapter 3: The Enigma of the Bayou

Nathan felt a pull in his chest as they ventured deeper into the heart of the Bayou. The whispers grew stronger, urging him forward. Lucy felt the hairs on the back of her neck stand on end, sensing subtle shifts in the air around them.

Hadley's eyes darted around, searching for hidden signs, and Ayden's cross glowed with a divine light, guiding them towards their destination. As they pushed through the dense undergrowth, the sounds of chirping insects and rustling leaves filled the air.

The family was drawn to a secluded clearing, its lush greenery untouched by human hands. Tall ancient trees loomed overhead, creating a natural canopy that blocked out all but slivers of sunlight. In the center of the clearing, vibrant wildflowers burst forth from the earth, their petals shimmering in an array of colors.

Nathan's gaze was immediately drawn to a small mound of leaves near his feet. Something about it called out to him, beckoning him closer. "Hey guys, come look at this," Nathan called out, crouching down to brush away the layers of dust and decay. His fingers tingle with anticipation as he exposes an ancient, crumbling book hidden beneath the mound.

Lucy knelt beside him, her fiery red hair falling over her shoulders as she peered at the book. "Wow, this looks like it's been here for ages," she remarked, her voice filled with awe. Hadley joined them next, her emerald eyes widening with curiosity.

"I've never seen anything like it. It's like we stumbled upon a hidden treasure," she murmured. Ayden approached cautiously, his kind eyes scanning the pages. "There must be something significant about this book.

The Bayou led us here for a reason," he said softly. Carefully flipping open the fragile cover, they were met with pages filled with intricate symbols and enigmatic messages written in a language long forgotten. The words seemed to dance across the yellowed parchment, elusive yet captivating.

Nathan traced his finger along one of the symbols, his mind racing with possibilities. "We need to decipher these clues," he declared, determination shining in his piercing eyes. Lucy nodded in agreement, her fierce gaze fixed on the words before her.

"Agreed. If there's knowledge hidden within these pages, it could help us understand our roles as protectors better." Hadley squinted at one of the messages, her sharp intellect trying to make sense of it all. "It won't be easy, but I'm up for the challenge.

We've come this far; we can't turn back now." Ayden's voice was filled with quiet confidence as he spoke, "Together, we will unravel the mysteries locked within these pages and unlock our true potential as guardians.

" They settled into a circle around the book, engaging in lively discussions and debates about possible interpretations and connections between different clues.

Excitement coursed through their veins as they uncovered fragments of knowledge that hinted at Ember Bay's ancient prophecies and its mystical forces. Hours turned into minutes as they became engrossed in their task, each revelation bringing them closer to understanding their intertwined destinies.

The clearing seemed to hum with an otherworldly energy, amplifying their determination and fueling their desire for answers. "In unison they both said 'we can do this.' They knew that together they would overcome any obstacle that stood in their way.

" Deciphering the Clues The sun began its slow descent, casting long shadows across the clearing as the family immersed themselves in deciphering the enigmatic text. Thoughts clashed and intertwined, intertwining theories and ideas.

Excitement bubbled within them as they pieced together fragments of knowledge and shared their findings. Nathan's eyes narrowed, his mind sharp with ninja-like focus as he traced his finger over a series of interconnected symbols.

"These symbols seem to represent different elements," he said, his voice tinged with excitement. "And look here, this could be a map, guiding us to sacred locations within Ember Bay." Lucy leaned closer, her fiery hair falling over her expressive eyes as she studied the pages. "I think you might be right, Nathan.

And these intricate patterns...they resemble the supernatural creatures we've encountered. Perhaps they hold the key to understanding their weaknesses." Hadley's gaze darted from page to page, her sharp instincts picking up patterns and connections others might have missed. "There's a recurring symbol here," she pointed out, her voice filled with intrigue.

"It appears to be linked to ancient rituals and traditions. Maybe it holds the power to unlock hidden abilities within us." Ayden's gentle presence radiated calmness as he absorbed the information before him. "These messages hint at a delicate balance between light and darkness," he mused, his voice soothing like a cool breeze on a warm day.

"Perhaps by embracing our own shadows and utilizing the light within us, we can tap into the full extent of our powers." The family exchanged glances, their eyes shining with determination and newfound understanding. They had always known they were connected to the supernatural forces of Ember Bay, but now they were beginning to grasp the intricacies of their roles as protectors.

Each revelation propelled them forward, fueling their motivation to unravel the mysteries that lay before them. As they continued their exploration of the ancient book, time seemed to stand still within that secluded clearing. Hours turned into minutes, and yet their vigor did not waver. The language of the text became familiar to them, whispers of forgotten truths settling deep within their souls.

In unison, they would discuss different interpretations and theories, each bringing their unique insights to the table. They debated ideas passionately yet respectfully, cherishing both the similarities and differences in their perspectives. Their conversations echoed through the clearing, mingling with the rustling leaves and distant calls of wildlife.

The air crackled with anticipation as they delved deeper into the enigmatic text, slowly unlocking the secrets long kept hidden within its pages. As night fell upon Ember Bay, stars dotted the velvety sky above them like celestial guideposts on their journey of discovery.

The family huddled together around the ancient book, their connection growing stronger with each passing moment. "We're getting closer," Nathan whispered, his voice filled with determination.

Lucy nodded beside him, her fiery gaze ablaze with newfound purpose. "Together, we will unveil every secret this book holds. We won't stop until we understand our destinies." Hadley's eyes gleamed in the moonlight as she chimed in, her voice steady and confident. "No challenge is too great for us. We will uncover every clue and rise above any obstacle that stands in our way.

" Ayden placed a comforting hand on Nathan's shoulder, his soothing presence radiating wisdom and reassurance. "Remember our mantra - 'Unity in purpose.' Together, we are unstoppable." With renewed energy and a shared determination burning within their hearts, they returned their attention to the ancient book before them.

With every word deciphered and every symbol understood, they moved one step closer to embracing their true potential as Elemental Guardians. As their voices melded together in conversation and debate, a profound unity settled over them - a unity that would challenge darkness itself and safeguard Ember Bay from all supernatural threats.

Their resolve was unshakable; their bond unbreakable. In that secluded clearing amidst the heart of Ember Bay's mystical realm, destiny beckoned them with promises of trials and triumphs yet to come. And together, they would embark on this extraordinary journey, armed with ancient knowledge and an unwavering spirit.

"In unison they both said 'we can do this.' They knew that together they would overcome any obstacle that stood in their way." Revelations and New Paths The crackling sound of a campfire filled the air as the family settled back into their campsite, their minds still swirling with the enigmatic knowledge they had uncovered.

The flickering flames cast dancing shadows across their faces, mirroring the mix of emotions that coursed through their veins. Nathan stared into the fire, his thoughts consumed by the weighty responsibility that had been placed upon their shoulders.

His eyes flickered with determination, a silent promise to protect his family and the Bayou's mystical realm from the impending darkness. Lucy reached out and clasped Nathan's hand, her fiery touch grounding him in reality.

She could sense his worries, but she also knew that they were stronger together. "We'll face whatever challenges come our way," she said, her voice brimming with conviction. "We have each other and the knowledge we've gained. We won't let anything or anyone stand in our way." Hadley leaned against a log, her eyes fixed on the distant horizon.

The moon cast an ethereal glow upon her face as she whispered, almost to herself, "No secret will remain hidden from us.

We will uncover every truth, no matter how veiled it may be. We have the power within ourselves to shape our destiny." Ayden sat cross-legged, his eyes twinkling with understanding. He had always believed in the inherent goodness of humanity and its ability to overcome darkness.

"We are connected to something greater than ourselves," he mused softly. "The Bayou has chosen us for a reason, and I believe that reason is to restore balance and harmony to this mystical realm." The sound of rustling leaves interrupted their thoughts, and they turned to find Jack, Gizmo, and Ellie emerging from the darkened forest.

Each animal companion exuded an aura of unwavering loyalty and strength as they settled beside their respective guardians. Jack stood tall and proud, his light brown fur glistening in the firelight. He nuzzled against Hadley's side, reminding him of a great power they possessed together. Gizmo transformed into his large black wolf form, his sharp teeth glinting faintly as he locked gazes with Nathan.

It was a silent reminder of their shared purpose - to protect and defend Ember Bay at all costs. And Ellie, majestic as ever in her white lion form, roared softly, embodying the regal authority that would guide Lucy on her path. The family exchanged knowing glances, their hearts swelling with gratitude for these magical creatures who had become more than just companions - they were symbols of hope and unity.

"We're not alone in this journey," Nathan said, his voice filled with a newfound resolve. "Together with Jack, Gizmo, and Ellie by our side, we have a bond that cannot be broken." Lucy nodded in agreement, her fiery hair reflecting the dancing flames.

"Our connection to these creatures and the Bayou itself is strong. We must embrace it fully if we are to succeed." Hadley watched the animals with a hint of awe in her piercing green eyes. "They're more than just animals now," she said softly. "They're our allies and guides in this mystical realm. We must trust them as much as they trust us.

" Ayden reached out to stroke Jack's fur, feeling a surge of warmth spread through his fingertips. "Their presence reminds us of the unity we share," he said, his voice calm yet infused with passion. "As long as we stand together, no darkness can prevail against us." In that moment, a profound silence enveloped their campsite - a silence that held a promise of unwavering support and unbreakable bonds.

With every passing second, they felt their connection deepen and strengthen. The night sky stretched above them like an endless tapestry of stars, illuminating their path forward. The ancient book lay nearby, its pages filled with knowledge waiting to be unlocked.

They were on the brink of discovering secrets that would shape not only their destinies but also the future of Ember Bay itself. "In unison they both said 'we can do this.

They knew that together they would overcome any obstacle that stood in their way." As they settled down for the night, sleep evaded them - visions of trials and triumphs danced in their minds.

But it was not fear that kept them awake; it was anticipation - an anticipation fueled by determination and an unwavering belief in their collective purpose. With each passing moment, they grew closer to embracing their true potential as Elemental Guardians - protectors chosen by destiny itself to safeguard Ember Bay from all supernatural threats.

And so, beneath the watchful gaze of a star-studded sky, they awaited the challenges that awaited them with open hearts and unyielding spirits. "In unison they both said 'we can do this.' They knew that together they would overcome any obstacle that stood in their way."

Wisdom From the Elder The family set out on a new day, guided by the wisdom of their newly found ancestral knowledge. Their path led them to a quaint cottage nestled at the edge of a tranquil lake, surrounded by lush vegetation. A sense of calm settled within their hearts as they approached the dwelling.

Inside, the cottage was adorned with relics and treasures from Ember Bay's rich history. Weathered books lined wooden shelves, their faded spines hinting at stories yet untold. Mysterious artifacts whispered tales of forgotten customs and rituals, waiting to be unearthed. As they entered the cottage, a sweet aroma filled the air - a blend of dried herbs and aged parchment, mingling with the scent of nature that permeated Ember Bay.

Sunlight streamed through the windows, casting dancing rays upon a sage-colored carpet. In the center of the room stood an elderly figure in flowing robes, their eyes shining with knowledge and experience. The elder exuded an aura of wisdom and grace as they welcomed the family with open arms.

"Welcome, seekers of knowledge," the elder greeted them, their voice carrying a melodic lilt that transcended time itself. "I have anticipated your arrival, for the whispers of the Bayou have carried your names to me." Nathan stepped forward first, his footsteps light but purposeful. "We seek understanding," he stated, his voice steady and determined.

"The Bayou has revealed fragments of our destiny, and we hope you can shed light on our path." Lucy followed suit, her fierce gaze fixed upon the elder. "We have discovered an ancient book that has unlocked secrets about our roles as protectors," she explained.

"With your guidance, we hope to assimilate this knowledge and honor our ancestors." Hadley's observant eyes took in every detail of the room as she spoke. "We seek to uncover forgotten customs and rituals associated with our journey," she said.

"We believe these traditions hold valuable wisdom that will aid us in our quest to protect Ember Bay." Ayden approached last, his gentle presence emanating warmth and compassion. "We yearn to connect with our predecessors, to understand their struggles and triumphs," he expressed. "By embracing ancestral wisdom, we hope to find harmony within ourselves and bring peace to Ember Bay.

" The elder smiled knowingly, their eyes crinkling at the corners. "You have come seeking answers that lie within your own hearts," they responded. "But I can offer guidance and share stories passed down through generations." Seated around a weathered wooden table, the family leaned in eagerly as the elder began to speak.

Their voices carried an ethereal quality, highlighting each word's significance. "The protectors who came before you faced similar battles against supernatural threats," the elder recounted, their voice a comforting melody amidst quiet reverence. "They fought with unwavering resolve and forged paths paved with courage and sacrifice.

" As the elder spoke, images danced in their minds - epic battles waged against mythical creatures, ancient rituals performed under moonlit skies, and sacrifices made for the greater good. Each story captivated their hearts, weaving threads of connection between past and present. "These stories offer more than just entertainment; they carry lessons and teachings," the elder continued.

"Through them, you will gain insight into forgotten customs and hidden symbols that have been bestowed upon you as protectors." With every word spoken by the elder, a deeper understanding settled within their souls. They absorbed tales of unity and perseverance, honoring those who had come before them while forging their own destinies. In unison, they listened - their minds absorbing ancestral wisdom like sponges soaking up water - gaining insights into ancient practices that would guide them on their journey.

"In unison they both said 'we can do this.' They knew that together they would overcome any obstacle that stood in their way." Tales Etched in Time The flickering firelight cast a warm glow within the cottage as the family settled into comfortable positions, their eyes
fixed on the elder. Their hearts beat with anticipation, eager to hear tales that would bring their ancestors to life.

The elder's voice carried a melodic rhythm as they began to speak, each word laced with the weight of history. "Long ago, before the Bayou was surrounded by civilization, there existed a harmonious balance between mortals and the supernatural realm," they began. "Ember Bay was a place where mythical creatures roamed freely, coexisting with the protectors who sought to maintain order and safeguard the delicate equilibrium," the elder continued.

"One such creature was the Bayou Serpent, known for its immense power and ability to control water." Lucy leaned forward, her fiery gaze fixed upon the elder. "What happened to this creature?" she asked, curiosity burning in her voice. A wistful smile played upon the elder's lips as they recounted the tale. "Legend has it that a fierce battle erupted between the protectors and an ancient evil force seeking to harness the Bayou Serpent's power for their own malevolent purposes," they explained.

"In a final act of sacrifice and heroism, the last protector of that era called forth a surge of celestial energy that sealed away both the Bayou Serpent and the darkness." Ayden nodded solemnly, his voice soft yet filled with reverence. "They sacrificed themselves to protect Ember Bay," he whispered. The elder's eyes gleamed with pride at Ayden's observation. "Indeed, young healer," they said.

"Their bravery serves as an inspiration for your own journey. Their sacrifices paved the way for you to stand against the encroaching darkness." Hadley's gaze was steady as she absorbed every word, her mind piecing together fragments of the past. "Is there anything we can learn from their battles? Any weaknesses we should be aware of?" she inquired.

The elder nodded, leaning forward slightly as they shared further tales. "Each mythical creature possesses unique vulnerabilities," they explained. "For example, the Spirit Guardian of the Ancient Woods can be weakened by earth-imbued artifacts or incantations.

" Nathan's eyes gleamed with determination, his focus sharpening on the insights provided. "We must gather knowledge about these creatures and exploit their weaknesses when we encounter them," he proclaimed, his voice filled with resolve.

Ayden interjected calmly, his voice like a soothing balm amidst the growing excitement. "Remember that our strength lies not only in exploiting weaknesses but also in maintaining unity among ourselves," he reminded them.

"Just as our ancestors fought together, we too must stand united in our purpose." With each tale shared by the elder, bonds were strengthened between past and present, weaving a tapestry of ancestral knowledge that now guided their path.

The family listened intently, absorbing every detail of battles fought and won. As time slipped away within those hallowed walls, characters emerged from forgotten pages - protectors long gone but forever etched within Ember Bay's history. Their victories became stepping stones for the family, guiding them towards triumph against all odds.

The atmosphere within the cottage shimmered with an otherworldly presence as story after story wove itself into their collective consciousness. Their minds became repositories of wisdom passed down through generations - customs, rituals, and chants meant to forge connections between protectors and their elemental counterparts.

"In unison they both said 'we can do this.' They knew that together they would overcome any obstacle that stood in their way." Assimilating Ancestral Wisdom The elder's voice fell to a whisper as they began to share the ancient customs and rituals that had guided protectors of Ember Bay for centuries. The family leaned in, their eyes shining with anticipation and respect.

"The power of the elements is woven into the very fabric of Ember Bay," the elder began, their voice filled with reverence. "To fully harness this power, you must commune with the natural world and embrace the sacred rituals passed down through the ages." Nathan listened intently, his mind absorbing every word.

"How do we establish this connection?" he asked, his voice filled with eagerness. The elder smiled knowingly, their eyes twinkling with ancient wisdom. "Through deep meditation and attuning your senses to the rhythm of nature, you will open yourself to its energy," they explained. "Listen to the whispers of the wind, feel the caress of water on your skin, and let the earth ground you.

" Lucy furrowed her brow, her fiery spirit burning with determination. "And what about fire?" she questioned. "How can we connect with its powerful energy?" The elder nodded approvingly. "Fire is both destructive and transformative," they mused. "Through controlled flames and focused intent, you can find harmony with this element. Channel its energy and allow it to guide your path.

" Hadley's eyes gleamed with curiosity as she posed her question. "What about the mysteries of the night? How can we embrace darkness and make it our ally?" The elder's gaze shifted to Hadley, their voice taking on a more mysterious tone.

"The night holds secrets only unveiled to those who dare to venture into its depths," they said softly. "Blend into shadows, trust your intuition, and learn to navigate the darkness without fear." Ayden's gentle presence filled the room as he sought clarity on his own connection to celestial energies. "How can I enhance my abilities in channeling divine vibrations?" he asked humbly.

The elder's eyes sparkled with understanding as they responded. "Your connection to celestial forces is profound," they said. "In moments of stillness and pure intentions, call forth celestial energy, and let it flow through you like a river of healing." As the family absorbed these teachings, a newfound sense of purpose settled within their hearts. They understood that true power came not just from physical strength but from aligning their spirits with the natural order of Ember Bay.

Together, they practiced deep breathing exercises, focusing their minds on the elements surrounding them - feeling the cool touch of air against their skin, envisioning flames dancing before their closed eyelids, grounding themselves by connecting with the earth beneath. Hours turned into minutes as they honed their abilities, allowing ancestral knowledge to infuse their every action.

Their bond grew stronger as they shared experiences and supported one another in unlocking their individual potentials. "In unison they both said 'we can do this.' They knew that together they would overcome any obstacle that stood in their way." As daylight faded and shadows lengthened across the cottage floor, the family emerged from their meditative state - transformed by the ancestral wisdom that now coursed through their veins.

They stood, a united front brimming with determination and purpose. The knowledge bestowed upon them would guide their every step forward as protectors of Ember Bay. The elder clasped each family member's hands in turn, their touch filled with reassurance and pride. "You have embraced your destinies with open hearts," they declared, their voice resonating with admiration.

Nathan's gaze met Lucy's; Hadley nodded affirmatively at Ayden. They shared an unspoken vow - to honor their ancestors' sacrifices and forge a new path for future generations. With renewed resolve and a deep connection to Ember Bay's mystical heritage, they stepped out into the night - prepared to face whatever challenges lay ahead.

Their journey had just begun, but they were ready - armed not only with powers bestowed upon them by the Bayou but also with wisdom carried through generations. "In unison they both said 'we can do this.' They knew that together they would overcome any obstacle that stood in their way."

Chapter 4: Heart of the Bayou

The family and the group of rival protectors stood face-to-face in a clearing bathed in the ethereal light of the Bayou. The air crackled with tension as each side asserted their claim to Ember Bay's mystical powers, their auras pulsating with raw energy. Nathan's eyes narrowed as he locked gazes with the leader of the rival protectors.

"We won't let you take what rightfully belongs to the guardians of Ember Bay," he declared, his voice steady and determined. Lucy stepped forward, her fiery red hair gleaming in the sunlight. "This is our duty. We will defend this land with everything we have," she added, her tone laced with conviction.

The rival protector smirked, his voice dripping with arrogance. "You think you stand a chance against us? You're nothing but a bunch of amateurs," he scoffed. Hadley, always observant, analyzed the rival protector's posture and expressions. "Arrogance often blinds one to their true weaknesses," she remarked, her voice carrying an air of mystery.

Ayden, ever the calm presence, spoke softly but with unwavering authority. "We were chosen for this role. Our dedication to protecting Ember Bay cannot be undone by empty words," he stated, his words resonating with quiet power. With tensions escalating, the characters' faces reflected the intensity of their emotions.

Nathan's jaw clenched, his eyes reflecting a steely resolve. Lucy's fiery gaze burned with determination as she stood tall and unyielding. Hadley's piercing green eyes scanned the rival protectors, analyzing their every move.

Ayden's kind eyes held a depth of wisdom and compassion that belied his inner strength. The rival protector sneered, his voice dripping with malice. "You're nothing more than a nuisance. Step aside before you get hurt," he taunted. Nathan's lips curled into a wry smile as he met the rival protector's gaze head-on.

"We've faced greater threats than you. The Bayou chose us for a reason," he retorted, his voice filled with quiet confidence. Lucy's grip tightened on her weapon as she took a step forward. "We won't back down. We'll fight for what we believe in until the very end," she stated firmly, her fiery spirit shining through her words.

Hadley's voice sliced through the tension like a blade, both mysterious and resolute. "You underestimate us at your own peril. We possess powers that you cannot comprehend," she warned, her words carrying an air of warning.

Ayden's calming presence radiated through his words as he took a step forward. "Our purpose goes beyond personal gain or pride. It is about protecting what is sacred and preserving the balance," he explained gently, his voice resonating with a profound sense of purpose. As their verbal exchanges intensified, the atmosphere grew increasingly charged with electricity.

The whispers of the Bayou seemed to echo through the trees, heightening the sense of mysticism and danger in the air. In the midst of this confrontation, Jack, now transformed into a mighty bear, growled menacingly beside Hadley.

Gizmo, the teacup Chihuahua turned wolf, prowled silently at Nathan's side. Ellie, a regal white lioness now by Lucy's side, emitted a low rumble that reverberated through the clearing. "Their animal companions are but physical manifestations of their inner strength and connection to Ember Bay," Hadley observed quietly.

Nathan cast a sideways glance at Gizmo and grinned. "Together, we will show them that we are more than just amateurs," he said confidently. As tensions reached their peak, both sides prepared for what lay ahead - a clash of elemental powers that would determine the fate of Ember Bay and test their strength in ways they had never imagined.

Verbal Exchanges and Battle of Wills The rival protectors, their faces twisted with arrogance and determination, matched the family's resolve with their own cutting remarks. The air crackled with hostility as they hurled insults and belittled the guardians of Ember Bay.

"You fools think you can beat us? You're nothing compared to our power," sneered one of the rival protectors, his voice dripping with contempt. Lucy's fiery spirit blazed even brighter as she shot back, her words laced with defiance.

"We may be amateurs in your eyes, but our determination and unity make us stronger than you'll ever be," she declared, her voice ringing with conviction. Hadley's piercing green eyes narrowed as she firmly met the gaze of another rival protector. "Arrogance often blinds one to their true weaknesses.

Your overconfidence will be your downfall," she stated calmly, her words laced with a hint of mystery. Ayden stepped forward, his calming presence cutting through the tension. "This battle is not about proving who is superior. It is about protecting what is sacred and preserving the harmony of Ember Bay," he emphasized, his voice carrying an air of wisdom and compassion.

The rival protectors scoffed, their laughter echoing through the clearing. "You speak of harmony and balance as if it means something! Your ideals are nothing more than empty platitudes," one of them spat, his voice filled with disdain. Nathan's eyes blazed with determination as he locked gazes with the leader of the rival protectors.

"Because we believe in something greater than ourselves, we have the strength to face any challenge that comes our way," he retorted, his voice steady and unwavering. As tensions continued to escalate, the rival protectors unleashed their elemental powers, igniting a dazzling display of brilliance that illuminated the clearing.

Flames erupted from one protector's hands, casting an intense glow and sending waves of scorching heat towards Nathan and Lucy. Nathan swiftly dodged the fiery projectiles with his exceptional ninja skills, his reflexes honed from years of training. He lunged forward, landing behind a large tree trunk for cover. His piercing eyes narrowed as he prepared to counterattack.

Lucy conjured force fields with her newfound powers, creating a protective barrier that shielded her from the oncoming flames. Her quick thinking allowed her to regroup and strategize her next move. Gizmo, now a large black wolf, moved stealthily through the shadows cast by the flames.

He utilized his agility and keen senses to navigate through the chaotic battleground, finding openings to strike against the rival protectors from unexpected angles. Ellie prowled alongside Lucy, her majestic presence radiating regality and authority. With a mighty roar, she launched herself at a rival protector, claws extended.

Her attack was swift and precise, aimed at incapacitating her opponent without causing permanent harm. Amidst the chaos and fierce exchanges of elemental powers, Nathan's agile movements allowed him to close in on one of the rival protectors. With lightning speed, he launched a series of devastating strikes, using his precision and exceptional ninja skills to weaken his opponent.

Backed by Ayden's healing abilities that soothed and restored balance, the family fought together as a united front. Their unity multiplied their strength exponentially as they defended each other from onslaughts that threatened to overwhelm them. As their battle raged on, their determination grew even stronger.

They refused to let arrogance or doubt cloud their minds. Each setback was met with resilience and determination—a testament to their unyielding spirit and unwavering belief in their purpose. Unleashing Elemental Powers As the rival protectors continued to unleash their elemental powers, the battleground became a spectacle of dazzling brilliance. The air crackled with raw energy and the ground trembled beneath the weight of their abilities.

Nathan, evoking the shadows, maneuvered gracefully through the chaos, blending into the darkness like a phantom. With each calculated move, he left his opponents disoriented and vulnerable. His exceptional ninja skills allowed him to strike swiftly and silently, nullifying their attacks before they could fully manifest.

Lucy, surrounded by a pulsating force field, stood tall and resolute. She channeled her fiery energy, amplifying her defensive capabilities. Flames licked at the edges of her protective barrier, but she held firm, refusing to allow her adversaries to breach her defenses. Her quick reflexes allowed her to retaliate with ferocity whenever an opening presented itself. Hadley, utilizing her mastery of teleportation, moved with unparalleled agility and grace.

She appeared in one location and vanished in the blink of an eye, making it nearly impossible for her opponents to anticipate her movements. Like a ghostly apparition, she traversed the battleground effortlessly, striking from unexpected angles and disappearing before her foes could react. Ayden focused his celestial energies, channeling divine vibrations that resonated with healing properties.

With a gentle touch and soothing words, he counteracted the destructive forces unleashed by the rival protectors. His presence brought balance to the chaos, restoring harmony amidst the cacophony of elemental powers. Gizmo, transformed into a large black wolf, moved with swift precision through the chaos.

His agility and keen senses enabled him to traverse the frenzied battleground unscathed. He utilized his lupine instincts to anticipate his opponents' moves, launching precise and strategic attacks that disrupted their concentration. Ellie, now a majestic white lioness, roared with regal authority as she engaged her adversaries head-on.

Her powerful paws delivered punishing blows while her sharp claws tore through any defenses in their path. She fought with unwavering determination and fearlessness, determined to protect those she held dear. In the heart of the dense woodland, where ancient trees intertwined their branches like mythical guardians, Jack, the formidable light brown bear, stood as a majestic sentinel.

His massive frame, a testament to untamed strength, dominated the forest landscape. The air crackled with tension as protesters, defiant and resolute, challenged the very essence of nature's might. Jack, with a thunderous growl that echoed through the woods, rose on his hind legs, his fur catching the dappled sunlight filtering through the foliage.

As he swiped through the air, a tempest of leaves danced around him, and the protesters were catapulted into a chaotic ballet. Jack's every movement seemed like a declaration, a primal symphony that resonated with the untamed energy of the wilderness. The onlookers, both awe-stricken and terrified, witnessed a spectacle of raw power clashing with human determination.

Jack, undeterred and resolute, continued to defend his domain with an innate fierceness that left an indelible mark on the forest's ancient tapestry. The clash of elemental powers created a symphony of destruction and resilience. Fire consumed the air as bursts of flame erupted from both sides. Winds whipped through the clearing, carrying debris and creating chaotic whirlwinds.

Earth trembled underfoot as stone constructs rose from the ground and clashed with powerful impacts. Amidst the chaos, the family's unity forged an unbreakable bond. Each member fought with unrivaled determination and unwavering trust in one another. Their coordinated efforts blended seamlessly as if they were extensions of one another—each movement intertwined with purpose and precision.

As the battle raged on, the rival protectors soon realized that their arrogance had blinded them to the true strength of their opponents. The family's exceptional skills, amplified by their newfound powers, began to overpower their adversaries.

The tide of battle shifted—a testament to the family's resilience and unwavering resolve. Through determination and strategy, Nathan managed to outmaneuver his opponent and deliver a crushing blow. The rival protector stumbled backward, dazed and disoriented. Lucy's force fields grew even stronger as she tapped into her inner fire.

Bolstered by her unwavering spirit, she launched herself at another rival protector with renewed ferocity, overpowering their defenses and forcing them onto the defensive. Hadley's teleportation abilities allowed her to evade attacks effortlessly while capitalizing on her opponents' momentary confusion.

She struck swiftly and silently from various vantage points, keeping her adversaries off balance and uncertain. Ayden's healing abilities flowed through him like a calming river. As he reached out to neutralize destructive forces, he also infused his allies with renewed strength and resolve.

His celestial energy weaved through them, bolstering their resilience as they faced off against their rivals. Gizmo weaved seamlessly through the chaos, his agility and keen senses allowing him to avoid attacks with near-superhuman reflexes. Guided by his bond with Nathan, he launched coordinated strikes alongside his partner—a seamless dance between man and beast that left their opponents reeling.

Ellie's ferocity knew no bounds as she lunged at another rival protector, her regal presence commanding attention. With each swipe of her mighty paw and roar that echoed through the clearing, she diminished their forces and forced them onto the defensive.

As the intensity of battle heightened, cracks began to form in the once-unbreakable facade of the rival protectors. Doubt tainted their expressions as they realized that they had underestimated their adversaries—warriors fueled by unity, determination, and an unwavering belief in themselves. With every strike landed and every defense shattered, the family's power surged forward like an unstoppable force—unalterable in their dedication to protect Ember Bay from any threat that dared to challenge its harmony.

Repercussions of Battle - Bonds Strengthened in Adversity After the intense battle subsided, silence settled over the scene, broken only by the faint sound of crackling embers and the distant echoes of their adversaries retreating. The air hung heavy with the scent of smoke and charred earth, a stark reminder of the destruction left in the wake of their clash.

Nathan surveyed the aftermath, his eyes scanning the clearing strewn with fallen trees and smoldering debris. The devastation weighed heavily on his heart, a profound realization of the cost of their conflict. He turned to Lucy, determination shining in his eyes. "We must rebuild what has been lost," he said softly, his voice carrying a note of resolve.

Lucy nodded, her gaze lingering on the damaged landscape. "Together, we will restore the Bayou to its former glory," she replied, determination shining in her fiery eyes.

Hadley approached them, her movements cautious yet purposeful. She surveyed the scene with a keen eye, searching for any signs of hidden danger or remaining foes. Her thoughts were focused on uncovering secrets that lay buried beneath the wreckage.

"Allies or rivals, this destruction affects us all," Hadley remarked, her voice tinged with hints of mystery. "We must find common ground and work together to heal what has been broken." Ayden joined them, his gentle presence a soothing balm amidst the turmoil. His gaze swept over the clearing, taking in the charred remnants and scattered debris. A sense of purpose radiated from him as he reached out to touch a scorched tree trunk. "In time, new life will emerge from these ashes," Ayden said softly, his voice carrying a tone of hope.

"Just as we have faced adversity and grown stronger, so too shall Ember Bay rise again."

Their bond as protectors deepened through their shared experience of battle and its consequences. In the face of destruction, they found unity and strength that transcended their individual roles. The rival protectors, once adversaries, had retreated into the shadows—leaving behind a trail of introspection and contemplation.

Lucy's fiery spirit blazed even brighter as she looked around at her family, her comrades-in-arms. "We may have fought against each other moments ago, but now we must find a way to unify our strengths," she declared passionately.

Nathan nodded in agreement. "Our true enemy lies beyond these internal conflicts," he said, his voice tinged with conviction. "If we are to protect Ember Bay from its impending darkness, we must learn from our mistakes and work together." Hadley's mysterious green eyes sparkled with understanding as she stepped forward.

"The strength of Ember Bay resides in each of us," she stated cryptically. "Only when we unite can we truly harness its power." Ayden placed a comforting hand on Lucy's shoulder, his voice carrying a note of compassion. "We all have our weaknesses and flaws," he said gently. "But it is through forgiveness and unity that we can channel our collective strength and protect what is sacred.

" As they stood together amidst the wreckage of battle, a newfound sense of camaraderie enveloped them like a warm embrace. They understood that alliances were forged not just through shared purpose, but also through acknowledging each other's strengths and resilience. The whispers of the Bayou seemed to echo through the air once more—a gentle reminder that their unity was essential in protecting Ember Bay.

The characters cast aside their differences and embraced their shared destiny—the preservation of harmony amidst chaos. With hands clasped and hearts filled with determination, they vowed to rebuild what had been destroyed. The path ahead was uncertain, but they faced it as one united force, ready to protect Ember Bay against any threat that dared to challenge its tranquility.

Realization of Futility and Common Ground As the dust settled and the echoes of battle faded, a somber silence settled over the clearing. The once-rival protectors now nursed their wounds and reflected on the consequences of their actions.

The destruction that lay before them served as a stark reminder of the futility of their rivalry. One by one, they cast aside their pride and approached the family, their expressions tinged with regret and acceptance.

Their arrogance had been humbled, replaced by a shared understanding of the true enemy that threatened Ember Bay. The leader of the rival protectors stepped forward, his voice laced with remorse. "We were blinded by our own ambition," he confessed, his words carrying a heavy weight. "But now we see the error in our ways and the impact it has had on this land.

" Lucy met his gaze, her fiery spirit tempered by compassion. "We have all made mistakes," she acknowledged, her voice softening. "What matters now is how we move forward and protect what truly matters.

" Hadley, ever observant, studied the rival protectors' expressions. "Our internal conflicts only serve to weaken us," she remarked cryptically. "It is unity and understanding that will lead us towards victory.

" Ayden's calming presence radiated through his words as he extended forgiveness. "Let us not dwell on past mistakes," he said gently. "Instead, let us recognize the strength we possess when we fight together for a common purpose.

" The rival protectors exchanged glances, remnants of their previous animosity still lingering but slowly dissipating. They understood that their true enemy lurked beyond their internal rivalries—the impending darkness that threatened to consume Ember Bay. With weariness etched into their features, they surveyed the destruction around them—a testament to the toll of their conflict.

Fallen trees looked like giants on the charred earth, reminders of the cost of their arrogance. Nathan approached the rival protectors, his eyes reflecting both weariness and determination. "We have witnessed firsthand the devastation our battles can bring," he stated solemnly. "Let us not repeat these mistakes.

Instead, let us come together for the greater good." The rival protectors nodded in agreement, their pride giving way to humility. They knew that unity was imperative if they were to stand a chance against the encroaching darkness that threatened to consume Ember Bay. Lucy extended her hand in a gesture of goodwill, her fiery gaze softening.

"Let us rebuild what has been broken," she proposed earnestly." Together, we can restore balance and protect this land from any threat." The rival protectors hesitated momentarily before accepting Lucy's outstretched hand—one by one, they joined in a circle, forming an unbreakable bond between former adversaries.

In this moment, they let go of ancient prejudices and embraced the strength that came from unity. Hadley's mysterious green eyes gleamed with newfound hope as she spoke softly yet assuredly. "Together, we are stronger than any darkness that seeks to consume us," she declared, her voice carrying an air of quiet determination.

Ayden closed his eyes momentarily as he tapped into his healing energy—the same energy that had mended physical wounds moments ago. With a renewed sense of purpose, he whispered words of peace and harmony, channeling celestial vibrations throughout the clearing.

As their collective energies intertwined, a sense of serenity filled the clearing—a reminder that even amidst chaos and destruction, there is always hope for restoration and renewal. The whispers of the Bayou seemed to echo through the air once more—a gentle reassurance that unity would prevail against any darkness that dared to challenge Ember Bay's tranquility. In this moment of reconciliation and acceptance, alliances were forged that transcended personal gain or pride—common ground rooted in a shared purpose to protect what was sacred.

From this point forward, they would face whatever challenges lay ahead with unwavering resolve and unwavering belief in each other.

As they stood together amidst the remnants of battle, they knew that their journey was far from over. But with forgiveness in their hearts and unity in their souls, they were prepared to face any darkness that sought to extinguish the light within Ember Bay.

And so, united by purpose and bound by resilience, they set forth on a path guided by a newfound harmony—a harmony that echoed through the Bayou and resonated within each protector's heart. Forgiveness and Unity The charred landscape stood as a testament to the fierce battle that had taken place.

Faded embers still smoldered, casting a dim glow upon the clearing. The air was heavy with the scent of smoke, a lingering reminder of the destruction that had transpired. Amidst the wreckage, the family and the rival protectors found themselves in an unexpected moment of respite. The intensity of battle had subsided, replaced by a solemn calmness as they assessed the aftermath of their clash.

Lucy's fiery spirit burned bright within her as she looked around at the fallen trees and scorched earth. She took a deep breath, centering herself amidst the devastation. "We have witnessed firsthand the consequences of our conflicts," she spoke with a conviction that resonated through the clearing.

Nathan nodded, his gaze focused on the rival protectors. "It is in moments like these that we must find strength in forgiveness and unity. Only through working together can we truly protect Ember Bay," he emphasized, his voice carrying a note of determination. The rival protectors exchanged hesitant glances, their pride still lingering within them.

They had been adversaries for so long, their rivalry deeply rooted in history. But now, faced with the consequences of their actions, they began to realize the futility of their disputes. One of the rival protectors stepped forward, their expression reflecting a newfound humility.

"We have caused great harm in our pursuit of power," they admitted, their voice laced with remorse. "But we are willing to set aside our differences for the greater good.

" Hadley observed them silently, her piercing green eyes taking in their words and expressions.

She had always been adept at reading between the lines and deciphering hidden truths. Now, she saw genuine remorse etched on their faces - a sign that they were willing to change. Ayden, ever attuned to the emotions of others, approached them with a gentle smile. "In forgiveness lies healing," he said softly, his voice carrying a soothing presence.

"Let us acknowledge our mistakes and work towards unity. Together, we can create a stronger force against the impending darkness." As his words hung in the air, silence enveloped the clearing once more.

The rival protectors hesitated, their hearts conflicted between old beliefs and newfound understanding. But ultimately, they understood that cooperation was necessary if they were to protect what they held dear. With a nod of agreement, one by one, they approached the family and extended their hands in reconciliation.

The tension that had once gripped the clearing dissipated as they formed a circle—an unbreakable bond forged through forgiveness. Lucy clasped hands with one of the rival protectors, her fiery gaze softening with compassion.

"The past cannot be undone, but together we can build a better future," she spoke with warmth in her voice. Nathan shook hands with another rival protector, his eyes conveying both strength and acceptance.

"We each possess unique strengths that can complement one another," he acknowledged. "Let us combine our powers for the greater good.

" Hadley, ever observant, offered her hand to another rival protector and met their gaze with sincerity. "Unity makes us stronger than any darkness we may face," she remarked cryptically yet reassuringly. Ayden completed the circle by extending his hand to the last remaining rival protector.

His kind eyes held no judgment, only empathy and understanding. "Let us embrace forgiveness and work towards safeguarding Ember Bay with unwavering resolve," he said gently. In the midst of swirling enchantment, Jack, formerly a doodle hound, underwent a captivating metamorphosis, emerging as a powerful light brown bear. Alongside him, Gizmo, the teacup Chihuahua, experienced a transformation of his own, evolving into a sleek and cunning wolf.

Simultaneously, Ellie, the regal white lioness who had momentarily taken on the guise of a Chihuahua, gracefully reverted back to there true form. In that moment of unity and forgiveness, the whispers of the Bayou seemed to echo through the air once more—a reminder that healing could emerge even from the darkest of battles.

The characters felt a surge of renewed hope as they stood united against the impending darkness. As they released their grasp on each other's hands, an undeniable sense of purpose settled over them all. They knew that challenges lay ahead, but they also knew that by embracing forgiveness and working together, they could overcome any obstacle that threatened Ember Bay.

And so, amidst the charred remains of battle, alliances were forged and bonds were strengthened. The family and former rivals now stood side by side—not just as protectors of Ember Bay but as guardians bound by a shared purpose and unwavering belief in one another. They turned towards the path that lay before them—the path towards protecting what was sacred and preserving harmony amidst chaos.

With every step taken together, they were reminded of the power that lay in forgiveness and unity—an indomitable force capable of conquering any darkness that dared to encroach upon Ember Bay's tranquility. For in Ember Bay's protection, their destinies intertwined—a destiny bound by forgiveness, unity, and an unwavering hope for a brighter future.

Chapter 5: A Historical Connection

The family arrived at the local historian's residence, a quaint cottage nestled on the outskirts of the Bayou. The historian, an elderly man with a twinkle in his eyes and a wealth of knowledge etched on his face, welcomed them warmly. "Welcome, young guardians," the historian greeted, his voice carrying a sense of wisdom.

"I have been expecting you." Nathan, Lucy, Hadley, and Ayden exchanged glances, their curiosity piqued by the historian's words. They followed him into a dimly lit room adorned with ancient relics, maps, and yellowed books that lined the shelves. "Sit, sit," the historian motioned toward a worn-out wooden table, covered in manuscripts and artifacts. "Let us delve into the secrets of Ember Bay's past.

" As they took their seats, Nathan couldn't help but feel a sense of awe. "So much history lies within these walls," he whispered to Lucy beside him. The historian began recounting tales of past protectors, their valiant struggles against supernatural threats, and the sacrifices they made to safeguard Ember Bay. His voice carried both wonder and respect for those who came before. "The first protectors battled against the forces of darkness long ago," the historian explained, his gaze wandering as if lost in memory.

"They possessed extraordinary powers and faced unimaginable trials in their quest to uphold the balance between the realms." Lucy leaned forward, captivated by the stories. "What kind of trials did they face?" she asked eagerly. The historian smiled at her eagerness. "They encountered creatures from other realms, faced treacherous landscapes filled with traps and challenges. Some even had to confront their own inner demons to prove their worthiness as guardians.

" Hadley's eyes sparkled with curiosity. "And how did they overcome these trials?" "They relied on their strengths as individuals but also learned the power of unity," the historian replied. "They understood that each one had a role to play in protecting Ember Bay, and only by working together could they vanquish the darkness.

" Ayden listened intently, his gentle demeanor radiating with compassion. "Were there any notable protectors who stood out amongst the rest?" he asked. The historian nodded thoughtfully. "Indeed, there were those whose bravery and sacrifice echoed throughout generations," he said. "Their names have become legends, forever etched in Ember Bay's history." Nathan leaned closer, his voice filled with anticipation.

"Could you tell us more about them? Their stories inspire us." The historian's eyes sparkled with delight as he delved into tales of heroic protectors who faced insurmountable odds, battling powerful adversaries to preserve peace in Ember Bay. Each story evoked a sense of determination within the family members, igniting a fire within their hearts.

"These protectors fought not only for themselves but for future generations," the historian concluded, his voice filled with reverence.

"Their spirits still linger in this land, guiding you along your journey." Silence enveloped the room as the family absorbed the weight of responsibility placed upon their shoulders. They felt a connection to those who came before them and realized that they were part of something much greater than themselves.

"We will do whatever it takes to protect Ember Bay," Lucy asserted, her gaze unwavering. Nathan nodded in agreement. "We won't let their sacrifices be in vain." Hadley glanced around at her fellow companions and offered a reassuring smile. "Together, we are stronger than any darkness that may come our way.

" Ayden placed a comforting hand on Lucy's shoulder. "We will bring harmony and light back to this sacred land." The historian watched them with pride brimming in his eyes. "You are true guardians," he said softly.

"Ember Bay is fortunate to have such dedicated protectors like yourselves." With newfound determination burning in their hearts, the family left the historian's cottage. They now understood the importance of their roles and felt connected not only to each other but also to the protectors who had walked this path before them.

As they ventured further into the heart of Ember Bay's mysteries, they carried with them the wisdom and courage of those who came before—ready to face whatever challenges lay ahead and restore balance to this mystical realm they called home.

Uncovering Ancient Artifacts - Portals to Other Realms Guided by their intuition and ancient maps, the family ventured further into the hidden recesses of the Bayou. They stumbled upon a concealed cave entrance tucked away behind overgrown foliage, its secrets waiting to be discovered. The air grew charged with anticipation as they cautiously stepped inside, their flashlight beams illuminating ancient markings on the walls.

The cave opened up into a vast chamber filled with ornate pedestals displaying various artifacts shimmering with mystical energy. Each pedestal seemed to call out to them, beckoning them closer. Nathan's eyes widened as he approached one specific pedestal, drawn to an intricately carved amulet adorned with swirling patterns.

Lucy reached out a hand to stop him, her voice laced with concern. "Nathan, be careful. We don't know what these artifacts can do." Nathan nodded, acknowledging her cautious words. "You're right, Lucy. We must proceed with caution." He extended his hand towards the amulet but paused just inches away.

As if sensing his hesitation, Ayden offered words of encouragement. "Trust your instincts, Nathan. If it is meant for you, it will guide you." Taking a deep breath, Nathan steeled his resolve and made contact with the amulet. In an instant, a surge of energy enveloped him, transporting him through a portal to a realm teeming with fantastical creatures and breathtaking landscapes.

Wide-eyed and filled with wonder, Nathan found himself standing in the midst of an enchanted forest where ethereal beings flitted among towering trees. The air was tinged with magic, and every breath he took seemed to fill him with renewed strength. The vibrant colors of the realm danced before his eyes, captivating his senses.

Meanwhile, Lucy, Hadley, and Ayden watched in awe as Nathan disappeared before their very eyes. They exchanged surprised glances before turning their attention back to the pedestals filled with artifacts. "I suppose it's our turn now," Hadley mused, eyeing a dagger that emanated an aura of mystery.

Lucy stepped forward confidently, placing her hand on a polished shield that seemed to pulse with power. "May this shield protect us on our journey," she whispered. Ayden walked towards a staff adorned with celestial symbols and closed his eyes in prayer.

He reached out and gently touched the staff, feeling a surge of warmth flow through him as he too was transported through a portal. In their individual realms, Lucy faced formidable enemies whose every strike she parried skillfully with her shield.

Hadley navigated treacherous terrain using her teleportation abilities to evade traps while simultaneously gathering vital information about the realm's mysteries. Ayden found himself in a tranquil sanctuary where he tended to wounded creatures using his healing touch and solaced those who had lost hope amidst the chaos.

Though separated by realms, the family felt connected by an invisible thread of strength and resilience. They drew comfort from knowing that while their trials were unique, they were united in purpose and unwavering in their commitment to protect Ember Bay. As each of them overcame their respective challenges in their own realms, new insights and revelations began to unfold.

Ancient secrets were unearthed, shedding light on Ember Bay's origins and the interwoven connections between realms. With each passing trial and discovery, the family grew more adept at harnessing their powers and understanding the intricate web of magic that bound Ember Bay together. They realized that these trials were not merely tests of physical strength but also tests of character and determination.

Hours turned into days as they delved deeper into their realms, forging alliances with inhabitants who shared a common cause in preserving harmony between realms. Lessons were learned, friendships were formed, and bonds were strengthened. Finally, the time came when each family member had completed their trials and gathered enough knowledge to return to the Chamber of Artifacts.

With newfound wisdom etched in their minds and hearts, they stepped through portals that led them back to the central chamber. As they reunited in front of the pedestals once more, a profound sense of unity washed over them. Their experiences had shaped them individually and as a family, reinforcing their commitment to protect Ember Bay with unwavering devotion.

"We have faced our trials and returned stronger than ever," Ayden said softly, his voice filled with pride. Lucy nodded in agreement. "Now we must integrate what we have learned and work together as a unified force against any darkness that threatens Ember Bay." Hadley held up a fragment of an ancient scroll she had acquired during her adventures.

"The pieces are slowly coming together," she said cryptically.

"We must continue our journey to uncover the full truth." Nathan's eyes sparkled with determination as he looked at his fellow protectors. "Let us press on. There is much more to be discovered about Ember Bay's past and its connection to these realms.

" With their resolve strengthened and their spirits soaring high, the family left the Chamber of Artifacts behind them. They were ready to face whatever challenges lay ahead as they pursued the truth behind Ember Bay's mysteries – confident in their abilities and united as elemental guardians against any darkness that threatened their beloved home.

Echoes of the Past - Ancestral Whispers The family set out on their quest, their steps guided by the whispers of the Bayou. The foliage seemed to part before them, revealing a hidden path that led deeper into the heart of Ember Bay. As they walked in silence, the air carried a tangible energy, as if the spirits of the past protectors were watching over them.

The songs of birds took on a mystical quality, and shadows danced playfully in the sunlight. It was as if nature itself acknowledged their presence and filled them with a sense of purpose. In a secluded clearing, bathed in golden rays of sunlight, they stumbled upon a circle of ancient stones.

The stones seemed to hum with power, resonating with an energy that pulsed through their very beings. Nathan knelt down to examine the stones, his fingertips tracing over the intricate engravings etched into their surface. As he did, he felt a surge of warmth spreading through him, connecting him to all those who had stood before him as protectors.

"These stones are a link to our ancestors," Ayden spoke softly, his voice barely audible above the rustling leaves. "They hold the wisdom and guidance we seek." Lucy's eyes shimmered with a mixture of excitement and reverence.

"What do we do now?" she asked, her voice filled with anticipation. Hadley's gaze darted around the clearing, her instincts guiding her actions. "We must commune with the spirits," she said confidently. "They will reveal to us the knowledge we seek.

" With a shared understanding, they joined hands and formed a circle within the ring of stones. In unison, they closed their eyes and let their minds become still, opening themselves up to the messages that awaited them. At first, there was only silence and stillness. Then, gradually, whispers began to fill their minds—a chorus of voices from generations past.

Fragments of memories and emotions flooded their consciousness, guiding them deeper into Ember Bay's history. Visions danced behind their closed eyelids—images of battles fought with unwavering determination, sacrifices made for the greater good, and moments of triumph against insurmountable odds. They saw the faces of long-forgotten protectors who had laid down their lives to safeguard Ember Bay's delicate balance.

Tears welled in Ayden's eyes as he felt their pain and struggles intertwine with his own. "They faced so much darkness," he murmured, his voice laced with a mix of admiration and sorrow. Lucy squeezed Hadley's hand tightly as she witnessed the strength and resilience shown by their predecessors. "Their spirits live on within us," she said determinedly. "We carry their legacy forward.

" Nathan's voice broke through their reverie, his words filled with conviction. "We have been chosen to continue their fight—to protect Ember Bay from all supernatural threats." As they embraced this newfound connection to their ancestral protectors, a deep-seated knowledge settled within their hearts.

They understood that they were not alone in this journey—that they were part of an unbroken chain that stretched back through time. With renewed purpose burning within them, they opened their eyes and released each other's hands. The clearing seemed brighter somehow—as if even nature rejoiced in their communion with the spirits.

"We carry the strength of our ancestors," Hadley said softly, her gaze glowing with determination. "And together, we will ensure that Ember Bay remains safe for generations to come." Ayden nodded in agreement, his voice calm but resolute. "Their sacrifices will not be in vain. We will honor their memory by protecting this land.

" Nathan rose to his feet and looked out at the Bayou stretching beyond the clearing. "Let us forge ahead," he declared. "With our ancestral protectors guiding our steps, we will overcome any obstacle that comes our way." As they walked forward, their steps infused with newfound purpose and resolve, they could almost hear echoes of past protectors' whispers intertwining with the wind that rustled through the trees.

Their journey had taken on even greater significance as they united not only with each other but also with those who had paved the way for them. With hearts ablaze and spirits connected to something far greater than themselves, they ventured forth into Ember Bay—ready to face whatever challenges lay ahead and ensure that its mystical spirit would endure for eternity.

Uncovering Ancient Artifacts - Portals to Other Realms Guided by their intuition and ancient maps, the family ventured further into the hidden recesses of the Bayou. They stumbled upon a concealed cave entrance tucked away behind overgrown foliage, its secrets waiting to be discovered. The air grew charged with anticipation as they cautiously stepped inside, their flashlight beams illuminating ancient markings on the walls.

The cave walls seemed to whisper secrets of the past as the family made their way deeper into the chamber. Their footsteps echoed through the darkness, each sound carrying a sense of mystery and anticipation. As they rounded a corner, their flashlights illuminated an awe-inspiring sight—a vast chamber filled with ornate pedestals displaying various artifacts shimmering with mystical energy. Lucy's eyes widened in wonder as she took in the sight before her.

"Look at all these artifacts," she whispered, her voice filled with awe. "They seem to hold unimaginable power." Nathan nodded in agreement, his gaze scanning the room. "Each pedestal seems to be calling out to us," he remarked, his voice filled with intrigue. "But we must choose wisely. These artifacts could hold the key to unlocking new knowledge and abilities." Hadley's gaze shifted from pedestal to pedestal, her instincts guiding her choices. "I believe our choices will reveal something about ourselves," she said thoughtfully.

"We must trust our instincts and choose the artifact that resonates with us." Ayden's gentle voice chimed in, his eyes shining with curiosity.

"Let us proceed with caution but also embrace the possibilities that lie within this chamber," he suggested. "Together, we will uncover the true purpose of these artifacts." With determination in their hearts, the family approached different pedestals, drawn towards artifacts that seemed to call out to them.

Nathan's gaze fell upon a gleaming staff adorned with celestial symbols—symbols that mirrored his own connection to celestial energy. He reached out tentatively, allowing his fingertips to graze the staff's surface. In an instant, a warm glow enveloped him, transporting him through a portal to a realm filled with ethereal light and floating islands.

Lucy's eyes were drawn to a polished shield that seemed almost translucent, as if it could create a barrier against any threat. She extended her hand hesitantly, feeling a surge of energy course through her as she made contact with the shield. In an instant, she was transported through a portal to a realm engulfed in flames—a world of fire and heat that tested her bravery and resolve.

Hadley's attention was captured by an intricately crafted dagger—its blade glinting with an iridescent hue. She couldn't resist reaching for it, feeling a rush of energy flow through her veins as her fingertips grazed its surface. Suddenly, she found herself standing in a realm of shadows and darkness, where every step required careful navigation and cunning strategy.

Ayden's gaze settled on a delicate amulet embedded with healing gemstones—gems that mirrored his own ability to heal and restore balance. With gentle hands, he picked up the amulet, feeling a comforting warmth emanating from it. In an instant, he was transported through a portal to a realm of lush greenery and wounded creatures—a place where his healing touch was needed most.

As each family member embarked on their individual journeys through these realms connected to Ember Bay, they were faced with unique challenges that tested their strengths and pushed them beyond their limits. Nathan found himself facing celestial beings who challenged his spiritual connection; Lucy battled fire-breathing creatures while trying to protect innocent lives; Hadley navigated treacherous terrain using her stealth and agility; Ayden became immersed in a world where balance had been disrupted, forcing him to tap into his healing abilities like never before.

In these realms, amidst trials and tribulations, the family discovered not only more about themselves but also about Ember Bay's interconnectedness with other realms. They encountered beings who shared their commitment to protecting the balance between worlds and forged alliances rooted in mutual respect and understanding.

Days turned into nights as each family member delved deeper into their respective realms—gaining wisdom from encounters with mythical creatures, learning from ancient wise beings, and embracing their newfound abilities with an unwavering resolve.

Meanwhile, back in the chamber of artifacts, time stood still as each artifact pulsed with energy—waiting for its chosen guardian to return once their journey through these realms was complete. Within the mystical realm of fire, Lucy fought against the inferno that threatened to consume her.

Flames licked at her shield as she reflected wave after wave of fiery projectiles, her determination pushing her forward. She could feel the scorching heat seep into her bones, but she refused to let it weaken her resolve. "Stay focused, Lucy," she reminded herself, gritting her teeth and summoning all her strength.

With a powerful thrust of her shield, she sent a burst of energy towards her adversaries, causing them to stagger back momentarily. It was in that moment of vulnerability that Lucy saw her opportunity. Taking a deep breath, she charged forward, shield held high.

With each step, she felt the flames part before her, creating a path towards victory. The heat intensified, but Lucy pushed through it, fueled by a sense of duty that burned brighter than any fire. As her adversaries grew fewer in number, Lucy's confidence soared. She could see the end in sight—a triumph over the flames that sought to consume Ember Bay.

With one final burst of energy, she unleashed a force field imbued with all her might, extinguishing the flames and leaving only smoldering embers in their wake. Adrenaline coursed through Lucy's veins as she stood amidst the aftermath of her battle. The air was thick with smoke and the scent of victory. She took a moment to catch her breath, surveying the scene before her.

The realm of fire had been tamed by her courage and determination. In a realm cloaked in shadows, Hadley used her teleportation abilities to navigate treacherous landscapes. She moved from one shadowy alcove to another, blending seamlessly into the darkness around her. Her movements were swift and calculated, her eyes trained on every detail that might give away an advantage or present a lurking threat.

The realm seemed alive with hidden traps and shifting shadows, testing Hadley's resourcefulness and observant nature. But she was undeterred. She had faced countless challenges throughout her life, and this realm was no exception. With careful precision, Hadley traversed narrow ledges and avoided deadly pitfalls.

She relied on her natural nimbleness and intuition to guide every step. As she neared the heart of the realm, she sensed a presence lurking nearby—a formidable adversary awaiting its moment to strike. Her senses heightened, Hadley prepared herself for what lay ahead. Shadows wrapped around her like a protective cloak as she drew closer to the looming figure. Then, with lightning-fast reflexes, she struck—darting out from the darkness to deliver a decisive blow. The figure recoiled in pain, but it was not defeated. It retaliated with a ruthless attack that sent Hadley sprawling to the ground.

For a moment, doubt flickered within her—a nagging voice that whispered of weakness and defeat. But Hadley refused to succumb to it. Summoning every ounce of strength within her, she rose to her feet and faced her adversary head-on. Shadows swirled around her as she launched herself into a relentless assault—a dance between light and darkness that showcased both her skill and resilience. With each strike, Hadley grew more confident. Her adversary faltered under the weight of her determination, its strength waning with each passing moment.

And then, in one final act of defiance, Hadley delivered a blow that shattered the darkness surrounding them—the realm of shadows now bathed in light.

Breathing heavily, Hadley stood victorious amidst the shattered remains of her battle. The realm had tested her limits and pushed her to the brink, but she emerged stronger than ever—a beacon of resilience in a world consumed by darkness. In a serene sanctuary filled with wounded creatures, Ayden embraced his role as a healer and restorer of balance.

He moved with gentleness and grace amidst the injured beings, his touch soothing their pain and bringing comfort to their weary souls. With each healing intervention, Ayden tapped into his deepest well of compassion—an endless reservoir that flowed through him like a gentle current. He understood their suffering intimately—healing not only their physical wounds but also offering solace to those whose spirits had been broken by darkness.

As he tended to each creature's needs, Ayden offered words of encouragement—a soft reassurance that they were not alone in their struggles. His presence radiated serenity and peace, bringing an atmosphere of hope into even the most dire circumstances. With each healing touch and kind word spoken, Ayden witnessed transformative moments—a flicker of light returning to a desolate gaze or a wounded heart finding solace amidst chaos.

Every act of healing felt like coming home—a reminder of his purpose as a guardian and symbol of harmony in Ember Bay. As Ayden moved from one creature to another within the sanctuary, he felt a sense of unity—a sacred bond that connected him not only to these beings but also to Ember Bay itself.

It was in this realm that he realized the true power of healing—not just mending physical wounds but also restoring faith and rejuvenating hope. His heart swelled with gratitude as he surveyed the sanctuary—once broken and now teeming with newfound life and vitality. Within these walls, Ayden had found his place—his purpose as a healer forever intertwined with Ember Bay's delicate balance. As time passed within these realms connected to Ember Bay, each family member underwent trials that pushed them beyond their limits and tested their resolve.

They encountered mystical beings, navigated treacherous landscapes, battled formidable adversaries, and witnessed miracles unfold before their eyes. These realms served as crucibles—the fires through which their strengths were forged and their weaknesses were confronted. As Nathan emerged from the celestial realm with new insights into his connection to celestial energy; Lucy triumphed over fire itself; Hadley mastered shadows and unveiled hidden truths; Ayden restored balance and offered solace within his realm—their journeys rekindled something within them.

They felt more connected than ever—to each other and to their shared purpose as protectors of Ember Bay. With their individual trials complete, the family members returned through portals back to the central chamber—back to where their journey began amidst pedestals adorned with artifacts shimmering with mystical energy.

As the family members returned from their respective realms, the energy in the central chamber seemed to shift. The artifacts pulsed with a renewed intensity, as if they awaited the presence of those who had unlocked their true potential. Nathan, Lucy, Hadley, and Ayden stood in a circle, their eyes filled with a mixture of excitement and anticipation.

They gazed at each other, their experiences etched into their very beings, and a shared understanding passed between them. They were no longer just individuals; they were now a unified force, ready to face whatever challenges lay ahead. "We have been tested and transformed," Nathan said, his voice filled with conviction.

"These realms have shown us the extent of our abilities and the strength that lies within us." Lucy nodded in agreement. "We have faced fire, shadows, healing crises—a testament to our resilience and the power of unity." Hadley's gaze darted from one family member to another, her heart bursting with pride.

"Together, we have proven that we are more than just protectors; we are warriors destined to safeguard Ember Bay." Ayden's calming presence radiated through the room as he spoke softly. "Our trials have not only honed our individual skills but also deepened our connection to this mystical realm. We are united with its energy." With a shared sense of purpose, they approached the pedestals once again—this time guided not only by intuition but also by the wisdom gained from their experiences. Each family member chose an artifact that resonated with them—the one that represented their newfound strengths and understanding. Nathan's hand gravitated towards a finely crafted bow imbued with celestial energy—an embodiment of his connection to the stars.

As he held it, he felt a surge of power coursing through his veins—a reminder of his role as a celestial guardian. Lucy's fingers brushed against a gauntlet pulsating with fiery energy—a symbol of her triumph over flames. She felt a sense of empowerment as she donned the gauntlet—knowing that fire would bend to her will and protect what she held dear. Hadley's touch landed on a pendant adorned with intricate shadow motifs—a token of her mastery over darkness.

As she fastened it around her neck, she knew that her ability to navigate unseen paths and uncover hidden knowledge was now amplified. Ayden's hand reached for a staff adorned with celestial gemstones—a reflection of his gift for healing and restoring balance. As he held it, he felt an even deeper connection to the celestial energies that flowed through him—knowing that he could bring harmony to both body and soul. As each family member embraced their chosen artifact, the central chamber seemed to come alive with energy.

A symphony of colors danced around them, blending seamlessly with their auras—a tangible representation of their unity and purpose. "We are no longer just protectors," Nathan declared solemnly. "We are guardians bound by destiny and tethered to Ember Bay's eternal magic." Lucy nodded in agreement, her eyes shining with determination. "From this day forward, we will stand together against any darkness that threatens this realm—drawing upon our individual strengths and unwavering bond.

" Hadley's voice rang out boldly. "We will uncover the secrets of Ember Bay's past and journey into uncharted territories—undaunted by what lies ahead." Ayden's serene presence enveloped the room as he spoke softly yet powerfully. "With compassion as our guide, we will heal wounds inflicted by both physical and emotional darkness—bringing peace and harmony to this sacred land."

As their voices faded into the ether, a quiet stillness settled over the central chamber.

The artifacts shimmered with approval, recognizing the newfound resolve within each family member. They understood that these protectors were no longer ordinary—they were Elemental Guardians united by purpose and fueled by the immense power residing within them. With every step they took forward, beams of light illuminated their path—a testament to their connection with Ember Bay's enchantment.

They were ready to face whatever lay ahead—uncovering ancient secrets, vanquishing supernatural threats, and protecting this mystical realm at all costs. As they left the central chamber behind—the artifacts pulsating with energy behind them—they carried with them newfound strength and a sense of purpose imprinted deep within their souls.

The journey continued, but now they walked as more than just a family—they were warriors bound by destiny and guided by the very essence of Ember Bay itself. Together, they would shape its future and ensure that its magical legacy endured for generations to come.

And so, hand in hand, hearts ablaze with determination—they ventured forth into the unknown—ready to embrace every challenge as Elemental Guardians united in their quest to safeguard Ember Bay and preserve its eternal magic.

Chapter 6: The Bayou's Ancient Guardians

As the family followed the ancient maps and cryptic clues deeper into the heart of the Bayou, they couldn't help but feel a sense of anticipation building within them. The atmosphere grew increasingly mystical, with every step guided by the flickering light filtering through the dense canopy above. Nathan's keen eyes scanned the surroundings, searching for any signs of danger or hidden secrets.

He felt a tingling in his fingertips as if the very air was charged with an unknown energy. Lucy's fiery hair shimmered in the dappled sunlight, her determined gaze fixed on the path ahead. She could sense subtle shifts in the air, whispers that seemed to beckon her forward. Her warrior instincts kicked in, and her grip tightened around her gauntlets. She shared a knowing glance with Nathan, their unspoken connection strengthening their resolve.

Hadley moved with a grace that was almost ethereal, her midnight black hair swaying gently with each step. Her piercing green eyes darted from tree to tree, taking in every detail of their surroundings. The mysterious energy calling to her grew stronger with each passing moment, guiding her through the thick vegetation towards their destination.

Ayden walked with a calm presence, his soft-spoken words carrying a sense of wisdom beyond his years. His healing staff glowed softly, its celestial energy intertwining with the enchantment of the Bayou itself. He took solace in the knowledge that they were on the right path, guided by forces greater than themselves.

Finally, they arrived at a secluded clearing bathed in golden light. The air was heavy with a sense of anticipation, as if nature itself held its breath in anticipation of what was to come. Before them stood a statue-like figure made entirely of stone and soil, towering over them like an ancient guardian. Nathan's piercing eyes met those of the earth guardian, his stealthy nature mirroring the stillness of the figure before him.

"We've been called here," he said, his voice barely above a whisper. "We're ready to prove ourselves." Lucy's voice rang out confidently, her fierce determination shining through her words. "We are warriors forged in fire and steel," she declared.

"We stand ready to face any challenge that lies before us." Hadley stepped forward, her slender frame emanating an air of mystery and resilience. "We have journeyed through darkness to find our purpose," she stated. "We are prepared to uncover the hidden truths of this land." Ayden's kind eyes met the guardian's stony gaze, a gentle smile forming on his lips. "We come with open hearts and boundless compassion," he said softly.

"Our purpose is to heal and restore balance." The earth guardian's expression softened ever so slightly, as if acknowledging their determination and purpose. With a slow nod of approval, it beckoned them forward into the clearing. They followed, their steps guided by an invisible force leading them closer to their destiny. The clearing was a serene oasis amidst the mystical chaos of the Bayou.

Moss-covered ground greeted their feet as they entered the sacred space, where wildflowers bloom in vibrant hues all around them. The scent of damp earth mingled with fragrant petals, creating an intoxicating aroma that filled their senses. Nathan's agility was put to the test as he navigated through a treacherous obstacle course of boulders and fallen trees.

Each movement required precision and balance, his heightened ninja skills shining through as he effortlessly leaped and twisted through the hazardous terrain. Lucy's strength was tested as she faced massive stones that stood in her path.

With every ounce of power she possessed, she summoned force fields around herself and pushed against the formidable obstacles. Sweat trickled down her brow as she poured every ounce of her fiery spirit into overcoming the challenge. Hadley closed her eyes for a moment, allowing herself to be guided by the natural rhythms surrounding her.

As she began to sing, her voice harmonized with the whispers of leaves and the babbling of nearby streams. The music resonated with the very heartbeat of the earth itself, infusing her trial with a melodic beauty that showcased her deep connection to nature. Ayden stood centered amidst fertile soil, his healing staff glowing softly in his grasp.

With each gentle touch, life sprouted forth from barren patches of ground, revealing his ability to nurture and restore balance to even the most desolate areas. He closed his eyes and allowed himself to become one with nature as he channeled his celestial energy into rejuvenation. Together, they faced their trials with unwavering determination and commitment to their newfound roles as guardians.

The earth guardian observed each trial intently, its stony expression betraying nothing but an underlying sense of validation. As Nathan completed his final hurdle and landed gracefully on solid ground, he looked towards Lucy with a triumphant smile. "We did it," he exclaimed breathlessly. Lucy's voice was filled with pride as she met Nathan's gaze.

"We make a great team," she replied, her fiery spirit shining through every word. Hadley approached Ayden with a sense of wonderment in her emerald-green eyes. "Who would have thought our destinies would lead us here?" she mused.

Ayden's calm demeanor exuded contentment as he regarded his fellow protectors. "It is no coincidence," he said softly. "This is where we are meant to be." In unison, they turned towards the earth guardian who had been silently observing their trials throughout. Its stony expression softened ever so slightly, a hint of approval twinkling in its eyes.

Nathan couldn't help but feel a surge of adrenaline coursing through his veins as he prepared to face his next trial. The earth guardian's gaze held a challenge in its stony eyes, urging him to push himself further. With a deep breath, he steadied himself and leaped into action. The obstacle course before him was a labyrinth of treacherous underground tunnels. In the dim light, Nathan relied on his exceptional ninja skills and keen senses to navigate the winding path.

The earth beneath his feet seemed to respond to his every step, guiding him away from potential pitfalls and traps. As he moved with agility and precision, Nathan's mind focused solely on his goal—to reach the end of the tunnel unscathed.

Doubts tried to creep into his mind, whispering that he might not be skilled enough or fast enough to conquer this challenge. But he shook off those thoughts, reminding himself of his purpose and the importance of protecting Ember Bay. Lucy watched Nathan's every move with bated breath.

Her heart swelled with pride as she witnessed his swift movements and unwavering determination. She knew that he had the strength and skill to overcome any obstacle that stood in his way. With each step he took, Nathan could feel the energy of the earth pulsating through him.

It fueled his resolve and sharpened his senses, allowing him to anticipate any danger that lay ahead. He gracefully maneuvered through tight spaces, his lithe frame barely making a sound as he evaded potential hazards. There were moments when Nathan found himself surrounded by complete darkness, unable to rely on his eyes alone.

In those instances, he tapped into his other senses—listening for the faintest sounds, feeling vibrations under his fingertips—to guide him forward. He trusted in his training and in the connection he had forged with the earth. As Nathan neared the end of the tunnel, a surge of triumph coursed through his body. He emerged from the darkness into a small chamber bathed in soft light—a testament to his success.

Breathing heavily, he looked back at the labyrinth he had conquered, feeling a sense of accomplishment wash over him. Lucy rushed forward to embrace him, her fiery hair cascading around them both as she hugged him tightly. "You did it," she whispered against his ear, her voice filled with pride and awe.

Nathan grinned as he wrapped an arm around Lucy's shoulders. "We did it together," he replied, never forgetting the importance of their unity as a family and as protectors of Ember Bay. Meanwhile, Hadley observed Nathan's trial with a mix of admiration and curiosity in her piercing green eyes. She had always admired his stealthy nature and precision, but seeing him in action brought a newfound appreciation for what he was capable of.

She knew that her own trial awaited her—challenging her to harness her unique abilities and unveil her true potential. As Nathan and Lucy rejoined the group, Ayden offered Nathan a nod of acknowledgement. He understood the challenges that Nathan had faced underground—the doubts that threatened to cloud one's mind as they navigated the darkness.

Ayden had experienced similar moments during his trials, where self-doubt tried to chip away at his confidence. Hadley took a deep breath, mentally preparing herself for what lay ahead. She felt a renewed sense of determination radiating throughout her being. It was time for her to confront her fears and embrace the role of the Night Owl.

With a shared understanding amongst them, the family turned their attention towards Hadley as she stepped forward to face her own trial. Her lithe figure moved with grace as she approached the designated area—a pool of water shimmering under the sunlight streaming through gaps in the foliage overhead.

The water guardian awaited her arrival—a figure made entirely of cascading water droplets that shimmered with an ethereal glow. Its presence exuded calmness and tranquility, yet held an air of mystery that drew Hadley closer. As Hadley met the water guardian's tranquil gaze, she could feel her heartbeat quicken with anticipation.

This trial would test not only her physical abilities but also her emotional resilience—a challenge that struck at the heart of who she was as an individual. She hesitated for a moment, taking a last calming breath before stepping into the pool of water ahead. As soon as her foot touched the liquid surface, ripples spread outwards—echoes of her presence within this mystical realm.

Hadley's slender form disappeared beneath the water's surface, plunging into a world unknown—a realm where she would be forced to confront her deepest fears and insecurities head-on. As Hadley descended into the watery depths, her senses were immediately engulfed by a surreal tranquility.

The water embraced her like a second skin, guiding her through a labyrinth of underwater passages with an otherworldly grace. She moved with ease, her slender form blending seamlessly with the ethereal environment. With each passing moment, Hadley felt the currents of the water guardian's energy swirling around her. It whispered ancient secrets, encouraging her to confront the doubts and fears that had plagued her for far too long. She knew that this trial would require her to trust in herself and fully embrace her role as the Night Owl.

Amidst the gentle ebb and flow of the water, images began to materialize before Hadley's eyes—visions of moments where she had faltered in her path, questioning her own worth and purpose. These memories threatened to overwhelm her, but deep within her, a flicker of determination burned bright. Drawing on her inner strength, Hadley mustered every ounce of resolve she possessed. With an elegant stroke, she propelled herself forward, determined to break free from the chains of self-doubt that had held her back for far too long.

The water seemed to respond to her newfound sense of purpose, guiding her towards a chamber bathed in a soft blue glow. As Hadley emerged from the depths, she found herself standing before a mirror-like pool surrounded by glowing lily pads. In its crystalline surface, she caught sight of her reflection—a moment frozen in time. Her midnight black hair hung loose around her shoulders, her piercing green eyes shining with an unwavering determination. It was a stark contrast to the doubt that had once clouded her gaze.

A voice resonated within Hadley's mind—a soothing melody that seemed to be carried on the very currents of the water itself. "Embrace the shadows within you," it whispered. "They are not a barrier but a source of strength." Hadley studied her reflection intently, taking in every detail. She saw not only the flaws and imperfections but also the resilience and determination that shone through them.

Each scar represented a battle fought, each moment of doubt overcome. In that reflection, she saw the true potential that lay dormant within her. With renewed confidence coursing through her veins, Hadley extended a hand towards the mirror-like pool.

As her fingertips made contact with the water's surface, gentle ripples spread across its stillness—a tangible manifestation of her acceptance and embrace of her own inner shadows. In that moment, Hadley realized that her uniqueness was not something to be feared or hidden away—it was a gift that set her apart as a protector of Ember Bay.

She understood that her ability to blend into shadows was not a weakness but a strength—an asset that could be used to navigate unseen dangers and uncover hidden truths. The water guardian observed Hadley's transformation with a sense of satisfaction and approval. It recognized in her a newfound sense of purpose—the willingness to face darkness head-on in order to protect what was dear.

As Hadley emerged from the chamber, dripping with water yet radiating an undeniable confidence, the rest of the family welcomed her with open arms. Nathan pulled her into a tight embrace, his voice filled with pride. "You did it," he murmured against her ear. Lucy's fiery spirit blazed brightly as she hugged Hadley tightly.

"You've unlocked your true potential," she declared, admiration evident in her voice. Ayden met Hadley's gaze with a gentle smile. "We always knew you were capable of greatness," he said softly. In that moment, surrounded by the unwavering support and love of her family, Hadley felt a profound sense of belonging—knowing that they were bound together by their shared destiny as protectors of Ember Bay.

With their trials complete, the family gathered at the center of the clearing where the earth and water guardians awaited them. The two elemental beings bowed their heads in acknowledgement—silent testament to the family's worthiness and their readiness to fulfill their roles as protectors.

Words needn't be spoken between them—it was an unspoken understanding forged through countless trials and challenges faced together. They stood united, ready to face whatever lay ahead, fueled by their newly discovered powers and unwavering determination. The elemental beings guided them towards their next destination—the realm of fire and air—where even greater challenges awaited them.

But as they journeyed deeper into the mystical heart of the Bayou, one thought echoed through their minds: They were no longer just four individuals—they were now The Elemental Guardians, bound by destiny and united in their commitment to protect Ember Bay from supernatural threats. And so they pressed onward, prepared for whatever trials lay ahead—their hearts brimming with hope and their spirits ablaze with purpose.

The Bayou's Ancient Guardians - The Fire Within The family followed the guidance of the earth guardian, their footsteps echoing through the dense undergrowth as they ventured deeper into the heart of the Bayou. A warm glow permeated through the foliage, casting an ethereal light on their path. There was a sense of anticipation in the air, a crackling energy that fueled their excitement and resolve. As they approached a secluded part of the woods, a blazing inferno came into view. It danced and flickered with an intensity that both captivated and intimidated. The fire guardian awaited them, a figure wreathed in flames that seemed to pulse with its own fiery life.

Lucy's fierce gaze remained fixed on the fire guardian, her hands tightening around her gauntlets in anticipation. She could feel the heat radiating from it, warming her skin and igniting a passionate fire within her. Her warrior spirit burned hot as she prepared to face her trial. Nathan stood tall beside Lucy, his keen eyes scanning their surroundings for any potential threats.

He felt the heat seep into his bones, energizing him with an intensity that mirrored the flames before him. His ninja instincts kicked in, urging him to stay agile and alert. Hadley observed the fire guardian with a mixture of curiosity and caution.

The mysterious figure exuded power and strength, its fiery presence captivating her attention. She could sense the raw energy emanating from it, beckoning her forward to embrace her own inner fire. Ayden approached the fire guardian with calmness and serenity, undeterred by the intense heat that engulfed them all.

His compassionate nature allowed him to see beyond the flames, recognizing the transformative power they held within. He knew that this trial would test his ability to harness his healing powers in the face of adversity. The family stood together, their collective presence radiating determination and unity. They shared a knowing glance, an unspoken acknowledgement of the challenges that lay ahead.

In unison, they stepped forward to face their trials, fully embracing the fire within themselves. Lucy's trial began with a wall of flames that seemed insurmountable. The intense heat threatened to overwhelm her as she stepped closer, but she refused to falter. With a surge of energy, Lucy summoned her force fields, creating a protective barrier around herself as she pushed through the scorching flames.

Each step brought her closer to victory, her fiery spirit fueling her determination. Nathan's trial was a test of agility and precision amidst ever-shifting pillars of fire. The searing heat licked at his skin as he weaved through the towering inferno with grace and ease. He relied on his exceptional ninja skills to dodge each flaming obstacle that came his way, his movements mirroring the flickering flames around him.

Hadley's trial called upon her to harness her love for music to ignite passion amid searing flames. As she stood amidst roaring fires, she closed her eyes and allowed herself to be consumed by the music within her. Her voice soared through the air, harmonizing with the crackling flames as they danced together in perfect synchrony.

Through melody and rhythm, Hadley created a symphony of hope in the midst of chaos. Ayden faced scorching temperatures that tested his ability to remain calm and centered in order to access his healing powers. The intense heat threatened to overwhelm him, but he drew upon his inner wellspring of tranquility and focused his celestial energy on soothing the flames rather than extinguishing them.

With each gentle touch, he brought balance and harmony to the fiery realm. As each family member completed their trials, a sense of triumph washed over them. They emerged from the inferno with renewed strength and purpose, their connection to fire deepened by their individual experiences. The fire guardian observed their trials with an approving gaze, its flames swaying in appreciation of their resilience and determination.

It recognized in them the capacity to wield fire responsibly—for protection rather than destruction—knowing that they would honor its power. With newfound confidence coursing through their veins, the family turned towards one another once more. Their eyes met in silent acknowledgment, a shared understanding that they had conquered this trial together.

In that moment, surrounded by roaring flames yet unscathed by their heat, they understood what it meant to be The Elemental Guardians—the chosen protectors of Ember Bay. As the family emerged from the realm of fire, their spirits ablaze with newfound confidence, they found themselves standing on the precipice of a great expanse—a seemingly endless sky that stretched out before them.

The air crackled with energy, carrying whispers of ancient knowledge and wisdom. Above them, billowing clouds swirled in shades of fiery red and cool blue, reflecting the ever-shifting balance between fire and air. They watched as gusts of wind danced through the treetops, leaving a gentle rustle in their wake. It was in this realm that they would face their next trial—the domain of the air guardian.

Lucy's eyes sharpened with anticipation as she surveyed the scene before her. The winds stirred her fiery hair into a frenzy, mirroring her own untamed spirit. She flexed her gauntleted fists, ready to harness the power of the air as she prepared to face her trial. Nathan's keen senses honed in on the subtle currents of air around him. He could feel the invisible threads weaving through his environment, whispering secrets only the wind understood.

As he moved through this ethereal realm, he knew his agility and precision would be put to the test. Hadley's slender form seemed to sway amidst the gentle breeze, her midnight black hair dancing in rhythm with the wind's whispers. She closed her eyes for a moment, letting the current carry away any lingering doubts or fears.

In this realm, she felt a sense of freedom—a calling to embrace her own inner flight. Ayden's calm presence seemed to merge seamlessly with the tranquility of the air. With each breath, he felt a connection to something greater—an unseen force that carried healing and harmony. His journey through this realm would require him to channel his celestial energy into uplifting those around him.

Together, they stepped forward into this vast expanse, fully immersing themselves in the embrace of the air guardian's realm. The wind beckoned them forward with a gentle caress, guiding them towards their individual trials. Lucy's trial began as she stood atop a high precipice overlooking a swirling vortex of air currents. Her gauntlets hummed with energy as she extended her arms and leaned into the rush of wind.

The gusts grew stronger, threatening to push her back, but she stood firm and focused. With each step closer to the edge, Lucy summoned her force fields to create a shield against the powerful currents. She gracefully maneuvered through the tempestuous winds, maintaining her balance and control even as they raged around her.

Nathan's trial took place amidst a labyrinth of swirling gusts that threatened to disorient him. He relied on his ninja training to navigate through these invisible mazes of wind—each step precise and deliberate. Using his heightened senses, he anticipated changes in direction and adjusted his movements accordingly.

His body became one with the wind, mirroring its fluidity and grace. Hadley's trial called upon her to embrace her affinity for music in order to harmonize with the symphony of the wind. She closed her eyes and let herself be carried by the currents, trusting in their guidance as she began to sing. Her melodic voice shimmered through the air—rising and falling in perfect harmony with the wind's own melodies.

As her song resonated with ethereal beauty, it created pockets of calm within the turbulence—a testament to her ability to find serenity amidst chaos. Ayden's trial required him to channel his celestial energy into uplifting those caught in turbulent winds below. He descended from above, his healing staff glowing softly as he focused his energy on soothing and calming those buffeted by the stormy currents.

With gentle touches and whispered words of comfort, he brought a sense of tranquility to those who needed it most—restoring balance amidst chaos. As each family member completed their trials, they felt a deep connection not only to themselves but also to each other—their individual strengths harmonizing with one another in perfect unity. The air guardian observed their trials with an approving gaze, its currents undulating in appreciation of their resilience and adaptability.

It recognized in them a profound understanding of how air could be harnessed responsibly—for protection and for flight—knowing that they would honor its power. With triumphant smiles on their faces, the family regrouped at the epicenter of this vast sky realm—a serene oasis where gentle breezes caressed their skin and whispered secrets only they could understand. In unison, they turned towards one another, finding strength and solace in their shared experiences.

They knew that their trials had not only forged them into stronger individuals but also bound them together as a family—the Elemental Guardians entrusted with protecting Ember Bay. As they ventured further into this mystical realm—the final domain—their hearts brimming with hope and determination, they couldn't help but wonder what awaited them at its end. But for now, they would savor this moment—the unity they had found within themselves and within each other—as they prepared for whatever challenges lay ahead. As the family moved deeper into the mystical realm of fire and air, they could feel a change in the atmosphere—a crackling energy that filled the air and stirred their spirits. Before them lay a vast expanse of swirling flames, dancing in harmony with gusts of wind that seemed to call out to them.

Lucy's fiery hair billowed behind her as she stepped forward, her gauntlets radiating a warm glow. She could feel the heat of the flames lapping against her skin, yet it did not burn. Instead, it fueled her determination, igniting a fire within her that burned brighter than ever before. Nathan's keen eyes scanned their surroundings, searching for any signs of danger lurking amidst the dancing flames.

The air currents whispered secrets only he could understand, guiding his movements with a precision that mirrored the agility he possessed. He knew that this trial would push him to his limits, testing his ability to navigate through the ever-shifting elements. Hadley stood at the edge of the inferno, her slender figure swaying gracefully in the currents of wind. Her midnight black hair danced in rhythm with the gusts, reflecting her adaptability and resilience.

She closed her eyes for a moment, allowing herself to be carried by the whispers of the wind, trusting in its guidance to lead her through this trial. Ayden's calming presence seemed to merge effortlessly with the fiery and airy realms. His soft-spoken words carried on the wind, soothing the flames and bringing balance to their chaotic dance.

He understood that this trial would require him to harness his celestial energy in order to restore harmony and tranquility. Together, they stepped forward into the swirling maelstrom—a delicate balance between fire and air. The flames leapt and twirled around them, the wind carrying their voices as they prepared to face their individual trials. Lucy's trial began amidst a sea of flames that rose and fell in a mesmerizing dance.

She felt the intense heat envelop her, but instead of fear, she felt a surge of adrenaline fueling her every move. With each step she took, she summoned her force fields to protect herself from being consumed by the inferno. Her gauntlets hummed with energy as she pushed through the flames, her determination unwavering. Nathan's trial challenged his agility and reflexes as he navigated through a labyrinth of fiery obstacles suspended in mid-air.

The gusts of wind added an extra layer of complexity, threatening to knock him off balance at every turn. But Nathan relied on his ninja skills and honed senses, anticipating each shift in the flames and adjusting his movements accordingly. He moved with grace and precision, easily navigating through the fierce obstacles before him.

Hadley's trial called upon her to find harmony within chaos—to blend her enchanting melodies with the roaring flames and gusts of wind swirling around her. As she raised her voice, her songs resonated with the very essence of fire and air, creating a symphony that brought solace amidst the tumultuous elements. She allowed herself to be carried by the currents of wind and embraced by the warmth of the flames, blending seamlessly with both realms.

Ayden's trial required him to channel his celestial energy into bringing healing and restoration to those caught in the midst of fiery turmoil. He extended his healing staff towards those consumed by flames or struggling against powerful gusts of wind. With gentle touches and calming words, he soothed their fears and restored balance within their beings. His celestial energy merged effortlessly with fire and air, bringing tranquility wherever it was needed.

As each family member completed their trials, a sense of triumph swept over them. They emerged from the depths of fire and wind unscathed but forever changed—they had harnessed the power within themselves and discovered a deeper connection to their elemental roles.

The fire guardian observed their trials with an approving gaze, its flickering flames dancing in appreciation of their resilience and mastery over the elements. It recognized in them a profound understanding of how fire and air could be wielded responsibly—for protection and transformation—knowing that they would honor its power.

With smiles on their faces and hearts ablaze with purpose, they regrouped in the center of this fiery realm—the convergence point between fire and air. In that moment, surrounded by swirling flames and gusts of wind, they felt an unbreakable bond—a unity forged through shared experiences and unwavering determination.

The family turned towards one another once more—eyes filled with pride and admiration for what they had accomplished together. Each individual had faced their own trials but had done so knowing they were supported by their loved ones—an unbreakable team bound by destiny. As they ventured further into this mystical realm—the final domain—they did so with hearts brimming with hope and determination.

Chapter 7: The Guardian's Vision

In the heart of the mystical Bayou, the family gathered in a secluded clearing, surrounded by towering cypress trees and a gentle babbling stream. The atmosphere was charged with ancient whispers as they prepared to delve into Ayden's prophetic dream. Nathan, his piercing eyes reflecting a sense of determination, motioned for everyone to gather closer.

"Alright, everyone, let's hear what Ayden has seen," he said, his tone filled with anticipation. Ayden took a deep breath, his voice steady yet tinged with excitement. "In my dream," he began, his eyes focused on each family member in turn, "I saw a great darkness descending upon Ember Bay.

It was a force unlike anything we have faced before." Lucy's fiery red hair seemed to ignite with a newfound resolve as she listened intently. "What did it look like? How did it make you feel?" she asked, her voice laced with curiosity. Ayden paused for a moment, searching for the right words to convey the depth of his experience. "It was an all-encompassing darkness, like an impenetrable mist that swallowed everything in its path," he explained. "And it filled me with a sense of foreboding and urgency, as if time itself were running out.

" Hadley, her midnight black hair blending seamlessly with the shadows around her, leaned forward. "Were there any symbols or visions alongside the darkness?" she inquired, her voice carrying a hint of mystery.

Ayden nodded, his expression thoughtful. "Yes, there were symbols... intricate patterns carved into ancient stones. They seemed to hold a hidden message, but I couldn't decipher their meaning," he confessed. As Ayden spoke, a sense of unity enveloped the family. They exchanged knowing glances, understanding the weight of their shared destiny. Each member brought their own unique perspective to unraveling the enigma before them. Nathan reached out and placed a reassuring hand on Ayden's shoulder. "Your dream is more than just a glimpse into our future," he declared. "It is a call to action, a warning that we must prepare ourselves for whatever lies ahead.

" Ayden's eyes sparkled with determination as he looked at his fellow guardians. "We cannot simply stand idly by and watch as the darkness consumes Ember Bay," he said firmly. "We have been chosen for a reason, given these powers for a purpose. We are meant to be its protectors.

" Lucy nodded in agreement, her fierce gaze fixated on Ayden. "You're right. We must bring forth our full potential and face this threat head-on," she urged, her voice filled with conviction. Hadley's piercing green eyes shone with determination as she added her own thoughts. "The symbols you saw... they hold clues to our path forward," she said. "We will analyze them together and unearth their hidden meanings.

" Ayden smiled gratefully at his companions. "Thank you all for your unwavering support," he said sincerely. "Together, we will confront this darkness and protect Ember Bay from its clutches.

" With renewed resolve and a shared vision of their purpose in mind, the family set out on their quest for knowledge and guidance. They knew that they were not alone and that their collective strength would guide them through the challenges that awaited them.

As they left the peaceful clearing behind, each step forward solidified their commitment to one another and their duty as protectors of Ember Bay. Little did they know that their journey would lead them to discover even more about themselves and the interconnectedness of their destinies.

As the family ventured deeper into the Bayou, guided by ancient maps and cryptic clues, they stumbled upon an overgrown path that led them to an ancient ritual site. The air crackled with energy as they stepped into the sacred space, surrounded by tall, slender columns adorned with intricate carvings. Nathan glanced at his family members, their eyes filled with anticipation and curiosity.

"This place is steeped in ancient power," he whispered, his voice carrying traces of awe. Lucy's fiery red hair seemed to dance with excitement as she took a step closer to one of the altars. "These carvings... they depict elemental symbols," she observed, her voice brimming with eagerness. "I think this is where we can unlock the full potential of our elemental powers.

" Hadley, her eyes reflecting newfound determination, nodded in agreement. "If there's any place that can help us harness the true essence of our abilities, it's here," she said, her voice tinged with a hint of mystery. Ayden closed his eyes for a moment, his hands gently touching the worn stone surface of an altar. "I can feel the ancient wisdom coursing through this place," he murmured, his voice reverent. "The spirits of the past are whispering their secrets to us.

" Nathan raised an eyebrow in curiosity. "What do the spirits say?" he asked, his voice filled with intrigue. Ayden opened his eyes and met Nathan's gaze. "They speak of a forgotten ritual, passed down through generations," he explained. "A ritual that can connect us even more deeply to Ember Bay's elemental forces." Lucy clasped her hands together, her eyes shining with excitement.

"We have to learn this ritual," she declared, her voice filled with determination. "It may hold the key to unlocking our true potential as protectors." The family turned their attention back to the altars, examining the worn inscriptions and symbols etched into the stone. They knew that their journey had brought them to this moment - a chance to embrace their destiny and delve deeper into their connection with the elemental forces of Ember Bay. A figure cloaked in flowing robes appeared before them, their presence commanding yet nurturing.

It was their enigmatic mentor, who had guided them thus far on their path. The mentor smiled knowingly and began to explain the steps of the forgotten ritual. Each family member listened attentively, committing every detail to memory. The mentor emphasized the importance of focus and intention, urging them to tap into their inner strength as they performed the ritual. With newfound knowledge and determination burning in their hearts, they began to practice the ritual together.

The air around them shimmered with ethereal energy as they chanted ancient words and moved in synchrony with one another. Nathan felt a surge of earth energy envelop him, grounding him in a sense of stability and resilience. He could almost feel the pulse of the earth beneath his feet, connecting him to the very essence of Ember Bay. Lucy's movements became imbued with fiery passion as she channeled her inner flame.

She felt a rush of power coursing through her veins, burning away any doubts or fears that lingered within. Hadley seemed to blend seamlessly into the shadows as she tapped into her innate ability to manipulate darkness. Her form became elusive, almost ethereal, as she danced with the night itself.

Ayden's body radiated celestial energy as he reached out to the heavens, connecting with the divine forces that flowed through him. He felt a sense of peace wash over him, calming any restless thoughts or uncertainties that plagued his mind. As they completed the ritual together, their bond strengthened even further. They knew that this was just the beginning - a stepping stone towards fully embracing their roles as protectors and defenders of Ember Bay. With renewed determination and enhanced understanding of their elemental powers, the family set forth from the ancient ritual site.

They were ready to face whatever challenges lay ahead, knowing that they were equipped with both individual strengths and collective unity. Little did they know that this newfound connection with elemental magic would open doors to even greater revelations about themselves and Ember Bay's hidden truths. But for now, they could only marvel at how far they had come on their journey and eagerly anticipate what awaited them on their path. As they left the ancient ritual site behind, the family couldn't help but feel a renewed sense of purpose and determination.

The power of the elemental forces coursed through their veins, intermingling with their own unique abilities. They knew that they were now ready to face the impending darkness that threatened Ember Bay. Nathan led the way, his ninja skills allowing him to navigate through the dense underbrush with ease. "We've unlocked a power within ourselves that we never knew existed," he said, his voice filled with quiet confidence. "Now it's time to put that power to good use.

" Lucy nodded, her fiery red hair gleaming in the sunlight as she followed closely behind Nathan. "We won't let this darkness consume our home," she declared, her voice ringing out like a battle cry. "We'll fight with everything we have and protect Ember Bay with our lives." Hadley, her eyes gleaming with newfound strength, melded seamlessly with the shadows as she joined the others. "I can feel the night itself embracing me," she whispered, her voice filled with a sense of awe.

"I'm ready to confront whatever challenges lie ahead." Ayden walked alongside them, his celestial energy radiating a soothing presence. "We must remember to stay true to ourselves and to each other," he reminded them, his voice gentle yet firm. "Through unity and trust, we will overcome any obstacle that comes our way." The family pressed onward, their path illuminated by beams of sunlight that filtered through the dense foliage above.

As they made their way deeper into the heart of the Bayou, they couldn't help but notice a subtle change in the air. The whispers of the ancient spirits grew stronger, guiding them towards their next destination. Suddenly, an ethereal figure appeared before them - a spirit of one of Ember Bay's ancient guardians.

The spirit's translucent form seemed to dance on the edge of reality as it spoke in a hushed voice. "Children of Ember Bay," the spirit began, its words resonating deep within each family member's soul. "The darkness you seek to defeat is more powerful than you can imagine. But fear not, for your destiny has been written in the stars.

Lucy stepped forward, her eyes narrowing with determination. "Tell us what we need to do," she insisted, her voice unwavering. "We are ready to face this darkness head-on." The spirit smiled knowingly and raised its translucent hand. A map materialized in front of them - a map that revealed hidden passages and long-forgotten paths within Ember Bay. "This map will guide you to places where ancient artifacts and knowledge can be found," the spirit explained.

"Each artifact will grant you new insights and powers that will aid you in your battle against darkness." Nathan studied the map intently, memorizing every twist and turn, every symbol and landmark. He looked up at the spirit with determination burning in his eyes. "We won't rest until we've obtained every artifact and harnessed every ounce of power we can," he vowed. The spirit nodded approvingly and faded away, leaving behind an air of mystery and anticipation. The family knew that their journey had just begun - a journey that would take them to distant lands within Ember Bay and beyond.

With the map in hand and their hearts filled with resolve, the family continued on their path. They were prepared to face whatever challenges awaited them - challenges that would test their strength, unity, and unwavering commitment to protecting Ember Bay. Little did they know what lay ahead - trials that would push them to their limits and revelations that would shape their destinies forever.

But one thing was certain - together, they were unstoppable. Secrets of Elemental Magic: An Ancient Ritual Unveiled As the family continued their journey through the Bayou, guided by the ancient map they had discovered, they found themselves standing before a hidden cave. Its entrance was obscured by vines and moss, seeming to guard the secrets within. Nathan, his eyes scanning the cave's exterior, turned to face his family.

"This could be the place we've been searching for," he said, his voice filled with anticipation. "The map leads us here, to uncover the secrets of elemental magic." Lucy nodded in agreement, her fists clenched with determination. "If there's any place that can reveal the true potential of our powers, it's this cave," she asserted, her voice brimming with confidence. Hadley stepped forward, her green eyes shining with curiosity. "Let's not waste any more time," she suggested eagerly. "There's so much we have yet to learn about ourselves and the mystical forces within Ember Bay.

" Ayden, his face illuminated by a soft smile, added his own thoughts. "We've come this far on our journey," he reminded them gently. "It's time to unlock the full extent of our abilities and embrace our destinies as protectors.

" With a collective nod, the family entered the cave, their footsteps echoing in the darkness. They could feel the air grow cooler and heavier as they ventured further into the cavernous depths. Tall stalagmites lined their path, casting eerie shadows that danced on the walls. The faint sound of dripping water echoed through the silence, creating an otherworldly ambiance.

As they walked deeper into the cave, they came upon a small chamber bathed in soft, ethereal light. In the center stood an ornate stone pedestal, adorned with ancient engravings depicting elemental symbols. Lucy couldn't help but gasp in awe at the sight before her. She reached out to touch one of the symbols etched into the stone, feeling a tingle course through her fingertips.

"These symbols hold great power," she whispered reverently. "They can unlock our connection to elemental magic." Hadley's eyes widened as she observed the intricate carvings. "It's as if these symbols are alive," she commented, her voice filled with wonder. "They seem to pulse with energy." Ayden stepped closer to the pedestal, his hand hovering over one of the symbols.

"We must respect and honor these ancient forces," he said solemnly. "Let us proceed with reverence and gratitude." Nathan nodded in agreement, his gaze fixed on the symbols before him. "Each symbol represents an element - earth, fire, water, and celestial energy," he explained. "Through this ritual, we will learn to tap into the essence of these elements and harness their power." With their intentions aligned, the family gathered around the stone pedestal and began to recite ancient incantations passed down through generations. The air crackled with energy as they chanted together, their voices mingling and harmonizing.

Each family member felt a surge of elemental energy coursing through their veins - earth grounding Nathan, fire igniting Lucy's passion, water flowing effortlessly through Hadley's thoughts, and celestial energy strengthening Ayden's connection with divine forces. Their bodies seemed to glow with an inner light as they completed the ritual. A sense of peace settled over them, their newfound abilities pulsing with raw potential. Lucy looked at her family members, her eyes gleaming with excitement. "We've just scratched the surface of what we're capable of," she said confidently.

"Together, we can unlock even greater powers and protect Ember Bay from any threat that comes our way." Nathan smiled at Lucy's words, his gaze filled with pride. "You're right," he agreed. "This ritual has opened doors to a realm of possibilities. We must continue to train and explore our newfound abilities.

" Hadley's gaze darted between each family member as she nodded in agreement. "Our connection to elemental magic is stronger than ever," she proclaimed. "We must embrace this power fully and use it for the good of Ember Bay.

" Ayden placed a comforting hand on Hadley's shoulder, his serene presence calming any lingering doubts or fears. "Our journey has only just begun," he assured them softly. "But together, we have unlocked a part of ourselves that will guide us towards our shared destiny.

" With their hearts filled with a renewed sense of purpose and determination, the family left the chamber behind and continued their path through the mystical Bayou. They knew that they had tapped into something extraordinary - something that would forever change their lives and enable them to fulfill their roles as guardians of Ember Bay.

As the family ventured deeper into the ancient cave, an ethereal glow illuminated their path. The air crackled with electricity as they stepped into a vast chamber, its walls adorned with faded murals depicting the mastery of elemental magic. Nathan's eyes widened in awe as he took in the grandeur of the chamber.

"This place... it's like stepping into a world where magic reigns supreme," he marveled, his voice filled with wonder. Lucy surveyed the room, her fiery red hair flickering with excitement. "Look at these murals," she exclaimed, her voice tinged with anticipation. "They show us the true potential of elemental magic.

We have only scratched the surface." Hadley's gaze flitted from mural to mural, her keen eyes absorbing every detail. "It's as if these paintings are alive, capturing the essence of each element," she observed, her voice reverent. Ayden approached one of the murals, his touch barely grazing its weathered surface. "These images hold ancient wisdom," he said softly. "They can guide us in our journey to master elemental magic." With reverence and determination in their hearts, the family set about studying the murals, each member focusing on a specific element that resonated with them.

Nathan's gaze fixated on the earth mural, depicting lush vegetation and towering mountains. He traced the intricate lines with his finger, feeling a surge of strength and stability surging through him. "The earth is a foundation, a source of grounding and resilience," he murmured, his voice reflecting newfound confidence.

Lucy's eyes were drawn to the fire mural, capturing the dance of flames and the intensity of its heat. She closed her eyes and allowed herself to be consumed by the passion and determination that radiated from the mural. "Fire is a catalyst for change and transformation," she whispered, her voice filled with fiery resolve.

Hadley found herself captivated by the water mural, its tranquility and fluidity calling out to her. She could almost feel the gentle lapping of waves against her skin as she immersed herself in its imagery. "Water is adaptable and powerful," she mused, her voice echoing with a deep understanding of its nature.

Ayden's attention was drawn towards the celestial energy mural, depicting stars twinkling amidst a cosmic canvas. He felt a connection to something greater than himself as he studied the image, his heart filling with divine purpose. "Celestial energy is a beacon of guidance and harmony," he reflected, his voice carrying a sense of serenity.

As they absorbed the wisdom within each mural, a collective realization washed over them - mastering their individual elements would require unity and collaboration. Nathan turned to his family members, his eyes shining with resolve. "We must learn from one another, share our knowledge, and train together," he proclaimed, his voice firm yet compassionate.

Lucy nodded in agreement, her fiery spirit aflame with determination. "By combining our strengths and abilities, we will become an unstoppable force," she declared, her voice resonating with unwavering conviction. Hadley's eyes sparkled with excitement as she embraced this newfound perspective.

"Together, we will create a symphony of elements - earth grounding us, fire fueling our passion, water flowing through our thoughts, and celestial energy guiding our every move," she envisioned, her voice filled with awe.

Ayden placed a gentle hand on Hadley's shoulder, his celestial energy infusing them all with a sense of purpose and unity. "Let us invoke the power of our elements and embark on this journey together," he suggested warmly, his voice radiating kindness. With their hearts aligned and their bond fortified by their shared understanding, the family formed a circle in the center of the chamber.

They closed their eyes and channeled their individual elemental energies, allowing them to merge and intertwine within their midst. A warm glow enveloped them as their elemental powers intertwined like threads weaving a tapestry of unity.

In this moment, they felt an unbreakable connection to Ember Bay itself - guardians chosen to wield elemental magic and protect their home from darkness. As they opened their eyes and released their combined energies into the chamber, it came alive with vibrant hues of earthy browns, fiery oranges, tranquil blues, and ethereal purples.

The room seemed to pulse with life as if acknowledging their newfound mastery. As they left the ancient chamber behind and continued their journey through the mystical Bayou, they carried with them not only elemental powers but also an unshakable solidarity - an unbreakable bond forged by shared aspirations and unwavering determination.

Little did they know what awaited them on their path or how these newly harnessed powers would shape their destinies. But one thing was certain - armed with ancient wisdom and united in purpose - they were prepared to face any challenge that threatened Ember Bay.

An Ancient Ritual Unveiled As the family delved deeper into the ancient cave, a soft glow illuminated their path. They felt a faint hum in the air, as if the very essence of elemental magic surrounded them. Nathan led the way, his footsteps echoing through the cavernous space. "We're getting closer," he said, his voice filled with anticipation. "I can feel the power of the elements growing stronger." Lucy nodded, her fiery red hair reflecting the ambient light.

"There's so much we have yet to learn about our connection to elemental magic," she remarked, her voice brimming with excitement. "I can't wait to see what awaits us." Hadley's green eyes sparkled with curiosity as she observed their surroundings. "This cave holds ancient wisdom," she mused, her voice filled with wonder. "I can sense that we are on the verge of unlocking something truly extraordinary.

" Ayden walked beside them, his serene presence soothing any lingering doubts or fears. "The secrets of elemental magic are within our grasp," he assured them gently.
"Now, it's up to us to embrace this knowledge and wield it responsibly."

As they ventured further into the cave, they came upon a large chamber bathed in an ethereal light. In the center stood a pedestal made of shimmering crystal, adorned with symbols representing each element.

Lucy's eyes widened with awe as she approached the pedestal. "These symbols... they hold the key to unlocking our true potential," she whispered, her voice filled with reverence. "Through them, we can tap into the very essence of elemental magic." Nathan placed a hand on Lucy's shoulder, his gaze focused on the symbols before them.

"These elements - earth, fire, water, and celestial energy - are intertwined with our world and our own beings," he explained, his voice carrying a sense of deep understanding. "By harnessing their power, we can become even more powerful protectors of Ember Bay.

Hadley traced her fingers along the smooth surface of one of the symbols, feeling a surge of energy course through her veins. "It's as if these symbols are alive," she marveled, her voice tinged with awe.

"They hold ancient wisdom and untapped potential." Ayden studied the symbols thoughtfully, his senses attuned to the subtle vibrations emanating from them. "Let us perform a ritual to awaken our connection to these elements," he suggested softly. "Through this ritual, we will unlock greater depths of our powers.

" With unanimous agreement, the family gathered around the pedestal and began to recite ancient incantations passed down through generations. Their voices blended harmoniously, resonating with the very fabric of elemental magic. As they chanted, their bodies became
enveloped in radiant light that corresponded with their chosen elements - Nathan emanating an earthy hue, Lucy radiating fiery warmth, Hadley surrounded by watery currents, and Ayden basking in celestial luminosity.

The air crackled with energy as their connection to elemental magic intensified. They could feel their abilities deepening, tapping into reservoirs of power they hadn't known existed. Lucy's force fields became stronger and more resilient, capable of deflecting even the most formidable attacks. Nathan's ninja skills reached new heights of precision and agility, his movements blending seamlessly with the natural world around him.

Hadley's teleportation became instantaneous and effortless, allowing her to travel great distances with a mere thought. Ayden's healing abilities transcended previous boundaries, bringing soothing restoration to even the most dire wounds. As they completed the ritual, their bodies basked in the afterglow of their newfound powers.

The room seemed to pulse with energy as if acknowledging their growth and potential. With renewed purpose and determination shining in their eyes, the family stepped away from the pedestal and continued their journey through the enchanted cave. They knew that their connection to elemental magic was just beginning - there were still many lessons to learn and challenges to face.

Chapter 8: The Spirit of the Bayou

The mist wrapped around the family like a cloak, obscuring their vision as they waded through the waist-deep waters of the Bayou. Nathan led the way, his footsteps silent as he carefully navigated through the treacherous terrain. Lucy followed closely behind, her eyes scanning the surrounding trees for any signs of movement.

Hadley and Ayden brought up the rear, both feeling a strange energy pulsing through the air. "Keep your senses sharp," Nathan whispered, his voice barely audible above the chorus of insect sounds. "There's something different about this part of the Bayou." Lucy nodded, her fiery red hair glinting in the dappled sunlight that seeped through the dense foliage. "I can feel it too," she replied. "It's like we're being watched.

" Hadley's emerald green eyes darted from tree to tree, her slender figure blending effortlessly into the shadows. "I sense a presence," she murmured, her voice tinged with excitement. "Something ancient and powerful." Ayden, his soft-spoken voice carrying an air of calmness, raised his hand to quiet the group.

"I feel it too," he said. "A divine vibration in the very essence of this place." As they ventured deeper into the heart of the Bayou, the mist began to thicken, swirling around them in mesmerizing patterns. Phosphorescent lights flickered on the water's surface, guiding them further into the unknown. Without warning, the mist coalesced before them, forming ethereal figures that swayed and flowed with the currents of the swamp.

The Swamp Sirens emerged from the depths, their translucent forms shimmering with a timeless beauty. Their haunting melodies filled the air, stirring something deep within each family member's soul. Nathan took a step forward, his piercing eyes fixed on the mesmerizing sight before him.

"Who are you?" he called out, his voice steady despite the awe he felt. The Swamp Sirens responded in a chorus of voices that echoed through the stillness of the swamp. "We are the guardians of these mystical waters," they sang, their ethereal voices intertwining to create a haunting melody. "We have watched over this place since time immemorial.

" Lucy stepped forward, her determination shining through her fierce gaze. "Why have you revealed yourselves to us?" she asked, her voice strong and unwavering. The Swamp Sirens swayed in unison, their movements graceful and ethereal. "You have been chosen as protectors of Ember Bay," they replied. "Only those who possess a deep connection to the elements are worthy of this task.

" Hadley's curiosity got the better of her as she peered closer at the Swamp Sirens. "What do you require of us?" she asked, her voice full of wonder. The ethereal figures swirled around Hadley, their ghostly touch sending shivers down her spine. "You must prove your worthiness," they whispered in unison, their voices like a gentle breeze rustling through leaves. Ayden stepped forward, his calming presence radiating from him like a warm embrace. "How shall we prove ourselves?" he asked, his voice filled with compassion.

The Swamp Sirens glimmered in response, their forms growing brighter as they spoke. "Each of you will face a trial that aligns with your connection to an element," they explained. "Through these trials, you will demonstrate your strength and resolve as protectors of Ember Bay." Nathan nodded solemnly, his determination shining in his eyes. "We accept your challenge," he declared.

Lucy echoed his sentiment, her fiery spirit undaunted by what lay ahead. "We will prove ourselves worthy," she said firmly. Hadley's gaze was filled with anticipation as she awaited her trial. "We are ready," she stated, her voice filled with confidence. Ayden's gentle smile spoke volumes as he prepared himself for what was to come.

"We will show you our commitment to this sacred task," he promised. As one, the family stood together in silent agreement, ready to face whatever trials awaited them. The mist swirled around them like a cloak of anticipation as they took their first steps towards becoming true guardians of Ember Bay.

The Swamp Sirens led the family deeper into the heart of the Bayou, their ethereal forms floating just above the water's surface. A sense of serenity washed over the family as they followed in their wake, their anticipation growing with each step. Nathan's trial awaited him, a test of his connection to the element of shadow. The mist thickened around him, obscuring his vision and creating an eerie atmosphere. He felt the weight of his responsibility settle on his shoulders as he prepared himself for what lay ahead.

"Trust in your instincts," whispered one of the Swamp Sirens, her voice like a gentle breeze in his ear. "Embrace the darkness within you." Nathan nodded in understanding and took a deep breath. With each exhale, he let go of his doubts and allowed himself to become one with the darkness. His body seemed to dissolve into the shadows, merging seamlessly with the surroundings.

He navigated through the labyrinthine tunnels beneath the Bayou, his agile movements guided by intuition alone. The darkness became his ally, concealing his presence from any lurking dangers. He relied on his exceptional ninja skills, honed through years of training, to navigate the treacherous terrain with ease. The sound of distant footsteps echoed through the tunnels, alerting Nathan to a potential threat.

He moved swiftly and silently, blending into the shadows to observe his surroundings. As he peered around a corner, he spotted a group of shadowy figures, their sinister energy palpable even from a distance. With precision and grace, Nathan sprang into action.

He unleashed a flurry of punches and kicks, striking with lightning speed and accuracy. His moves were executed flawlessly, leaving his opponents disoriented and unable to counterattack. The battle was fierce but brief. Nathan emerged victorious, his enemies defeated and scattered across the tunnel floor. He paused for a moment to catch his breath, feeling a surge of pride in his accomplishments. The shadows receded, releasing him from their grasp as he returned to his normal form.

Lucy's trial awaited her next - a test of her connection to the element of force fields. She watched as the Swamp Sirens guided her towards a clearing where a raging river roared alongside her path.

The swift currents crashed against rocks with such intensity that it sent shivers down her spine. "Harness your inner strength," whispered one of the Swamp Sirens, her voice filled with encouragement. "Create a barrier that can withstand any force." Lucy closed her eyes and focused her energy. She summoned an invisible shield around her body, feeling the surge of power flowing through her veins.

As she stepped onto a narrow bridge spanning across the rapids, she could feel every tremor beneath her feet. The rushing water threatened to sweep her away with its raw power, but Lucy stood strong and resolute. With each step forward, she reinforced her force field, pushing back against the relentless currents that sought to overpower her.

She faced various challenges along the way - massive waves crashing against her shield, powerful gusts of wind threatening to knock her off balance - but she stood firm in her resolve. Her force field held steady against every obstacle thrown her way. As she reached the end of the bridge, Lucy released her force field with a sigh of relief.

Her connection to this element had been tested and proven steadfast. She rejoined her family, feeling a renewed sense of purpose and confidence. Hadley's trial was next - a test of her connection to the element of healing energy. She followed the Swamp Sirens deeper into the Bayou until they arrived at a secluded grove filled with vibrant flowers and lush greenery.

The air was heavy with tranquility and Hadley's heart swelled with anticipation. "Channel your healing powers," whispered one of the Swamp Sirens, her voice melodic and soothing. "Let your voice be an instrument of restoration." Hadley took a deep breath and closed her eyes. She focused on calming her mind and allowing her healing energy to flow freely through her being. When she opened her eyes again, she sang out an enchanting melody that resonated through the grove.

Plants bloomed before Hadley's eyes as she continued to sing, their vibrant colors enriching the once-dormant landscape. The air was infused with an invigorating energy that brought life back into every blade of grass and petal on each flower. A wounded bird fluttered down from its perch, drawn by Hadley's soothing voice. It landed gently on her outstretched hand as she continued to sing.

Light radiated from her palm and enveloped the injured bird, mending its broken wing. When Hadley finished singing, she watched in awe as the bird flew away with newfound strength. Her connection to this element had been tested and proven true - she possessed unparalleled abilities to heal and restore.

As Nathan, Lucy, and Hadley reunited with Ayden after completing their respective trials, they stood together in silent reverence for what they had accomplished. The Swamp Sirens surrounded them once more, their ethereal forms glowing brighter than before. "We have witnessed your unwavering resolve," they sang in unison, their voices cascading harmoniously through the stillness of the Bayou.

"You have proven yourselves worthy protectors of Ember Bay." The family exchanged knowing glances and shared smiles filled with gratitude and determination.

Their trials had only strengthened their bond as protectors and deepened their understanding of their roles in safeguarding Ember Bay from supernatural threats. With newfound confidence and heightened abilities, they set forth towards their next challenge - ready to face whatever lay ahead in their quest to protect the mystical realm they called home.

The Swamp Sirens swirled around the family, their ethereal forms shimmering with an otherworldly light. A sense of anticipation filled the air as they prepared to guide each family member through their individual trials. Ayden's trial awaited him - a test of his connection to the element of celestial energy.

The Swamp Sirens led him to a sacred clearing bathed in moonlight, where the stars above seemed to dance and twinkle with divine energy. Ayden could feel the vibrations of the cosmos resonating deep within his soul.

"Tap into the celestial power that lies within you," whispered one of the Swamp Sirens, her voice carrying a timeless wisdom. "Harness its healing essence and let it flow through your every breath." Ayden closed his eyes and took a deep breath, centering himself in the presence of the celestial energies that surrounded him.

As he exhaled, a soft glow emanated from his body, illuminating the clearing with a gentle radiance. He raised his arms towards the heavens, feeling the energy course through his fingertips. With each movement, he channeled the celestial power into the earth below, soothing its restless tides and bringing balance to its volatile nature.

As Ayden focused his energy, he sensed a disturbance in the natural order. He opened his eyes and saw a wounded animal lying on the ground before him, its pained cries echoing through the night. Without hesitation, Ayden approached the creature and knelt beside it. He placed his hand gently on its fur, allowing the celestial energy to flow from his fingertips into its wounded body.

The glow intensified as the creature's injuries slowly began to heal. As he continued to channel his celestial energy, Ayden felt a profound connection with all living beings. He understood that his role as a protector was not only to defend Ember Bay against supernatural threats but also to bring healing and harmony wherever he went.

When Ayden finished, he watched as the once-injured creature stood up and looked at him with gratitude shining in its eyes. It darted away into the night, restored and ready to face whatever challenges lay ahead. As Nathan, Lucy, and Hadley completed their own trials, they reunited with Ayden in the sacred clearing.

Their newfound powers shimmered around them, blending with the celestial energy that enveloped them all. "We are now bound by these elements," Nathan said, his voice filled with conviction. "Our connection to Ember Bay and our duty as protectors is stronger than ever." Lucy nodded in agreement, her fiery spirit burning bright. "We have been tested and proven worthy," she affirmed. "No matter what challenges come our way, we will face them united." Hadley's eyes shone with determination as she spoke.

"Through these trials, we have discovered our true potential," she declared. "We are no longer just individuals – we are a force to be reckoned with." Ayden smiled softly, his calm presence radiating with a sense of inner peace. "With our newly awakened powers and unwavering commitment," he said, "we shall bring balance and harmony to Ember Bay.

" The Swamp Sirens encircled the family once more, their ethereal forms glowing with pride. "You have exceeded our expectations," they sang in unison. "Your connection to the elements is unbreakable. Go forth and fulfill your destiny as protectors of Ember Bay.

" As they bid farewell to the Swamp Sirens and ventured back through the mist-shrouded Bayou, each family member felt a renewed sense of purpose and unity. They knew that their trials were only stepping stones on their journey towards protecting Ember Bay from the impending darkness. Hand in hand, they walked together, ready to face whatever challenges lay ahead.

Their bond grew stronger with each step forward - a testament to their unyielding resolve and their shared destiny as Elemental Guardians. Legacy of Legends - A Journey into the Past The family pressed on, following the guidance of ancient maps and cryptic clues that led them deeper into the heart of the Bayou. The path grew treacherous, with vines winding around their ankles and thick undergrowth obscuring their vision.

But their determination remained unwavering as they sought to uncover the stories and legends of Ember Bay's past protectors. Torchlight flickered against the moss-covered walls of a hidden cave, illuminating faded murals that depicted legendary protectors engaged in epic battles against supernatural forces. The scenes came alive before their eyes, frozen in time yet pulsing with energy.

Nathan approached one mural, his gaze fixed on a figure with dark, piercing eyes. "This must be one of the ancient protectors," he remarked, tracing the outline of the warrior's silhouette with his finger. Lucy joined him, her fiery red hair casting a warm glow in the dimly lit cavern. "Look at the determination on their faces," she marveled. "They fought fearlessly to protect Ember Bay." Hadley and Ayden huddled close, studying the details of another mural depicting protectors using their unique abilities to defend against supernatural threats. Hadley pointed to a figure blending into the shadows. "That must be one of our predecessors," she said.

"They possess powers similar to mine." Ayden's gentle voice carried a sense of reverence as he whispered, "These murals tell a story of sacrifice and triumph. We are part of a legacy that stretches far beyond our own lives.

" The family continued to venture deeper into the hidden cave, each step leading them closer to forgotten relics and artifacts that held glimpses into Ember Bay's history. They discovered handwritten journals filled with tales of heroic exploits, faded photographs capturing moments of triumph and camaraderie, and oral traditions passed down through generations.

As they explored further, they unearthed an ancient relic - a tattered map inscribed with symbols and coordinates that hinted at hidden knowledge waiting to be discovered. The map seemed to whisper secrets, guiding them towards their next destination.

With renewed determination, the family embarked on a journey through forgotten ruins and hidden chambers closely guarded by time itself. Their footsteps echoed through silent corridors as they encountered relics imbued with magic and power.

One artifact revealed itself to be a portal stone - an ancient artifact capable of opening gateways to other realms. It pulsed with energy, beckoning them to step through its ethereal threshold. Curiosity ignited within them as they cautiously stepped forward, their bodies tingling with anticipation.

The family found themselves transported to a realm unlike anything they had ever seen before. Mythical creatures roamed freely, their existence intertwined with magical energies that pulsated through the air. Unique challenges awaited them, tests that would push their limits while revealing deeper truths about Ember Bay's origins.

As they navigated this new landscape, they uncovered clues that tied this realm to Ember Bay's ancient past. Relics and whispers carried echoes of long-forgotten tales, speaking of a time when protectors from different realms collaborated in defense against shared threats. Nathan's eyes widened as he gazed upon an artifact depicting an emblem that mirrored the symbol emblazoned on his chest.

"This emblem is the key," he exclaimed. "It represents unity among protectors from different realms." Lucy nodded in agreement, her eyes sparkling with excitement. "There is power in diversity," she said. "Just as our animal companions come from different backgrounds but fight alongside us, it seems protectors from different realms once joined forces.

" Hadley's keen observance led her to decipher an ancient script etched into stone tablets scattered throughout the realm. "These tablets speak of an impending darkness that threatens all realms," she revealed. "Our purpose goes beyond protecting just Ember Bay - we must unite all protectors against this common enemy." Ayden's compassionate heart resonated with this newfound knowledge.

"Harmony among realms is vital for our success," he affirmed. "Together, we can restore balance not just to Ember Bay but to all realms affected by this darkness." With each discovery, the family's understanding of their interconnectedness deepened. They realized that their roles as protectors extended beyond defending Ember Bay alone; they were part of a greater tapestry woven with mystical threads that connected realms and protectors alike. As they prepared to return to Ember Bay armed with this newfound wisdom, the family felt an overwhelming sense of responsibility weighing on their shoulders.

The echoes of ancient prophecies reverberated through their minds, reminding them of the magnitude of the task ahead. Hand in hand, they vowed to honor their legacy - both as guardians of Ember Bay and as ambassadors for unity among realms.

Their journey had only just begun, but their spirits burned bright with determination and hope. The family stood in awe as they entered the hidden cave within the Bayou. Torchlight cast eerie shadows on the walls, revealing faded inscriptions and arcane symbols etched into stone. The air felt charged with energy, tingling with the presence of ancient magic.

Nathan carefully examined the chamber, his eyes drawn to a pedestal at the center of the room. Resting upon it was an artifact unlike any they had ever seen before – a polished obsidian orb pulsating with an otherworldly glow.

Lucy stepped forward, her gaze fixed on the mysterious artifact. "What is this?" she wondered aloud, her voice filled with curiosity. Hadley approached cautiously, her slender fingers reaching out to touch the smooth surface of the orb.

As her hand made contact, a surge of energy coursed through her body, illuminating her midnight black hair and piercing green eyes. "I feel a connection," Hadley whispered, her voice barely audible above the hum of power around them.

"This orb... it feels like a key to another realm." Ayden's kind eyes sparkled with intrigue as he joined the others. "Perhaps this artifact is a gateway," he mused. "A portal to realms beyond our own." Nathan nodded thoughtfully, his mind racing with possibilities. "If that's true," he said, "then we have the opportunity to explore other realms and gather valuable insight and allies in our fight against darkness.

" With newfound purpose and determination, the family gathered around the obsidian orb. The room seemed to tremble as they channeled their combined energies into activating the ancient artifact. Suddenly, the air crackled with energy, and a brilliant burst of light engulfed the chamber.

The walls seemed to dissolve as the family was transported to a realm bathed in ethereal hues. They found themselves standing on a vibrantly colored landscape, surrounded by exotic flora and fauna unlike anything they had ever seen before. Creatures with feathered wings fluttered overhead, while shimmering beings traversed shimmering paths of light.

"This is incredible," Lucy gasped, her eyes wide with wonder. "Look at this vibrant realm! It's teeming with life." Hadley nodded in agreement, her senses overwhelmed by the beauty and energy that surrounded them. "It's as though magic flows freely here," she whispered in awe. Ayden closed his eyes and took a deep breath, absorbing the harmony and tranquility of this foreign realm.

"This place radiates balance and serenity," he said softly. "We can learn much from these beings about maintaining inner peace." Nathan surveyed their surroundings, his focus shifting to an elevated platform in the distance. Perched upon it was a figure with wise eyes and a regal presence – a being who exuded ancient knowledge and untamed power. "We should seek guidance from that figure," Nathan suggested, pointing towards the enigmatic being.

"They may hold answers to our questions." As they approached the figure, they discovered that it guarded a hidden chamber filled with scrolls, books, and relics of lost civilizations. Each artifact told a story – tales of triumph over darkness, alliances forged between realms, and ancient prophecies hinting at their shared destiny.

The figure turned towards them, its eyes filled with wisdom and recognition. "Welcome, protectors," it spoke in a voice that seemed to echo through time itself. "You have ventured far to seek knowledge and unite realms against impending darkness.

" The family exchanged glances, their hearts filled with anticipation and respect for this wise guardian of knowledge. They nodded simultaneously, acknowledging their purpose and eagerness to learn from this enigmatic being. "Tell us your story," Nathan requested respectfully.

"Help us understand our place in this vast tapestry of protectors." The figure smiled knowingly before sharing tales of legendary protectors who rose above challenges and bridged gaps between realms. They recounted stories of battles fought side by side with allies from different realms – warriors whose strengths complement one another in their quest for balance and harmony.

With each word spoken, the family's understanding deepened, fortifying their bond as protectors committed to preserving peace across realms. They absorbed every lesson learned – the importance of unity and cooperation, embracing diversity in abilities, and finding strength in their shared purpose. Before bidding farewell, the figure entrusted them with ancient scrolls containing prophecies that foretold future trials and revealed glimpses of distant realms yet to be explored.

With gratitude and renewed determination burning within them, the family accepted these sacred gifts, knowing that their journey had only just begun. As they returned to Ember Bay through the obsidian orb portal, they brought back not only relics and knowledge but also an unbreakable spirit of collaboration among realms.

They were now armed with insights that would guide their actions, inspire unity among protectors and prepare them for whatever challenges lay ahead. Hand in hand once more, they stepped forward into their shared destiny – protectors united across realms in defense of all that was sacred and precious. The family emerged from the hidden cave, their hearts filled with awe and wonder at the knowledge they had acquired.

They knew that their journey to uncover Ember Bay's past was far from over, but they felt a deep sense of gratitude for the glimpses they had been granted into the realm's rich history. As they trekked back through the Bayou, the sun's rays filtered through the dense foliage, casting a warm glow on their path.

The weight of their discoveries settled upon them, filling them with a renewed sense of purpose and determination. Nathan led the way, his footsteps deliberate as he contemplated the stories of legendary protectors he had unearthed. He realized that their struggles mirrored their own - battles against darkness, sacrifices made for the greater good, and an unwavering commitment to protecting Ember Bay.

Lucy walked alongside Nathan, her fiery spirit burning bright as she reflected on the courage and bravery displayed by those who came before them. She recognized that their journey was not just about defending Ember Bay but also about preserving the legacy of protectors who fought for its well-being. Hadley followed closely behind, her mind buzzing with newfound knowledge. She marveled at how the stories of ancient protectors were woven together, each chapter building upon the last to create a tapestry of hope and resilience.

She understood the importance of passing down these stories to future generations, ensuring that the flame of protection would continue to burn brightly.

Ayden walked beside Hadley, his gentle presence emanating a sense of calm and tranquility. The lessons learned from Ember Bay's past protectors resonated deeply with him - compassion, healing, and finding inner harmony. He knew that these virtues were essential in their quest to safeguard Ember Bay from darkness.

As they approached their campsite near the Bayou, a profound silence fell upon the group. They sat around the crackling fire, sharing stories and insights gleaned from their journey into Ember Bay's past. The flames danced and flickered, casting shadows that seemed to echo the spirits of those who had come before.

"We have been entrusted with a great responsibility," Nathan began, his voice steady and resolute. "The stories we have uncovered remind us that we are part of something much larger than ourselves. We must honor the legacy of protectors who fought selflessly for Ember Bay." Lucy nodded in agreement, her fiery gaze unwavering. "We carry their torch," she declared. "Their spirits reside within us as we face our own trials and challenges.

" Hadley leaned forward, her eyes shining with determination. "It is our duty to share these stories," she said. "The wisdom and guidance they offer will strengthen future protectors and ensure that Ember Bay remains a beacon of light." Ayden's kind eyes scanned the faces of his loved ones, filled with compassion and hope.

"We are united in our purpose," he affirmed. "Our connection to Ember Bay's past gives us strength and reminds us of the power we hold within ourselves." As they sat together under the starlit sky, a new understanding settled upon their hearts.

Their journey through Ember Bay's history had brought them closer not only to their role as protectors but also to one another as a family bound by destiny. With renewed resolve, they extinguished the fire and settled into peaceful sleep, knowing that they would awaken ready to face whatever challenges lay ahead.

Their bond was unbreakable, fortified by the lessons learned from Ember Bay's past protectors. In the depths of their dreams, visions of battles won and unity among realms filled their minds. They saw themselves standing shoulder-to-shoulder with protectors from different lands, their combined strength overpowering darkness and restoring balance to Ember Bay and beyond.

When they awoke, the sun rose on a new day - a day filled with possibilities and opportunities to continue writing Ember Bay's story. United by purpose, guided by wisdom earned from their exploration of Ember Bay's past, they embarked on their next chapter as guardians of this mystical realm.

Chapter 9: The Lost Prophecy

The family approached the hidden cottage nestled deep within the Bayou, its weathered exterior blending seamlessly with the surrounding trees. The air was thick with anticipation as they stepped onto the creaking porch, their eyes drawn to the intricately woven tapestries adorning the walls. Nathan took a deep breath, his gaze fixed on the mysterious symbols etched into the woodwork.

As they entered the cottage, a warm glow enveloped them, emanating from the flickering candles scattered throughout the room. Their presence seemed to awaken something ancient within the cottage, and the air hummed with an otherworldly energy. Lucy glanced around in awe, her eyes tracing the tapestries that depicted battles fought long ago.

The seer awaited them, her silver hair cascading down her back in gentle waves. Her eyes shone with wisdom garnered from years of communing with the supernatural forces that surrounded them. "Welcome, guardians of Ember Bay," she said softly, her voice carrying a melodic lilt. Nathan's heart pounded in his chest as he listened to the seer's words.

He had always believed in the unseen world that lay beyond human perception, and now he stood on its threshold as a chosen protector. "What do you know of our destiny?" he asked, his voice steady despite the turmoil of emotions within him.

The seer smiled knowingly. "You are part of a prophecy that stretches back countless generations," she began, her voice taking on an ethereal quality. "Ember Bay has faced darkness before, and now a new threat looms on the horizon. It is written that only those chosen by the Bayou's enchantment can stand against this darkness.

" Lucy exchanged a glance with Nathan, her excitement mingling with trepidation. She had always felt a calling to protect others, and now she realized that her purpose went far beyond what she had ever imagined. "Tell us more," she urged, her voice filled with determination.

The seer's eyes sparkled with ancient knowledge as she continued. "You possess unique powers granted to you by the elemental guardians of the Bayou," she explained. "As protectors, it is your duty to master these powers and unite them in order to defend Ember Bay from Juggernaut." Hadley leaned forward, her curiosity piqued by the mention of Juggernaut. "Who is Juggernaut?" she inquired, her voice laced with intrigue. The seer's expression grew grave as she spoke of their formidable foe.

"Juggernaut is an ancient being of immense power, seeking to claim Ember Bay for its own dark purposes," she warned. "It will stop at nothing to spread chaos and destruction, but you have been chosen to oppose it." Ayden's eyes brimmed with compassion as he absorbed the weight of their mission.

"What must we do?" he asked softly, his calming presence grounding the others. The seer nodded solemnly. "First, you must gather the scattered fragments of an ancient prophecy," she revealed. "These fragments hold the keys to Juggernaut's defeat and will guide you on your path.

" Nathan's gaze drifted to his fellow protectors, a flicker of determination in his eyes. "We will retrieve these fragments and fulfill our destiny," he declared, his words echoing with unwavering resolve. With a nod of approval, the seer reached into a velvet pouch on her side and retrieved a fragment of parchment.

As she handed it to Nathan, a surge of energy coursed through him, connecting him deeper to Ember Bay's mystical forces. "May your journey be guided by light and may your spirits remain unyielding in the face of darkness," she said softly, her voice carrying a blessing that resonated deep within each family member.

Leaving the cottage behind them, the family felt a renewed sense of purpose burning within their hearts. They knew that their path would not be easy, but they were ready to face whatever challenges lay ahead.

Together, they would gather the fragments and unravel the secrets that would lead them to victory over Juggernaut. The fate of Ember Bay rested in their hands, and they were determined not to let it fall into darkness. As the family ventured back into the Bayou, the weight of their mission pressed upon them like an invisible force. Each step brought them closer to discovering the scattered fragments of the ancient prophecy, but it also intensified their awareness of the looming threat that awaited them.

Nathan's footsteps were purposeful and determined, his eyes scanning their surroundings for any signs or clues that would lead them to their next destination. He could feel the energy of Ember Bay coursing through his veins, empowering him with a sense of clarity and focus. "Stay alert, everyone," he cautioned, his voice tinged with a quiet intensity.

"We must be prepared for any challenges that come our way." Lucy nodded in agreement, her hand instinctively resting on the hilt of her sword. Her fiery hair danced in the wind as she scanned the landscape with hawk-like precision.

"We can handle anything that comes our way," she reassured the group, her voice filled with unwavering confidence. "Together, we are unstoppable." Hadley remained silent, her eyes darting from tree to tree as she used her night vision to navigate through the dense foliage. She had always been attuned to the shadows and unseen worlds, and now she relied on her instincts to guide them towards their goal.

The moonlight cast an enchanting glow on her features, enhancing her air of mystery and intrigue. Ayden walked beside Hadley, his presence emanating a calming aura that enveloped the group like a warm embrace. His eyes held a gentle wisdom gained through years of healing and compassion. He reached out a hand to steady Hadley as she stumbled over a hidden root. "We will find the fragments," he assured her softly.

"Trust in our unity and the power within us." Hours turned into days as they journeyed deeper into the heart of the Bayou, following the cryptic clues left behind by their ancestors. The chorus of frogs and insects served as their soundtrack, a constant reminder that nature itself was both their ally and their guide.

They could sense Ember Bay's presence growing stronger with each passing moment. Finally, they arrived at a clearing marked by an ancient stone monument etched with symbols long forgotten by time. The air crackled with anticipation as they gathered around, their eyes intently studying the engravings that told stories of triumph and sacrifice.

Lucy traced her finger along one of the symbols, her touch sending ripples of energy through the stone. A surge of realization washed over her as she deciphered their meaning. "This is it," she whispered in awe. "This is where we find our first fragment." With renewed vigor, Nathan approached the stone monument, his gaze focused and unwavering. He placed a hand on its weathered surface and closed his eyes, tapping into his ninja training to heighten his senses.

Within moments, he sensed a subtle vibration beneath his palm. Digging into his pocket, Nathan retrieved a small vial containing shimmering dust made from crushed moonstone. Carefully sprinkling it onto the stone monument, he watched as it revealed hidden writing etched into its very core. A gasp escaped Hadley's lips as she read the words aloud, her voice infused with wonder.

"Through shadow's embrace, behold your destiny." Their hearts quickened as realization dawned upon them - this was no ordinary stone monument. With a collective breath, they stepped closer to it until their own shadows merged with its silhouette. In an instant, they found themselves transported into a realm cloaked in darkness and mystery. Stars twinkled overhead, casting an ethereal glow on their surroundings.

They stood awestruck in this surreal landscape, knowing well that they had arrived at a place pivotal to their quest. "This is where we will find the fragment," Ayden said softly, breaking the silence that had settled over them. His voice carried both reverence and determination. As they ventured deeper into this mysterious realm, they encountered trials designed to test their mettle and resolve. Nathan moved stealthily through an intricate series of obstacles testing his agility and precision while Lucy faced waves of illusions meant to challenge her focus and determination.

Hadley used her teleportation skills to traverse treacherous chasms and overcome seemingly insurmountable barriers, while Ayden tapped into his healing powers to restore balance in an environment tainted by darkness. With every trial conquered and every challenge faced head-on, they felt themselves growing stronger - individually and as a team. The connection between them deepened even further as they leaned on one another for support and guidance.

Finally, they arrived at an ancient altar adorned with shimmering crystals radiating with otherworldly light. Resting upon it was a glowing fragment of parchment - the first piece of the lost prophecy.

As each family member reached out to touch it, a surge of energy coursed through them once more - this one more powerful than before. Their bond with Ember Bay's mystical forces grew stronger as they held the fragment in their hands. "We are one step closer to fulfilling our destiny," Nathan declared with conviction, his voice ringing out in triumph.

The family stood together at the altar, their hands intertwined around the fragment, savoring this moment of unity and victory. They knew that challenges still lay ahead - battles yet to be fought and sacrifices yet to be made - but for now, they revealed in the triumph of finding their first piece of the prophecy.

With renewed determination burning within their hearts, they returned to Ember Bay's earthly realm ready to face whatever lay in store for them next. Their spirits were emboldened by this newfound strength, fueled by the knowledge that as elemental guardians chosen by ancient prophecies, they possessed the power to protect Ember Bay from Juggernaut's darkness.

As they made their way back to the seer's cottage, the weight of their mission felt heavier than ever. The scattered fragments of the ancient prophecy that they had managed to retrieve so far were carefully concealed within a pouch, each piece serving as a reminder of the challenges that lay ahead. Silence enveloped them as they walked, each lost in their own thoughts. Ayden glanced at his fellow protectors and couldn't help but feel a surge of pride for how far they had come.

They had faced numerous trials, forged unbreakable bonds, and discovered powers within themselves they hadn't known existed. Now, with the seer's guidance, they were inching closer to their ultimate goal. As they entered the seer's cottage once again, the air seemed charged with anticipation.

The candles flickered as if in acknowledgement of their return, casting dancing shadows on the tapestries adorning the walls. The room exuded a sense of comfort and familiarity, a sanctuary amidst the chaos that awaited them. The seer awaited them with a serene smile upon her face, her eyes gleaming with unwavering faith in their abilities.

"You have returned," she said softly, her voice carrying a soothing melody that calmed their restlessness. Nathan stepped forward, his voice steady and determined. "We have retrieved several fragments of the prophecy," he stated, extending the pouch towards the seer.

We are ready to learn more." The seer accepted the pouch with gracefully gloved hands, her fingers delicately caressing its surface. "You have done well," she commended them gently. "Your determination and unity have brought you this far." Lucy couldn't help but feel a swell of pride at the seer's words. She had always believed in the power of teamwork and now it was being validated in this pivotal moment.

She exchanged glances with Nathan and a silent understanding passed between them - they were stronger together than apart. The seer withdrew one fragment from the pouch and held it up to examine it closely, as if searching for hidden messages within its delicate script.

"This fragment speaks of a long-forgotten ritual," she began, her voice carrying a hint of reverence. "A ritual that must be performed to unlock the true power of the prophecy." Hadley's eyes widened with curiosity as she listened intently.

She had always been intrigued by ancient rituals and their metaphysical properties. Her mind whirled with questions, eager to uncover the secrets that lay hidden within this particular rite.

The ritual requires you to gather at a sacred site deep within Ember Bay," the seer continued, her voice low and reverent. "Once there, you must recite an incantation that will awaken the dormant powers woven within your very souls.

" Ayden leaned forward, his eyes narrowed with concentration. He had always possessed an affinity for spiritual practices and knew that this ritual would require focus and intention. He wondered what kind of power it would unleash within him and his family. "It is during this ritual that you will fully embrace your destiny as elemental guardians," the seer explained. "Your bond with Ember Bay will strengthen, allowing you to tap into its limitless energies.

" A mixture of excitement and trepidation filled the room as the family absorbed the seer's words. This ritual marked another milestone on their journey - a gateway to unlocking even greater potential within themselves. They knew that they had come too far to turn back now. "When do we perform this ritual?" Nathan asked, his voice steady despite the growing anticipation in his chest.

The seer smiled knowingly. "The time draws near," she replied cryptically. "You will know when the stars align and the elements guide you to the sacred site." As if on cue, a gentle gust of wind blew through the open window, causing the tapestries to sway with mystic grace.

The family exchanged glances, a shared understanding passing between them - they would heed nature's call when she deemed them ready. With gratitude in their hearts, they bid farewell to the seer and stepped out into Ember Bay once again. The air felt charged with energy as they ventured out into the night, guided by an invisible force drawing them closer to their destiny.

As they walked beneath a canopy of ancient trees, their footsteps echoing through the dense undergrowth, an unspoken determination settled over them like a cloak of protection. They knew that they were on the cusp of something extraordinary - a ritual that would bind them even closer to Ember Bay and unveil powers beyond their wildest imaginings.

Deep in their souls, they could feel the echoes of fate resonating within each beat of their hearts. Though challenges lay ahead and sacrifices would need to be made, this was their path - one that would define them not only as protectors but as guardians of hope in a world threatened by darkness.

Quest for Fragments - Unveiling Cryptic Messages As the family ventured deeper into the heart of the Bayou, their determination burned brightly, fueling their search for the scattered fragments of the ancient prophecy. Each step brought them closer to their goal, but it also amplified the weight of their mission, reminding them of the impending darkness that threatened Ember Bay.

Nathan led the way, his eyes scanning every nook and cranny for any signs or clues that would guide them to the next fragment. His instincts as a ninja sharpened by years of training kicked into high gear, enabling him to navigate through the dense foliage with grace and precision.

"Keep your senses keen," he urged, his voice carrying an undercurrent of urgency. "The next clue could be hidden in plain sight." Lucy walked closely behind Nathan, her fiery hair serving as a beacon in the dimly lit forest. Her warrior spirit burned within her, fueling her determination to overcome any challenges that arose.

She scanned their surroundings with hawk-like precision, every muscle tensed with readiness. "Let nothing escape your attention," she reminded the group, her voice resolute. "We cannot afford to miss even the slightest detail.

Hadley moved gracefully through the shadows, her keen night vision guiding her path as if she were an extension of the darkness itself. The vibrant hues of her midnight black hair blended seamlessly with the surrounding shadows, making her almost imperceptible to those who did not possess her knack for blending in.

She observed their surroundings with unwavering focus, noting every anomaly with a sharp eye. "We must remain vigilant," she whispered softly, her voice barely audible. "The answers we seek may lie in places unseen.

" Ayden walked beside Hadley, his calming presence offering solace and reassurance to the group. His gentle eyes radiate warmth and kindness, imbued with an understanding of the interconnectedness between nature and its protectors.

He reached out a hand to steady Hadley as she stumbled over a hidden root, his touch emanating a soothing energy that banished any lingering doubts. "Trust in our unity and the guidance of Ember Bay," he encouraged, his voice gentle yet firm.

"Together, we will find what we seek." Hours turned into days as they delved deeper into the heart of the Bayou, following cryptic clues left by their ancestors. The sounds of chirping frogs and singing insects served as a constant reminder that nature itself was both their ally and their guide. They could feel Ember Bay's presence growing stronger with each passing moment, its mystical energies intertwining with their own.

Finally, they arrived at a clearing marked by an ancient stone monument adorned with symbols long forgotten by time. The air crackled with anticipation as they gathered around it, their eyes intensely studying the engravings etched upon its weathered surface. Nathan ran his fingers along one of the symbols, feeling a faint vibration resonating from deep within the stone. A surge of realization washed over him as he deciphered their meaning. "This is it," he whispered with awe.

"This is where we find our next clue." With renewed vigor, Nathan stepped forward towards the stone monument, his gaze focused and unwavering. He placed a hand on its weathered surface and closed his eyes, tapping into his enhanced senses honed through years of training.

Almost instantly, he felt a subtle vibration beneath his palm - a sign that he had found something significant. Reaching into his pocket, Nathan retrieved a small vial containing shimmering dust made from crushed moonstone. Carefully sprinkling it onto the stone monument, he watched as hidden writing etched into its core began to reveal itself.

Letters formed words and words formed sentences until a cryptic message emerged. Lucy's eyes widened with excitement as she read aloud what was etched into stone, her voice infused with wonder and anticipation. "Open your heart to nature's harmony," she recited slowly, savoring each syllable.

The family exchanged glances filled with curiosity and determination - this clue held a promise of enlightenment and progress on their quest. They knew that they had to unlock nature's harmony within themselves in order to discover what lay ahead. Ayden stepped forward, his voice filled with reverence for nature's intricate balance.

"Let us heed this message and seek harmony within ourselves," he suggested, his words carrying weight and significance. Agreeing wholeheartedly, Nathan extended his hand towards Lucy and Hadley, inviting them to join him in forming a circle.

As they grasped each other's hands firmly yet gently, they closed their eyes and allowed themselves to become attuned to nature's rhythm. In unison, they took deep breaths and focused on their connection to Ember Bay's mystical forces - its earthy scents, whispering winds, rustling leaves - allowing these natural elements to permeate their beings.

They felt a stirring within themselves as they let go of individual thoughts and surrendered to the collective harmony enveloping them. A sense of tranquility settled upon them as they stood there in silent communion with nature's essence. They could sense their energies intertwining with that of Ember Bay itself - a chorus of voices united in purpose and intent.

When they opened their eyes once more, they saw before them a trail bathed in a soft green light leading deeper into the Bayou. It was a pathway illuminated by nature's affirmation of their unity and synchronicity. "We have found our next clue," Hadley said softly, her voice carrying a hint of excitement laced with calm assurance.

Lucy tightened her grip on Nathan's hand as they prepared to venture down the path together. "Our unity has led us here," she affirmed confidently. "And it will continue to guide us towards our destiny." With rejuvenated spirits and a renewed sense of purpose burning within them, they set forth down the luminous path - ready to uncover what secrets awaited them at journey's end.

Quest for Fragments - Unveiling Cryptic Messages The family had been walking for what felt like hours, following the illuminated path that led them deeper into the Bayou. The soft green light cast a gentle glow on their faces, filling them with a sense of anticipation and wonder.

They knew that they were drawing closer to their next destination - a place that held another fragment of the ancient prophecy. Nathan's footsteps were purposeful as he guided the group through the dense undergrowth.

His eyes scanned their surroundings, searching for any signs or clues that would lead them to their next clue. Every sense was heightened, his ninja training sharpening his instincts as he moved silently through the shadows. Lucy kept pace beside Nathan, her fiery hair flowing behind her like a beacon in the night.

Her grip on her sword tightened, ready to defend against any potential threats that might cross their path. She trusted Nathan's guidance implicitly, knowing that he would lead them safely through whatever challenges they might face. Hadley, ever observant, used her night vision to navigate through the darkness.

Her agile movements allowed her to move effortlessly through the thick foliage, as if she were an extension of the shadows themselves. She studied every nook and cranny, searching for any hidden symbols or signs that might reveal their next clue. Ayden walked beside Hadley, his calming presence offering solace and support to the group.

His healing abilities resonated with nature's harmony, giving him a unique insight into their surroundings. He listened intently to the sounds of the Bayou - the calls of nocturnal creatures, the rustling of leaves - using these cues to guide their path. Suddenly, Nathan stopped in his tracks, his senses tingling with anticipation. He pointed towards a faint glimmer of light up ahead, barely visible through the dense trees. The family gathered around him, their eyes filled with curiosity and excitement.

As they approached the source of the glimmering light, they saw before them a shimmering pool nestled in a clearing. The water sparkled like liquid moonlight, ethereal and enchanting. The air carried a faint scent of night blooms, adding to the mystical atmosphere that surrounded them. Carefully stepping towards the edge of the pool, Lucy peered into its depths. What she saw took her breath away - symbols and writing danced across the surface of the water, forming a cryptic message that seemed to shift and change with every passing moment.

Hadley tilted her head slightly, her eyes narrowing as she studied the ever-changing symbols. She recognized some of them from ancient texts and whispered incantations she had come across in her research. "This is no ordinary pool," she said softly, her voice filled with awe and curiosity.

Ayden stepped forward and extended his hand towards the water. As he did so, his connection to celestial energy resonated within him, his fingertips tingling with an otherworldly warmth. "There is power in this pool," he stated confidently. "It is waiting to be unlocked." Nathan looked at his fellow protectors, determination burning in his eyes.

He knew that this pool held another piece of the puzzle - another step along their journey towards fulfilling their destiny. "We must find a way to decipher the cryptic message," he declared, his voice resolute.

Together, they brainstormed ideas on how to unlock the pool's secrets. Each family member offered their own perspective based on their unique abilities and strengths. They spoke words of encouragement and support to one another, knowing that their unity was paramount in overcoming any obstacle.

Finally, a plan began to take shape. Lucy stepped forward and drew her sword from its sheath. With a swift but controlled motion, she directed her blade towards the shifting symbols on the water's surface. As if obeying an unseen command, the symbols stilled and aligned into a coherent message.

The family leaned in closer to read what had been revealed: "In shadows' embrace, A riddle you must face. Seek wisdom from above, To unlock truth and love. In unity you'll find, "the fragment left behind." A collective gasp escaped their lips as they absorbed the message before them. It was clear that they needed to solve a riddle in order to proceed. Excitement mingled with anticipation as they racked their brains for answers.

Hadley's eyes lit up with understanding as she recalled an ancient riddle she had come across in her research. "I think I know what we must do," she said confidently. With Hadley guiding them through each step of the riddle-solving process, they worked together as a well-oiled machine.

Their minds complemented one another's, each bringing a unique perspective and insight to unraveling the puzzle. After what felt like an eternity of contemplation and discussion, they finally arrived at an answer that seemed to fit perfectly with the riddler's clues. As they spoke it aloud in unison, an invisible force seemed to ripple through the air.

The waters of the pool stirred with an otherworldly energy until they calmed once more, revealing a glowing fragment resting on a bed of shimmering stones at its center. They glanced at one another with triumphant smiles, knowing that they had once again conquered a challenge set before them.

Their combined efforts had unlocked another piece of the ancient prophecy - a fragment that would bring them closer to fulfilling their destiny as elemental guardians. As they reached out together to retrieve it from its resting place on the stones, their hands touched briefly before closing around it as one unit.

A surge of energy coursed through them once more - a reminder of their unity and shared purpose. With renewed determination burning within their hearts, they left behind the shimmering pool and continued along their path through Ember Bay. The quest for fragments continued - each one bringing them closer to unlocking the full power of the prophecy and ultimately facing Juggernaut head-on.

Little did they know what challenges awaited them at every turn - trials that would test not only their individual abilities but also their unwavering bond as a family.

But with each challenge overcome and each fragment retrieved, they grew stronger - individually and as a united front against darkness. Their journey was far from over, but they were ready to face whatever lay ahead with courage in their hearts and hope shining brightly within them.

As the family continued their quest for the scattered fragments of the ancient prophecy, they could feel the weight of their mission pressing upon them. The challenges they had faced thus far had tested their mettle and resolve, but they knew that the most difficult trials still lay ahead.

Nathan led the way through the dense foliage, his footsteps purposeful and determined. His every movement exuded a quiet intensity, fueled by his unwavering commitment to protect Ember Bay and fulfill his destiny as a chosen guardian.

He glanced back at his family every so often, ensuring they were still following closely behind. Lucy walked by Nathan's side, her fiery hair glimmering in the dappled sunlight filtering through the trees.

Her gaze remained fixed on their surroundings, ever vigilant for any signs or clues that might lead them to their next fragment. She had become a fierce warrior since accepting her role as a protector, her determination and courage unmatched. Hadley moved with grace and stealth, blending seamlessly into the shadows as if she were an extension of the very darkness itself.

Her keen eyes scanned every inch of their path, searching for hidden symbols or messages that might reveal their next destination. Though quiet and observant, her steadfast resolve burned brightly within her. Ayden walked beside Hadley, emanating a calming presence that soothed even the most frayed nerves.

His gentle eyes reflected an inner serenity, and his touch brought comfort and healing to those in need. The family drew strength from his wisdom and compassion, knowing that his presence was a guiding light in their darkest moments.

As they ventured deeper into the Bayou, the air grew thick with tension and anticipation. They sensed that they were drawing closer to a significant breakthrough in their quest - a pivotal moment that would propel them towards Juggernaut's defeat. Each step forward brought them closer to unlocking the power of the ancient prophecy.

Finally, they arrived at a crumbling ruin hidden within a dense thicket. The structure stood as a testament to both time's relentless march and its connection to Ember Bay's mystical forces. Intricate symbols adorned the walls, whispering stories of forgotten battles and triumphs. Nathan stepped forward, his fingers tracing the intricate carvings etched into the stone.

He could almost hear echoes of ancient voices reverberating through his touch - voices that held wisdom and guidance he hoped to uncover. "There's something hidden here," he said quietly, his voice tinged with anticipation. Lucy's eyes widened with excitement as she joined Nathan at the wall. Together, they deciphered the symbols and pieced together their meanings.

It became clear that they were on the verge of discovering a vital clue that would bring them closer to achieving victory against Juggernaut. Hadley's curiosity compelled her to explore further.

She moved around the ruins, her nimble movements avoiding loose stones and overgrown foliage. Her sharp eyes caught sight of a small crevice in the wall - one that seemed too deliberate to be coincidental.

With careful precision, Hadley reached into the crevice and retrieved a weathered parchment. Its edges crumbled slightly under her touch, but its contents remained remarkably intact. Delicately unfolding it, she revealed ancient writing that spoke of a hidden chamber located deep within Ember Bay.

Excitement coursed through their veins as they listened to Hadley recite what she read. The hidden chamber was said to hold not just a fragment of the prophecy but also secrets crucial to understanding Juggernaut's vulnerabilities.

It was an opportunity they couldn't pass up. Ayden placed a reassuring hand on Hadley's shoulder, his voice filled with gratitude for her discovery. "We are fortunate to have your keen observations," he said warmly.

"This hidden chamber may hold answers that will guide us on our path." The family exchanged glances brimming with determination and hope. They knew that entering this hidden chamber would be no easy task - it would test their abilities and challenge them in ways they had yet to face.

But they also knew that it was a necessary step on their journey towards protecting Ember Bay from Juggernaut's imminent threat. With their resolve unshaken, they made preparations to venture into the hidden chamber together. They equipped themselves with what little knowledge they had acquired thus far, ready to face whatever awaited them within its depths.

As they approached the chamber's entrance, a surge of anticipation filled the air around them. They took one last look at each other, sharing silent reassurances and reminders of their bond as protectors. Together, hand in hand, they crossed into the unknown - ready to confront the challenges within, unlock secrets long forgotten, and claim yet another fragment of the ancient prophecy.

They were propelled forward by unwavering faith in each other and an unyielding resolve to protect Ember Bay at all costs. The quest for fragments continued, and with each step forward, their destiny became clearer.

But little did they know how much more awaited them within the hidden chamber - revelations that would reshape their understanding of Ember Bay's past and present, and prepare them for an epic battle against Juggernaut.

Chapter 10: The Nexus Rises

As the family stood at the entrance of the legendary Nexus, their eyes filled with anticipation and determination. Nathan glanced at his companions, a silent understanding passing between them. This was a pivotal moment in their journey as protectors of Ember Bay. Nathan took a step forward, his footsteps reverberating through the charged air.

His connection with the earth element surged within him, empowering him with unwavering strength. He focused his gaze on a stone panel engraved with intricate earth symbols, each one pulsating with energy. With a deep breath, he extended his hand and channeled his inner power.

"I am the guardian of the earth," Nathan whispered, his voice carrying a weight of conviction. "I call upon the essence of the earth to guide me." A tremor rippled through the ground as Nathan's touch awakened the ancient magic within the stone panel. The symbols beneath his fingertips glowed with an earthy hue, resonating with his presence. He closed his eyes, allowing the Earth's energy to flow through him, merging his own spirit with that of the land. Lucy watched her brother intently, her fiery spirit burning brightly within her.

She had always been drawn to the element of fire, its passion and force resonating deeply within her soul. As Nathan completed his task, she knew it was now her turn to unlock their path to the Nexus. With steely determination, Lucy stepped forward, her every movement radiating confidence.

She faced a row of fire glyphs that lay dormant before her, waiting to be ignited by her power. Flames danced in her eyes as she extended her palms towards the glyphs. "I am the guardian of fire," Lucy declared, her voice laced with an undeniable strength.

"I call upon the essence of fire to guide me." In a burst of fiery energy, flames erupted from Lucy's outstretched hands, engulfing each glyph in a vibrant inferno. The room became awash with a warm glow as the glyphs responded to her command. Lucy felt a surge of exhilaration coursing through her veins as she harnessed the power of fire, allowing it to fuel her every move.

Hadley observed her siblings' actions with a keen eye, her mysterious demeanor giving way to a sense of purpose. Her connection with the element of air had always been profound, granted by the Bayou's mystical enchantment. Now it was time for her to unveil it. Moving with grace and agility, Hadley approached a pattern of air symbols etched into the ground before her.

They seemed to shimmer with hidden potential, waiting for her to breathe life into them. She lifted her hand and traced her fingers lightly across the symbols. "I am the guardian of air," Hadley murmured, her voice drifting gently like a whisper carried in the wind. "I call upon the essence of air to guide me.

" As if responding to her touch, gusts of wind swirled around Hadley, creating an invisible dance in the air.

The symbols beneath her fingertips glowed with an ethereal blue light, carried by the breeze that echoed through the chamber. Hadley closed her eyes, letting herself become one with nature's gentle embrace.

Ayden watched each member of his family connect with their respective elements, feeling both humbled and inspired by their unwavering dedication. He knew it was his turn now – to call forth the energy of water and channel its calming essence.

Ayden approached a series of water glyphs carved delicately onto a nearby wall. Their flowing curves evoked images of tranquil streams and glistening raindrops. His hands hovered above them, palms tingling with anticipation.

"I am the guardian of water," Ayden uttered softly, his voice carrying an almost melodic quality. "I call upon the essence of water to guide me." A soft glow enveloped Ayden's hands as water droplets materialized from thin air and cascaded gracefully onto each glyph.

The symbols reacted eagerly to Ayden's touch, shimmering with crystalline brilliance. As Ayden connected deeply with the water element, he felt a sense of serenity washing over him – a comforting reassurance that he was fulfilling his purpose as he embarked on this journey alongside his family. Together, Nathan, Lucy, Hadley, and Ayden united their elemental powers in unlocking the doorway to the Nexus.

Each symbol pulsed with energy as they merged their individual essences into one harmonious symphony of elements. The ground rumbled beneath their feet as if acknowledging their unity. As the doorway began to open slowly, bathing them in blinding light, excitement coursed through their veins.

They exchanged determined glances before stepping through the portal together – their footsteps echoing in this otherworldly realm where destiny awaited them. The Path Unveiled As the family entered the Nexus, they found themselves surrounded by a kaleidoscope of swirling colors, each hue representing a different elemental force.

The air crackled with raw energy, creating an otherworldly atmosphere that seemed to vibrate with power. They stood in awe, their senses overwhelmed by the grandeur and reverberations of the Nexus. The intertwining forces of earth, fire, air, and water swirled around them in a mesmerizing dance.

The family felt a deep connection to this mystical place, an understanding that they were meant to be here – that their destinies as protectors of Ember Bay lay within this realm. Nathan was the first to break the silence, his voice filled with determination.

"We have come this far together. Let us continue our journey with unwavering resolve." Lucy nodded in agreement, her fiery gaze reflecting the determination burning within her.

"We have faced numerous challenges and triumphed as one. We will face whatever lies ahead together." Hadley's eyes gleamed with curiosity as she surveyed their surroundings. "The secrets and knowledge hidden within these depths are vast.

We must stay united and embrace what we discover." Ayden's calming presence radiated assurance. "In unity, we shall uncover the truth and fulfill our purpose as protectors. Let us press on and steer Ember Bay towards its rightful path." With their resolve firm, the family delved deeper into the Nexus, guided by an instinctual pull that drew them forward.

As they walked through the swirling mist of elemental energies, they could feel a subtle shift in the air – a change that heightened their awareness and attuned their senses to new possibilities. They soon came across shimmering reflections of past battles fought by legendary protectors of Ember Bay.

Images danced before their eyes – moments frozen in time where protectors unleashed their elemental powers to defend their home from darkness. Nathan placed a hand on his heart, his eyes tracing the flickering images before him. "These visions give us a glimpse into the countless battles fought by those who came before us.

We carry their legacy within us." Lucy stepped closer, her fiery hair framing her determined expression. "Their strength and courage pave the way for us. We shall honor their memory by fulfilling our duty with unwavering conviction.

" Hadley's penetrating green eyes scanned the images with a sense of solemn appreciation. "Their stories are etched deep into the fabric of this realm. We must learn from them and continue their fight against darkness." Ayden's voice carried a soothing tone as he absorbed the wisdom embedded in each reflection.

"Through these glimpses of the past, we see echoes of our own destiny unfold. May their guidance guide us as we navigate the challenges that lie ahead." With every step forward, the family's bond grew stronger, bolstered by their shared purpose and the weight of responsibility resting upon their shoulders.

They knew that the journey ahead would test them in ways they had yet to fathom but remained steadfast in their commitment to protect Ember Bay from the impending darkness. As they continued on, they couldn't help but feel a hum of anticipation building within them – an intangible energy that drove them forward, drawing them closer to their ultimate destiny.

The Nexus resonated with their presence, whispering ancient secrets that only those worthy of embracing the elemental forces could comprehend. The family pressed on, united by their unyielding determination and fueled by a deep-rooted belief in the power of unity. They knew that whatever challenges awaited them within the Nexus would pale in comparison to the strength they derived from one another.

With each passing moment, they grew more attuned to the intricacies of this mystical realm – sensing its power coursing through their veins, igniting a fire within them that would guide them through darkness and lead Ember Bay to its rightful path. Triumph and Self-discovery. As the family faced off against their elemental foes, they felt a surge of adrenaline coursing through their veins. Every movement was instinctive, guided by the newfound mastery of their elemental powers.

Each battle became a dance of power, where strength and strategy melded seamlessly together. Nathan's opponent, an earth elemental being, loomed before him with unwavering determination. The ground shook beneath Nathan's feet as his adversary unleashed waves of rock and soil.

With every dodge and parry, Nathan's ninja skills came to life, his body becoming an extension of the earth itself. "I will not falter," Nathan declared, his voice resolute and focused. "I stand as the guardian of the earth – strong and unyielding." With a swift strike, Nathan slipped past his opponent's defenses, striking a blow that shattered the earth elemental's core.

As the being crumbled into pieces, motes of elemental energy swirled around Nathan before dissipating into the air. Lucy faced off against a fire elemental being that matched her fierce determination.

Flames leapt and twisted around them as Lucy conjured her force fields to shield herself from scorching attacks. Her own flames burned brightly, intertwining with those of her adversary. "I am the guardian of fire,

" Lucy proclaimed, her voice crackling with fiery intensity. "I embrace the flames and harness their power." With a final burst of energy, Lucy unleashed a torrent of flames that engulfed her opponent. The heated battle raged on until her adversary let out one last roar of defiance before succumbing to defeat.

Hadley confronted an air elemental being that moved with an ethereal grace, its form shifting like whispers in the wind. Her keen night vision pierced through the swirling vortexes created by her opponent as she prepared to use her teleportation skills to gain the upper hand.

"I am the guardian of air," Hadley stated, her voice tinged with enigmatic resolve. "I move between worlds, unseen yet ever present." Using her ability to blend into shadows, Hadley evaded her adversary's attacks effortlessly. With each precise teleportation, she drew closer and closer to her opponent until she was within striking range.

A calculated move allowed her to sever the connection between the air elemental and its source of power, causing it to dissolve into misty remnants of air. Ayden's opponent was a water elemental being that surged with unruly waves and currents.

Ayden felt a soothing calm wash over him as he connected with his healing abilities and embraced his role as a channeler of celestial energy. "I am the guardian of water," Ayden said softly yet with unwavering conviction. "I bring harmony and balance to all that is wounded." With gentle gestures and bursts of celestial radiance, Ayden mended any wounds inflicted upon his allies while redirecting the water elemental's own energy back towards it.

The battle reached its peak as Ayden's opponent dissipated into nothingness – a mere ripple in the water before vanishing entirely. As the battles concluded, each family member took a moment to catch their breaths and reflect on their individual growth throughout the intense trials.

They had come face-to-face with their own strengths and weaknesses, embracing them wholeheartedly as they fought for Ember Bay's safety. Nathan realized that his aloofness and self-doubt no longer defined him. Through his ninja skills and connection to the earth element, he had emerged stronger than ever – a true embodiment of resilience and fortitude.

Lucy acknowledged her impulsive nature and stubbornness but saw them transformed into traits that fueled her determination. She was no longer just a fierce warrior but an unstoppable force, protecting Ember Bay with every fiber of her being.

Hadley recognized that her trust issues and struggles with vulnerability were not hindrances but stepping stones towards self-discovery. Her mysterious persona took on new meaning as she learned to trust in herself and embrace her true potential as the Night Owl.

Ayden understood that his emotional reservedness and doubts about using his healing powers did not make him weak but showcased his capacity for empathy and compassion. He had unlocked his ability to bring peace and harmony to others while finding harmony within himself.

In this moment of reflection, their triumphs became guiding lights, illuminating their path forward as protectors of Ember Bay. They were more than individuals now; they were united in purpose, driven by unity even in their moments of vulnerability.

The battles had tested their limits and revealed hidden reservoirs of strength within themselves. Each had discovered depths they hadn't known existed, cementing their confidence in facing whatever challenges awaited them beyond the Nexus.

As they shared glances filled with silent understanding, a renewed sense of purpose washed over them. The victories they had achieved were not only physical but also deeply rooted in personal growth and transformation.

They had uncovered their full potential as protectors – not just wielders of elemental powers but beacons of hope for Ember Bay's future. With hearts ablaze and spirits ignited by this newfound resolve, they continued onward into the depths of the Nexus – ready to face whatever awaited them as they fulfilled their destinies as Elemental Guardians.

The family entered the Nexus, their footsteps echoing in the vast chamber as vibrant colors swirled around them. The air crackled with energy, charged with the convergence of elemental forces. They found themselves face-to-face with powerful elemental beings, towering figures wreathed in their respective elements.

Nathan squared his shoulders, his eyes locked onto his opponent – a massive earth elemental being. Rocks and soil swirled around it, forming a formidable shield. Nathan's ninja instincts kicked in as he analyzed his adversary's movements. "I am the guardian of the earth," Nathan declared, his voice ringing with determination. "I will bring your reign of darkness to an end." With unparalleled agility, Nathan leaped into action.

He darted between rock formations and struck with precision, exploiting any weaknesses in his opponent's defenses. His movements were fluid and calculated, mirroring the grace and strength of the earth. Meanwhile, Lucy faced off against a fire elemental being that blazed with intensity.

Flames danced at its fingertips, ready to scorch anything in its path. Lucy summoned her force fields and channeled her fiery spirit. "I am the guardian of fire," Lucy asserted, her voice resolute. "I will extinguish your destructive flames." Lucy's force fields flickered around her like ethereal shields, protecting her from the scorching heat.

She retaliated with swift and powerful attacks, channeling her inner inferno to engulf her opponent in waves of searing flames. Hadley took on an air elemental being that shifted and twisted like gusts of wind. Its presence was ephemeral yet undeniably daunting. Hadley embraced her enigmatic nature and tapped into her teleportation skills.

"I am the guardian of air," Hadley whispered, her voice carried on the wind. "I will unravel your illusions and bring forth clarity." With each teleportation, Hadley evaded her opponent's attacks with astounding grace. She moved like a shadow, striking swift blows whenever an opportunity presented itself.

Her ability to blend into shadows allowed her to traverse the battlefield undetected, giving her an advantage over her ethereal foe. As for Ayden, he faced a water elemental being that surged with unpredictable waves and currents. Its power was overwhelming, threatening to drown anyone who stood in its way. Ayden drew upon his healing abilities and celestial connection. "I am the guardian of water," Ayden murmured, his voice gentle yet resolute. "I will calm your tumultuous waters and restore harmony.

" Ayden's touch spread healing warmth through his allies, mending their wounds and shielding them from the water elemental's assaults. He radiated celestial light as he channeled his powers, unleashing radiant blasts that disrupted the elemental's control over water. The battles raged on as each family member unleashed their full potential – exploiting their opponents' weaknesses while capitalizing on their own strengths. Sweat trickled down their brows, mingling with the vibrant colors swirling around them.

Nathan pressed forward relentlessly, launching a final devastating attack that shattered his opponent's stony exterior. The earth elemental crumbled into dust, its essence dissipating into the air. Lucy matched her adversary's fiery fury blow-for-blow until she harnessed an immense blaze that consumed her opponent entirely.

The flames died down to reveal nothing but ashes. Hadley outmaneuvered her ethereal foe at every turn until she landed a crushing strike that dispersed it into thin air. It dissolved into a gentle breeze that carried remnants of its essence away. Ayden's celestial radiance grew more intense until it overwhelmed his adversary completely.

The water elemental evaporated into misty droplets that dispersed throughout the chamber. As dust settled and echoes of battle faded away, the family stood together – triumphant and in awe of what they had accomplished. They felt a deep sense of satisfaction knowing they had harnessed their elemental powers to their fullest extent.

Breathing heavily, Nathan wiped sweat from his brow and turned to his siblings. "We fought valiantly, my siblings. We have proven ourselves worthy of this noble task." Lucy grinned, feeling the heat of victory still coursing through her veins. "Indeed! We have shown the elemental beings that we are not to be underestimated.

" Hadley's eyes gleamed with newfound confidence as she adjusted her stance gracefully. "Our unity has prevailed against these formidable foes. Our combined strengths are unstoppable." Ayden's serene presence radiated reassurance as he offered a soft smile.

"We have truly embraced our roles as protectors of Ember Bay today. Our commitment to one another is unwavering." In this triumphant moment, the family basked in their collective achievement – understanding that they were more than just individuals with extraordinary powers.

They were a united force that would stand against any darkness threatening Ember Bay. Their battles within the Nexus had revealed not only their physical strength but also their unwavering resolve and unbreakable bond as protectors. They had discovered depths within themselves they had never imagined existed – depths that held tremendous power and unwavering determination.

As they prepared to continue their journey through the Nexus, they breathed deeply and exchanged glances filled with silent understanding. The challenges ahead would test them further, but their victories here served as a reminder that they were capable of overcoming any obstacle when united. Together, they stepped forward into the swirling currents of energy within the Nexus – ready to face whatever awaited them next on their path as Elemental Guardians.

The Elemental Beings As the family ventured deeper into the Nexus, they found themselves surrounded by a swirling vortex of elemental essences. Vibrant colors merged and clashed around them, forming ethereal beings that embodied the very essence of earth, fire, air, and water. Nathan faced an earth elemental being, towering above him with massive boulders forming its impenetrable armor.

The ground trembled beneath its weight as it unleashed a barrage of stone projectiles towards Nathan. With his ninja agility, Nathan dodged the onslaught, his movements blending seamlessly with the earth itself. "I am the guardian of the earth," Nathan declared fiercely, his voice cutting through the chaos. "I will not let your darkness consume Ember Bay." With lightning-fast strikes, Nathan flipped and twisted amidst the rock formations, launching calculated blows at his opponent's vulnerable spots.

Each strike reverberated with the strength of the earth, causing cracks to form in the elemental being's stony exterior. As the final blow landed, the earth elemental shattered into fragments that melded back into the swirling vortex.

Lucy stood face-to-face with a fire elemental being, flames raging in its eyes and dancing wildly around its body. Intense heat radiated from its presence, threatening to engulf everything in its path. But Lucy would not back down. "I am the guardian of fire," Lucy proclaimed firmly, her voice channeling her fiery determination.

"I will extinguish your destructive flames and protect Ember Bay." Summoning her force fields, Lucy created a barrier that shielded her from the intense heat. With each strike of her flaming fists, she disrupted the fire elemental's chaotic energy.

She weaved through the flames with grace and agility, countering every attack with a fierce determination. As her final blow connected, an explosion of embers filled the air before dissipating into wisps of smoke. Hadley confronted an air elemental being that twirled and swirled like a tempestuous storm.

Its presence was both mesmerizing and dangerous, but Hadley was undeterred. "I am the guardian of air," Hadley declared confidently, her voice carried on an invisible breeze. "I will unravel your illusions and bring clarity to Ember Bay.

" Using her teleportation abilities, Hadley moved with incredible speed and precision. She phased in and out of existence, striking her opponent when it's least expected. Her movements were like whispers in the wind, her attacks disorienting and disruptive to the air elemental's control over its surroundings.

With one final burst of energy, Hadley outmaneuvered her opponent entirely, causing it to dissipate into a gentle breeze that carried away its essence. Ayden faced a water elemental being that surged with tidal waves and crashing currents. Its power threatened to drown anyone who dared challenge it.

But Ayden remained resolute in his purpose. "I am the guardian of water," Ayden spoke softly yet with unwavering conviction. "I will calm your tumultuous waters and restore harmony within Ember Bay." Drawing upon his healing abilities and celestial connection, Ayden radiated a soothing aura that quelled even the most turbulent waters.

He directed his celestial energy towards the water elemental, disrupting its control over its own element. As celestial light enveloped his opponent, it gradually dispersed until nothing remained but shimmering droplets – a peaceful reflection of what once was. As each family member triumphed over their respective elemental foes, they could feel a bond between them growing stronger than ever before.

They stood together amidst the swirling vortexes of elemental energies – their victory serving as a testament to their unity and unwavering determination. Breathing heavily from their battles, they exchanged glances filled with pride and admiration for one another. The challenges they had overcome within the Nexus were not only physical trials but also tests of their character and resolve as protectors. Nathan's eyes met Lucy's fiery gaze as he spoke, his voice filled with awe.

"We have proven ourselves today – not just as wielders of elemental powers but as a united force defending Ember Bay." Lucy nodded, her expression reflecting a newfound sense of purpose. "Together, we are unstoppable. Our connection grows stronger with every battle we face." Hadley's piercing green eyes shone with deep-rooted confidence as she added, "We have witnessed our unity in action today.

No obstacle can stand in our way when we stand shoulder to shoulder.

" Ayden's calm presence radiated reassurance as he concluded, "Our victories here are not only for ourselves but for all those who believe in us – past, present, and future protectors of Ember Bay." With their hearts full of accomplishment and their spirits resolute, the family pressed onward into the depths of the Nexus.

Whatever challenges awaited them beyond these battles, they knew they would face them head-on – united in purpose and ready to fulfill their destinies as Elemental Guardians. Triumph and Self-discovery As the battles within the Nexus came to a close, the family stood in the aftermath – their triumphant breaths mingling with the lingering energies of elemental clashes.

They looked at each other, their eyes filled with mutual respect and admiration for the strength and determination they had displayed. Nathan's chest rose and fell with each deep breath as he surveyed his siblings. "We have proven ourselves worthy as protectors of Ember Bay. Our unity and unwavering resolve have brought us victory." Lucy nodded, a proud smile on her face.

"Together, we are an unstoppable force. We have tapped into the depths of our elemental powers and harnessed them to their fullest potential." Hadley's eyes gleamed with newfound confidence as she adjusted her stance gracefully. "Our journey has forged us into warriors of light, ready to embrace any challenge that lies ahead." Ayden's serene presence radiated reassurance as he offered a soft smile.

"We have learned to trust in one another and in ourselves. Our connection as a family has made us stronger, allowing us to unlock our full potential." In this moment of shared triumph, they felt a deep understanding that their journey as protectors went beyond mere physical battles. It was a journey of self-discovery, of embracing their inner strengths, and of finding the courage to face their own vulnerabilities.

Nathan stepped forward, placing a hand on each sibling's shoulder. "Let us not forget the lessons we have learned along this path. We are more than just wielders of elemental powers – we are beacons of hope for Ember Bay." Lucy's fiery gaze met Nathan's, her voice resolute. "Indeed, our purpose extends far beyond ourselves. We fight not only for our loved ones but for all those who call Ember Bay home.

" Hadley glanced between her siblings, a renewed sense of determination in her eyes. "As protectors, we carry the burden of defending this mystical land. But we also carry its people's hopes and dreams within us." Ayden's gentle presence enveloped them all, a calming reassurance amidst the battles they had faced. "With every victory, we inch closer to fulfilling our destiny as the Elemental Guardians of Ember Bay.

Let us continue forward with unwavering conviction." In unison, they took a moment to soak in their achievements and reflect on how far they had come since their first encounter with the enchanted stones.

Their individual journeys had merged into one collective quest – a quest that would test their mettle, forge unbreakable bonds, and lead them towards their ultimate purpose. With hearts ablaze and spirits ignited by this shared victory, they prepared to venture deeper into the Nexus – ready to face whatever challenges awaited them next.

For no matter what darkness might lurk ahead, they knew that unity was their greatest strength, and together they could overcome anything that threatened Ember Bay. As they stepped forward into the swirling currents of energy within the Nexus once more, their footsteps echoed with determination.

Their path was clear – they were guardians of light in a world threatened by darkness, and they would fight relentlessly to protect their beloved home. And so, with renewed resolve burning in their hearts, Nathan, Lucy, Hadley, and Ayden pressed on – united as elemental guardians forging their legacy in the annals of Ember Bay's history.

The battles they had faced within the Nexus were just the beginning of their journey towards greatness – a journey that would test their limits, challenge their beliefs, and ultimately shape their destinies. Together, they would bring light where darkness loomed, restore balance where chaos reigned, and safeguard Ember Bay from all supernatural threats that dared to encroach upon its mystical lands.

The Elemental Guardians had emerged victorious within the Nexus, but now their true tests awaited them beyond its concealed depths. They carried within them the weight of their ancestors' legacies and the hopes of future generations. With unwavering determination and an unbreakable bond as siblings and protectors alike, they marched bravely onward – ready to face whatever trials may come their way.

For Ember Bay was counting on them. And as long as they remained together – steadfast and united – there was no force in this realm or any other that could extinguish the light burning within their souls. And so they ventured forth into the unknown, guided by their elemental powers, strengthened by their unity, and driven by an unyielding commitment to protecting what truly mattered – family, love, and the boundless magic of Ember Bay.

Chapter 11: Celestial Dreams Unveiled

Under the enchanting glow of the blood moon, the family finds themselves drawn to a secluded clearing in the heart of the Bayou. The air is thick with an otherworldly energy as they lie down on the soft ground, gazing up at the star-studded sky. Slowly, they close their eyes, surrendering to the celestial magic that surrounds them.

As their dreams unfold, Nathan finds himself in a shadowy realm. He moves with agility and precision, his ninja skills honed to perfection. In his dream, he battles shadowy figures, his movements blending seamlessly into the darkness. Doubts about his abilities dissipate as he embraces his role as the Ninja of the Bayou and channels the power of his ancestors.

Lucy's dream takes her to a fiery landscape. She stands tall and fierce, conjuring powerful force fields to protect her loved ones. Flames dance around her as she faces formidable adversaries, her determination unwavering. In her dream, she recognizes her true strength and understands that she has the power to overcome any obstacle that stands in her way.

Hadley's dream unfolds in a mysterious forest shrouded in darkness. She moves silently through the shadows, her every step guided by intuition. As she navigates through the dense foliage, she encounters ancient spirits who test her resolve and trustworthiness. In her dream, she realizes that her enigmatic nature is not a weakness but a unique strength that allows her to uncover hidden truths.

Ayden's dream transports him to a tranquil meadow bathed in celestial light. He stands among celestial beings, his hands emanating a gentle healing energy. In his dream, he heals wounded creatures and brings harmony to the land with his soothing presence. Ayden embraces his role as a healer and discovers that his ability to restore balance goes beyond physical wounds—it extends to emotional scars as well.

As each family member dreams, emotions surge within them—fears subside, hopes soar, and determination swells. Nathan awakens with newfound confidence, ready to embrace his destiny as the Ninja of the Bayou and overcome his self-doubt. Lucy opens her eyes with fiery determination burning in her gaze, knowing that her strength will shield those she loves from harm.

Hadley rises from her dream with an air of mystery surrounding her, knowing that her journey will lead to profound discoveries about the ancient civilization. Ayden awakens bathed in celestial light and feels a deep sense of purpose within him. He knows that healing is not just his duty but also his calling—a calling that goes beyond physical ailments and extends into the realms of emotional well-being.

With their dreams still fresh in their minds, the family gathers around the campfire at dawn. The crackling flames mirror the growing connection between them—a connection forged by shared experiences and a common purpose. Their eyes meet, filled with understanding and unwavering determination. Nathan takes a deep breath and breaks the silence.

"In my dream," he begins, his voice steady and resolute, "I embraced my role as the Ninja of the Bayou like never before. I fought with agility and precision, feeling the power of my ancestors flow through me. I know now that I am meant for this path.

" Lucy's fiery spirit radiates from her as she speaks next. "I stood amidst flames in my dream," she says, her voice filled with conviction. "I conjured force fields without hesitation, protecting those I love with all my might. My dream showed me that I have the strength to face any challenge head-on.

" Hadley's eyes shimmer with intrigue as she shares her experience. "In my dream," she murmurs softly, "I moved through shadows effortlessly, embracing my role as the Night Owl. I felt a deep connection to the ancient spirits that dwell within the Bayou—their trust in me reassured me that my mysterious nature is not something to fear but something to embrace.

" Ayden looks at each family member with kind eyes before speaking from his heart. "In my dream," he says gently, "I was surrounded by celestial beings and felt their healing energy flow through me. I knew then that my purpose is not only to heal physical wounds but also to bring emotional healing—to offer solace and restore balance." As they share their visions and insights, a sense of unity fills the air—a unity born from a deep understanding of their collective destiny as protectors of Ember Bay.

They understand now that their individual strengths are essential pieces of a greater whole—a whole that will stand against Juggernaut and protect what they hold dear. The fire crackles and dances before them, mirroring their unyielding determination and illuminating their path forward.

They rise from their seats, their eyes locked together in silent communion. In this moment, there is no doubt or hesitation—only certainty and conviction. "We can do this," Nathan says, breaking the silence. Lucy nods and adds, "Together, we are unstoppable." Hadley's voice resonates with mystique as she says, "Our destinies are intertwined—no obstacle can stand in our way." Ayden's calming presence envelops them all as he says softly, "Let us embrace our roles fully and face our journey with unwavering resolve.

" With these words of unity echoing in their hearts, they leave the clearing behind, ready to face whatever lies ahead on their quest to protect Ember Bay. Emotions run high as the family members express their fears, hopes, and determination in light of the shared visions. A sense of vulnerability lingers in the air as they open their hearts to one another, laying bare their deepest fears and doubts.

Nathan's voice trembles slightly as he begins, "I've always felt this weight on my shoulders, doubting whether I'm truly capable of fulfilling my role as the Ninja of the Bayou. But in my dream, I saw myself moving with such grace and precision, confidence radiating from every fiber of my being.

It made me realize that I have the strength within me to overcome any hurdle." Lucy's eyes shimmer with a mixture of determination and vulnerability as she speaks next. "For so long, I've tried to be strong for everyone else, but sometimes I doubt if I can truly protect them.

In my dream, though, I saw myself standing tall amidst fierce flames, summoning force fields without hesitation. It showed me that my strength is not just physical—it comes from deep within, fueled by love and an unwavering desire to shield those I hold dear.

" Hadley's voice carries a sense of wonder and mystery as she recounts her dream. "I've always felt like an outsider, someone who never quite fits in. But in my dream, I moved through shadowy realms effortlessly, connecting with ancient spirits who saw the value in my enigmatic nature.

They helped me understand that being different doesn't make me less valuable—it's what sets me apart and gives me the power to uncover hidden truths." Ayden's gentle voice washes over the group, bringing a sense of peace and reassurance. "Throughout my life, I've grappled with doubts about my abilities and whether I can truly bring healing to those who need it most.

But in my dream, I stood among celestial beings, channeling their energy to heal both physical and emotional wounds. It reminded me that healing is not just a task—it's a calling that comes from deep within my soul." As they share their vulnerabilities and doubts, a sense of understanding and empathy grows between them.

They realize that they are not alone in their struggles—that together, they can overcome any obstacle that stands in their way. Nathan reaches out and places a hand on Lucy's shoulder, his touch conveying both strength and support. "You've always been a pillar of strength for us, Lucy," he says softly. "But it's important to remember that we all have moments of doubt. We're here for you, just as you've always been there for us." Lucy offers him a small smile of gratitude before turning to Hadley.

"Your unique nature has always intrigued me," she admits, her voice filled with admiration. "In your dream, it showed me that being different is not something to be feared—it's what makes us strong as a team. We each bring something special to the table, and together, we create an unbreakable bond.

" Hadley's eyes shine with appreciation as she replies, "And Ayden, your calming presence brings us solace when our hearts are heavy. Your dream reminded us that healing goes beyond physical wounds—it extends to the emotional burdens that weigh us down. Your gift is invaluable to our mission.

" Ayden nods gratefully and takes a moment to gather his thoughts before speaking again. "We all have our doubts and fears," he says, his voice soothing yet resolute. "But together, we are stronger than any darkness that may come our way. We have seen glimpses of our destiny in these dreams, and they tell us one thing—we are meant to face this journey together.

" The atmosphere around the campfire becomes charged with renewed determination as each family member absorbs the support and understanding flowing between them. Nathan stands up first and extends a hand towards Lucy. "Let's stand united against whatever challenges await us," he says firmly. Lucy rises without hesitation and grasps Nathan's hand firmly in her own.

"No matter what comes our way," she declares with conviction, "we'll face it head-on—together." Hadley joins them next, her gaze steady and unwavering. "Our individual strengths become magnified when combined," she adds resolutely. "There's nothing we can't accomplish when we embrace our unique abilities.

" Finally, Ayden rises gracefully from his spot by the fire and places a hand on each family member's shoulder. "Let us approach this journey with open hearts and trust in one another," he says softly but with profound certainty.

With their hands joined in unity once more, the family looks towards the future with newfound resolve. Their shared visions have solidified their bond and reawakened their determination to protect Ember Bay at all costs. As they extinguish the campfire that has brought them together, they step into the unknown—their hearts ablaze with hope and determination.

Their dreams have shown them their true potential as protectors of Ember Bay—and with each other by their side—they are ready to face any challenge that lies ahead. Together, they walk towards their destiny—united as one—ready to confront Juggernaut and safeguard Ember Bay from its impending darkness.

As the family shares their visions and insights, a sense of unity fills the air—a unity born from a deep understanding of their collective destiny as protectors of Ember Bay. The crackling fire dances before them, mirroring their unyielding determination and illuminating their path forward.

Each word spoken strengthens their resolve, preparing them for the challenges that lie ahead. Nathan takes a deep breath, his gaze steady and unwavering. "In my dream, I embraced my role as the Ninja of the Bayou like never before," he begins.

"I fought with agility and precision, feeling the power of my ancestors flow through me. It made me realize that I have the strength within me to overcome any hurdle." Lucy's fiery spirit radiates from her as she speaks next. "For so long, I've tried to be strong for everyone else, but sometimes I doubt if I can truly protect them," she admits.

"But in my dream, I saw myself standing tall amidst fierce flames, summoning force fields without hesitation. It showed me that my strength is not just physical—it comes from deep within, fueled by love and an unwavering desire to shield those I hold dear." Hadley's eyes shimmer with a mixture of wonder and mystery as she recounts her dream.

"I've always felt like an outsider, someone who never quite fits in," she confesses. "But in my dream, I moved through shadowy realms effortlessly, connecting with ancient spirits who saw the value in my enigmatic nature. They helped me understand that being different doesn't make me less valuable—it's what sets me apart and gives me the power to uncover hidden truths.

" Ayden's gentle voice washes over the group, bringing a sense of peace and reassurance. "Throughout my life, I've grappled with doubts about my abilities and whether I can truly bring healing to those who need it most," he shares. "But in my dream, I stood among celestial beings, channeling their energy to heal both physical and emotional wounds.

It reminded me that healing is not just a task—it's a calling that comes from deep within my soul." As they share their vulnerabilities and doubts, a sense of understanding and empathy grows between them. They realize that they are not alone in their struggles—that together, they can overcome any obstacle that stands in their way.

Nathan reaches out and places a hand on Lucy's shoulder, his touch conveying both strength and support. "You've always been a pillar of strength for us, Lucy," he says softly. "But it's important to remember that we all have moments of doubt. We're here for you, just as you've always been there for us.

" Lucy offers him a small smile of gratitude before turning to Hadley. "Your unique nature has always intrigued me," she admits, her voice filled with admiration. "In your dream, it showed me that being different is not something to be feared—it's what makes us strong as a team. We each bring something special to the table, and together, we create an unbreakable bond.

" Hadley's eyes shine with appreciation as she replies, "And Ayden, your calming presence brings us solace when our hearts are heavy. Your dream reminded us that healing goes beyond physical wounds—it extends to the emotional burdens that weigh us down. Your gift is invaluable to our mission.

" Ayden nods gratefully and takes a moment to gather his thoughts before speaking again. "We all have our doubts and fears," he says, his voice soothing yet resolute. "But together, we are stronger than any darkness that may come our way. We have seen glimpses of our destiny in these dreams, and they tell us one thing—we are meant to face this journey together.

" The atmosphere around the campfire becomes charged with renewed determination as each family member absorbs the support and understanding flowing between them. Nathan stands up first and extends a hand towards Lucy. "Let's stand united against whatever challenges await us," he says firmly. Lucy rises without hesitation and grasps Nathan's hand firmly in her own.

"No matter what comes our way," she declares with conviction, "we'll face it head-on—together." Hadley joins them next, her gaze steady and unwavering. "Our individual strengths become magnified when combined," she adds resolutely. "There's nothing we can't accomplish when we embrace our unique abilities." Finally, Ayden rises gracefully from his spot by the fire and places a hand on each family member's shoulder.

"Let us approach this journey with open hearts and trust in one another," he says softly but with profound certainty. With their hands joined in unity once more, the family looks towards the future with newfound resolve. Their shared visions have solidified their bond and reawakened their determination to protect Ember Bay at all costs.

As they extinguish the campfire that has brought them together, they step into the unknown—their hearts ablaze with hope and determination.

Their dreams have shown them their true potential as protectors of Ember Bay—and with each other by their side—they are ready to face any challenge that lies ahead. Together, they walk towards their destiny—united as one—ready to confront Juggernaut and safeguard Ember Bay from its impending darkness.

Shared Visions and Renewed Determination As the first rays of dawn illuminate the family's campsite, they gather around the remnants of the campfire, their faces bathed in a warm glow. The air is charged with anticipation and a sense of unity that can only come from sharing profound experiences. In this moment, they are no longer separate individuals but a united force bound by destiny.

Nathan breaks the silence, his voice steady and resolute. "In my dream," he begins, "I embraced my role as the Ninja of the Bayou like never before. I fought with agility and precision, feeling the power of my ancestors flow through me. It made me realize that I have the strength within me to overcome any hurdle.

" Lucy listens attentively, her fiery gaze reflecting the determination that burns within her. "For so long," she admits, "I've tried to be strong for everyone else, but sometimes I doubt if I can truly protect them. But in my dream, I saw myself standing tall amidst fierce flames, summoning force fields without hesitation. It showed me that my strength is not just physical—it comes from deep within, fueled by love and an unwavering desire to shield those I hold dear.

" Hadley's eyes shimmer with wonder as she recounts her dream. "I've always felt like an outsider, someone who never quite fits in," she confesses. "But in my dream, I moved through shadowy realms effortlessly, connecting with ancient spirits who saw the value in my enigmatic nature. They helped me understand that being different doesn't make me less valuable—it's what sets me apart and gives me the power to uncover hidden truths.

" Ayden's gentle voice washes over the group, bringing a sense of peace and reassurance. "Throughout my life," he shares, "I've grappled with doubts about my abilities and whether I can truly bring healing to those who need it most. But in my dream, I stood among celestial beings, channeling their energy to heal both physical and emotional wounds. It reminded me that healing is not just a task—it's a calling that comes from deep within my soul.

" As each family member speaks, their vulnerabilities and fears dissolve into a shared understanding. They realize that their dreams are not just individual experiences but fragments of a larger tapestry—a tapestry that reveals their true purpose and their interconnectedness. Nathan reaches out, placing a hand on Lucy's shoulder.

"You've always been a pillar of strength for us, Lucy," he says softly. "But it's important to remember that we all have moments of doubt. We're here for you, just as you've always been there for us." Lucy offers him a small smile of gratitude before turning to Hadley. "Your unique nature has always intrigued me," she admits, her voice filled with admiration. "In your dream, it showed me that being different is not something to be feared—it's what makes us strong as a team.

We each bring something special to the table, and together, we create an unbreakable bond." Hadley's eyes shine with appreciation as she replies, "And Ayden, your calming presence brings us solace when our hearts are heavy.

Your dream reminded us that healing goes beyond physical wounds—it extends to the emotional burdens that weigh us down. Your gift is invaluable to our mission." Ayden nods gratefully and takes a moment to gather his thoughts before speaking again. "We all have our doubts and fears," he says soothingly, yet with profound resolve.

"But together, we are stronger than any darkness that may come our way. We have seen glimpses of our destiny in these dreams, and they tell us one thing—we are meant to face this journey together." The atmosphere around the campfire becomes charged with renewed determination as each family member absorbs the support and understanding flowing between them.

Nathan stands up first and extends a hand towards Lucy. "Let's stand united against whatever challenges await us," he says firmly. Lucy rises without hesitation and grasps Nathan's hand firmly in her own. "No matter what comes our way," she declares with conviction, "we'll face it head-on—together.

" Hadley joins them next, her gaze steady and unwavering. "Our individual strengths become magnified when combined," she adds resolutely. "There's nothing we can't accomplish when we embrace our unique abilities." Finally, Ayden rises gracefully from his spot by the fire and places a hand on each family member's shoulder.

"Let us approach this journey with open hearts and trust in one another," he says softly but with profound certainty. With their hands joined in unity once more, the family looks towards the future with newfound resolve. Their shared visions have solidified their bond and reawakened their determination to protect Ember Bay at all costs.

As they extinguish the campfire that has brought them together, they step into the unknown—their hearts ablaze with hope and determination. Their dreams have shown them their true potential as protectors of Ember Bay—and with each other by their side—they are ready to face any challenge that lies ahead. Together, they walk towards their destiny—united as one—ready to confront Juggernaut and safeguard Ember Bay from its impending darkness.

With their hands joined in unity, the family sets off on their path, the weight of their shared purpose driving them forward. They walk through the Bayou with a newfound determination, leaving behind the remnants of their campsite and the comfort of familiarity. As they journey deeper into the mystical realm, they encounter fellow protectors who have also felt the call to defend Ember Bay.

These encounters serve as reminders of the importance of unity and collaboration in their mission. They share stories, exchange knowledge, and offer support to one another, forming an unbreakable bond woven by a shared purpose. Their conversations are filled with a mix of excitement and trepidation. Each protector brings a unique perspective and set of skills that will prove essential in their collective battle against Juggernaut.

Through these interactions, they gain valuable insights into the supernatural threats that loom over Ember Bay and solidify their resolve to protect it at all costs. In the midst of their preparations, they stumble upon ancient texts and artifacts that reveal more about Juggernaut's history and its connection to Ember Bay.

The family pours over these discoveries, piecing together information and formulating strategies to counteract Juggernaut's destructive power. With each new revelation, their determination swells. They realize that this battle is not just about protecting the physical realm but also safeguarding the spiritual essence of Ember Bay—a place steeped in magic and ancient wisdom. As night falls, they gather around a sacred fire in a secluded clearing—a makeshift altar where they can collectively channel their energies and intentions.

In this moment of quiet reflection, they reaffirm their commitment to one another and to the land they hold dear. Nathan steps forward, his eyes burning with conviction. "We stand here together as guardians of Ember Bay," he begins, his voice resonating with strength. "We have been chosen for a reason—to face these challenges head-on and protect what we hold dear. Let us honor the trust placed upon us and fight with unwavering resolve.

" Lucy nods, her fiery gaze reflecting her determination. "We are stronger together than we could ever be alone," she says, her voice echoing with certainty. "Let us embrace our roles fully and unleash our true potential. Ember Bay needs us now more than ever." Hadley's piercing green eyes gleam with determination as she speaks next.

"Our paths have brought us here for a reason," she says softly but firmly. "We are the ones who will uncover the hidden truths and confront the darkness that threatens our home. Let us do so with courage and unwavering resolve." Ayden's calming presence envelopes them all as he adds his voice to theirs. "In healing both physical and emotional wounds," he says softly, "we restore balance to Ember Bay—a balance that has been disrupted by Juggernaut's impending presence.

Let us bring light to the shadows and restore harmony to this land." The family stands in a moment of collective silence, feeling the weight of their shared purpose settle upon them. As they open their eyes, their gazes meet, sparking an unspoken understanding that transcends words. With renewed determination pulsing through their veins, they step away from the sacred fire, ready to face whatever lies ahead.

Their dreams have shown them glimpses of their destiny—of battles fought and victories won—but it is their unity that will ultimately guide them through this journey. Armed with their individual strengths and bolstered by their unbreakable bond, they make their way towards Juggernaut, ready to confront this formidable adversary head-on. Ember Bay awaits—their destiny awaits—and the Elemental Guardians are ready to fulfill their role as protectors. The family's journey continues, their hearts filled with determination and their spirits intertwined.

They navigate treacherous terrain and face countless challenges along the way, but they do not falter. Each obstacle becomes a stepping stone, solidifying their bond and honing their skills.

As they travel deeper into the heart of the Bayou, they encounter ancient allies who offer guidance and wisdom. These mentors impart valuable knowledge about Juggernaut and the ancient prophecies that foretell its rise.

The family listens intently, absorbing every word, knowing that this information is essential to their mission. With each passing day, their confidence grows. They train relentlessly, harnessing the elemental powers within them and mastering new techniques. Nathan refines his ninja skills, moving with even greater agility and precision.

Lucy pushes her limits, conjuring force fields that are more impenetrable than ever before. Hadley delves deeper into her enigmatic abilities, embracing her role as the Night Owl with unwavering confidence. Ayden delves into ancient healing practices, discovering ways to channel celestial energy more effectively.

Their training sessions become moments of unity—a symphony of movement and power that reaffirms their collective purpose. They move as one, each member complementing the others, their abilities intertwining seamlessly. It is in these moments that they truly understand the strength they possess as a team—the strength of a family bound by destiny. As they approach the final stages of their journey, the remaining fragments of the prophecy weigh heavy on their minds. The seer's words echo through their thoughts, urging them to find the scattered fragments and unlock Juggernaut's weaknesses.

They search tirelessly, uncovering clues and deciphering cryptic messages. The quest for the fragments takes them to hidden caves and forgotten ruins, where they confront both physical and mental challenges. They face ancient guardians tasked with protecting these fragments—guardians who test not only their physical prowess but also their resolve and understanding of Ember Bay's history.

With each fragment retrieved, they feel a surge of power flowing through them—a power directly linked to Ember Bay itself. The fragments pulsate with energy, resonating with the family's united purpose. And as they gather all the fragments together, a complete picture begins to form—a picture that reveals not only Juggernaut's vulnerabilities but also the true potential of the Elemental Guardians themselves.

In the final moments before their confrontation with Juggernaut, the family gathers in quiet contemplation. They stand together under the light of a full moon, their eyes locked in a shared understanding. It is a moment of reflection—an acknowledgment of how far they have come and how much they have grown.

Nathan looks at his family—Lucy, Hadley, and Ayden—with pride shining in his eyes. "We are ready," he says softly but with unwavering conviction. "We have faced our fears and embraced our strengths. Now it is time to fulfill our destiny—to protect Ember Bay from the darkness that threatens it." Lucy nods beside him, her fiery gaze burning brightly. "Together," she says firmly, her voice resolute. "No matter what challenges we may face, we will face them head-on—as one." Hadley steps forward next, her piercing green eyes filled with determination.

"Our journey has brought us here," she declares boldly. "Every step has led us closer to this moment—to confront Juggernaut and protect Ember Bay with everything we have."

Ayden adds his voice to theirs, his gentle presence radiating warmth and reassurance. "We carry the hopes and dreams of those who came before us," he says softly but with profound certainty. "Let us honor their legacy—and our own—by standing strong against Juggernaut's darkness.

" As they prepare to face Juggernaut—to fulfill their collective destiny—the family takes one last moment to draw strength from each other's presence. They raise their hands together, palms touching in a symbol of solidarity—a symbol of unity in the face of adversity. Their hearts beat as one—bound by love and determined resolve.

Ember Bay awaits—their destiny awaits—and together, as Elemental Guardians, they are prepared to face whatever lies ahead. They will protect Ember Bay at all costs—for it is not just a mystical realm—it is their home—and it is worth fighting for. With these thoughts echoing in their minds and hearts, they venture forth—ready to confront Juggernaut head-on—and protect Ember Bay from its impending darkness. Their journey continues—their destinies intertwined—the Elemental Guardians stand united.

Chapter 12: Confronting the Master of Shadows

The family stood on the edge of a desolate landscape, their eyes locked on the Master of Shadows' who radiated an ominous aura. The air crackled with dark energy, sending shivers down their spines. Nathan tightened his grip on his ninja daggers, his body poised and ready for battle.

Lucy squared her shoulders, her fiery red hair blazing in defiance. Hadley's green eyes glinted with determination as she clutched a small amulet, her gateway to teleportation. Ayden took a deep breath, channeling celestial energy through his veins, feeling the power surge within him. Nathan locked eyes with the Master of Shadows' a silent challenge passing between them.

"You won't get away with this," he growled, his voice laced with a steely determination. "We will protect Ember Bay, no matter the cost." Lucy stepped forward, her voice clear and commanding. "You may be powerful, the Master of Shadows' but we have something you don't - unity and love for one another. We will never let darkness prevail." Hadley, ever observant, watched the Master of Shadows' every move.

You may think you're unstoppable, but we've faced adversity before. We know how to adapt and overcome. Prepare to face defeat." Ayden's calm voice resonated with wisdom and compassion. "Master of Shadows' your reign ends here. We will use our powers not just to defeat you, but to heal and bring balance back to Ember Bay.

" The Master of Shadows' menacing laugh echoed through the air as he summoned dark tendrils of energy around him. "You underestimate my power, Elemental Guardians. You were chosen for a reason - to serve as mere pawns in my conquest. But I will show you that your abilities are no match for true darkness." With a sudden surge of power, the Master of Shadows' lunged at the family with terrifying speed.

Nathan dodged and weaved through the Master of Shadows' attacks, his ninja skills allowing him to dance through the shadows unscathed. He struck back swiftly, landing precise blows that seemed to have little effect on their formidable foe. Lucy raised her hands, summoning force fields that shimmered brightly in the air.

She deflected the Master of Shadows' strikes with ease, protecting her family from harm. Sparks flew as their powers collided, each clash showcasing the strength of their resolve. Hadley utilized her night vision and agility to blend into the shadows, striking from unexpected angles. Her teleportation abilities allowed her to appear and disappear in a flash, keeping the Master of Shadows' off balance and unable to anticipate her moves.

Ayden focused his healing abilities, reaching out with his celestial energy to soothe both physical and emotional wounds inflicted by the Master of Shadows' onslaught. His presence brought a sense of calm amidst the chaos, bolstering his family's strength and giving them renewed energy to fight.

The battle raged on, each member of the family tapping into their elemental powers with unwavering determination. Bruises and wounds began to mark their bodies as they pushed themselves beyond their limits. Sweat dripped down their brows as they exchanged blows with the Master of Shadows. "This fight is not over," Nathan said breathlessly.

Lucy grinned, her fiery hair reflecting her pride. "We will fight together and conquer." Hadley nodded in agreement. "No enemy can break our bond or extinguish our light." Ayden smiled softly. "Through love and unity, we have shown the darkness our limits.

" As the battle with the Master of Shadows' intensified, the family unleashed their elemental powers with a ferocity they had never before experienced. Nathan moved with an agility and precision that seemed almost supernatural. His ninja training allowed him to dodge and deflect the Master of Shadows' attacks effortlessly, his every move calculated to exploit his opponent's weaknesses.

With each strike, he aimed for critical areas, hoping to weaken the Master of Shadows' defenses. Lucy's force fields shimmered brightly as she summoned them around herself and her family. Like impenetrable barriers, they absorbed the Master of Shadows' powerful blows and redirected his attacks back at him. Energy crackled in the air as the force fields clashed with the Master of Shadows' dark energy, creating dazzling displays of light and power.

Hadley used her enchantment of teleportation to her advantage, disappearing from one spot and reappearing elsewhere in the blink of an eye. She struck with precision and stealth, catching the Master of Shadows ' off guard and leaving him disoriented. Her quick reflexes and keen night vision allowed her to anticipate his moves, giving her a strategic advantage in the battle.

Ayden channeled the celestial energy within him, using it to heal and restore his family's strength in the face of the Master of Shadows' relentless assault. With a gentle touch and soothing words, he mended their wounds and bolstered their resolve. His calming presence radiated a sense of peace amidst the chaos, providing a much-needed respite for his weary comrades. With each passing moment, the intensity of the battle grew.

Sweat dripped down their brows as they traded blows with the Master of Shadows' the ground beneath them shaking with the force of their clash. Bruises and wounds began to mark their bodies, evidence of the sacrifices they were willing to make to protect Ember Bay. But even as exhaustion set in, their determination remained unwavering. They drew strength from one another, relying on their unbreakable bond to push through the pain and press on. Each strike became fueled by love for their family, their friends, and the mystical realm they called home.

Nathan darted in and out of shadows, using his exceptional ninja skills to deliver swift strikes at the Master of Shadows' vulnerable spots. He landed blow after blow, pushing himself beyond his limits despite the strain on his body. There were moments when self-doubt threatened to consume him, but the love he felt for his family propelled him forward. He knew he couldn't let them down. Lucy's force fields shimmered brightly as she deflected blow after blow from the Master of Shadows'.

The strain of maintaining them was immense, but she refused to let them falter. In her heart, she carried a fierce determination to protect those she loved and ensure that darkness would never prevail. Every strike against the Master of Shadows' was a testament to her unwavering strength. Hadley moved with grace and precision, striking swiftly from the shadows and disappearing just as quickly.

Her enchantment allowed her to blend into darkness like a ghost, making her movements unpredictable. Doubts plagued her mind at times, whispering that she wasn't strong enough or skilled enough. But she pushed those thoughts aside, drawing strength from the support of her family and embracing her role as the Night Owl. Ayden stood at the center of the battlefield, channeling healing energy to mend his family's wounds.

Despite his gentle nature, he understood the importance of fighting for what was right. He refused to let darkness consume Ember Bay or its inhabitants. Doubts occasionally crept into his mind, causing him to question whether he was truly fulfilling his potential as a healer. But he channeled those doubts into determination and doubled his efforts to protect and bring harmony. The battle raged on, each member of the family tapping into their elemental powers with unwavering determination.

They fought not just for themselves but for all those who called Ember Bay home. Every strike against the Master of Shadows sent shockwaves through their foe's dark form. In the final climactic moment, fueled by love for one another and an indomitable spirit, the family unleashed a combined attack that sent the Master of Shadows reeling. His defenses faltered momentarily as they capitalized on this moment of vulnerability.

Landing blow after blow, they delivered a decisive strike that left the Master of Shadows' staggered. A blinding light enveloped the battlefield as the Master of Shadows' was consumed by their unified attack. The brilliance overwhelmed him, weakening his grip on power. As the light dissipated and silence settled over the desolate landscape, the family stood together, breathing heavily but triumphant.

Their victory lay not just in their individual achievements but in their unwavering unity and unwavering belief in one another. "We did it," Nathan said breathlessly, wiping sweat from his brow. "We stood together and conquered." Lucy grinned defiantly. "No enemy can break our bond or extinguish our light." Hadley nodded in agreement. "Darkness may be relentless, but we are stronger." Ayden smiled softly. "Through love and unity, we have shown darkness its limits." They stood there for a moment longer, basking in the glow of their victory before turning their attention toward what lay ahead.

The battle may have been won but there were still challenges awaiting them on their mission to protect Ember Bay. But as long as they had each other - united by an unbreakable bond forged through trials and triumphs - they knew that they would continue to defend Ember Bay until their very last breath. The family retreated to a tranquil clearing within the Bayou, seeking solace and respite after the intense battle with the Master of Shadows. Exhausted and bruised, they gathered around a small stream, its babbling waters providing a soothing backdrop to their weariness.

Nathan winced as he peeled his ninja outfit away from his skin, revealing an array of cuts and bruises. Lucy carefully poured cool water over his wounds, gentle fingers tracing the edges of his injuries. "You took quite a beating back there," she murmured, her voice laced with concern. Nathan grinned sheepishly. "Yeah, but it was worth it.

We showed the Master of Shadows' that we won't back down." Lucy's fiery hair framed her face as she leaned in closer, searching his eyes for any signs of hidden pain. "I'm just glad you're alright," she whispered, breathing a sigh of relief.

Hadley crouched beside them, her slender fingers expertly wrapping bandages around Nathan's injured wrists. Her piercing green eyes held a hint of worry as she muttered, "You're lucky it's just a sprain. That could've been much worse." Nathan nodded appreciatively, his gaze flickering between Lucy and Hadley. "I owe you both my gratitude," he confessed, touched by their unwavering support. Ayden sat nearby, his calming presence washing over the group like a gentle breeze.

With soft hands, he attended to the minor wounds and scrapes on his own body before turning his attention to Lucy. "How are you holding up?" he asked softly, brushing a strand of fiery red hair away from her face. Lucy managed a wry smile. "A few bumps and bruises won't keep me down," she replied, her voice filled with determination. "I'm ready to keep fighting." Ayden's eyes sparkled with admiration as he continued tending to her wounds. "Your strength never ceases to amaze me," he whispered, his voice filled with awe.

Meanwhile, Hadley inspected her blackened eye in a small mirror. She turned her head this way and that, appreciating the battle scars etched across her face. "I may look like I've been through a storm," she mused, "but these wounds will serve as a reminder of our victory against the Master of Shadows'.

" Nathan regarded her with respect in his eyes. "You fought with incredible courage and skill," he said sincerely. "You're an invaluable member of our team." Hadley's lips twitched into a shy smile as she accepted the compliment, her gaze flitting between Nathan and Ayden. "Thank you," she murmured, grateful for their unwavering belief in her abilities. Ayden finished cleaning his own scrapes and turned his attention to Hadley's injuries. His touch was gentle as he dabbed at the deep gash along her arm, his soft voice filled with warmth and reassurance.

"You were exceptional out there," he praised her. "Your teleportation skills saved us more times than I can count." Her green eyes softened as she met Ayden's gaze. "It means a lot coming from you," she replied sincerely. "Your healing abilities played a crucial role in our victory." Together, they tended to each other's wounds with a tenderness born out of love and friendship. As they worked, their conversation shifted to lighter topics - memories of past battles, moments of triumphs and failures, and hopes for the future.

In the background, the sounds of nature provided a soothing symphony. Birds chirped melodiously above them while leaves rustled gently in the breeze. The tranquility of the Bayou offered respite from their weary bodies and minds. As Nathan watched Ayden skillfully bandage Hadley's arm, a sense of gratitude welled up within him.

They were not just teammates or friends; they were family bound by shared experiences and mutual trust. Finally, when all the wounds had been tended to and the physical pain eased, they settled into comfortable silence. Their bodies may have been scarred but their spirits burned brighter than ever before.

In this moment of stillness and healing, they found solace in one another's presence. Each bruise and wound became a symbol of their resilience and unwavering determination to protect Ember Bay. With renewed strength and unity coursing through their veins, they looked ahead into the unknown challenges that awaited them on their journey. But whatever lay ahead, they were prepared to face it together – stronger than ever before.

As the physical pain began to fade and their wounds tended to, the family turned their attention to the emotional toll that the battle with the Master of Shadows' had taken. They gathered in a small circle, their faces reflecting the weariness and weight of the challenges they had faced. Nathan spoke first, his voice filled with a mixture of relief and grief. "We did it," he said softly, his eyes searching each family member's face.

"But at what cost? The sacrifices we made... they weigh heavy on my heart." Lucy nodded solemnly, her fiery gaze flickering with a mix of pride and sorrow. "It's true," she whispered, her voice choked with emotion. "We fought with everything we had, but we can't ignore the toll it took on us." Hadley's voice was steady but laced with vulnerability. "I can't help but question if my abilities were enough," she admitted, her gaze falling to the ground.

"There were moments when I doubted myself, when I wondered if I truly belonged among all of you." Ayden's gentle presence wrapped around them like a comforting embrace. His kind eyes held compassion and understanding as he spoke. "We all have our doubts and fears," he said softly. "But that's what makes us human. It's through acknowledging those doubts that we find strength and grow." Nathan reached out and clasped Lucy's hand, squeezing it gently.

"We faced our darkest fears together," he said, his voice filled with determination. "And despite our doubts, we emerged stronger than ever before." Lucy returned the squeeze, her grip firm and unwavering. "That's right," she said fiercely. "No matter what doubts we may have, we will face them head-on. Because together, we are unstoppable." Hadley looked up, meeting Ayden's gaze with a hint of a smile. "You're right," she said, her voice stronger now.

"Our doubts don't define us. It's how we overcome them that truly matters." Ayden's expression softened as he spoke words of wisdom and comfort. "In our vulnerability lies our greatest strength," he said gently. "It's through acknowledging our doubts and fears that we find the courage to move forward." Silence settled over the clearing as their words hung in the air, each family member reflecting on their shared experiences and individual journey of growth.

Then, as if in silent agreement, they leaned into one another - connecting through touch, through shared warmth, and through unspoken understanding. They drew strength from one another, finding solace in their unity and resilience.

"We may have faced darkness today," Nathan said, his voice steady, "but it is our unwavering love for each other that will lead us forward." Lucy nodded firmly, her gaze meeting each family member's eyes as she declared, "No matter what challenges lie ahead, we will face them together - united as one.

" Hadley's eyes sparkled with newfound determination as she whispered, "Our doubts may attempt to cloud our path, but they will not deter us from fulfilling our destiny." Ayden smiled softly at his family, his voice filled with quiet confidence.

"Through love and unity," he concluded, "we have shown that even in our vulnerability, we are invincible." With their hearts anchored by love and fortified by unity, they knew that no challenge would be too great to overcome. As they sat there in the tranquil clearing, basking in the healing warmth of one another's presence, a renewed sense of purpose settled over them.

Together, they would face whatever lay ahead - their bond unbreakable against any darkness. The physical and emotional wounds were tended to, leaving the family with a renewed sense of clarity and determination. As they sat together in the peaceful clearing within the Bayou, their minds turned towards the future challenges that awaited them. Nathan broke the silence, his voice strong and resolute.

"We have overcome the Master of Shadows' but we cannot rest on our laurels," he said, his eyes meeting the gaze of each family member. "There are still threats that lurk in the shadows, waiting to test our strength and unity." Lucy nodded in agreement, her fiery spirit burning brightly. "We must remain vigilant," she emphasized.

"Our victory against the Master of Shadows' has shown us that darkness will always regroup and seek to regain its hold. We must be prepared for whatever comes our way." Hadley's green eyes glittered with newfound determination. "We should seek guidance from our allies," she suggested.

"There are others who have faced similar battles and triumphed. Their wisdom and experience may prove invaluable as we face new challenges." Ayden's calming presence soothed their anxieties as he spoke. "We must also refine our abilities," he said softly. "In the heat of battle, we discovered new depths to our powers. Through further training and exploration, we can unlock even greater potential within ourselves.

" Nathan's voice grew stronger as he continued, his gaze fixed on the path ahead. "We should seek out ancient knowledge," he proposed. "Ember Bay holds many secrets, and if we can uncover more about its history and the supernatural forces at play, we can better understand the nature of the challenges we may face.

" Lucy's eyes sparkled with excitement as she added her own idea. "We should strengthen alliances," she suggested eagerly. "There are protectors beyond our own realm who could provide us with valuable insights and support. By forging bonds with like-minded individuals, we can create a network of shared knowledge and resources." Hadley's words held a note of caution as she expressed her concerns.

"We must be careful not to let our rival protectors exploit any divisions in our ranks," she warned. "Unity is our greatest strength, and if we allow internal conflicts to weaken our bonds, we risk falling into disarray." Ayden's words resonated with certainty as he spoke from the heart. "Our focus should always be on protecting those who cannot protect themselves," he said gently.

"We must never lose sight of our purpose - to bring harmony and peace to Ember Bay." Silence settled over the family as they absorbed each other's ideas and perspectives. The weight of their collective responsibility hung in the air, but so did a sense of hope and possibility. Nathan stood up abruptly, his voice filled with conviction.

"Let it be known then," he declared, his eyes shining with unwavering determination. "We shall seek guidance, refine our abilities, uncover ancient knowledge, forge alliances, and above all else, protect Ember Bay with every fiber of our being." Lucy rose to her feet next to him, her fiery hair swirling around her as she echoed his sentiment.

"Together, we are the Elemental Guardians - a united force against darkness," she proclaimed, her voice carrying across the clearing. Hadley followed suit, her green eyes aflame with purpose. "May our steps be guided by wisdom and courage," she intoned solemnly.

Chapter 13: Uncovering The Ancient Chamber

The family cautiously stepped into the hidden divination chamber, their footsteps reverberating against the ancient stone walls. The air inside was heavy with anticipation and mystery, as if time itself held its breath in this sacred space. Torches flickered, casting dancing shadows on the intricate carvings and symbols that adorned the chamber. Nathan's heart pounded in his chest as he took in the grandeur of the chamber.

The walls seemed to whisper secrets long forgotten, their weathered stone telling tales of ancient prophecies and hidden powers. His fingers trembled as he reached out to touch one of the inscriptions, feeling a surge of energy coursing through his fingertips.

Lucy's eyes widened with awe as she gazed at the elaborate carvings that depicted powerful beings and swirling currents of elemental forces. She couldn't help but feel a deep connection to this place, as if it were calling to her, beckoning her to unlock its mysteries. She took a hesitant step forward, her hand hovering just above the smooth surface of the divination table.

Hadley's gaze darted around the chamber, her keen eyes absorbing every detail. The delicate strands of cobwebs that clung to the walls seemed to sway gently in an otherworldly breeze, adding an ethereal touch to the atmosphere. She felt a magnetic pull toward the table, a sense that there was something important waiting for them there. Ayden's breath hitched in his throat as he stepped further into the chamber.

He could feel the weight of centuries past pressing down on him, yet there was also a gentle warmth in the air—a comforting presence that whispered of ancient wisdom and divine guidance. He knew deep in his soul that this place held answers they desperately sought. As each family member approached the divination table, they felt a mixture of excitement and trepidation. Their hands hovered above the smooth obsidian surface, their fingers tingling with anticipation.

And then, as if responding to their touch, a surge of energy surged through their bodies—a tangible current of power. Visions flickered before Nathan's eyes—shadows dancing across moonlit landscapes, his form slipping effortlessly through darkness like an extension of himself. He glimpsed fleeting scenes of battles fought and victories won, his mind filled with whispers of destiny and purpose. A sense of determination welled within him as he withdrew his hand, his resolve hardening. In Lucy's vision, she stood at the center of a swirling storm of fire—a tempest of flames controlled by her will alone.

Her force fields crackled with fiery energy, shielding those she loved from harm. She saw herself standing tall and unyielding against powerful opponents, her strength radiating like a beacon in the darkness.

Hadley's vision took her deep into the heart of an underwater world—lush coral reefs stretching out before her like a vast tapestry woven by nature itself. She heard her voice resonating with magical energy, commanding water to do her bidding.

The sense of freedom and power that surged through her veins made her realize the untapped potential within her, waiting to be unleashed. For Ayden, celestial dreams unfolded before his eyes—an aurora borealis illuminating the night sky with brilliant hues, his hands glowing with healing energy as he mended wounds both physical and emotional.

He saw himself becoming a symbol of hope and restoration, bringing balance and harmony wherever he went. As these visions faded away, each family member stood in silence for a moment, their minds spinning with fragments of insight and enlightenment. They shared knowing glances, understanding that they had caught glimpses of their shared destiny—as protectors of Ember Bay.

"We have been chosen," Nathan said solemnly, his voice filled with determination. "And we must embrace our roles," Lucy added, her fiery gaze reflecting unwavering resolve. Hadley nodded slowly, a mysterious smile playing at the corners of her lips. "These visions are not mere fantasies but glimpses into what lies ahead.

We must trust in ourselves and in each other." Ayden's voice was soft yet filled with conviction as he spoke. "Together, we can face whatever challenges await us. We have been given these gifts for a reason." In unison they said with renewed purpose and unity, "We can do this." The divination table seemed to hum with a low vibration as the family members took turns touching its smooth surface.

As Lucy reached out, a surge of fiery energy coursed through her fingertips, causing her whole body to tingle with anticipation. Flames danced across her vision, swirling and flickering in a mesmerizing display of power. Visions of battles fought and won enveloped Lucy's mind. She saw herself standing tall and unyielding against powerful opponents, her force fields crackling with fiery energy as they shielded those she loved from harm.

The intensity of the flames mirrored her own determination, igniting a fire within her that burned brighter than ever before. Nathan watched Lucy's face, his eyes filled with pride and admiration. He had witnessed her strength and resilience before, but now he saw it in an entirely new light.

She was a warrior, fierce and unstoppable—a force to be reckoned with. And he knew that with her by his side, they could face any challenge that came their way. Hadley approached the table next, hesitant yet curious. As her fingertips brushed against the obsidian surface, she felt a cool rush of water wash over her senses.

Her vision shifted to an underwater world, where vibrant coral reefs stretched out before her like a vast tapestry woven by nature itself. Her voice resonated with magical energy, commanding water to do her bidding.

She watched in awe as currents obeyed her every command, parting before her like a curtain revealing hidden wonders deep beneath the surface. The sense of freedom and power that surged through her veins made her realize the untapped potential within her, waiting to be unleashed.

Nathan observed Hadley's transformation with fascination. The way she moved with such grace and fluidity reminded him of a creature at one with the water—a true guardian of the depths. He knew that her ability to blend into shadows and navigate unseen made her an invaluable asset to their mission.

Ayden stepped forward with quiet confidence, his eyes shining with celestial light. As he touched the divination table, a gentle warmth spread through his fingertips, radiating up his arms and filling his entire being with a soothing energy. Celestial dreams unfolded before his eyes—an aurora borealis illuminating the night sky with brilliant hues.

In his visions, he saw himself becoming a beacon of hope and healing, his hands glowing with divine energy as he mended wounds both physical and emotional. He witnessed moments of serenity and restoration, where darkness gave way to light and pain transformed into peace. Ayden recognized the immense responsibility that came with his gift—the power to heal and bring balance to those who needed it most.

Lucy gazed at Ayden, captivated by the sense of calm and wisdom that emanated from him. She had always known him as a compassionate healer, but now she understood that his abilities went beyond physical wounds. He possessed a gift for soothing troubled hearts and restoring harmony—a rare quality that would be vital in their journey.

As each family member withdrew their hand from the divination table, they found themselves standing together in silent contemplation. They had caught glimpses of their shared destiny—the challenges they would face, the battles they would fight. "We have been chosen," Nathan said with unwavering conviction, breaking the silence that hung over them. "And we must embrace our roles," Lucy added, her voice filled with determination as she locked eyes with each member of their group.

Hadley nodded slowly, a mysterious smile playing at the corners of her lips. "These visions are not mere fantasies but glimpses into what lies ahead. We must trust in ourselves and in each other." Ayden's voice was soft yet filled with conviction as he spoke. "Together, we can face whatever challenges await us. We have been given these gifts for a reason." In unison, they stood together—Nathan with his piercing gaze, Lucy with her fiery determination, Hadley with her enigmatic presence, and Ayden with his calming strength—and said with renewed purpose and unity, "We can do this.

" The echoes of their words filled the chamber, carrying their resolve beyond its stone walls and into the world beyond. The family gathered around the divination table, their eyes locked on one another as they shared their visions. The room seemed to hold its breath, the air thick with anticipation and a sense of profound connection.

Nathan's voice was steady but filled with emotion as he spoke first. "In my vision, I saw myself moving through the darkness with grace and ease. Shadows wrapped around me like a second skin, concealing my presence from those who would seek to harm us. It was as if the very essence of the night flowed through my veins." Lucy's eyes sparkled with determination as she recounted her own experience.

"I stood at the center of a blazing inferno, flames licking at my fingertips.

My force fields crackled with fiery energy, forming an impenetrable shield around us. In that moment, I felt invincible—like nothing could stand in our way." Hadley's voice was hushed yet brimming with excitement.

"I found myself in an underwater world, surrounded by shimmering coral reefs and gentle currents. I could command water to move in harmony with my will, parting before me as if following a hidden song. It was as if I had become one with the very essence of the Bayou itself." Ayden's words were filled with serenity and light. "In my vision, I was a beacon of healing and compassion.

Celestial energy flowed through my hands, mending wounds and soothing troubled hearts. I saw myself bringing balance and harmony to those who needed it most—guiding them towards peace." As each family member shared their visions, a sense of awe settled over them. They were no longer just individuals—each possessing unique gifts and abilities—but a united front bound together by a shared destiny.

Nathan reached out his hand, his gaze steady yet filled with vulnerability. "We have been given these visions for a reason. They show us what we are capable of and remind us of the responsibility we bear as protectors of Ember Bay. It won't be easy, but together, we can face anything." Lucy stepped forward, her fiery spirit radiating from within her.

"Our visions are like puzzle pieces that fit together to form a larger picture—a picture of strength, unity, and unwavering resolve. We must trust in ourselves and in each other." Hadley's gaze was enigmatic yet determined.

"The Bayou has chosen us for this task. It has placed its faith in us to protect it from the encroaching darkness. We must honor that trust by embracing our roles and using our gifts to their fullest extent." Ayden's voice was soft yet filled with conviction. "We have been prepared for this journey—tested and forged like weapons in fire.

The challenges we face may be great, but so is our potential to overcome them. We have each other's backs, and that is our greatest strength." In unison, the family raised their hands and brought them together in a symbol of unity—a reminder of the bond they shared and the strength they drew from one another. "We are the Elemental Guardians," Nathan declared, his voice resonating through the room. "And together, we will protect Ember Bay," Lucy added, her voice joining Nathan's in perfect harmony.

Hadley smiled mysteriously, her eyes alight with determination. "Our destinies are intertwined with the very fabric of this mystical realm. Together, we will rise above any challenge that comes our way." Ayden's voice was filled with hope and healing as he spoke the final words.

"Let us go forth with unwavering resolve and bring light to the darkness that threatens Ember Bay." And so, united by their visions and bound by their shared sense of purpose, the family stepped forward into the unknown—their hearts aflame with courage and determination. They were ready to face whatever challenges lay ahead, armed not only with their individual gifts but with the unbreakable bonds they had forged along the way.

The family stood before the enigmatic blacksmith, their hearts beating with a mixture of excitement and anticipation. His workshop was filled with the scent of smoldering embers and the glow of soft candlelight, creating an otherworldly atmosphere that seemed to heighten their senses.

Nathan's eyes roamed over the rows of gleaming tools and weapons, his fingers tingling with anticipation. He knew that this place held the key to unlocking their full potential as protectors of Ember Bay. The blacksmith stood beside a roaring forge, his weathered hands stained with soot, yet emanating a sense of wisdom and mastery.

As they approached the blacksmith, his gaze met there's—a knowing look passed between them as if he understood the weight of their mission. Each family member was aware that they were about to embark on a transformative journey—a journey that would require not only their courage but also the weapons that would amplify their elemental abilities. Nathan stepped forward first, gripping the hilt of his shadow-infused weapon firmly in his hand. The blade glinted in the dim light, its surface reflecting his determined expression.

The blacksmith studied Nathan's weapon with keen eyes, nodding in approval. "This blade is forged from the rarest metal infused with shadows," the blacksmith explained. "It will enhance your already exceptional ninja skills, allowing you to move through darkness with even greater stealth and precision." Nathan's heart swelled with pride as he felt the weight of the weapon in his hand—it was an extension of himself, a symbol of his commitment to protect Ember Bay.

He thanked the blacksmith with a nod, silently vowing to wield his newfound power with honor and integrity. Lucy approached next, her eyes fixed on the fiery gemstones embedded within her weapon. As she reached out to touch it, a surge of energy coursed through her fingertips—the same fiery energy that had flickered in her visions. She gripped her weapon tightly, feeling its crackling power course through her veins.

"This weapon harnesses the very essence of fire," the blacksmith explained. "It will allow you to command flames with even greater control, creating formidable force fields that can shield those you hold dear from harm." Lucy's heart soared as she held her weapon aloft—fire danced within her grasp, ignited by her unwavering spirit. It felt like second nature to her, as if this weapon had always been a part of who she truly was.

She thanked the blacksmith with a smile, ready to unleash her newfound power in defense of Ember Bay. Hadley approached next, her fingers tracing delicate patterns etched into the sleek surface of her weapon. A cool rush of water washed over her senses as she grasped it firmly—a tangible connection to the underwater world that had captivated her in her visions.

"This weapon is crafted with mercurial substances," explained the blacksmith. "It will amplify your ability to move effortlessly through water and blend into shadows, enhancing your already impressive stealth and observation skills." Hadley felt a surge of excitement as she held her weapon—the weight was familiar yet exhilarating.

It was a tool that would allow her to tap into the very essence of the Bayou itself—a testament to her role as the Night Owl.

She thanked the blacksmith with a nod, fully embracing her destiny as a protector of Ember Bay. Ayden approached last, his gentle demeanor juxtaposed against the glowing celestial fragments adorning his weapon. As he touched it, a sense of serenity enveloped him—a soothing energy that resonated deep within his soul.

"This weapon is imbued with celestial light," explained the blacksmith. "It will enhance your natural healing abilities and enable you to channel divine energy with unmatched precision and potency." Ayden's heart swelled with gratitude as he held his weapon aloft—the celestial glow reflected in his kind eyes mirrored the hope and healing he aimed to bring to Ember Bay.

It was an embodiment of his purpose—a symbol of harmony and restoration. He thanked the blacksmith with a soft smile, ready to embrace his destiny as a healer for both body and spirit. As each family member held their newly forged weapons in their hands, they could feel an undeniable surge of power coursing through their veins—a connection to something greater than themselves. They gazed at one another with newfound understanding—each individual piece now part of a greater whole.

The blacksmith smiled knowingly, observing their transformed presence and sense of purpose. "You have proven yourselves worthy," he declared. "Remember, these weapons are not just objects—they are an extension of who you are. Wield them with respect and honor the trust that Ember Bay has placed in you." With gratitude and determination etched on their faces, the family thanked the blacksmith for his guidance and craftsmanship.

They left his workshop armed not only with physical weapons but also with an unbreakable resolve—to protect Ember Bay at all costs. As they emerged from the blacksmith's workshop, their spirits lifted—they were ready to face whatever challenges lay ahead. With their elemental weapons in hand and hearts blazing with courage, they embarked on their journey—as united protectors bound by destiny—ready to defend Ember Bay from darkness's relentless grip.

The blacksmith led the family to a separate area of his workshop, where various materials and tools were laid out before them. Each family member's eyes widened in awe as they took in the array of rare substances and intricate instruments that would play a vital role in their weapons' construction. Nathan's gaze fixated on a dark metal ingot, shimmering with an otherworldly glow. The blacksmith explained that this metal was infused with the essence of shadows, granting it exceptional strength and the ability to meld seamlessly with its surroundings.

With steady hands, Nathan grasped the ingot and placed it upon an anvil, ready to shape it into his desired weapon. The blacksmith handed him a specially crafted hammer, which seemed to hum with power as he held it. Nathan closed his eyes, channeling the shadows within him as he struck the ingot with precise force.

The rhythmic sounds of metal meeting metal filled the air, punctuated by sparks that danced like fireflies. Under Nathan's skillful blows, the ingot began to take shape—a slender and agile blade, honed to perfection.

As Nathan quenched the blade in water to cool its fiery temper, he couldn't help but marvel at how it had transformed from a mere ingot into a formidable weapon—a symbol of his commitment to protect Ember Bay with stealth and precision. Lucy's attention, however, was drawn to a collection of vibrant gemstones.

They glimmered like miniature suns, radiating intense heat that made her palms tingle with anticipation. The blacksmith explained that these gemstones held the essence of fire itself, capable of harnessing its power in ways unimaginable. With steady hands and focused determination, Lucy carefully selected the gemstones that resonated most strongly with her fiery spirit.

She arranged them in a precise pattern along the length of her weapon—a staff that crackled with raw energy. As she pressed each gemstone into place, she could feel their fiery energy merging with her own. It was as if she had become one with the flames—their warmth flowing through her veins and fueling her resolve to protect Ember Bay with unwavering passion.

Hadley gazed upon a shimmering pool of mercurial liquid, captivated by its ethereal beauty. It beckoned to her, calling forth memories of her visions—of an underwater world where she could move with grace and mystique. With graceful movements, Hadley dipped her weapon—a sleek and slender dagger—into the liquid mercury. As it coated the blade, it seemed to come alive—as fluid and elusive as the depths of the Bayou itself. In silence, Hadley marveled at how something so ordinary could be transformed into something extraordinary.

The blade now mirrored her own enigmatic presence—a fitting tool for navigating shadows and revealing hidden truths. Ayden's attention turned to clusters of celestial fragments—tiny shards that glowed with divine radiance. These fragments had been imbued with healing energy, capable of mending not only physical wounds but also soothing troubled souls.

Carefully collecting each fragment, Ayden arranged them along the hilt of his staff—a staff that seemed to emanate a gentle warmth as he held it. He marveled at how these humble fragments held such immense power—to bring peace and balance to those in need. Ayden closed his eyes and allowed himself to become attuned to the celestial vibrations that thrummed through his fingertips.

He whispered a silent prayer—a vow—to use this weapon not only for healing but also for dispelling darkness wherever it may lurk. As each family member completed their weapons, an air of reverence settled over them. The blacksmith watched with pride as they stood together—weapons in hand—each reflecting their individual strengths and abilities. They were no longer separate entities but a united force—a reflection of Ember Bay's elemental harmony.

With gratitude in their hearts, they expressed their thanks to the blacksmith for his guidance and expertise. They felt humbled by his wisdom and honored to carry these weapons forged from ancient elements.

As they stepped out of the blacksmith's workshop, their spirits soared—they were now armed not only with physical weapons but also with a deep sense of purpose and unity. They knew that together they could face any challenge that lay ahead—an unbreakable bond forged in fire, shadows, water, and light.

As they set off on their journey, weapons gleaming in hand, they did so with heads held high—knowing that they were ready to protect Ember Bay from whatever darkness may come their way.

The blacksmith watched with a sense of pride as the family approached him, each holding their newly forged weapons. He could see the determination and unity reflected in their eyes, knowing that these weapons were more than just tools—they were symbols of their commitment and strength.

"You have all surpassed my expectations," the blacksmith said, his gravelly voice carrying a hint of admiration. "These weapons are not simply tools of war but extensions of your very beings. Wield them with honor and use your elemental powers for the greater good of Ember Bay." Nathan, his shadow-infused weapon glinting in the sunlight, nodded in understanding.

"I will be the guardian of darkness, embracing the shadows to protect those I hold dear." Lucy tightened her grip on her fiery staff, determination burning in her eyes. "With the power of fire, I will shield Ember Bay from harm and light the way through the darkest times." Hadley's enigmatic smile hinted at the mysteries that lay within her as she held her mercurial dagger.

"In the depths of water and shadows, I will uncover hidden truths and guard against deceit." Ayden's staff glowed with celestial energy, reflecting his calming presence. "With healing light, I will bring solace and harmony to those in need and restore balance to Ember Bay." The blacksmith nodded approvingly, his wise eyes gleaming with understanding.

"Remember, it is not only the physical form of these weapons that holds power—it is also the unity and unwavering spirit of those who wield them. Stay true to yourselves, stay united, and you will overcome any obstacle that stands in your way." With gratitude in their hearts, the family bid farewell to the blacksmith, ready to embark on their next chapter as protectors of Ember Bay.

They walked away from his workshop, each holding their weapons close to their chests—the physical embodiment of their newfound purpose and determination. As they looked out over Ember Bay, a renewed sense of responsibility settled upon them.

The journey ahead would not be easy—their visions had shown them glimpses of the challenges they would face—but they were prepared. United by their elemental powers and armed with their weapons, they knew that together they could face anything that threatened their beloved home.

Chapter 14: Suspicion and Doubt

The family gathered in a secluded clearing, the dappled sunlight filtering through the dense tree canopy above. Nathan's hand trembled slightly as he held out the small piece of parchment he had found, his eyes filled with a mix of anger and disbelief.

"Look what I found," he said, his voice laced with bitterness. Lucy leaned forward, her fiery red hair framing her determined face. Her eyes scanned the words written on the parchment, her brows furrowed in confusion.

"But...how? How could they betray us like this?" she exclaimed, her voice filled with hurt. Hadley crossed her arms tightly over her slender chest, her voice tinged with frustration. "We trusted them with our lives, and they stabbed us in the back," she said, her piercing green eyes flashing with anger. "I can't believe we were so blind.

" Ayden, his usual calm demeanor wavered for a moment, his voice filled with a mix of disappointment and sadness. "It's true. We put our faith in them, only to have it shattered," he said, his kind eyes clouded with sorrow. "What are we going to do?" Nathan clenched his fists, his gaze fixed on the ground. "We need answers," he said through gritted teeth. "They need to explain themselves and face the consequences of their actions.

" As the family exchanged glances, emotions surged within each of them - betrayal, anger, confusion, and a profound sense of loss. Their once-solid bond had been fractured, and they struggled to make sense of it all. Lucy spoke up after a moment, her voice shaking with suppressed fury. "We're not going to let this divide us," she declared, her fiery determination shining through.

"We are still a family, and we will face Juggernaut together." Hadley nodded in agreement, her voice filled with steely resolve. "This betrayal won't break us," she said firmly. "If anything, it has made us stronger. We know now who we can truly trust." Ayden reached out a comforting hand to Lucy, his gentle voice cutting through the tension. "You're right," he said softly, his voice filled with compassion.

"We must remember why we fight - to protect Ember Bay and those we love. This setback will only strengthen our resolve." Nathan took a deep breath, his muscles tensing as he let go of his anger. "We will confront our ally," he said firmly, determination flickering in his eyes. "We deserve answers, and they deserve to face the consequences of their actions." With renewed determination, the family stood together in their shared goal - to protect Ember Bay at all costs.

Despite the betrayal that lingered like a dark cloud over them, they knew they couldn't afford to let it tear them apart. In unison, they nodded their heads in agreement. They would confront their ally and demand an explanation. No matter how painful it may be, they had to uncover the truth and find a way to move forward.

The secluded clearing seemed to hold its breath as the family prepared themselves for what lay ahead.

The path ahead was uncertain and treacherous, but they would face it together - a united front against Juggernaut and anyone who dared stand in their way. With their eyes firmly set on their shared destiny, the family turned as one and set off towards their ally's hiding place. Though doubt lingered in their hearts, they would not let it consume them. For Ember Bay's sake and for their own sake as well, they would find the strength to overcome this betrayal and continue fighting for what they believed in.

And so the Elemental Guardians moved forward together, ready to face whatever challenges awaited them on this path of uncertainty and redemption. A Desperate Alliance The family ventured through the dense undergrowth of the Bayou, their footsteps muffled by the thick layers of leaves and moss.

The air was heavy with anticipation as they approached the dilapidated cabin that would serve as their meeting place with their newfound allies. Nathan's heart pounded in his chest as he pushed open the creaking door, revealing a dimly lit interior filled with shadows. The scent of decay and dampness hung in the air, adding to the sense of foreboding that filled the room.

The family exchanged wary glances, their eyes meeting in silent agreement to proceed cautiously. As they stepped further into the cabin, their eyes adjusted to the gloom,
revealing a mismatched group of individuals awaiting them. The leader of the group, a weathered man with a grizzled beard and piercing blue eyes, stepped forward to greet them. His voice was gravelly yet commanding.

"Welcome," he said, his gaze sweeping over the family. "I am Joshua, leader of this resistance." Lucy tensed at Joshua's words, her fiery spirit burning bright within her. "Why should we trust you?" she demanded, her tone laced with suspicion. "We know what betrayal feels like. What makes you any different?" Joshua's eyes bore into Lucy's, unflinching in the face of her doubt.

"I understand your skepticism," he replied calmly. "But we have been fighting against Juggernaut for years, long before you arrived on the scene. We share a common enemy, and it is in our best interest to join forces against him." Hadley spoke up next, her voice tinged with curiosity. "What can you offer us?" she asked, her gaze unwavering. "We have been betrayed once before.

How do we know you won't do the same?" A solemn expression crossed Joshua's face as he locked eyes with Hadley. "All I can offer you is my word," he said earnestly. "We have lost loved ones to Juggernaut's darkness, and our only goal is to see him defeated. We may not be perfect allies, but we share a common purpose." Ayden stepped forward, his calming presence radiating through the room.

"Unity is crucial if we are to stand a chance against Juggernaut," he said, his voice resonating with wisdom. "We must put aside our doubts and work together for the greater good." Nathan remained silent, his eyes scanning the room as he assessed their potential allies. After a moment of contemplation, he spoke with a firm resolve in his voice.

"We will take a chance on this alliance," he declared. "But make no mistake - if we sense any hint of betrayal or treachery, we will not hesitate to sever ties.

" Joshua nodded solemnly, accepting Nathan's terms without hesitation. "Understood," he said, his voice tinged with gravity. "Our success against Juggernaut relies on our collective efforts. We must overcome our differences and work towards a shared goal.

" As the room fell silent, both families stared at each other - strangers united by a common enemy and forced to rely on one another in order to prevail. Doubts still lingered in their hearts, but they understood that they had reached a pivotal moment in their fight against Juggernaut.

With renewed determination, they began discussing strategies and sharing information about Juggernaut's movements and weaknesses. They studied maps and devised plans for future battles, each side bringing valuable insights and unique skills to the table. The atmosphere in the cabin shifted from one of uncertainty to one of camaraderie as bonds began to form between the two groups.

Trust was still fragile, but it had begun to take root amidst their shared purpose. As they left the cabin hours later, night had fallen over Ember Bay, casting an eerie glow over their surroundings. They stood outside under the starlit sky as Joshua turned to address them one final time. "Remember," he said firmly, his voice carrying across the quiet night air. "Juggernaut's power lies in division and fear. But together, we can overcome anything he throws at us.

" The Elemental Guardians nodded in agreement, their eyes shining with determination beneath the moonlit canopy of trees. Though uncertain of what lay ahead, they were ready to face Juggernaut as a unified front. With their newfound allies by their side, they set off towards their shared destiny - a destiny filled with challenges and sacrifices but also hope and triumph.

And so they marched forward into the night - friends turned allies turned family - ready to face whatever darkness awaited them as they fought for peace and protection in Ember Bay. Consequences of Conflict - Healing Wounds The family gathered around a flickering campfire in the heart of the Bayou, their weary bodies seeking solace and comfort after the intensity of their battle with Juggernaut.

The warmth of the fire brought a sense of calm to their souls as they tended to their wounds, both physical and emotional. Nathan winced as Lucy gently cleaned a deep gash on his arm, her touch firm yet gentle. "Thank you," he murmured, his voice filled with gratitude. "I couldn't have done it without you.

" Lucy glanced up at him, a soft smile tugging at the corners of her lips. "We're a team, Nathan," she replied, her tone filled with unwavering loyalty. "We've always got each other's backs." Ayden sat quietly beside them, his hands emitting a soft glow as he channeled healing energy into their wounds. His presence brought a soothing calmness to the air, his compassionate nature radiating through every gesture. Hadley watched Ayden work, her eyes filled with admiration.

"Your healing abilities are truly remarkable," she whispered, her voice barely above a breath. "Thank you for using your powers to help us." Ayden's gaze met Hadley's, a hint of vulnerability shining in his eyes.

"It is my purpose to heal," he said softly, his voice filled with quiet determination. "I couldn't bear to see any of you suffer." As the family tended to physical wounds, they also addressed the emotional scars left by their battle with Juggernaut.

The weight of their fight and the sacrifices they had made were etched onto their faces, lines of exhaustion and sadness marking their features. Nathan sighed heavily, his voice tinged with weariness.

"I never expected it would be this difficult," he admitted, his words carrying the weight of their recent experiences. "The toll it takes on us...physically and emotionally." Lucy reached out and took his hand in hers, offering a reassuring squeeze. "We're all feeling it," she said softly, her voice filled with empathy.

"But we can't let it break us. We have to keep going." Hadley nodded in agreement, her voice laced with determination. "We've faced challenges before," she said firmly, her eyes meeting each family member's turn. "And we'll face them again. Together." Ayden added his voice to the conversation, his tone gentle yet resolute.

"We must take time to heal our wounds - both inside and out," he said wisely, his words resonating with each family member. "But we can't lose sight of our goal - protecting Ember Bay and each other.

" As the embers in the fire crackled and danced, the family found solace in each other's presence - in the bond that connected them beyond words and actions. They may have been battered and bruised, but their spirits remained unbroken. In the quiet moments between conversation and healing, they reflected on the consequences of their conflict with Juggernaut. They realized that every action had a ripple effect - that their fight against darkness carries great weight and sacrifice.

But they also understood that they were stronger for it. The wounds they carried would become scars - reminders of their resilience and unwavering dedication to their cause. As they continued to tend to one another's wounds, both physical and emotional, an unspoken understanding settled over them.

They had faced great adversity together and emerged on the other side stronger and more united than ever before. With renewed determination and fortified bonds, they prepared themselves for what lay ahead. Their path was still treacherous and uncertain, but they faced it with unwavering resolve. The fire crackled and popped as the night wore on, casting dancing shadows upon their worn faces.

They knew that every step forward would bring new challenges and tests of strength. But as long as they stood together - as long as they remained loyal to one another and fought for what they believed in - there was nothing that could stand in their way. And so they sat, shoulder to shoulder, bound by love and shared purpose, ready to face whatever darkness awaited them in Ember Bay.

The family ventured through the dense undergrowth of the Bayou, their footsteps muffled by the thick layers of leaves and moss.

The air was heavy with anticipation as they approached the dilapidated cabin that would serve as their meeting place with their newfound allies. Nathan's heart pounded in his chest as he pushed open the creaking door, revealing a dimly lit interior filled with shadows.

The scent of decay and dampness hung in the air, adding to the sense of foreboding that filled the room. The family exchanged wary glances, their eyes meeting in silent agreement to proceed cautiously. As they stepped further into the cabin, their eyes adjusted to the gloom, revealing a mismatched group of individuals awaiting them.

The leader of the group, a weathered man with a grizzled beard and piercing blue eyes, stepped forward to greet them. His voice was gravelly yet commanding. "Welcome," he said, his gaze sweeping over the family.

"I am Joshua, leader of this resistance." Lucy tensed at Joshua's words, her fiery spirit burning bright within her. "Why should we trust you?" she demanded, her tone laced with suspicion. "We know what betrayal feels like. What makes you any different?" Joshua's eyes bore into Lucy's, unflinching in the face of her doubt.

"I understand your skepticism," he replied calmly. "But we have been fighting against Juggernaut for years, long before you arrived on the scene. We share a common enemy, and it is in our best interest to join forces against him." Hadley spoke up next, her voice tinged with curiosity. "What can you offer us?" she asked, her gaze unwavering.

"We have been betrayed once before. How do we know you won't do the same?" A solemn expression crossed Joshua's face as he locked eyes with Hadley. "All I can offer you is my word," he said earnestly. "We have lost loved ones to Juggernaut's darkness, and our only goal is to see him defeated.

We may not be perfect allies, but we share a common purpose." Ayden stepped forward, his calming presence radiating through the room. "Unity is crucial if we are to stand a chance against Juggernaut," he said, his voice resonating with wisdom. "We must put aside our doubts and work together for the greater good.

" Nathan remained silent, his eyes scanning the room as he assessed their potential allies. After a moment of contemplation, he spoke with a firm resolve in his voice. "We will take a chance on this alliance," he declared. "But make no mistake - if we sense any hint of betrayal or treachery, we will not hesitate to sever ties." Joshua nodded solemnly, accepting Nathan's terms without hesitation.

"Understood," he said, his voice tinged with gravity. "Our success against Juggernaut relies on our collective efforts. We must overcome our differences and work towards a shared goal." As the room fell silent, both families stared at each other - strangers united by a common enemy and forced to rely on one another in order to prevail. Doubts still lingered in their hearts, but they understood that they had reached a pivotal moment in their fight against Juggernaut.

With renewed determination, they began discussing strategies and sharing information about Juggernaut's movements and weaknesses. They studied maps and devised plans for future battles, each side bringing valuable insights and unique skills to the table.

The atmosphere in the cabin shifted from one of uncertainty to one of camaraderie as bonds began to form between the two groups. Trust was still fragile, but it had begun to take root amidst their shared purpose.

As they left the cabin hours later, night had fallen over Ember Bay, casting an eerie glow over their surroundings. They stood outside under the starlit sky as Joshua turned to address them one final time. "Remember," he said firmly, his voice carrying across the quiet night air. "Juggernaut's power lies in division and fear.

But together, we can overcome anything he throws at us." The Elemental Guardians nodded in agreement, their eyes shining with determination beneath the moonlit canopy of trees. Though uncertain of what lay ahead, they were ready to face Juggernaut as unified front. With their newfound allies by their side, they set off towards their shared destiny - a destiny filled with challenges and sacrifices but also hope and triumph.

And so they marched forward into the night - friends turned allies turned family - ready to face whatever darkness awaited them as they fought for peace and protection in Ember Bay. The family gathered around a large wooden table in the heart of the forest, their allies joining them as they finalized their plans to confront Juggernaut.

Maps and diagrams were strewn across the table, symbols and markings highlighting strategic points and potential weaknesses. Nathan leaned forward, his eyes narrowing as he studied the maps. "We have to exploit Juggernaut's vulnerabilities," he said, his voice filled with determination.

"We know he draws power from darkness, so our best chance is to bring him out into the light." Lucy chimed in, her fiery gaze focused on the maps. "Agreed," she said, her voice brimming with confidence. "If we can expose him to the elements, weaken his dark forces, we'll have a better chance of defeating him." Hadley nodded in agreement, her gaze shifting between the maps and her fellow guardians.

"And we must use our elemental powers strategically," she said, her voice tinged with excitement. "Each of us has a unique connection to the elements that we can harness to our advantage." Ayden interjected softly, his calming presence bringing a sense of balance to the discussion. "Our unity will be key," he said, his voice resonating with wisdom.

"We must work together seamlessly, combining our abilities and coordinating our efforts for maximum effectiveness." Joshua, the leader of their newfound allies, leaned back in his chair, his weathered face showcasing years of battle experience.

"Our knowledge of Juggernaut's strengths and weaknesses will be crucial," he said, his voice steady. "We've been fighting him for years, and we've learned a great deal about his tactics." The room fell silent as each member of the alliance absorbed Joshua's words. They were no longer alone in this fight against Juggernaut; they had the guidance and expertise of those who had faced him before.

The weight of responsibility mingled with a newfound hope. Determined to capitalize on their collective knowledge, they spent hours dissecting strategies and honing their plans.

Each family member contributed their unique insights, their passions ignited by a shared purpose. As the night wore on, they refined their battle plan further, leaving no stone unturned. Their alliance had grown stronger, trust solidifying amidst shared strategizing and open dialogue.

Eventually, they rose from the table, exhausted yet energized by their progress. The sun had begun to rise over Ember Bay, casting a warm glow across the forest clearing. Lucy turned to Joshua, gratitude shining in her eyes. "Thank you for your guidance," she said sincerely. "You've given us invaluable information that will undoubtedly make a difference in this fight." Joshua nodded solemnly.

"The pleasure is all mine," he replied. "It has been an honor to share what I know with you all. Together, we have a chance at putting an end to Juggernaut's reign of darkness." With their plans in place and their resolve strengthened, the Elemental Guardians stood united at the edge of the clearing. A sense of anticipation hung heavy in the air as they prepared to embark on their final mission.

Nathan drew in a deep breath and spoke for them all: "It's time to face Juggernaut head-on," he declared boldly. "Today marks the beginning of the end for him. We fight for Ember Bay and everyone who calls it home." His words resonated among them, fueling their determination and igniting a fire within each guardian's heart. There was no turning back now; they knew they would face unimaginable challenges and sacrifices.

But as they locked eyes with one another and felt the strength of their bond, they found solace and courage. Hand in hand, the Elemental Guardians and their newfound allies stepped forward into the dawning light, ready to take on Juggernaut and whatever darkness awaited them. With their plans in place and their resolve strengthened, the Elemental Guardians prepared to embark on their final mission.

The air crackled with anticipation as they stood at the edge of the clearing, ready to face Juggernaut head-on. Nathan turned to his family, his voice firm and resolute. "We've come this far together," he said, his eyes locking with each of their gazes. "No matter what lies ahead, we will face it as one.

" Lucy nodded, her fiery hair catching the morning sunlight. "We are stronger together," she affirmed, her voice filled with conviction. "Juggernaut may be powerful, but we have something he doesn't - unity." Hadley stepped forward, her midnight-black hair contrasting against the brightening sky.

"We've formed alliances and overcome betrayal," she stated, determination burning in her piercing green eyes. "This fight is not just about us anymore; it's about protecting all those who call Ember Bay home." Ayden took a deep breath, his calming presence radiating a sense of peace amidst the tension. "Our purpose is clear," he said softly, his voice carrying strength and wisdom.

"We fight not only for ourselves but also for the balance and harmony of this sacred land." Joshua and his allies stood alongside the Elemental Guardians, their faces mirroring determination and resolve. Joshua stepped forward, his voice steady and filled with conviction.

"Today we forge an unbreakable alliance," he declared, his words carrying the weight of years of resistance against Juggernaut. "Together, we will bring an end to his darkness and restore peace to Ember Bay." As the sun bathed them in its warm embrace, casting long shadows across the clearing, the two groups joined hands in a symbol of unity.

A surge of energy passed through them, intertwining their destinies and strengthening their bond. In that moment, doubts and fears dissolved as a wave of unwavering determination washed over each member of the alliance. They had faced their own trials and challenges, experienced betrayal and loss, but now they stood firmly united.

With synchronized steps, they embarked on their journey through the Bayou, each footfall echoing with purpose and determination. As they ventured deeper into the mystical forest, familiar sounds and scents surrounded them - the whisper of wind through leaves, the rustle of wildlife in the underbrush. The path before them was treacherous, shrouded in shadows and uncertainty.

Yet they pressed on, guided by courage and fueled by hope. Their footsteps echoed through the stillness as they moved forward, leading each other through dense undergrowth and navigating obstacles together. Each guardian drew strength from their allies' presence, trusting that they would have each other's backs no matter what lay ahead.

Hours turned into days as they journeyed deeper into the heart of Ember Bay. Along the way, they encountered remnants of Juggernaut's darkness - crumbling ruins tainted by his malevolent energy. But with every obstacle they faced, their unity grew stronger.

They shared laughter and camaraderie around campfires at night, uplifted each other during moments of doubt or fatigue. Their connection went beyond mere friendship or alliance; it was an unbreakable bond forged through adversity and shared purpose.

As they neared their destination - the heart of Juggernaut's lair - a sense of both trepidation and excitement settled within them.

The final battle loomed on the horizon, its outcome uncertain yet filled with promise. They knew that it would take all of their combined strength and abilities to defeat Juggernaut.

But united as one force - the Elemental Guardians and their newfound allies - they were ready to face him head-on.

And so they continued their march towards destiny, hearts aflame with courage and hope. Together, they would confront Juggernaut, wielding their elemental powers and fierce determination.

Ember Bay awaited its protectors' arrival - a beacon of light in a world consumed by darkness. And as they stepped closer to their ultimate test, they knew deep in their souls that unity would be their greatest strength in the fight for justice and harmony.

Chapter 15: Trials of Unity

As the family entered the hidden clearing in the Bayou, Nathan's piercing eyes scanned their surroundings, his stealthy demeanor alert and focused. Lucy's fierce determination mirrored in her fiery red hair, a testament to her readiness to face any challenge that came their way.

Hadley, with her midnight black hair and piercing green eyes, observed the stone pillars with a mysterious curiosity, her resourceful mind already anticipating what lay ahead.

Ayden, with his kind eyes filled with compassion, radiated a calming presence amidst the anticipation. The first trial stood before them, a daunting obstacle course demanding physical agility and coordination.

Nathan took the lead, gracefully maneuvering through narrow logs suspended above murky waters. He looked back at his family, his voice barely above a whisper. "Stay focused and trust in your abilities. We can conquer this together.

" Lucy nodded, her fiery determination igniting as she leapt onto a swinging rope, her quick reflexes propelling her forward. "I've got this," she said confidently.

"Just keep moving and don't look down." Hadley hesitated for a moment, her slender figure blending seamlessly into the shadows cast by the towering trees. She took a deep breath, her eyes scanning the path ahead.

"Teleportation will be my ally in this challenge," she murmured softly to herself. With a sudden burst of energy, she vanished into thin air, reappearing on a distant platform. Ayden watched his family navigate the obstacles with awe, his compassionate heart driving him forward. He stepped onto a narrow log, its unsteady surface testing his balance.

"Balance is key," he reminded himself, his voice echoing with wisdom. With each step, he found equilibrium within himself and in his movements. As they pushed through the trials with determination and unity, tensions began to rise.

Nathan's aloof nature made it difficult for him to express his fears and frustrations openly. Lucy's impulsive nature clashed with Ayden's cautious approach, causing clashes along the way. Hadley's tendency to keep her thoughts to herself gave way to doubts about her own value. With each obstacle they faced, their weaknesses were laid bare before their family members.

Nathan struggled with his fear of heights as he balanced precariously on a high wire bridge. His hands trembled slightly as he called out to Lucy for support. "Lucy! I need your force fields!" he called out urgently, his voice laced with vulnerability.

Lucy's impatience had threatened to overshadow her support for Nathan earlier in their journey. But in that moment, she realized the importance of setting aside her own desires for the sake of their unity.

"Of course, Nathan!" she replied without hesitation. A shimmering force field materialized around him, stabilizing his footing and allowing him to continue across the bridge with renewed confidence. Hadley watched from a distance, the doubts that had plagued her throughout the trials resurfacing once again.

She had always been hesitant to rely on others, preferring to work alone. But as she observed her family's unwavering support for one another, she began to question her own reluctance. "I...I need your guidance," she admitted reluctantly, her voice barely above a whisper.

Nathan turned towards Hadley, recognizing the vulnerability in her eyes. "We're here for you, Hadley," he assured her gently. "Trust us." And trust she did. As Hadley faced her own individual challenges within the trial, she found solace in knowing that her family had her back. Their words of encouragement echoed in her mind as she summoned every ounce of strength within herself.

With each completed obstacle, their bond grew stronger. The trials tested not only their physical abilities but also their ability to communicate effectively and understand one another's strengths and weaknesses. At last, they reached the final challenge of the trial - a towering wall that seemed insurmountable at first glance.

But as they gathered around it in a circle, their hands clasped together tightly, they realized that their unity was their greatest strength. "We've come so far together," Ayden said softly, his voice resonating with unwavering belief.

"This wall may seem formidable, but together we can overcome anything." Lucy nodded in agreement, her fiery determination burning brighter than ever. "We've faced our fears and doubts head-on," she declared boldly.

"There's nothing we can't accomplish as long as we're united." Their voices merged into one collective affirmation of their bond and resolve. "In unison they both said 'we can do this'" Energized by their unity and fortified by their shared experiences during the trials, the family prepared themselves mentally and emotionally for what lay ahead - an impending battle against Juggernaut and his dark forces threatening Ember Bay.

As they stepped back from the wall and embraced one another tightly, a renewed sense of purpose filled their hearts. Together, they were unstoppable. Reconciliation and Renewed Resolve The crackling campfire cast a warm glow on the family as they settled around it, its flickering flames mirroring their renewed determination.

The air was heavy with the lingering emotions of the trials they had just faced, but now they were ready to confront any lingering conflicts that had arisen. Nathan took a deep breath, his piercing gaze softening as he looked at each of his family members in turn.

"I want to apologize for my aloofness," he began, his voice tinged with sincerity. "I've realized that I need to express my fears and frustrations more openly. We're a team, and I want us to trust one another completely." Lucy's fiery determination softened as she listened to Nathan's words.

She reached out and gently squeezed his hand, her fierce gaze softening. "And I apologize for my impatience earlier," she admitted. "I tend to let my passion overshadow my support for you all. But from now on, I promise to listen more and be patient with each of you.

" Hadley shifted uncomfortably, her midnight black hair cascading over her shoulders as she struggled to put her thoughts into words. "I...I know I've been distant and hesitant to rely on all of you," she confessed, her voice barely above a whisper. "But seeing how you've supported one another throughout the trials has made me realize the strength in unity.

I want to be part of that." Ayden's kind eyes filled with warmth as he listened to his family's apologies and honest reflections. "In my role as the healer, I must confess that I sometimes struggle with my own doubts," he admitted with a gentle smile.

"But witnessing the unwavering trust and support you have shown me has given me the strength to overcome those doubts and fully embrace my abilities." As they each spoke their truths, tears glistened in their eyes, a reflection of the deep love and bond they shared. And in that moment, their vulnerabilities became their greatest strengths.

With their apologies accepted and forgiveness granted, their focus shifted toward their shared mission - protecting Ember Bay from Juggernaut's dark forces. Nathan leaned forward, his voice filled with determination.

"We've proven time and time again that we are stronger together," he declared. "Now it's time for us to strategize our next steps and prepare ourselves for what lies ahead." Lucy nodded in agreement, her fiery eyes gleaming with unwavering resolve. "We each bring unique strengths to this fight," she said, her voice firm.

"From Nathan's tactical expertise to Hadley's resourcefulness and Ayden's compassionate healing abilities, we have everything we need to face Juggernaut head-on." Hadley looked up at her family with newfound clarity in her piercing green eyes. "And we can't forget the importance of balance," she added softly.

"Just as our elemental powers complement one another, so too must we strike a balance within ourselves and our actions." Ayden smiled warmly at his family, his kind eyes shining with wisdom. "Our unity is our greatest strength," he reminded them gently. "As long as we support one another and stay true to our purpose, nothing can stand in our way.

" The family gathered closer together around the campfire, their hands clasped tightly together in a symbol of their unity and commitment. The crackling sound of burning wood kept them company as they discussed their plans, strategies taking shape based on their unique powers and experiences.

Leaving no stone unturned, they delved into the intricacies of their upcoming battle against Juggernaut, discussing potential challenges and possible ways to overcome them. Their voices blended together in harmonious synergy, each member contributing ideas and insights fueled by their newfound trust and resolve.

As the night wore on, the family realized the importance of rest and preparation before facing Juggernaut and his dark forces.

They extinguished the campfire but carried its warmth within their hearts. With one last embrace, they bid each other goodnight and retreated to their respective sleeping quarters. As they lay beneath the moonlit sky, their minds buzzed with anticipation for what lay ahead. Tomorrow would mark the beginning of the final phase of their journey – a battle where their unity would be tested once more.

But armed with a stronger bond and renewed sense of purpose, they felt ready to face whatever challenges awaited them. Together, they whispered in unison, "In unison they both said 'we can do this'" Equipped with a renewed sense of purpose and a strengthened bond, the family gathered around the towering wall that marked the final challenge of the trials.

The sheer magnitude of the obstacle stirred both awe and trepidation within them, but they knew that their unity would be their ultimate source of strength. Nathan took a step forward, his voice filled with determination. "This wall may seem insurmountable, but together we can overcome anything," he declared, his words resonating with unwavering belief.

Lucy nodded in agreement, her fiery determination burning brighter than ever. "We've faced our fears and doubts head-on throughout these trials," she affirmed boldly. "There's nothing we can't accomplish as long as we stay united." Hadley glanced at her family members, a mix of apprehension and hope flickering in her piercing green eyes.

"These trials have shown us the power of trust and collaboration," she mused softly. "I believe in each and every one of us. Together, we can conquer this wall." Ayden smiled warmly, his kind eyes shining with unwavering faith.

"We've proven time and time again that our unity is our greatest strength," he reminded them gently. "Let us stand side by side and face this final challenge together." With their resolve fortified, the family stepped back from the wall and clasped hands, creating a circle that radiated with shared determination.

They closed their eyes for a moment, allowing the energy of their connection to flow between them, drawing strength from one another. As they opened their eyes in unison, a surge of energy filled their beings. It was no longer four individuals facing an impassable obstacle; it was a united force ready to take on any challenge that stood in their way.

Nathan, Lucy, Hadley, and Ayden approached the wall as one cohesive unit, their movements fluid and synchronized. With Nathan leading the way, they began to scale the seemingly insurmountable surface, relying on one another for support and guidance.

A sense of harmony enveloped them as they seamlessly passed each other along the way, offering helping hands and words of encouragement. Nathan's agility complemented Lucy's strength, while Hadley's resourcefulness found its counterpart in Ayden's healing presence.

As they ascended higher and higher, inching closer to the top of the wall, doubts and fears melted away under the weight of their collective determination. Their hearts beat as one, fueled by unwavering belief in themselves and each other.

Finally, they reached the pinnacle of the wall - a breathtaking view awaited them on the other side. The shimmering waters of Ember Bay stretched out before them, mirroring the intensity of their resolve. They stood there for a moment, basking in the radiant glow of victory. Each member glanced at one another, a silent acknowledgment passing between them.

They had faced countless trials, confronted their inner demons, and emerged stronger than ever. "In unison they both said 'we did it'" The crackling campfire cast a warm glow on the family as they settled around it, their faces illuminated by the flickering flames.

The air was heavy with the weight of recent revelations and the knowledge that an impending battle against Juggernaut loomed before them. Despite the darkness that lay ahead, there was a newfound sense of determination and unity within the family. Nathan broke the silence, his voice filled with conviction.

"We've faced numerous trials together, and it's clear that our strength lies in our unity," he declared, his piercing eyes meeting the gaze of each family member. "But now, we must face an enemy who threatens not only Ember Bay but also our very existence.

" Lucy's fiery resolve burned brighter than ever as she locked eyes with Nathan. "You're right," she responded, her voice filled with determination. "Juggernaut may be powerful, but we have something he doesn't – the power of unity and love.

As long as we stay united, nothing can break us." Hadley, normally the quiet observer, spoke up with a renewed sense of purpose. "Our individual powers and unique abilities alone are formidable, but when combined, we become an unstoppable force," she noted, her gaze shifting from Nathan to Lucy, then to Ayden.

"I've seen firsthand the strength of our bond during the trials. Together, we can overcome anything." Ayden's compassionate eyes met each family member's gaze in turn before speaking softly but resolutely. "We have been chosen as the protectors of Ember Bay for a reason," he said.

"Our shared purpose connects us in ways that are beyond comprehension. It is this connection that will guide us through the darkness and help us triumph over Juggernaut." As they listened to one another's words, a palpable energy permeated through the air, solidifying their commitment to one another and their shared mission.

Though doubts and fears still lingered, they were overshadowed by the unwavering belief that together they were unstoppable. Nathan reached out a hand towards each family member, inviting them to join him in a symbolic gesture of unity. One by one, they grasped his hand with unwavering determination and unbreakable resolve.

"We may encounter unexpected challenges along this journey," Nathan began, his voice steady yet filled with anticipation. "And it's possible that we may have to form alliances with those who were once our rivals." He glanced at Lucy, Hadley, and Ayden before continuing. "But to protect Ember Bay and fulfill our destinies, we must set aside any personal differences and work together as one.

" Lucy nodded in agreement, her fiery red hair casting a fierce glow in the firelight. "We must remember that our ultimate goal is to defeat Juggernaut," she affirmed. "No matter what sacrifices or compromises are required, we will do whatever it takes to ensure Ember Bay's safety.

" Hadley's eyes gleamed with a mix of curiosity and determination as she spoke up. "If there are allies who possess knowledge or skills that can aid us in our battle against Juggernaut, we must put aside pride and embrace any assistance offered," she voiced, her words carrying a weight of wisdom beyond her years.

Ayden's gentle smile conveyed both compassion and wisdom as he added his thoughts. "Let us remember that unity does not mean uniformity," he reminded them gently. "Each of us brings unique strengths and experiences to this fight. By embracing our differences and working together, we can create a force that is greater than the sum of its parts.

" In unison they both said 'we can do this' As their hands remained joined in unison, a profound silence settled over the family. The crackling campfire provided a soothing soundtrack to their unspoken understanding – they were now united not only by destiny but also by a shared purpose.

The road ahead would be fraught with danger and uncertainty, but armed with newfound unity and resolve, the family knew they were ready. Tomorrow would mark the beginning of a desperate alliance forged amidst the looming threat of Juggernaut.

With their bond as their greatest weapon and their love for Ember Bay as their driving force, they would face their enemy head-on. Their voices merged into one collective affirmation: "Together...we are unstoppable.

" Challenges and Compromises The crackling campfire engulfed the family in its warm embrace as they settled closer, their faces illuminated by the flickering flames. The gravity of their impending battle against Juggernaut weighed heavily on their hearts, but they were determined to set aside personal differences and form alliances with unlikely allies. Nathan took a deep breath, his voice steady but tinged with a touch of vulnerability.

"In order to defeat Juggernaut, we may have to make compromises and form alliances that we once thought impossible," he acknowledged. "It won't be easy, but if it means protecting Ember Bay, then it's a sacrifice we must be willing to make." Lucy's fiery determination burned brighter as she nodded in agreement.

"We can't let pride or past grievances stand in the way of victory," she said firmly. "Our priority is the safety and well-being of Ember Bay, and if aligning ourselves with former rivals can help us achieve that, then it's a risk worth taking." Hadley listened intently, her midnight black hair framing her face as her eyes reflected the flickering flames. "Uncovering the truth often requires working alongside unexpected allies," she remarked thoughtfully.

"We must approach these alliances with caution, but also remain open to the possibility that they may hold crucial knowledge or skills that can aid us in our fight against Juggernaut.

" Ayden's compassionate gaze met each family member's eyes as he added his wisdom to the discussion. "Unity does not mean sacrificing our individuality," he reminded them gently. "While we may have differing approaches and perspectives, it is through the strength of our bond that we can find common ground and work towards our shared goal.

" As they contemplated their next moves, doubts and uncertainties lingered. They understood that forming alliances would require navigating treacherous waters and overcoming deep-rooted rivalries.

But they also knew that they had to put aside personal agendas for the greater good. Nathan's voice broke the silence that had settled over them. "Approaching these alliances with humility and clear intentions will be key," he emphasized.

"We must be prepared to listen and learn from those who were once our adversaries. Together, we can uncover strategies and insights that will aid us in our battle against Juggernaut." Lucy's fierce determination flared anew as she locked eyes with her family members. "Remember, our strength lies in unity," she reminded them firmly.

"By setting aside our differences and working together, we become an unstoppable force capable of overcoming any challenge that stands in our way." Hadley nodded in agreement, her observant gaze assessing the potential allies they might encounter. "Our goal remains the same – to protect Ember Bay at all costs," she affirmed.

"By being open-minded and resilient in the face of adversity, we can build bridges with those who share our purpose." Ayden's gentle smile radiated hope as he concluded their discussion. "Whatever challenges lie ahead, remember that love and unity will guide us through," he assured them softly. "Together, we can forge a path towards victory and safeguard the future of Ember Bay for generations to come.

" In unison, they repeated their mantra: "In unison they both said 'we can do this'" As their hands remained joined, a renewed sense of purpose settled over the family. They understood that forming alliances would require navigating delicate power dynamics and overcoming deeply ingrained mistrust.

Yet, armed with their unwavering belief in one another and their shared mission to protect Ember Bay, they were ready to face whatever lay ahead. With the warmth of the campfire still embracing them, they leaned closer together, their minds buzzing with anticipation for what awaited them in the days to come.

Tomorrow would mark the beginning of a desperate alliance forged amidst uncertainty and compromise. United by their common goal and fueled by their love for Ember Bay, they would face Juggernaut head-on. Their voices merged into one collective affirmation: "Together...we are unstoppable.

" A Fragile Alliance The crackling campfire bathed the family in its warm glow as they gathered closely, their eyes reflecting both determination and skepticism. The weight of their impending alliance with unlikely allies pressed upon their hearts, for they knew that trust and unity were fragile commodities in times of conflict. Nathan spoke first, his voice measured and filled with caution.

"Forming this alliance will not be without its challenges," he warned, his eyes scanning each family member's face. "We must approach this with open minds but also a sense of skepticism. We cannot afford to let our guard down completely.

" Lucy's fiery determination flickered alongside her skepticism as she nodded in agreement. "We must remember that our ultimate goal is the protection of Ember Bay," she stated firmly. "But we must also be wary of the potential for ulterior motives from our newfound allies.

Vigilance will be our best defense." Hadley's observant gaze swept the circle, her mind already racing through the complexities of forming an alliance. "To forge this delicate alliance, we must find common ground and understand both our own strengths and the strengths of those we seek to align with," she surmised.

"By finding synergy between our abilities, we can achieve greater success against Juggernaut." Ayden's compassionate eyes met each family member's gaze, his calming presence grounding them in the midst of uncertainty. "Compassion and empathy will be essential in forming this alliance," he reminded them gently.

"We must strive to understand the motivations and perspectives of our potential allies, fostering an environment where trust can grow amidst chaos." As they discussed the challenges ahead, their concerns and doubts remained ever-present.

They understood that alliances were not built overnight and often required compromise and sacrifice. But they also believed in the power of unity and its ability to overcome even the greatest obstacles. Nathan's voice broke through the silence, infused with a mixture of hope and caution.

"In forging this alliance, we must remember that our common purpose unites us," he emphasized. "Despite differences or past grievances, we share a mission to protect Ember Bay. It is this shared purpose that will guide us through this delicate dance." Lucy's determination ignited anew as she locked eyes with her family members.

"While there may be challenges along this path, we must let our shared purpose illuminate the way," she declared boldly. "Our differences can be strengths when harnessed properly, weaving a tapestry of resilience against Juggernaut.

" Hadley nodded in agreement, her piercing green eyes scanning the faces around her with a keen sense of clarity. "Our ability to overcome differences and work collaboratively will set us apart," she reflected thoughtfully. "By embracing diversity within our alliance, we can tap into a wellspring of innovation and strategic brilliance.

" Ayden's gentle smile radiated warmth as he concluded their discussion. "Through open communication, understanding, and a commitment to peace-building, we can navigate the treacherous terrain of forming an alliance," he assured them softly.

"It will require patience, but I believe that unity is a beacon that guides us towards a brighter future for Ember Bay.

" In unison, they repeated their mantra: "In unison they both said 'we can do this'" With their hands still clasped together, a renewed sense of purpose settled over the family.

They understood that this alliance would require careful navigation through murky waters and difficult compromises. Yet they also knew that their shared mission to protect Ember Bay was greater than any individual grievances or differences. As they leaned closer together around the campfire's warmth, their minds buzzed with plans and strategies for building bridges with their potential allies.

Tomorrow would mark the beginning of their quest for unity amidst uncertainty – an intricate dance marred by mistrust and conflicting agendas. But armed with unwavering belief in one another and a shared vision for Ember Bay's safety, they were ready to take their first steps towards forging an alliance that could withstand the storm.

Chapter 16: The Trial of Shadows

Nathan stood before the mysterious entity in the heart of the Bayou, his heart pounding with a mix of determination and trepidation. The entity, a towering figure shrouded in darkness, emanated an aura of foreboding that seemed to seep into every fiber of Nathan's being. His family stood behind him, their supportive gazes urging him forward.

The Bayou's mystical energies swirled around them, casting eerie shadows that danced across the ground. Nathan could feel the weight of his fear of failure pressing against his chest, threatening to consume him. But he knew he had to face this trial head-on if he wanted to prove himself as a worthy protector.

The entity extended a long, shadowy arm towards Nathan, beckoning him to step forward. As he took a hesitant step into the tangled corridors of the labyrinthine maze, the walls seemed to shift and twist, disorienting him within the depths of his own insecurities. "Remember, Nathan," Lucy's voice rang out behind him, filled with unwavering belief. "You are capable of so much more than you think.

" Nathan swallowed hard and steadied his breathing, determined to silence the voices of doubt that threatened to undermine his confidence. With each step he took, the walls closed in around him, tightening like a vice grip. But he refused to let them suffocate his spirit. As Nathan maneuvered through the intricate maze, illusions of past mistakes and missed opportunities haunted his thoughts.

Whispering voices filled the air, criticizing and mocking every decision he had made. Doubt crept into his mind like tendrils of fog, threatening to cloud his judgment. "You'll never be good enough," a voice sneered from the darkness. Nathan gritted his teeth and pushed through the uncertainty.

He summoned memories of past victories and moments of triumph to fuel his determination. Each time doubt threatened to overwhelm him, he drew strength from the support and belief of his family. Sweat dripped down Nathan's brow as he navigated through moments of uncertainty and near defeat.

The weight of exhaustion settled in his muscles, begging him to give up. But deep down, he knew that giving up was not an option. He could hear Lucy's encouraging words echoing in his mind. "You've faced tougher challenges than this before, Nathan. You can do this." With renewed resolve, Nathan pressed forward.

He tapped into a reserve of inner strength he didn't know existed, drawing upon his exceptional ninja skills and stealthy agility to navigate the labyrinth's complex twists and turns. Finally, as if testing him one final time, Nathan reached the heart of the labyrinth.

Before him stood a massive stone wall blocking his path. Doubt crept back in, threatening to paralyze him once again. But he took a deep breath and remembered the unwavering support of his family standing just beyond the maze.

"I can do this," he whispered to himself, summoning every ounce of courage within him. With determination shining in his eyes, Nathan scaled the seemingly insurmountable obstacle with ease. It was as if all of his training had led up to this moment – a testament to his growth and unwavering resolve.

At the peak of the wall, blinding light engulfed him, symbolizing his triumph over self-doubt and failure. His heart swelled with a sense of accomplishment as he emerged from the labyrinth victorious. As Nathan stepped out of the maze into the clearing where his family anxiously waited for him, a triumphant smile spread across his face.

He knew that he had conquered his inner darkness and proven himself as a formidable protector. "Well done," Hadley said softly, her voice filled with admiration. "You faced your fears head-on and emerged stronger because of it.

" Nathan nodded gratefully, feeling an indescribable sense of pride in himself. The understanding and support from his family had been vital in guiding him through this trial, reminding him that he never had to face these challenges alone. Together, they would overcome whatever obstacles lay ahead in their journey to protect Ember Bay from Juggernaut's malevolent influence.

As Nathan basked in the glow of his victory over the labyrinth, his family gathered around him in the clearing. They enveloped him in a tight embrace, their pride and admiration palpable in the air. The sense of unity and support warmed his heart, and he felt a renewed sense of purpose. Lucy gazed at him with awe shining in her eyes.

"I always knew you had it in you, Nathan. Your determination is truly inspiring." Nathan's cheeks flushed with modesty as he humbly accepted her praise. He looked around at his family, finding strength and encouragement in their unwavering love and belief in him.

 Each of them had faced their own trials, conquering their inner demons to emerge stronger than ever before. And together, they were an unstoppable force. Hadley stepped forward, her voice filled with admiration.

"You faced your fear of failure head-on, Nathan. That takes immense courage and resilience." Nathan nodded gratefully at Hadley's words, feeling a swell of pride within him. He had learned that failure didn't define him—it was merely an opportunity for growth and improvement. With every trial he faced, he discovered new layers of his strength and determination.

Ayden placed a comforting hand on Nathan's shoulder, his gaze filled with wisdom. "You've shown us all that we are more capable than we realize. Thank you for reminding us of our own potential." Nathan smiled warmly at Ayden's words, feeling a deep sense of gratitude for the bond they shared. Their journey had not only been about protecting Ember Bay; it had also been about discovering their true selves and unlocking their hidden strengths.

In the midst of their celebration, a soft breeze rustled through the trees surrounding them. It whispered secrets of ancient prophecies and untold destinies, reminding them that their journey was far from over.

There were still battles to be fought, challenges to be conquered, and darkness to be vanquished. "What lies ahead is not without its challenges," Ayden said solemnly, breaking through the joyous ambiance. "But we are stronger now, united as one.

" Nathan nodded thoughtfully, understanding the gravity of Ayden's words. Their individual triumphs over their trials had brought them closer together, strengthening their bond and instilling unwavering belief in their collective power.

Lucy interlocked her fingers with Nathan's, her fiery spirit burning brightly in her eyes. "Together, we can face anything—Juggernaut doesn't stand a chance against us." A wave of determination washed over Nathan as he squeezed Lucy's hand firmly. She was right—they were a force to be reckoned with. They had proven time and time again that when they stood united, no obstacle was insurmountable.

The family stood there under the moonlit sky, their hearts brimming with hope and resolve. They were ready to face whatever challenges lay ahead—whatever darkness Juggernaut had to throw at them. "So what's next?" Nathan asked, a hint of excitement lacing his voice. Hadley grinned mischievously, her eyes twinkling with anticipation. "We continue to prepare ourselves—physically, mentally, and emotionally—for the battles that lie ahead. We train harder, strategize better, and ignite the flames of our determination even brighter.

" Ayden nodded in agreement, his voice tinged with quiet confidence. "And we never forget the power that comes from our unity—the unbreakable bond that exists between us." Nathan felt a surge of pride and gratitude for his family as they filled the clearing with their unwavering determination.

They were not just protectors of Ember Bay; they were also each other's pillars of strength. With their hands clasped tightly together, they forged ahead into the unknown future—a future where darkness loomed but where hope burned ever brighter. The Trial of Shadows had tested Nathan's resolve and illuminated the path ahead.

As long as they remained united and unwavering in their beliefs, they would overcome any darkness that threatened Ember Bay. Together, they were invincible. And so, with newfound determination coursing through their veins, the family prepared themselves for the battles yet to come.

Nathan stood at the peak of the massive stone wall, the blinding light surrounding him serving as a symbol of his triumph over self-doubt and failure. He took a moment to catch his breath and let the magnitude of his achievement sink in. It was then that he heard a familiar voice in his mind – his father's soothing tone guiding him through the darkness.

"You've come so far, my son," his father's voice echoed. "I am proud of the ninja you've become." Tears welled up in Nathan's eyes as he felt an overwhelming surge of emotions. His father's words reminded him of where he came from and the strength that ran through his bloodline.

He knew that his father would always be with him, urging him forward with unwavering support. With newfound confidence and determination, Nathan descended from the wall and reentered the labyrinth.

The walls seemed to shift and twist around him, but now he faced them with a renewed sense of purpose. As he navigated through the intricate passages once more, Nathan encountered illusions that taunted him with his failures and insecurities.

Each step forward felt like an uphill battle, but he knew that his family's belief in him carried him through. "I believe in you, Nathan," Lucy's voice echoed in his mind. "I know that you have what it takes to overcome this trial.

" With every challenge that crossed his path, Nathan tapped into the resilience and agility that had defined him as a ninja. He leaped over pitfalls and ducked beneath low-hanging obstacles, never losing sight of his goal. In a particularly intense moment, Nathan found himself facing a mirror reflecting his own image.

The reflection showed not only his physical form but also his doubts and fears. It was a stark reminder of how easily he could succumb to self-doubt. But instead of shying away from his reflection, Nathan looked directly into its eyes. He saw strength and determination staring back at him – the embodiment of who he truly was. "I am more than my doubts," Nathan declared boldly.

"I am a protector – a guardian destined to defend Ember Bay." The illusion shattered, revealing another passage that led further into the labyrinth. Nathan pressed on, feeling a surge of confidence coursing through him. Finally, after what felt like an eternity of navigating through the darkness, Nathan reached the heart of the labyrinth once again.

This time, there was no stone wall awaiting him – only blinding light that enveloped him completely. As he emerged from the labyrinth victorious, Nathan was greeted by the triumphant cheers of his family. They rushed forward to embrace him, their love and pride palpable in the air.

Lucy hugged him tightly, her fiery spirit matching his own. "You did it, Nathan! You conquered your fear of failure and emerged stronger because of it." Hadley stepped forward, her eyes filled with admiration. "Your determination has always been your greatest asset, Nathan. It's an honor to stand by your side.

" Ayden placed a hand on Nathan's shoulder, his voice filled with wisdom. "You've proven time and time again that you are capable of greatness, my friend. Never doubt your own abilities." Overwhelmed with gratitude for his family's support and belief in him, tears streamed down Nathan's cheeks.

At that moment, he realized just how lucky he was to have them by his side. Together, they stood under the moonlit sky – a united front against whatever darkness Juggernaut had in store for them. They were no longer just individuals with their own trials – they were a family bound together by love and shared purpose.

"So what's next?" Ayden asked, curiosity gleaming in his eyes. Nathan smiled, feeling a renewed sense of purpose coursing through his veins. "We prepare ourselves for whatever challenges lie ahead," he replied confidently. "We train harder, strategize better, and ignite the flames of our determination even brighter." Lucy nodded enthusiastically.

"And we never forget the power that comes from our unity – the unbreakable bond that exists between us." As they gazed at one another with renewed conviction, their hearts swelled with hope and resolve. They were ready for whatever lay ahead – ready to face Juggernaut head-on and protect Ember Bay with everything they had.

Hand-in-hand, they took their first steps towards the future – a future brimming with uncertainties but also infinite possibilities. The trials they had faced had forged them into something stronger than ever before – a formidable force against any darkness that threatened their home.

With their heads held high and their spirits aflame, they embarked on this new chapter together – united as Elemental Guardians ready to face whatever challenges lay ahead on their journey to protect Ember Bay. Embracing Inner Strength - Uniting as a Stronger Force The family stood in a central clearing illuminated by the soft glow of the moonlight.

The air was filled with a sense of calm and serenity, contrasting with the intensity of their recent trials. They formed a circle, faces filled with exhaustion but also with an undeniable determination.

Nathan took a deep breath, his mind still reeling from the trial he had just overcome. He glanced at Lucy, her fiery spirit burning brightly in her eyes, and couldn't help but feel a surge of admiration for her unwavering strength.

Lucy locked eyes with Nathan and offered him a reassuring smile. "You did it, Nathan. You conquered your fear of failure and emerged stronger than ever before." Nathan's chest swelled with pride as he accepted Lucy's words.

Her belief in him, as well as the support of the rest of his family, had been crucial in guiding him through his trial. Hadley stepped forward, her voice filled with admiration. "Your determination knows no bounds, Nathan.

You faced your inner darkness head-on and emerged victorious." A mixture of gratitude and humility washed over Nathan as he looked at Hadley. Her observant nature and mysterious aura had always intrigued him, and her words resonate deeply within his heart.

Ayden placed a gentle hand on Nathan's shoulder, his voice tinged with quiet wisdom. "You've shown us all what true resilience looks like, my friend. Your journey has reminded us of our own inner strength.

" Nathan nodded gratefully at Ayden's words, feeling a renewed sense of purpose within him. The trials they had each faced had not only tested their individual strengths but had also highlighted the power that came from their unity as a family.

The clearing seemed to emit a warm glow as they watched each other with expressions filled with understanding and empathy. They could see the growth and transformation that had taken place within each member of the family.

In that moment of silence, Nathan felt an overwhelming surge of gratitude and love for his family. They had been there for him every step of the way—through triumphs and failures, doubts and fears—and their unwavering support had guided him through the darkest moments. Lucy broke the silence, her voice strong and determined.

"Together, we are unstoppable. Juggernaut doesn't stand a chance against the power of our unity." Her words echoed through the clearing, instilling confidence and conviction in each family member. They knew that as long as they remained united and stayed true to their purpose, they could face any challenges that lay ahead.

Nathan tightened his grip on Lucy's hand, feeling a sense of solidarity radiating between them. "We've come so far together," he said, his voice filled with emotion. "And we'll continue to push forward—together." Ayden joined their circle, his presence calming and reassuring. "Our unity is our greatest strength," he said softly.

"In this journey, we have learned that we are capable of more than we ever thought possible." The bond between them grew stronger with every word spoken—each member providing support and encouragement to their loved ones.

Their shared vulnerabilities had brought them closer together, creating an unbreakable trust that would guide them through even the darkest times. Hadley stepped forward once again, her voice filled with conviction. "As Elemental Guardians, we are bound by destiny to protect Ember Bay," she proclaimed.

"And together, we will rise above any challenge that comes our way." As if responding to her words, a gentle breeze rustled through the clearing, carrying with it whispers of ancient prophecies and untold destinies. The mystical energies of the Bayou seemed to converge around them, imbuing them with renewed strength and purpose.

Nathan looked around at his family—each face reflecting determination and resilience—and felt an overwhelming sense of hope for the future. They were more than just individuals; they were an unyielding force connected by love and an unbreakable bond. He squeezed Lucy's hand tighter and met the gaze of each family member with unwavering resolve in his eyes.

"Whatever lies ahead," he declared confidently, "we will face it together—with love, trust, and unwavering belief in one another." With those words lingering in the air like a sacred vow, the family embraced one another once more—a gesture that symbolized their unbreakable bond and commitment to protect Ember Bay.

They knew that the path ahead wouldn't be easy—that there would be battles to fight, sacrifices to make, and darkness to overcome—but they also knew that as long as they stood united, nothing could stand in their way. With hearts aflame and spirits united, they prepared themselves for what lay ahead—the daunting yet exhilarating journey of fulfilling their destiny as Elemental Guardians.

As the family stood in the central clearing, their eyes met one another's with a newfound sense of purpose and determination. The trials they had each faced had brought them closer together, cementing their bond as protectors of Ember Bay.

Hadley took a step forward, her voice filled with quiet resolve. "Our unity is our greatest strength," she said, her words carrying the weight of truth. "Together, we will face whatever challenges lie ahead and emerge victorious." Nathan nodded in agreement, feeling a surge of pride and gratitude for his family.

They had proven time and time again that when they stood united, nothing could stand in their way. Ayden's gentle presence added to the serene atmosphere, his voice resonating with wisdom. "We have come so far on this journey, but our purpose remains the same—to protect Ember Bay from the darkness that threatens it.

" Lucy's fiery spirit burned brightly as she interlaced her fingers with Nathan's. "And protect it we shall," she declared, her voice filled with determination. "Juggernaut doesn't stand a chance against the power of our unity and love for each other." The words hung in the air, carrying with them a sense of hope and resolve.

The family knew that challenges awaited them—battles against Juggernaut and his forces, the unknown perils of their destiny—but they also knew that together, they were prepared to face whatever lay ahead. Nathan looked around at his family, their faces etched with strength and determination.

He felt an overwhelming surge of love for each of them—their unwavering support had carried him through the darkest moments. With renewed conviction, Nathan spoke from the depths of his heart. "No matter what comes our way, we will face it together," he proclaimed. "Our bond is unbreakable, and our love for one another will guide us through even the darkest times.

" The clearing seemed to glow with an otherworldly light as they stood there, hearts aflame with determination. They had faced their trials individually, but now they were united as a stronger force—a family bound by destiny and love. As they embraced once more, their connection grew stronger—an unspoken understanding passing between them.

In each other, they found solace and strength—a reminder that they were never alone in this journey. "We are ready," Hadley stated, her voice resolute. "Ready to face whatever lies ahead and protect Ember Bay with everything we have." The family nodded in unison, their eyes alight with determination.

They knew that sacrifices would need to be made, that difficult choices lay ahead—but they were prepared to face it all with unwavering resolve. With one final look towards the moonlit sky, the family turned as a unified force towards their next steps. They knew that their journey was far from over—the battles against Juggernaut would be fierce and treacherous—but they also knew that together, they could overcome anything.

Hand-in-hand, they forged ahead into the unknown future—a future where darkness loomed but where hope burned ever brighter. Their unity would guide them through every trial, every obstacle. As Elemental Guardians destined to protect Ember Bay, they were ready to face whatever challenges lay ahead—with unwavering belief in themselves and their unbreakable bond.

And so, with renewed purpose and hearts intertwined in love and unity, the family set forth on their path—a path illuminated by courage, fueled by determination, and guided by unconditional love. Together, they marched forward—ready to confront Juggernaut head-on and protect Ember Bay with everything they had. The family remained in the central clearing, basking in the sense of unity and purpose that permeated the air.

Each member of the family had faced their own trials, conquered their inner demons, and emerged stronger than ever before. Nathan locked eyes with Lucy, his heart swelling with love and admiration. "Lucy, you've always been the fiercest warrior among us," he said, his voice filled with gratitude.

"Your strength and determination have inspired us all." Lucy blushed, her fiery spirit dimming slightly under Nathan's praise. "I couldn't have done it without each and every one of you," she replied honestly. "We're in this together, and we draw strength from one another." Hadley stepped forward, her green eyes shining with a newfound sense of purpose. "Nathan, your unwavering commitment to protecting Ember Bay is truly commendable," she said, her voice filled with respect.

"Your determination knows no bounds." Nathan met Hadley's gaze, feeling a wave of gratitude wash over him. Her support and belief in him had fueled his determination throughout his trials, reminding him of his own potential. Ayden placed a comforting hand on Nathan's shoulder, his soft voice brimming with wisdom.

"You have shown us what it means to embrace our inner strength, Nathan," he said, his eyes warm with admiration. "Your journey has inspired us all to confront our own fears and doubts.

" Deeply moved by Ayden's words, Nathan nodded gratefully. The bond they shared as friends and protectors ran deep, and he knew he could rely on Ayden for guidance and support whenever needed. The family stood together, their hearts connected by an unbreakable bond forged through trials and triumphs.

They had learned that their individual strengths were amplified when they united as one. A gentle breeze rustled through the clearing, carrying with it a whispered message of hope and resilience—a reminder that they were destined for greatness.

"We stand on the precipice of something extraordinary," Ayden said, his voice carrying a note of awe. "Together, we will face whatever lies ahead—rising above our own limitations to protect Ember Bay." Nathan took a deep breath, feeling the weight of responsibility settle upon his shoulders.

He glanced at each member of his family, finding solace in their unwavering belief in him. "We will protect Ember Bay with everything we have—our love, our strength, and our unbreakable unity," he declared, his voice ringing with unwavering resolve.

In that moment, the clearing seemed to glow with an ethereal light—the tangible manifestation of their commitment to the cause they held dear. The mystical energies of the Bayou wrapped around them like a protective embrace, their connection to Ember Bay growing stronger with each passing moment.

Lucy squeezed Nathan's hand tightly as an understanding passed between them. "No matter what challenges we face or how dark the path may seem," she said firmly. "We will never waver in our dedication to protecting Ember Bay.

" The rest of the family nodded in agreement—each member standing tall, ready to face whatever darkness lay ahead. Together, they embraced their collective destiny as Elemental Guardians—determined to defend Ember Bay against Juggernaut's malevolent influence. They knew that battles awaited them—hard-fought victories and heart-wrenching losses—but they also knew that as long as they stood together, their unity would be their greatest weapon.

Hand-in-hand, they stepped forward into the unknown future—a future teeming with challenges and endless possibilities. With love in their hearts and determination in their souls, they were prepared to face whatever came their way.

As Elemental Guardians bound by fate and driven by purpose, they were a force to be reckoned with—a united front against the darkness that threatened their beloved home. With resolute steps and unwavering belief in themselves and each other, the family set forth on their mission—to protect Ember Bay with everything they had.

Chapter 17: A Desperate Retreat

The air hung heavy with tension as the family found themselves surrounded by Juggernaut's forces, their hearts pounding in their chests. Nathan's piercing eyes scanned the area, assessing their chances of escape.

"We need to get out of here," he said, his voice steady but laced with urgency. Lucy nodded in agreement, her fiery red hair reflecting the determination in her eyes. "I'll create a diversion," she declared, summoning her force field abilities.

With a wave of her hand, a translucent shield materialized around her, shimmering with energy. Hadley, her piercing green eyes flickering with intensity, stepped forward. "I'll scout ahead and find us a way out," she stated, ready to rely on her teleportation skills to navigate the treacherous terrain.

Ayden, his calming presence radiating strength, placed a hand on Lucy's shoulder. "We must remain focused and united," he reminded them all. "Together, we can overcome any obstacle." With a nod of agreement, the family swiftly moved as one, their movements swift and stealthy like shadows in the night.

Their agile bodies weaved through the dense vegetation, blending seamlessly with the darkness that cloaked the Bayou. Branches snapped underfoot as they darted through narrow trails, their hearts racing with each step.

The gnarled branches overhead cast ominous shadows that seemed to reach out for them, threatening to ensnare their fleeting existence. Nathan's mind raced with thoughts of strategy and survival. He had always been the stealthy one, slipping through the shadows unnoticed like a phantom.

But now, with their lives hanging in the balance, his ability to navigate these treacherous grounds was paramount. Suddenly, Lucy halted in her tracks, a flash of panic in her eyes. "They're closing in," she whispered urgently. Her force field flickered with intensity, ready to repel any attackers that dared to come too close.

"We need to stay together," Hadley said firmly, her voice filled with determination. She glanced back at Ayden and gave him a reassuring smile before disappearing into the shadows once more. Ayden's gentle voice cut through the oppressive atmosphere.

"Remember," he said softly, his words carrying profound wisdom. "Fear is merely an illusion. We must rise above it." Nathan's senses sharpened as he scanned their surroundings once more.

He could feel the weight of uncertainty pressing upon them, threatening to crush their spirits. But he knew they had come too far to cower in fear. As they pushed deeper into the Bayou's labyrinthine paths, each family member confronted their darkest fears and insecurities. Nathan battled with self-doubt as he questioned his ability to lead them to safety.

Lucy grappled with her impulsive nature, struggling to control her anger and channel it into focused action. Hadley wrestled with trust issues, fighting against her instinct to rely solely on herself. And Ayden confronted his own doubts about his healing abilities and whether they would be enough to protect those he cared for.

Their minds became battlegrounds between light and darkness, their own insecurities fighting against their resolve. But as they pressed forward together, leaning on one another for support and finding strength in their unity, shadows began to recede and light pierced through the darkness.

In unison they both said "we can do this" The retreat grew more treacherous with each passing moment, the family's hearts pounding in their chests as they faced their inner fears head-on. In the midst of the Bayou's oppressive silence, fear manifested in vivid hallucinations and haunting visions, threatening to consume their thoughts and weaken their resolve. Nathan's agile movements faltered for a split second when he saw his worst nightmare materialize before him - a shadowy figure wearing a hauntingly familiar face.

Doubts flooded his mind as he questioned his ability to protect his loved ones and fulfill his role as the Ninja of the Bayou. But just as the darkness threatened to overtake him, his family's unwavering support echoed in his ears, urging him to cast aside his self-doubt. With a deep breath, he banished the apparition from his mind and focused on the path ahead.

Lucy's normally fierce gaze wavered for an instant as she found herself standing in the midst of a raging inferno, flames dancing dangerously close to her skin. The heat licked at her body, testing her control over her fiery temper. Memories of past conflicts and anger-driven actions flooded her mind, but she refused to let them define her.

Drawing strength from her family's love and acceptance, she forged a barrier of willpower within herself, extinguishing the flames and proving that she was more than just a vessel of raw emotions. Hadley's slender frame trembled slightly as she found herself alone in a vast expanse of murky water, the depths seemingly endless.

Doubts about her own worthiness gnawed at her soul as she grappled with self-trust and questioned whether she truly belonged among the protectors. But as she closed her emerald eyes and reached deep within herself, memories of her triumphs and moments of inspiration flooded her consciousness.

She realized that it was through unity and embracing vulnerability that true strength was found. With newfound determination, she burst through the surface of the water, embracing her role as the Night Owl with unwavering confidence.

Ayden's usually calm demeanor faltered as he became submerged in a world of relentless pain and suffering. He relieved moments when he couldn't save those he cared for, doubting his abilities as a healer and feeling overwhelmed by his own emotional reserve.

But as he delved deeper into his memories, he discovered resilience and hope hidden beneath layers of self-doubt.

The warmth of his family's love enveloped him, filling him with renewed purpose and reminding him that healing went beyond just physical wounds. With gentle compassion, he paved a path forward, channeling celestial energy to restore balance within himself and those around him.

As each family member confronted their inner fears and insecurities, their personal battles overlapped and intertwined in a symphony of growth and resilience. Their individual journeys mirrored one another, reinforcing the collective strength they possessed as the Elemental Guardians.

The weight of uncertainty continued to bear down upon them as they pressed forward through the Bayou's labyrinthine trails. Yet now, something had shifted within them - a sense of certainty that they were stronger together than apart.

Their footsteps grew surer, their voices steadier, as they propelled one another forward with unyielding determination. The shadows that once threatened to consume them now became mere remnants of doubt, dissolving in the face of their unwavering resolve.

With each step they took towards unity and self-acceptance, the oppressive atmosphere lifted ever so slightly, replaced by an ethereal light that seemed to guide their way through the darkest corners of their minds.

The Weight of Uncertainty - As the family pressed deeper into the Bayou's labyrinthine paths, uncertainty weighed heavily upon their hearts. Doubt and fear lurked at the edges of their consciousness, threatening to unravel their resolve. The path ahead seemed shrouded in darkness, an unknown abyss that left them questioning their chances of survival.

Nathan's mind raced with thoughts of strategy and survival. He had always been the one to devise plans, to calculate every move with precision. But now, faced with the overwhelming forces of Juggernaut, his mind was clouded by doubt.

Could they truly overcome this formidable enemy? Would their powers be enough to protect Ember Bay? Lucy's fiery spirit flickered momentarily as she battled her own insecurities. The weight of responsibility pressed upon her shoulders as she questioned her ability to lead her family through this treacherous journey.

Her impulsive nature clashed with the careful calculations needed for success, leaving her wondering if she was truly capable of guiding them to victory. Hadley's usually piercing gaze became clouded with hesitation as she grappled with trust issues. The recent betrayal had shaken the foundation of her belief in others, leaving her wary of forming new alliances.

She questioned whether they could truly rely on these newfound allies, and whether their unity would hold in the face of adversity. Ayden's gentle voice cut through the oppressive atmosphere, offering a ray of hope amidst the uncertainty. "We must remember," he said softly, his words carrying a profound wisdom, "that even in the darkest moments, there is always light.

We must not lose sight of our purpose or our collective strength." His words resonate deeply within each family member, providing a glimmer of hope that pushes aside the encroaching darkness. They leaned on one another for support, finding solace in their shared determination to protect Ember Bay from Juggernaut's malevolent influence.

With each step they took forward, their unity grew stronger, forging an unbreakable bond that defied the weight of uncertainty. They stood tall against the looming shadows, refusing to let doubt consume them.

Together, they would face whatever challenges lay ahead - united, unwavering, and unbeatable. Confronting Inner Demons - Shadows of Resilience The family found solace within the hidden sanctuary of the Bayou, their weary bodies and minds seeking respite from the constant onslaught of fear and uncertainty.

Amidst the tranquil beauty that surrounded them, they could feel the weight of their inner demons lurking, waiting to be confronted. Nathan stood at the edge of a serene pond, gazing at his reflection in the still waters. Doubts and insecurities swirled within him, threatening to drown his sense of purpose.

The troubling memories of past failures played over and over in his mind, each one a reminder of his own fallibility. But as he met his own gaze in the water, he saw determination flicker in his eyes. He vowed to overcome his self-doubt and rise above his past mistakes, knowing that only through embracing his flaws could he truly grow into the leader he needed to be.

Lucy sat beneath the shade of a towering oak tree, her fiery hair cascading around her like a crown. Guilt gnawed at her heart as she replayed moments when her anger had overwhelmed her better judgment. It was those moments that haunted her now, taunting her with the idea that her temper would ultimately lead to their downfall.

But as she closed her eyes and listened to the whispers of the wind through the leaves, she felt a renewed sense of control wash over her. She made a silent promise to herself - to channel her fiery nature into a force for good, to protect rather than destroy.

Hadley found herself drawn to a circle of moss-covered stones, their ancient energy pulsating beneath her fingertips. Trust issues had always been her greatest obstacle, a shield she had built to protect herself from the pain of betrayal. But as she knelt within the stone circle, she felt a subtle shift in her perception.

She saw her reflection in the polished surface of a small amethyst stone, and with a surge of clarity, she realized that it was not weakness to trust in others; it was strength. She vowed to embrace vulnerability and allow herself to lean on her newfound allies, knowing that unity and trust were essential in their fight against Juggernaut. Ayden walked along a path lined with vibrant flowers, their delicate petals dancing in harmony with the breeze.

Self-doubt weighed heavily on Ayden's gentle soul as he questioned his ability to heal both physical and emotional wounds. The memory of those he had failed haunted him, leaving him hesitant to fully embrace his role as a protector.

But as he observed the resilience of the flowers around him, their life force unyielding even in harsh conditions, he found inspiration. He vowed to let go of past regrets and trust in his own abilities, knowing that his healing presence brought comfort and hope to those who needed it most.

As each family member confronted their deepest fears and insecurities within this sacred sanctuary, an ethereal light seemed to illuminate their surroundings. The weight of their inner turmoil began to lift as they tapped into their hidden reservoirs of courage and determination.

In this incubator of self-reflection and growth, they shed old limitations and embraced their true potential. The shadows that once threatened to consume them gradually withdrew, revealing rays of hope that streamed through the cracks in their resolve.

Their shared purpose gathered strength with each passing moment as they rose from the ashes of their inner turmoil. United by their collective growth and unwavering bond, they emerged from the hidden sanctuary stronger and more determined than ever before. Battling Inner Turmoil The hidden sanctuary of the Bayou offered solace, but it also demanded confrontation.

As the family members delved deeper into their inner demons, their battles intensified, and the weight of their emotional turmoil threatened to consume them. Nathan found himself in a dimly lit chamber, his heart heavy with regret and self-doubt.

Shadows danced on the walls, whispering echoes of past failures and missed opportunities. The weight of the world seemed to rest on his shoulders as he grappled with the burden of leadership. But with each step he took towards acceptance, his shoulders straightened and his resolve hardened.

He realized that mistakes were inevitable, but it was how he learned from them that truly defined him as a leader. Lucy stood on the edge of a precipice, her fiery gaze fixated on the abyss below. Doubts gnawed at her soul as she questioned her worthiness and wondered if her impulsive nature would only lead to destruction.

But as she looked down into the darkness, she felt a spark within her ignite. She refused to let fear hold her back; instead, she embraced her passion and harnessed it as a force for good. In that moment, she understood that her fire could illuminate paths and drive away shadows.

Hadley wandered through a dense forest, a fog thickening around her as doubts clouded her mind. The whispers grew louder, fueling her insecurities and making her question if she truly belonged among the protectors. But as she reached out to touch the gnarled bark of a tree, strength surged through her veins.

She realized that her unique perspective and resourcefulness made her invaluable to their mission. With renewed purpose, she vowed to trust in herself and embrace her role as the Night Owl. Ayden found himself in a room filled with wounded souls, their cries for healing echoing in his ears.

Doubts plagued him as he questioned whether his abilities were enough to ease their pain. The weight of responsibility almost crushed him until he closed his eyes and allowed compassion to wash over him like a wave.

He understood that healing went beyond physical wounds; it required empathy and genuine connection. With a renewed sense of purpose, he vowed to channel his inner light and bring peace to those who needed it most.

In each battle against their inner demons, the family members confronted the darkest corners of their minds with honesty and courage. Their struggles mirrored one another, intertwining their stories into a powerful tapestry of growth and resilience.

As they faced their deepest fears head-on, the oppressive atmosphere within the sanctuary began to lift. Rays of sunlight filtered through the branches above, casting gentle warmth upon their faces. The whispers that once haunted them transformed into words of encouragement, urging them forward on their shared journey.

United by their individual triumphs over doubt and fear, they emerged from this sacred space with a newfound sense of purpose and unity. The weight of uncertainty had lifted from their shoulders, replaced by an unwavering determination to protect Ember Bay at all cost rising from the ashes.

The weight of uncertainty lifted as the family emerged from the hidden sanctuary, their spirits renewed and their hearts ablaze with purpose. The oppressive atmosphere dissipated, replaced by a gentle breeze that carried with it a sense of hope and clarity.

Nathan stood tall, his piercing eyes filled with determination. The shadows that once threatened to consume him had been replaced by an unwavering resolve. He understood that their mission was not without risks and challenges, but he also knew that they possessed the strength and unity to overcome anything.

Lucy's fiery spirit burned brighter than ever before. She had confronted her inner doubts and proved that her impulsive nature could be channeled into a force for good. She felt the weight of responsibility upon her, but instead of feeling burdened, she embraced it as an opportunity to protect those she loved. Hadley radiated confidence as she walked alongside her family.

The trust issues that had plagued her were replaced with a newfound understanding - she didn't have to face their battles alone. She had allies who stood by her side, ready to support and uplift one another in their fight against Juggernaut. Ayden's calming presence resonated with renewed purpose.

He had grappled with doubts about his healing abilities, but now he recognized that his compassion and ability to bring balance were essential in protecting Ember Bay. He vowed to use his gifts to soothe the wounds inflicted by darkness, both physical and emotional.

As a united front, they stepped forward into the unknown, their steps guided by a shared vision and the unbreakable bond they had forged through adversity. The family understood that their journey would not be easy, but they were prepared to face whatever lay ahead.

The Bayou seemed to come alive around them as if acknowledging their unity. Birds chirped in harmony, the winds whispered tales of courage, and the very essence of nature rejoiced in their presence. They felt the interconnectedness between themselves and the mystical realm they fought to protect.

Their voices carried on the wind, echoing through the trees as a testament to their unwavering belief in one another. With each step forward, they left behind traces of doubt and uncertainty until all that remained was an unshakable faith in their collective strength. The path ahead was still uncertain, but they faced it with newfound resilience and determination.

They knew there would be sacrifices along the way, moments of triumph and moments of defeat. But through it all, they would stand together, bound by love, trust, and a shared destiny. Ember Bay awaited their arrival - a place teetering on the edge of darkness but infused with the spark of hope. It was here, in this mystical realm they held dear, that they would confront Juggernaut and safeguard all that they cherished.

In unison, they took their first step towards their ultimate confrontation. As they ventured forth, their hearts filled with fierce determination - together they would overcome every obstacle, united they would protect Ember Bay from the grip of darkness.

As they strode forward hand in hand, the world watched in awe. The Elemental Guardians had risen from the ashes, ready to face Juggernaut and ensure that light would prevail over darkness.

Chapter 18: Unmasking the Enigma

Nathan cautiously stepped into the dimly lit cave, his heart pounding with a mixture of anticipation and trepidation. The air was heavy with an ancient energy that seemed to whisper secrets of the past. Lucy followed closely behind him, her fiery red hair catching the faint glow emanating from the artifacts scattered across the cave floor. "Can you feel it, Nathan?" Lucy whispered, her voice filled with a mix of excitement and reverence.

"There's something truly extraordinary about this place." Nathan nodded, his piercing eyes scanning the room as they settled on a peculiar scroll resting on a nearby pedestal. Its edges were frayed with age, but the text engraved upon it still held an otherworldly beauty. Hadley joined them, her midnight black hair cascading down her slender figure as she carefully examined the intricate symbols etched into an ancient artifact. Her piercing green eyes gleamed with intrigue as her fingers traced the grooves of each symbol.

"This is like nothing I've ever seen," Hadley murmured, her voice barely audible over the whispers echoing through the cave. "It feels...significant." Ayden, ever the calming presence, approached a weathered stone tablet adorned with swirling patterns. His gentle touch sent a shiver through his body as he closed his eyes and allowed the energy to flow through him.

"The essence of this place is undeniable," Ayden said softly, his voice carrying a sense of awe. "We are standing on hallowed ground, surrounded by echoes of our ancestors." As they continued to explore the cave, deciphering texts and piecing together fragments of forgotten history, a sense of urgency began to build within them.

They knew that whatever secrets lay hidden within these artifacts would have profound implications for their battle against Juggernaut. Hours turned into days as the family poured over the scrolls and artifacts, their minds racing with possibilities and revelations. Each new discovery added another layer to the enigmatic tapestry of Juggernaut's past, providing glimpses into the events that led to his descent into darkness. Nathan's hands trembled as he uncovered a scroll detailing Juggernaut's first encounter with the forces that now consumed him.

He could feel anger welling up inside him, fueled by a sense of betrayal. "We trusted him, believed in him," Nathan growled, his voice filled with a mix of rage and sorrow. "How could he let himself be consumed by such darkness?" Lucy placed a comforting hand on Nathan's shoulder, her fierce gaze softening with compassion. "We may never fully understand why he chose this path," she said, her voice filled with empathy. "But we can't let anger cloud our judgment. Our duty remains to protect Ember Bay from Juggernaut's malevolent influence.

" Hadley knelt beside a crumbling tablet, her slender fingers gently tracing faded inscriptions. A pensive look crossed her face as she searched for answers amongst the fragmented symbols. "There must be more to this story," Hadley mused aloud, her voice tinged with curiosity. "Hidden truths we have yet to uncover. " Ayden nodded in agreement, his kind eyes filled with determination.

"We must continue our search," he said, his words carrying both conviction and unwavering hope.

"The answers we seek are within our reach. " With renewed purpose and a newfound understanding of their adversary's origins, the family emerged from the secluded cave, ready to face Juggernaut head-on. The weight of their mission hung heavy in the air as they prepared themselves for the final confrontation. "We have come so far," Nathan said, his voice steady and resolute. "And now we know what we must do." Lucy nodded, her fiery hair framing her determined expression.

"Juggernaut may have succumbed to darkness," she said, her voice filled with unwavering resolve, "but we will not let him destroy Ember Bay without a fight." Hadley turned towards Ayden and offered a small smile filled with gratitude.

"Thank you for guiding us through this journey," she said softly. "Your wisdom and strength have been our guiding light." Ayden's gaze met each family member's in turn, his voice filled with compassion. "We are stronger together," he said, his words echoing through the depths of their souls.

"And together we will face whatever lies ahead." As they stood in unity, their hearts filled with renewed purpose, they felt an unbreakable bond between them – an unbreakable bond that would carry them through the impending battle against Juggernaut. With resolute determination shining in their eyes, they were ready to confront their darkest fears and protect Ember Bay from its most formidable foe yet.

The family gathered around the ancient artifacts, their eyes tracing the intricate engravings and symbols that adorned them. Nathan's fingers traced the lines of a weathered amulet, his touch seeming to awaken dormant memories within its surface. "This amulet… it carries a story," Nathan murmured, his voice filled with a mix of wonder and curiosity. "A story we must uncover."

Lucy's gaze fell upon a small vial filled with an iridescent liquid. She carefully picked it up, her eyes reflecting the vibrant colors swirling within. "I believe this liquid is imbued with ancient magic," Lucy spoke, her voice barely above a whisper. "It may hold the key to unlocking Juggernaut's secret power source." Hadley's attention was drawn to an ancient book, its pages seemingly untouched by time.

She delicately opened it, the scent of aged parchment filling the air. "This book… it contains spells and incantations," Hadley said, her voice filled with awe. "Spells that could tip the scales in our favor against Juggernaut." Ayden approached a cracked stone tablet, its surface etched with celestial symbols that seemed to shimmer under his gaze. "These symbols… they resonate with celestial energy," Ayden said, his tone filled with reverence. "They offer glimpses into divine guidance that can aid us in our battle."

As they delved deeper into their examination of the artifacts, a sense of connection began to form between them. The artifacts seemed to stir something within their very souls, intertwining their destinies and fueling their determination to defeat Juggernaut. Nathan held out the amulet for the others to see, his voice filled with conviction.

"This amulet… it was once worn by one of Juggernaut's most trusted allies. It holds secrets about his past that he may have written off as lost forever." Lucy nodded in agreement, her fiery eyes burning with determination. "And this liquid…" she trailed off, her gaze focused on the vial. "It has the potential to weaken Juggernaut's power, to expose his vulnerabilities."

Hadley flipped through the pages of the ancient book, her voice laced with excitement. "Here… these spells are designed to strip away Juggernaut's dark influence, to bring light back into his heart." Ayden closed his eyes, channeling celestial energy through his body. His voice resonated with unwavering certainty.

"These symbols… they guide us towards divine intervention, towards enlightenment even in the face of darkness." The artifacts became beacons of hope, guiding the family towards a newfound understanding of their enemy and his weaknesses. Each artifact represented a piece of the puzzle, unveiling a path towards victory against Juggernaut.

"We must combine our knowledge," Nathan stated with determination, his voice ringing out with an air of authority. "Only together can we unlock these artifacts' true potential and use them against Juggernaut." Lucy stepped forward, her aura radiating confidence and strength. "We need to share our discoveries and devise a plan," she said firmly.

"With each artifact, we strengthen our understanding of how to defeat him." Hadley nodded in agreement, her eyes shining with anticipation. "If we pool our resources and align our powers with these artifacts' ancient wisdom," she said eagerly, "we have a fighting chance against Juggernaut." Ayden placed a hand on each family member's shoulder, his voice filled with reassurance.

"These artifacts are not just objects," he said softly. "They represent the collective power within us all – a power that when harnessed together can bring down even the strongest of foes." As they stood united, their hearts aflame with purpose and determination, they began to brainstorm strategies for utilizing the artifacts against Juggernaut.

They shared their insights and visions and together formed a plan that maximized their individual strengths while leveraging the power of their newfound artifacts. They knew the road ahead would be challenging and fraught with danger, but armed with ancient wisdom and unified purpose, they were ready to face whatever awaited them.

The fight against Juggernaut had taken on new meaning – it wasn't just about protecting Ember Bay; it was about reclaiming what was lost and restoring balance in their world. With unity fueling their spirits and ancient artifacts empowering their every move, they set forth on their next step towards victory over Juggernaut.

No longer mere guardians but true Elemental Guardians forged by destiny itself, they were ready to unleash their full potential and rewrite the story that had been stained by darkness for far too long. Heightened Stakes and Intensifying Battle The weight of their revelations hung heavy in the air as the family emerged from the secluded cave. They knew that their battle against Juggernaut would be their most challenging yet, but armed with newfound knowledge, they were more determined than ever to protect Ember Bay.

Nathan's fists clenched at his sides as he stared out into the horizon, his mind filled with thoughts of revenge and justice. "Juggernaut may have succumbed to darkness, but we will not let him destroy Ember Bay without a fight," he declared, his voice filled with unwavering resolve.

Lucy nodded, her fiery hair casting a glow around her determined expression. "We've seen what he's capable of," she said, her voice laced with steely determination. "But we've also seen the strength that lies within us.

Together, we can overcome anything." Hadley joined them, her piercing green eyes reflecting the fierce spirit burning within her. "Juggernaut may have turned his back on the light," she stated, her words carrying a sense of quiet determination, "but we will remind him of the power of hope and the strength of unity. "

Ayden stepped forward, his calming presence radiating a sense of reassurance. "Our journey has prepared us for this moment," he said softly, his voice filled with unwavering faith. "We stand on the precipice of something extraordinary – a battle that will redefine our destinies and bring light back into the heart of Ember Bay.

" As they set off towards their next destination, the family carried with them a renewed sense of purpose and an unwavering belief that their shared destiny would guide them through the darkness. Thoughts of their fallen comrades and the sacrifices made weighed heavily on their hearts, fueling their resolve to bring an end to Juggernaut's reign of terror.

They felt a deep responsibility to honor those who had come before them and to protect future generations from the darkness that threatened to engulf their world. Their journey was not just about reclaiming Ember Bay from Juggernaut; it was about reclaiming their own identities and finding redemption in the face of overwhelming adversity. They would not only defeat Juggernaut but also prove that love, unity, and the power of good could triumph over even the deepest darkness.

As they walked together, their footsteps echoed with determination and their hearts beat in unison. The path ahead would be treacherous, filled with unforeseen challenges and unimaginable trials, but they faced it with an unbreakable spirit and an unwavering bond. The battles that awaited them were not only physical but also spiritual and emotional. They knew that defeating Juggernaut would require more than just brute force; it would require wisdom, compassion, and an unyielding belief in themselves and each other.

With every step they took, the family grew stronger – their spirits intertwined like threads in a tapestry woven by fate itself. They were no longer just protectors; they were Elemental Guardians bound by destiny and united by a common purpose. As they prepared themselves for the final battle against Juggernaut, their minds were filled with images of victory – images of Ember Bay bathed in light once more.

They embraced these visions, allowing them to fuel their determination and fortify their resolve. Together, they would face whatever challenges lay ahead. And together, they would emerge victorious – not just for themselves but for the countless lives that depended on their success.

The stage was set for an epic showdown between light and darkness – a battle that would determine the fate of Ember Bay. With each passing moment, their anticipation grew, knowing that their destiny awaited them just beyond the horizon. And so they pressed on, their hearts filled with courage and their spirits aflame with hope.

The Elemental Guardians were ready to confront Juggernaut head-on, armed with ancient artifacts and fortified by their unbreakable bond. Ember Bay awaited its heroes. And as they stood on the cusp of their final confrontation with Juggernaut, the family shared one last glance – a look that conveyed both determination and unwavering faith in one another. "We're in this together," Nathan said firmly, his voice carrying across the land.

"No matter what happens, remember that we are stronger as one." With a resounding chorus of agreement, the family moved forward as a united front – embracing their shared destiny and ready to give everything for Ember Bay. Guided by Visions The family emerged from the secluded cave, their minds buzzing with newfound knowledge and a renewed sense of purpose.

As they made their way to a sacred grove within the Bayou, a hush fell over them, the ancient trees towering above like stoic sentinels. They approached the center of the grove, where a sunlit clearing cast a warm glow upon the ground. Nathan stood at the edge of the clearing, his eyes scanning the surroundings with an air of anticipation.

"This is the place," he said, his voice filled with reverence. "Our ancestors have called us here for guidance." Lucy stepped forward, her fiery hair catching the sunlight. She closed her eyes and took a deep breath, allowing herself to be enveloped by the tranquility of the grove. "I can feel their presence," she whispered, her voice filled with awe. "They are waiting for us.

" Hadley joined them, her slender figure poised and observant. She glanced around the grove, her piercing green eyes searching for signs or symbols that would offer insight into their shared destiny. "Our ancestors have walked this path before us," she mused aloud, her voice carrying a mix of wonder and curiosity. "Their wisdom can guide us in our battle against Juggernaut." Ayden closed his eyes, his face turned towards the sky as rays of sunlight bathed his features.

He began to breathe deeply, focusing on the sounds of nature and allowing himself to connect with the spiritual energy surrounding them. "Our ancestors are ready to share their wisdom," he said softly, his voice carrying a soothing tone. "Let us open our hearts and minds to receive their guidance.

" As they stood in silence, a soft breeze rustled through the leaves, carrying with it whispers of distant voices. Visions began to flicker in their minds' eyes – fragmented scenes of battles fought long ago, words of encouragement from loved ones who had passed on, and symbols that held profound meaning.

Nathan's vision showed him facing off against Juggernaut, his shadowy nemesis laughing as darkness enveloped them both. But in a burst of light, Nathan saw himself standing tall and resolute, channeling his inner strength to overcome the darkness. Lucy's vision revealed her surrounded by a wall of fire, flames licking at her feet as Juggernaut bore down upon her.

But she saw herself summoning a force field so powerful that it pushed back against Juggernaut's dark forces. Hadley's vision showed her navigating through a treacherous maze, each twist and turn representing her personal doubts and fears. But she witnessed herself finding her way through with unwavering confidence and unmatched determination.

Ayden's vision depicted him standing atop a mountain peak shrouded in celestial light. He was bathed in healing energy as he reached out to those in need, bringing solace and restoration to even the darkest corners. The visions lingered in their minds even after they opened their eyes.

They shared what they had seen with one another, recognizing that these glimpses into their shared destiny were gifts from their ancestors – messages meant to reaffirm their purpose and offer guidance in their battle against Juggernaut. "We have been chosen for this great task," Nathan declared, his voice carrying an air of conviction. "Our ancestors have shown us the way forward – we must embrace our strengths and trust in ourselves."

Lucy nodded in agreement, a determined smile playing at her lips. "These visions have reminded us that we are capable of so much more than we realize," she said firmly. "We have the power within us to overcome any obstacle." Hadley placed a hand on Ayden's arm, her eyes shining with newfound clarity.

"Our ancestors have given us their blessings," she said softly. "It is now up to us to honor their legacy and protect Ember Bay with all our might." Ayden clasped Hadley's hand in his own, a serene smile gracing his features. "We are not alone in this battle," he said gently. "Our ancestors walk beside us, guiding our every step." As they stood together in the sacred grove, bathed in the warmth of ancestral wisdom, they felt an unbreakable bond linking them to those who had come before.

They knew that their journey was far from over and that challenges still awaited them – but armed with visions of hope and faith in one another, they were prepared to face whatever lay ahead. With renewed determination and a deep sense of gratitude for their ancestors' guidance, they left the grove – emboldened by visions that had solidified their shared destiny as Elemental Guardians.

The battle against Juggernaut loomed on the horizon, and as they continued on their path towards victory, guided by visions and bolstered by ancestral wisdom, they moved forward as one united force – ready to reclaim Ember Bay from darkness once and for all. Embracing Ancestral Wisdom The family approached a hidden grove within the Bayou, their steps gentle as they entered a space imbued with ancient energy. A sense of reverence hung in the air as they gathered in the center, surrounded by towering trees that seemed to whisper forgotten truths. Nathan closed his eyes and took a deep breath, allowing himself to become fully present in the moment.

He felt a connection to something greater than himself, a lineage of protectors who had come before him. "Our ancestors are speaking to us," he said, his voice filled with wonder. "Their wisdom is guiding us." Lucy placed a hand on her heart, her fiery gaze softening with gratitude. "We carry their legacy within us," she said, her voice filled with reverence. "Their strength and determination flow through our veins." Hadley looked up at the canopy of leaves above them, feeling a sense of awe wash over her.

"These trees have witnessed countless battles fought in defense of Ember Bay," she mused, her voice tinged with respect. "Their branches are intertwined with our stories." Ayden stood tall among them, his face radiant with inner peace. "Our ancestors' wisdom resides within us," he said, his voice carrying a soothing tone. "They have faced darkness before and emerged victorious. We must draw upon their teachings." As they closed their eyes and quieted their minds, the whispers of their ancestors grew louder.

Visions danced at the edges of their consciousness – scenes of battles fought and victories won, ancestral figures offering guidance and words of encouragement. Nathan saw himself standing atop a cliff, gazing out at a shimmering bay. The presence of his ancestors surrounded him, filling him with an unwavering belief in his purpose. Lucy's vision showed her running through a field of fire, flames licking at her heels.

But she was protected by an invisible shield – an ancestral forcefield that surrounded her and offered limitless protection. Hadley witnessed herself soaring through the night sky, her movements graceful and precise. The echoes of past protectors whispered in her ears, guiding her every move and filling her with unshakeable confidence.

Ayden's vision depicted him seated beneath a celestial waterfall, healing energy cascading down upon him. His ancestors wrapped themselves around him, infusing his spirit with divine guidance and unwavering faith. When they opened their eyes, the visions lingered; the presence of their ancestors reverberated within each member of the family.

They shared their experiences with one another, feeling the weight of their shared destiny and the depth of their bond. "We are not alone in this journey," Nathan declared, his voice carrying a note of conviction. "Our ancestors walk with us every step of the way." Lucy nodded in agreement, her fiery hair reflecting the determination burning within her.

"Their guidance will light our path forward," she said firmly. "Together, we can face any challenge." Hadley's eyes sparkled with newfound understanding as she spoke softly, her voice filled with gratitude. "We carry our ancestors' strength within us," she said gently. "Their courage flows through our veins." Ayden placed a hand on each family member's shoulder, his calming presence grounding them all. "Our ancestors have entrusted us with this sacred duty," he said softly.

"We must honor their legacy and protect Ember Bay with unwavering dedication. " As they stood together in the ancestral grove, they felt an unbreakable connection to those who had come before them. The wisdom passed down through generations fueled their resolve and bolstered their spirits. With renewed purpose and hearts emboldened by ancestral guidance, they left the grove – knowing that they were not alone in their quest to defeat Juggernaut.

As they stepped back onto the path ahead, they carried with them the collective strength and wisdom of their ancestors. And as they continued to march forward towards victory against Juggernaut, they did so with gratitude for those who had paved the way and faith in the power that resided within them.

Harnessing Ancestral Strength The family stood at the heart of the ancestral grove, their collective spirits resonating with the wisdom of generations past.

They closed their eyes and breathed in deeply, allowing the energy of their ancestors to flow through them, igniting a fire within their souls. Nathan's mind was transported to a battle fought centuries ago, where an ancestor faced a similar adversary to Juggernaut. He witnessed the ancestor's unwavering courage and determination as they faced insurmountable odds.

Nathan felt his own resolve strengthen, knowing that he carried the spirit of bravery within him. Lucy's vision showed her an ancestress enveloped in a sphere of pure light, emanating compassion and unconditional love. Lucy understood that she had inherited this immense capacity for empathy, recalling the words of her ancestress: "Love is the most powerful weapon against darkness.

" Hadley saw a line of Night Owls stretching back through time, each one discovering their unique gifts, embracing their enchantment, and stepping into their true power. She realized that her role as the Night Owl was not just an individual journey but part of a lineage dedicated to preserving the balance between light and dark. Ayden's vision depicted a line of healers standing side by side, channeling celestial energy to soothe the wounds of those affected by darkness.

Ayden embraced the responsibility of continuing this legacy, feeling the presence and guidance of his healer ancestors offering him strength and clarity. As they shared their visions with one another, a deep sense of gratitude washed over them. They knew that they were not alone in their fight against Juggernaut – they had the wisdom and power of their ancestors supporting them every step of the way. Nathan placed a hand on Lucy's shoulder, his voice filled with reverence.

"We carry our ancestors' stories within us," he said softly. "Their resilience and determination will guide us in the face of adversity." Lucy nodded, her eyes shining with gratitude. "We are not just protectors of Ember Bay," she said firmly. "We are torchbearers for our ancestors' legacies.

" Hadley joined them, her voice filled with awe. "Our ancestors have laid the foundation for our path," she said gently. "It is now our responsibility to honor their sacrifice and protect what they held dear. " Ayden's calming presence enveloped them all as he spoke words of reassurance. "We are vessels for their wisdom and strength," he said softly. "Together, we embody their legacy and have the power to shape Ember Bay's future.

" With renewed purpose and hearts aflame with ancestral strength, they left the grove – no longer mere individuals but representatives of a lineage devoted to safeguarding Ember Bay. They knew their journey would be filled with challenges, but armed with ancestral wisdom, they felt invigorated and ready to face whatever lay ahead. As they stepped onto the path before them, they felt a profound connection to their ancestors stretching back through time – a tapestry woven with threads of courage, love, resilience, and healing.

The names and faces may have changed over generations, but the spirit remained steadfast. With each step forward, they forged a deeper understanding of themselves and their place in history. Their journey was not just about defeating Juggernaut; it was about building upon the legacy left by those who had come before them and passing on that torch to future generations.

As the Elemental Guardians continued down the winding path towards their final battle with Juggernaut, they held tightly to the knowledge that they were never alone. Their ancestors walked beside them every step of the way – lending strength in times of doubt and guiding their hands in moments of uncertainty. With an unbreakable bond forged between past and present, they moved forward – ready to face Juggernaut and protect Ember Bay with unwavering determination.

Chapter 19: Echoes of Destiny

The family embarked on a treacherous journey through the heart of the Bayou, guided by ancient maps and cryptic clues left behind by previous protectors. The dense foliage and tangled roots obstructed their path, adding an air of mystique and danger to their quest.

As they ventured deeper into the Bayou, the landscape transformed into a twisted labyrinth of narrow paths and murky waters. Nathan led the way, his stealthy movements guiding the family through the treacherous terrain. His piercing eyes scanned their surroundings, searching for any signs of mythical creatures that may pose a threat.

Lucy followed closely behind, her fiery red hair contrasting against the shadows as she remained vigilant and ready to defend her loved ones at a moment's notice. Hadley moved with a grace that seemed almost supernatural, her agile movements allowing her to navigate even the most challenging obstacles with ease. Her piercing green eyes took in every detail, as if she could see beyond what was visible to the naked eye. Ayden, gentle and wise, brought up the rear, his calming presence providing solace amidst the eerie surroundings.

As they continued their journey, tensions rose within the family. Doubts and fears about the authenticity of the ancient ritual began to surface, threatening to dampen their spirits. Nathan paused for a moment, turning to face his family with a determined gaze. "I know this journey has been filled with uncertainty," he said in his calm yet commanding voice. "But we cannot let doubt cloud our judgment now. We are protectors of Ember Bay, chosen for a reason. Our faith in ourselves and each other is what will carry us through.

" Lucy nodded in agreement, her fiery spirit undeterred by the challenges they faced. "Nathan's right. We've come too far to let doubt consume us now. We have to believe in our purpose and trust that this ritual will awaken our hidden powers. " Hadley's mysterious aura seemed even more pronounced as she observed her family members. "I understand your doubts," she admitted softly.

"But sometimes, it is in times of uncertainty that our true strength shines through. We must have faith in ourselves and embrace the unknown." Ayden's gentle voice cut through the tension like a soothing melody. "Our connection to the Bayou is strong, as is our bond as a family," he said. "Let us not forget the trials we have overcome together. We are stronger than we think, and this ritual will only serve to awaken what lies dormant within us." The words hung in the air, resolute and determined. Their shared faith in their collective destiny gave them renewed strength to push forward.

They pressed on, navigating through narrow paths and wading through murky waters with a newfound determination. As they neared their destination, an air of anticipation and trepidation filled their hearts. They knew that completing this ancient ritual would mark a significant turning point in their journey as protectors of Ember Bay. Their unity and resolve were more important than ever as they prepared themselves mentally and emotionally for what lay ahead.

Tensions ran high within the family as they continued their journey to uncover the rare ingredients needed for the ancient ritual. Doubts and fears about the ritual's authenticity crept into their minds, threatening to undermine their faith in its power. Each family member carried a weight of uncertainty as they journeyed deeper into the heart of the Bayou. Nathan, mindful of the doubts brewing among his loved ones, called for a moment of pause.

The family gathered around him, their expressions a mix of anticipation and trepidation. "I sense the uncertainty that fills your hearts," Nathan began, his voice steady and determined. "But we must remember why we are here. We have witnessed the power of the Bayou first-hand; its mysteries and enchantments are real. We were chosen for a reason, and this ritual is our key to unlocking our full potential as protectors.

" Lucy nodded, her fiery gaze reflecting her resolve. "Nathan's right. We've seen too much to doubt now. We've faced trials and challenges that no ordinary people could overcome. This ritual is our opportunity to tap into those extraordinary abilities that lie dormant within us.

" Hadley observed her family members with her keen green eyes, her mysterious presence bringing an aura of wisdom to the group. "Doubt may be natural in times like these, but it can also be a distraction," she explained softly. "We must trust in our instincts and in the guidance of the Bayou. It has brought us this far for a reason." Ayden interjected with his gentle voice, radiating a calming energy that seemed to ease the tension in the air.

"Our connection to the Bayou runs deep," he said. "It has chosen us to be its protectors, and we must have faith in its wisdom. Remember the moments when we doubted ourselves in the past but overcame those doubts through unity and determination." The family fell silent, absorbing the wisdom each member shared. Doubt still lingered, but their shared bond and unyielding determination outweighed their uncertainties. They knew they had come too far to turn back now. With renewed conviction, they pressed forward, navigating through treacherous terrain and overcoming obstacles that tested their perseverance and determination.

Each family member supported one another through moments of doubt, offering words of encouragement and reminding each other of their shared purpose. As they ventured deeper into the heart of the Bayou, strange occurrences heightened their senses. Whispers floated on the wind, seeming to carry messages from unseen beings. Shadows danced in their peripheral vision, hinting at mystical forces at play. Despite these eerie signs, the family remained steadfast in their pursuit of the ritual's ingredients. With every challenge they faced, they learned more about themselves and their connection to Ember Bay. The path grew narrower as they approached a legendary tree with roots that reached deep into the ground.

The tree was said to hold the rare ingredient they sought: a single golden leaf imbued with ancient magic. Nathan reached out to touch one of the tree's gnarled roots, feeling a surge of energy rush through his body. He looked back at his family members, their faces reflecting determination and trust. "Together, we will find what we seek," Nathan declared, his voice filled with unwavering conviction.

The family joined hands, forming a circle around the tree. Their connection grew stronger as they channeled their combined energy into searching for the golden leaf. Time seemed to slow as they scanned the leaves above them until finally, Lucy's sharp eyes caught a glimmer of gold amid a cluster of dark green leaves. "There!" she exclaimed, pointing up with excitement. Nathan extended his hand towards the leaf, feeling a surge of power as he plucked it delicately from its branch.

The moment he grasped it, a soft golden light enveloped him before spreading throughout the entire circle. Their doubts began to dissipate as they felt the ancient magic course through their veins. The golden leaf represented their unwavering belief in themselves and their destiny as protectors of Ember Bay. Together, they took a collective breath, knowing that this golden leaf would be the catalyst for awakening their hidden powers during the forthcoming ritual.

Doubt lingered in their minds, but hope burned brighter than ever before. The family embarked on a treacherous journey through the heart of the Bayou, guided by ancient maps and cryptic clues left behind by previous protectors..." Despite their doubts and reservations, the family pushed forward, their unwavering belief in themselves and each other guiding them through the treacherous terrain of the Bayou.

Nathan, always the determined leader, led the way with his exceptional ninja skills and agile movements. His eyes remained focused on their destination, never wavering in his commitment to protect Ember Bay. Lucy, with her fierce spirit and powerful force fields, followed closely behind Nathan. Her fiery red hair seemed to ignite with each step, matching the fire that burned within her. She could feel the mystical energy of the Bayou surrounding her, urging her to tap into her true potential. Hadley, the mysterious and observant one, blended effortlessly into the shadows as she navigated the treacherous paths.

Her midnight black hair seemed to absorb the darkness around her, and her piercing green eyes allowed her to see what others couldn't. She was attuned to the hidden truths of the ancient civilization and felt a sense of purpose in uncovering their secrets. Ayden, ever compassionate and wise, brought up the rear with his calming presence. His soothing energy provided a sense of harmony amidst the chaos of their journey. Ayden's ability to heal wounds inflicted by both physical and emotional darkness was essential in their quest to protect Ember Bay.

As they ventured further into the heart of the Bayou, whispers filled the air, carrying snippets of ancient prophecies that foretold their destiny as protectors. The family listened intently, deciphering the messages woven through the wind and embracing the knowledge it bestowed upon them. With each step they took, their bond deepened, solidifying their unity as protectors of Ember Bay.

They knew that their individual strengths were amplified when combined, creating an impenetrable force against any supernatural threat that lurked in the shadows. Arriving at a secluded clearing surrounded by ancient trees bathed in moonlight, they knew they had reached their destination.

The air crackled with anticipation as they prepared for the ritual that would awaken their hidden powers. Nathan stepped forward, holding out the enchanted stones that had been bestowed upon them by the Bayou's mystical forces.

Each stone pulsated with a unique essence, resonating with the dormant powers within its bearer. As he handed a stone to each family member, their connection to Ember Bay grew even stronger. Lucy clasped the stone tightly in her hand, feeling its power surge through her. She closed her eyes briefly, allowing herself to surrender to its energy.

When she opened them again, she could see flickers of fire dancing across her fingertips. Hadley held her stone delicately between her palms, feeling a warmth spread throughout her body. She could sense a newfound ability to blend into shadows even more seamlessly than before. It was as if the night itself had become her ally.

Ayden cradled his stone gently, a sense of peace washing over him like a gentle wave. He connected with its celestial energy and felt his healing abilities intensify. The stone seemed to whisper ancient secrets only he could hear. Nathan looked at his family members with a renewed sense of determination in his eyes.

The time had come for them to embrace their powers fully and fulfill their destinies as protectors of Ember Bay. Together, they raised their hands toward the moonlit sky and recited an incantation passed down through generations. As they spoke the ancient words, a surge of energy enveloped them, causing their bodies to glow with an ethereal light. They could feel their latent powers awakening within them, bursting forth like flames from a long-dormant volcano. The family stood together, bathed in their newfound powers and united in purpose.

They could feel the energy of Ember Bay coursing through them, intertwining their individual strengths into a formidable force. In unison, they raised their voices in a chant that echoed through the clearing and reverberated throughout the Bayou. Their words carried their unwavering dedication and resolve as protectors: "We are the Elemental Guardians, United by destiny, Bound by love and strength, Together we shall protect Ember Bay.

" With each word spoken, their powers intensified until they radiated with an indomitable light that illuminated even the darkest corners of their souls. With their awakening complete, the family knew that there was no turning back now. Their duty as protectors had been sealed in this sacred ritual.

They were ready to face any challenge that came their way and stand united against Juggernaut's imminent threat. The family embarked on a treacherous journey through the heart of the Bayou, guided by ancient maps and cryptic clues left behind by previous protectors..." The family found solace in each other's shared faith and determination as doubts began to cast shadows over their minds.

Nathan's commanding voice cut through the air like a razor-sharp blade. "Listen," he said firmly but compassionately. "We've faced grave challenges before – trials that tested our mettle and proved our worthiness as protectors. This ritual is no different. We must believe in its power to awaken our hidden abilities. " Lucy nodded vigorously, her fiery red hair bouncing with affirmation.

"Nathan's right," she declared with conviction. "We've seen firsthand what this Bayou is capable of – its magic is real! We cannot let doubt cloud our judgment now.

" Hadley observed her family members carefully; her mysterious green eyes locked onto each one of them with purposeful intensity. "Allow yourselves to be vulnerable," she advised softly yet decisively. "Doubt is natural in times like these but remember, it is through vulnerability that we allow ourselves to grow." Ayden's voice resonated with wisdom as he gently interjected.

"The Bayou chose us for a reason," he reminded them all. "We have witnessed its wonders and felt its profound influence on our lives. This ritual will open doors we never thought possible; we just need to trust in its power.

" Their doubts slowly began to dissipate like morning mist beneath rays of sunshine as they absorbed each other's words. Tension released its grip on their hearts as unity took hold once more. Renewed strength coursed through them as they pressed on toward their goal: unveiling the ancient ritual that would awaken their hidden powers as protectors of Ember Bay. The family arrived at a secluded clearing, the air thick with an otherworldly energy.

Ancient stones encircled them, their significance and power palpable. Each family member stepped into the circle, their hearts pounding with anticipation. Nathan took a deep breath, feeling the weight of his responsibilities as the Ninja of the Bayou settled upon his shoulders.

He closed his eyes for a moment, grounding himself in the present moment. When he opened them again, his gaze was unwavering and determined. Lucy stood beside him, her fiery spirit radiating from every pore. She felt the force fields within her stir in response to the ancient energies surrounding them.

The anticipation coursed through her veins, igniting a fire within her that could not be extinguished. Hadley moved gracefully into the circle, her eyes scanning the surroundings with a sense of reverence. She had always been attuned to the hidden truths of the Bayou, and now she sensed that this ritual held secrets long forgotten by others. She knew that unlocking those secrets would reveal her true potential as the Night Owl.

Ayden joined them, his calming presence providing a sense of peace amidst the charged atmosphere. He knew that this ritual would enable him to harness his healing abilities to their fullest potential, bringing light and balance to Ember Bay. He closed his eyes and allowed himself to connect with the celestial energy that flowed through him.

The family members raised their hands simultaneously, their palms facing upwards in a gesture of openness and receptivity. They chanted ancient incantations that echoed through the clearing, their voices becoming one with the mystical energies swirling around them. A soft glow enveloped each family member as they channeled their intentions and aspirations into the universe.

Their desires intertwined like threads of golden light, weaving together a tapestry of unity and purpose. With every word spoken, the energy intensified until it reached its crescendo. A surge of power surged through the family members' bodies, causing them to gasp in awe at the sheer magnitude of the experience. As Nathan opened his eyes, he could see shadows dancing across his vision – not in darkness but in vibrant shades of light.

Lucy felt an invisible forcefield pulsating around her, crackling with electric energy that could both protect and defend.

Hadley's senses become heightened, allowing her to see beyond what was visible to others. She could feel herself merging with the shadows, becoming one with the night itself. Ayden's cross glowed with an ethereal light as celestial energy surged through him. His healing abilities amplified, radiating outwards with a warmth and gentleness that could lift spirits and restore harmony.

The realization washed over them like a tidal wave – they had awakened their hidden powers. Each family member stood in awe of what they had just experienced, recognizing the immense responsibility that came with these newfound abilities. They knew that this was only the beginning of their journey as protectors of Ember Bay. The ancient ritual had unlocked a door within them, revealing inner strength and potential they had yet to fully comprehend. As they looked at each other with renewed determination in their eyes, they understood that they were no longer ordinary individuals merely camping in the Bayou.

They were Elemental Guardians, destined to defend Ember Bay and safeguard its mystical energies from any threats that may arise. In that moment, unity and purpose bound them together – an unbreakable bond forged through trials, challenges, and now awakening. The family stood in the sacred clearing, their hearts racing with anticipation and a newfound sense of purpose.

The symbols etched into the ancient stones seemed to pulse with energy as they prepared for the next phase of the ritual. Nathan took a deep breath, his gaze focused on the task at hand. He extended his hand towards Lucy, who placed her palm against his, their connection solidifying their bond and shared determination. They looked at each other, a silent acknowledgment passing between them - they were ready to face whatever challenges lay ahead.

Hadley moved gracefully into position beside Ayden, her presence emanating a quiet confidence. She reached out to Ayden, her fingertips touching his lightly, forming a circle of unity. Ayden's serene expression mirrored Hadley's, his calmness radiating serenity and strength. As the family embraced the power of their collective energy, a warm golden light enveloped them.

Their individual abilities flickered like stars in the night sky, waiting to be unleashed. They closed their eyes and let their minds settle into a state of meditation, opening themselves to the guidance of the Bayou. With each breath, they allowed themselves to be fully present in this moment, ready to receive what the ritual had to offer.

Moments passed in stillness as they surrendered to the flow of energy surrounding them. In their minds, they visualized a connection of light that linked them together, forming an unbreakable chain forged through love and trust. A soft hum filled the air as their energies intertwined and merged, creating a harmonious symphony that resonated throughout their beings.

They could feel the power building within them, like a wellspring awaiting release. Together, they began to chant a melodic mantra passed down through generations - words that expressed gratitude, strength, and unity.

Their voices blended together, rising and falling in perfect synchrony as if guided by an unseen conductor. With every repetition of the mantra, their vibrational frequency increased, elevating their connection to higher realms of consciousness. Visions washed over them in waves - glimpses of battles fought and victories won, moments of joy and sorrow, and fragments of harmony and chaos.

The energy within them surged as they tapped into the wisdom of their ancestors and the elemental forces that flowed through Ember Bay. Their individual strengths were amplified by the collective power of their family bond.

A gust of wind swept through the clearing, carrying with it whispers from ancient guardians who had once tread these hallowed grounds. Each family member felt a presence beside them - a guiding force offering support and encouragement. As the chant reached its peak, the energy reached its crescendo.

The sky above them darkened as clouds swirled overhead. The very fabric of reality seemed to shift and shimmer with anticipation. Abruptly, the chanting stopped and silence descended upon the clearing. The family opened their eyes simultaneously and found themselves bathed in an ethereal glow that emanated from within. Their bodies seemed lighter than air as they reveled in their awakened powers.

Nathan felt an affinity with shadows, his movements becoming fluid and elusive as he melded seamlessly with darkness itself. Lucy's force fields crackled with intensity around her, shimmering like a protective shield that could repel any threat. Her fiery spirit burned brighter than ever before. Hadley's senses sharpened even further as she delved deeper into her connection with the Bayou. She could see beyond visible illusions and hear whispers carried on nocturnal breezes - a true Night Owl attuned to realms others couldn't perceive.

Ayden radiated a calming energy that soothed all who stood near him. His healing abilities expanded exponentially - he could mend both physical and emotional wounds with unparalleled grace and compassion. The family members marveled at their transformations, feeling both humbled and emboldened by their awakened powers. They understood that these abilities were gifts bestowed upon them by Ember Bay itself - tools to protect its sacred essence from darkness.

As they basked in the glow of camaraderie and newfound potential, they knew that their journey was far from over. The ritual had only unlocked the first layer of their abilities; there was still much more to learn and explore. But in this moment, surrounded by the ancient stones and infused with ancestral knowledge, they were filled with hope and certainty that they possessed what it took to face any challenge that Juggernaut presented.

They clasped hands once more, forming a circle that represented their unwavering unity. Their eyes locked together in solemn affirmation - they were bound not just by blood but by destiny itself. Together, they vowed to protect Ember Bay at all costs - harnessing their awakened powers and facing whatever challenges lay ahead with unwavering resolve. The family embarked on a treacherous journey through the heart of the Bayou, guided by ancient maps and cryptic clues left behind by previous protectors.

" The family stood in the sacred clearing, their hearts racing with anticipation and a newfound sense of purpose. The symbols etched into the ancient stones seemed to pulse with energy as they prepared for the next phase of the ritual. Nathan took a deep breath, his gaze focused on the task at hand.

He extended his hand towards Lucy, who placed her palm against his, their connection solidifying their bond and shared determination. They looked at each other, a silent acknowledgment passing between them - they were ready to face whatever challenges lay ahead. Hadley moved gracefully into position beside Ayden, her presence emanating a quiet confidence. She reached out to Ayden, her fingertips lightly touching his, forming a circle of unity. Ayden's serene expression mirrored Hadley's, his calmness radiating serenity and strength.

As the family embraced the power of their collective energy, a warm golden light enveloped them. Their individual abilities flickered like stars in the night sky, waiting to be unleashed. They closed their eyes and let their minds settle into a state of meditation, opening themselves to the guidance of the Bayou. With each breath, they allowed themselves to be fully present in this moment, ready to receive what the ritual had to offer. Moments passed in stillness as they surrendered to the flow of energy surrounding them.

In their minds, they visualized a connection of light that linked them together, forming an unbreakable chain forged through love and trust. A soft hum filled the air as their energies intertwined and merged, creating a harmonious symphony that resonated throughout their beings. They could feel the power building within them, like a wellspring awaiting release. Together, they began to chant a melodic mantra passed down through generations - words that expressed gratitude, strength, and unity.

Their voices blended together, rising and falling in perfect synchrony as if guided by an unseen conductor. With every repetition of the mantra, their vibrational frequency increased, elevating their connection to higher realms of consciousness. Visions washed over them in waves - glimpses of battles fought and victories won, moments of joy and sorrow, and fragments of harmony and chaos.

The energy within them surged as they tapped into the wisdom of their ancestors and the elemental forces that flowed through Ember Bay. Their individual strengths were amplified by the collective power of their family bond.

A gust of wind swept through the clearing, carrying with it whispers from ancient guardians who had once tread these hallowed grounds. Each family member felt a presence beside them - a guiding force offering support and encouragement. As the chant reached its peak, the energy reached its crescendo. The sky above them darkened as clouds swirled overhead. The very fabric of reality seemed to shift and shimmer with anticipation. Abruptly, the chanting stopped and silence descended upon the clearing.

The family opened their eyes simultaneously and found themselves bathed in an ethereal glow that emanated from within. Their bodies seemed lighter than air as they reveled in their awakened powers. Nathan felt an affinity with shadows, his movements becoming fluid and elusive as he melded seamlessly with darkness itself. Lucy's force fields crackled with intensity around her, shimmering like a protective shield that could repel any threat. Her fiery spirit burned brighter than ever before.

Hadley's senses sharpened even further as she delved deeper into her connection with the Bayou. She could see beyond visible illusions and hear whispers carried on nocturnal breezes - a true Night Owl attuned to realms others couldn't perceive. Ayden radiated a calming energy that soothed all who stood near him.

His healing abilities expanded exponentially - he could mend both physical and emotional wounds with unparalleled grace and compassion. The realization washed over them like a tidal wave – they had awakened their hidden powers. Each family member stood in awe of what they had just experienced, recognizing the immense responsibility that came with these newfound abilities. They knew that this was only the beginning of their journey as protectors of Ember Bay.

The ancient ritual had unlocked a door within them, revealing inner strength and potential they had yet to fully comprehend. But in this moment, surrounded by the ancient stones and infused with ancestral knowledge, they were filled with hope and certainty that they possessed what it took to face any challenge that Juggernaut presented.

They clasped hands once more, forming a circle that represented their unwavering unity. Their eyes locked together in solemn affirmation - they were bound not just by blood but by destiny itself. Together, they vowed to protect Ember Bay at all costs - harnessing their awakened powers and facing whatever challenges lay ahead with unwavering resolve.

Chapter 20: The Final Showdown Begins

Hadley's sharp voice cut through the tension. "This is the time to call for our pets!" In response, the air around them shimmered with an otherworldly energy. In the midst of the chaotic battle, Jack, now transformed into a mighty bear, growled menacingly beside Hadley.

Gizmo, the teacup Chihuahua turned wolf, prowled silently at Nathan's side. Ellie, a regal white lioness, stood proudly by Lucy's side, emitting a low rumble that reverberated through the clearing. The pets, infused with supernatural abilities, added a new dimension to the fight. Jack lunged at Juggernaut with immense strength, his claws slashing through the dark energy surrounding their adversary.

Gizmo darted between shadows, delivering swift bites that disrupted Juggernaut's focus. Ellie circled the battlefield, her mere presence disrupting the malevolent energy that enveloped their opponent. Nathan and Lucy, emboldened by the support of their supernatural companions, intensified their assault.

Nathan executed a series of acrobatic maneuvers, exploiting the distraction caused by the pets to land precise strikes on Juggernaut. Lucy's sword danced in the moonlight, cutting through the shadows with a grace that belied its deadly intent. Hadley and Ayden continued to coordinate their efforts. Ayden channeled celestial energy through his cross, creating radiant barriers that augmented Lucy's force fields. Hadley, with her keen sense of Juggernaut's weaknesses, directed the pets to exploit vulnerabilities in his defenses. The battlefield became a symphony of chaos and strategy, with each member of the family and their pets contributing to the intricate dance against Juggernaut.

The malevolent entity, though formidable, found himself surrounded by a united force determined to overcome the darkness he embodied. As the battle raged on, the moon cast an eerie glow over the Bayou, bearing witness to the clash between light and shadow. The family, joined by their supernatural companions, pressed forward with unwavering resolve, knowing that this confrontation would determine the fate of not just their lives, but the destiny of the world itself.

Hadley cast a quick look at Ellie, the majestic white lion who stood protectively by Lucy's side. The bond between them was unbreakable, their connection serving as a symbol of strength. "You ready, Ellie?" Hadley asked softly. Ellie let out a regal roar in response, affirming their shared determination to bring down Juggernaut. Jack, now transformed into a mighty bear, emitted a menacing growl by Hadley's side. Meanwhile, Gizmo swiftly traversed alongside Nathan, his sleek black wolf form seamlessly blending into the shadows of the Bayou.

His sharp instincts allowed him to track every move of Juggernaut, enabling him to anticipate and counter each attack with agility and precision. "We're not yielding without a fight," Nathan growled quietly as he skillfully evaded another of Juggernaut's powerful strikes.

Gizmo barked in agreement just as Lucy's voice echoed from across the battlefield, "We need to find a way to weaken him! Keep pushing!" Nathan nodded and drew upon his extraordinary ninja skills to outmaneuver Juggernaut. With lightning speed, he struck a decisive blow to Juggernaut's vulnerable point, causing the formidable adversary to stagger momentarily.

"For Ember Bay!" Lucy exclaimed, unleashing a rapid series of strikes upon Juggernaut's defenses. Nathan joined in, utilizing every ounce of his agility and precision to deliver relentless blows, gradually weakening their formidable foe. The family fought with unyielding determination and unity.

As Juggernaut's assaults intensified, the family members found themselves at the edge of their capabilities. His dark energy crackled and swirled, posing a threat to overwhelm them. Yet, they stood firm, resolute in their determination to protect Ember Bay at any cost. Lucy's force fields shimmered and glowed with intensified power, serving as an impervious shield against Juggernaut's relentless onslaught.

She deftly deflected his strikes, each force field pulsating with impenetrable strength. "Stay focused, Lucy!" Nathan's voice cut through the chaos. "You've got this!" Lucy gritted her teeth, blocking Juggernaut's assault with a forceful swing of her sword. "We won't let him win! Not while we still breathe!" Hadley utilized her teleportation abilities to maneuver swiftly around the battlefield, appearing and disappearing like a phantom.

She launched surprise attacks on Juggernaut, keeping him off balance and unable to fully concentrate on any single opponent. Ayden channeled celestial energy through his cross, emitting a soothing light that filled the clearing. He moved with grace and purpose, healing any wounds inflicted upon his family members and fortifying their strength. As Gizmo bounded alongside Nathan, the two moved in perfect synchronization.

Gizmo's agility mirrored Nathan's ninja skills, allowing him to evade Juggernaut's attacks effortlessly and strike back with precision. "We're wearing him down!" Nathan exclaimed as he landed a powerful blow on Juggernaut's weakened defenses. Gizmo barked in agreement, his black fur standing on end with excitement. Together, they pressed on, never wavering in their assault.

The air crackled with tension as each strike and parry reverberated through the clearing. The intensity of the battle reached its peak as Juggernaut's defenses weakened under the relentless assault from the family. Lucy felt an exhilarating surge of determination flow through her veins.

With a mighty roar, she directed her force fields into a concentrated blast of energy, launching it straight at Juggernaut. The impact sent him staggering backward, his imposing figure momentarily faltering. "Seize the moment!" Hadley exclaimed, taking immediate action.

Jack, the formidable light brown bear, lunged at Juggernaut with a ferocity that matched the wild, unleashing the full force of his mighty claws. Hadley teleported behind Juggernaut, landing precise strikes on his exposed vulnerabilities. Each blow struck true, weakening his dark energy and leaving him reeling.

Ayden moved closer to Juggernaut, his healing energy enveloping the family as he channeled it toward their wounded bodies. The celestial light washed over them like a soothing balm, rejuvenating their strength and resolve.

Nathan leapt back into action, his shadows weaving around him like a swirling cloak of darkness. With a fierce determination burning in his eyes, he unleashed a flurry of strikes upon Juggernaut. Each blow hit home, driving him further toward defeat. Gizmo darted between Juggernaut's legs with lightning speed, delivering swift bites that further weakened their adversary.

His agility and precision proved invaluable in disorienting Juggernaut's movements and creating openings for the others to exploit. As the family members fought with unwavering resolve, Juggernaut began to stumble under the weight of their combined assault. His dark energy wavered and flickered as cracks formed in his once impenetrable defenses.

"We're breaking him!" Nathan declared triumphantly as he landed a final devastating blow. With a resounding crash, Juggernaut collapsed to the ground, defeated and weakened. The family members stood over him, their chests heaving with exertion but their spirits soaring with victory.

"We did it," Lucy gasped between breaths. "We actually did it." Hadley gave Ayden a knowing look before turning to face the fallen form of Juggernaut. "He underestimated us. " Ayden nodded, his calm demeanor radiating relief and satisfaction. "He never stood a chance against our unity.

" Nathan approached Ellie, who had been a steadfast companion throughout the battle. He reached out to stroke her majestic white mane, gratitude shining in his eyes. "Thank you for being there with us," he murmured. Ellie let out a low rumble of contentment before nuzzling Nathan's hand affectionately. Gizmo trotted up beside them and barked playfully, his tail wagging wildly.

They shared a moment of camaraderie before turning their attention back to the defeated Juggernaut. Though they had emerged victorious from this battle, they knew that their mission was far from over. With Ember Bay still at risk from other supernatural threats, they would need to remain vigilant and prepared for whatever lay ahead. But in this moment of triumph over darkness, they allowed themselves a brief respite to bask in the glow of their accomplishment. The family members stood together as elemental guardians of Ember Bay – their bond unbreakable and their purpose unwavering.

As Juggernaut struggled to get back up, the family closed in on him, their determination burning brighter than ever. Nathan's eyes blazed with an intensity that matched the flickering flames surrounding them. "This ends now," Nathan vowed, his voice filled with a steely resolve.

Lucy and Hadley flanked Juggernaut, their weapons raised and ready to strike. Their movements were precise and calculated, fueled by the newfound powers that coursed through their veins. "Time to face the consequences of your actions," Lucy snarled, her fiery hair reflecting her unwavering determination.

Hadley's eyes glinted with an otherworldly determination as she warned, "Your reign of darkness ends here." Ayden stepped forward, his gentle presence radiating strength and compassion. He channeled celestial energy through his cross, illuminating the clearing with a calming light. "You had a choice, Juggernaut," Ayden spoke softly, his voice carrying across the battlefield.

"But you chose darkness over unity. " Juggernaut fought against the overwhelming force of the family's assault, his dark energy crackling and seething with anger. He lashed out with renewed ferocity, each strike aimed at weakening their spirit. But the family remained steadfast, unwavering in their commitment to protect Ember Bay.

They moved together in perfect synchrony, anticipating each other's movements and providing support when needed. Nathan darted in and out of Juggernaut's peripheral vision, striking with blinding speed and precision.

His shadows swirled around him like a cloak of protection, shielding him from harm while he focused on weakening their foe. Lucy's force fields acted as a shield not only for herself but also for her family members. She deflected Juggernaut's attacks while simultaneously launching her own offensive strikes, each blow filled with a fiery determination to bring him down. Hadley harnessed her teleportation prowess to confound Juggernaut.

She materialized and vanished in rapid, elusive flashes, launching assaults from myriad angles, rendering it impossible for him to predict her next maneuver. Meanwhile, Jack, the formidable light brown bear, assailed Juggernaut with a relentless onslaught, employing his formidable claws with unbridled might.

Ayden provided healing and support, bolstering the family's strength and resilience with his celestial energy. He channeled his inner power and directed it towards his allies, soothing their wounds and reinvigorating their spirits. Gizmo weaved between Juggernaut's legs, delivering quick bites and strikes that added to the onslaught against their adversary. His agility helped keep Juggernaut off balance, creating openings for the others to exploit.

Each member of the family fought with unwavering determination and unmatched skill. They pushed themselves to their limits, tapping into their newly awakened powers and using them in tandem to weaken Juggernaut further. With every strike and parry, Juggernaut's defenses weakened.

He stumbled under the relentless assault, his once impenetrable armor cracking under the pressure. The energy surrounding him flickered and waned, a sign of his impending defeat. Nathan seized the opportunity, launching one final strike that sent Juggernaut crashing to the ground. The impact reverberated through the clearing, signaling a pivotal moment in their battle against darkness.

The family members stood over Juggernaut's fallen form, their chests heaving with exhaustion but their spirits undeniably triumphant. They had faced unimaginable challenges, testing their strength and unity at every turn. And now, they had emerged victorious. "Ember Bay is safe once more," Nathan declared, his voice filled with satisfaction and relief.

Lucy nodded in agreement, a proud smile gracing her lips. "We did it together. As a family." Hadley glanced around at her fellow protectors, a sense of awe and gratitude filling her heart. "I couldn't have asked for a better group to fight alongside." Ayden stepped forward and placed a hand on Juggernaut's still form, his eyes filled with empathy.

"May you find peace in whatever lies beyond this existence." Gizmo barked softly as if in agreement, acknowledging their hard-fought victory against impossible odds. In this moment of triumph over darkness, they allowed themselves a rare moment of respite.

They took solace in the knowledge that they had fulfilled their purpose as guardians of Ember Bay. But they also understood that their journey was far from over. As they stood together in the aftermath of their battle against Juggernaut. Their unity had been tested and proven unbreakable.

And now more than ever, they were prepared to face whatever challenges lay ahead—together. And so, their journey continued—new adventures awaited them, new threats would emerge—but they would face them all as one... as The Elemental Guardians. Lucy approached Nathan, her breath coming in ragged gasps.

She reached out and placed a hand on his shoulder, offering a silent gesture of solidarity and gratitude. Together, they had faced seemingly insurmountable odds, but their unwavering determination had propelled them to this moment of triumph. "We're stronger than we ever imagined," Lucy said, her voice filled with awe.

Hadley joined them, a glint of mischief in her eyes. "Who would have thought a group of misfits could accomplish something so incredible?" Ayden stepped forward, his healing energy still emanating from his cross. He regarded his family with a gentle smile, his eyes shining with pride. "It is through our differences that we find strength. We are united by a common purpose.

" Gizmo barked excitedly, circling around the group in joyful celebration. His loyalty and fierce spirit had been integral to their victory, serving as a reminder of the unbreakable bond they shared. With Juggernaut defeated and Ember Bay safe for now, the family took a moment to catch their breaths and reflect on what they had achieved.

The clearing was bathed in the soft glow of moonlight, casting an ethereal ambiance over their triumphant scene. But even as they reveled in their victory, they understood that their journey was far from over. There were still supernatural forces lurking in the shadows, waiting to threaten the peace they had fought so hard to preserve.

Nathan turned his gaze to the horizon, his eyes scanning the darkness beyond. "This battle may be won, but there will always be new challenges." Lucy nodded in agreement, her fiery spirit undeterred by the unknown that lay ahead. "We must remain vigilant and continue to hone our powers. Ember Bay depends on us." Hadley glanced at Ayden and smiled knowingly.

"Our destiny as protectors has just begun. We'll face whatever comes our way." Ayden's expression grew serious as he contemplated their next steps. "We must seek further guidance and training to strengthen our abilities. There is much left to learn." Gizmo barked in agreement once more before settling down at Nathan's feet, ever faithful and unyielding in his commitment to their cause.

The family members stood together in silence, their hearts filled with hope and determination. This victory had not only solidified their bonds but also ignited a newfound sense of purpose within each of them. Ember Bay was safe for now, but they knew that there would always be battles to fight and darkness to overcome.

They were prepared to face the challenges head-on because together, united as elemental guardians, they were unstoppable. And so, with renewed strength and resilience coursing through their veins, the family members turned back towards Ember Bay—their home—ready to face whatever lay ahead as defenders of light against the encroaching shadows.

Their journey was not yet complete, but they carried the spirit of triumph over darkness within them—a reminder that no matter how daunting the task may seem, they had already proven that hope could prevail. As they embarked on the next chapter of their adventure, the family moved forward with heads held high and hearts ablaze with the fervor of protectors who had emerged victorious.

For in their unity and unwavering commitment to one another, they knew that no challenge could stand in their way. Ember Bay awaited their continued protection—their destinies forever intertwined with the mystical forces that coursed through its veins. And as long as these elemental guardians stood tall and fought alongside one another, light would always triumph over darkness.

The echoes of their victory reverberated through the clearing as the family members caught their breath and surveyed the aftermath of their battle.

Juggernaut's defeated form lay motionless on the ground, his once imposing presence reduced to mere remnants of dark energy. Nathan exhaled a sigh of relief, the weight of their hard-fought victory lifting from his shoulders. "We did it," he murmured, his voice filled with a mix of exhaustion and triumph. Lucy nodded, her fiery red hair framing her radiant smile.

"Against all odds, we've proven that light can conquer darkness." Hadley approached them, her eyes shining with admiration. "I've never been prouder to fight alongside such brave and resilient companions. " Ayden stepped forward, his calming presence permeating the air. "Ember Bay owes its safety to our unwavering unity and determination." Gizmo barked in agreement, his tail wagging enthusiastically. He had witnessed their shared strength firsthand, knowing that together they were an unstoppable force.

As the family members stood around Juggernaut's fallen form, a sense of solace washed over them. They had faced immense challenges and pushed themselves beyond their limits to protect Ember Bay. This triumphant moment was a testament to their unwavering commitment and resolve. But even as they relished in their victory, they knew that there would always be new battles to fight.

The struggle against darkness was an ongoing endeavor—one they were prepared to face head-on. "We must remain vigilant," Nathan proclaimed, his voice tinged with determination. "There will always be forces that seek to extinguish the light. We must be ready." Lucy nodded in agreement, her eyes gleaming with an undying fire.

"We will continue to strengthen our abilities and stand united against any threat that arises." Hadley glanced at Ayden, a knowing look passing between them. "Our journey is far from over," she said. "But with each battle we face, we grow stronger and more attuned to the powers that reside within us.

" Jack, the formidable light brown bear, unleashed a resounding roar that reverberated with potent intensity, accompanied by a powerful growl that echoed through the wilderness. Ayden offered a reassuring smile, his presence imbued with a profound sense of wisdom. "Our spirits are resilient, and our connection as a family is unbreakable. Together, we can overcome anything that comes our way.

" Gizmo barked eagerly, a testament to his unwavering loyalty and dedication. He had become an integral part of their family, a steadfast companion whose bond with each member strengthened their unity. In this moment of reflection and respite, the family members allowed themselves to savor the taste of victory. But deep within their hearts, they knew that darkness could never truly be eradicated. It lingered on the edges of existence, awaiting an opportunity to reclaim what it had lost. And so, with renewed determination and fortified spirits, the family turned toward the horizon—their eyes fixed on the challenges that lay ahead.

Their journey as Elemental Guardians continued, fueled by their shared purpose and unyielding belief in the power of light. As they set forth toward Ember Bay, their home and sanctuary, they carried within them the embers of triumph over darkness—a flame that would guide them through every trial they would face. Ember Bay awaited their return—their watchful eyes and unwavering resolve serving as a shield against whatever malevolent forces may seek to taint its beauty.

And so, with heads held high and hearts ablaze with determination, the family ventured forth into an uncertain future—united as guardians of light against the encroaching shadows. For as long as they remained together—as long as their spirits burned bright—Ember Bay would forever stand under their watchful protection. And wherever darkness dared to rear its head, it would find itself met with fierce resistance—a testament to the indomitable spirit of those who had emerged triumphant over its cruelty.

Jack, the once unassuming doodle hound now transformed into a formidable bear, Gizmo, the teacup Chihuahua turned sleek wolf, and Ellie, the Chihuahua metamorphosed into a regal white lioness, seamlessly reverted to their original selves. With a sense of gratitude, Hadley declared, "It's time for you to return home. Thank you for aiding us in our time of need.

" The battlefield fell silent as the echoes of battle faded into the night air. The family stood together, their bodies battered and bruised, their breaths heavy with exhaustion. Nathan leaned on his shuriken for support, feeling the weight of the battle settle on his weary shoulders. He surveyed the aftermath of their fight, taking in the fallen dark creatures scattered around them.

Lucy's fire had dimmed, her flames flickering weakly before extinguishing completely. She slumped to the ground, a mix of relief and weariness etched on her face. Her wounds throbbed with pain, a reminder of the intense fight they had just endured.

Hadley's voice, once filled with ethereal power, was reduced to a mere whisper as she struggled to find her breath. She sank to her knees, cradling her throat in her hands as she fought to regain her composure.

Her body ached from the strain of channeling so much energy during the battle. Ayden's serene expression masked the toll the battle had taken on him. He stood tall, but his healing powers were depleted, leaving him feeling drained and emotionally spent. His eyes flickered with concern as he assessed the injuries of his fellow protectors.

As Nathan's gaze shifted from one family member to another, he couldn't help but feel a sense of guilt. Each of them had carried their weight in the battle against Juggernaut, pushing themselves past their limits to protect Ember Bay. But at what cost? Their physical wounds were visible reminders of the sacrifices they had made. An overwhelming silence settled over them—a profound stillness that carried unspoken words and a shared understanding born from the crucible of their trials.

Collapsing onto the ground, they formed a circle, seeking solace in the presence of their steadfast companions. As they settled, their arms brushed against each other, the friction not just from fatigue but also a testament to the profound bond they forged through adversity. In the quietude, Nathan released a heavy exhale, shattering the silence.

"We did it," he uttered quietly, his voice a blend of relief and awe. Lucy, her voice strained yet filled with pride, added, "We fought bravely. We protected Ember Bay." Hadley nodded in agreement, her eyes reflecting gratitude and admiration for the family she had found in the midst of chaos. "I couldn't have asked for better companions in this battle," she rasped. Ayden, his voice steeped in compassion, contributed, "Take comfort in knowing that we defended our home with unwavering resolve.

" Together, they sat in shared contemplation, breathing in unison, savoring a moment of respite amid the battlefield's wreckage. The moon cast its gentle glow upon them, illuminating their weary faces while also casting long shadows over their fatigued bodies. As the echoes of the battle faded, a realization dawned upon them.

The time of guardianship had concluded, and a new day awaited. Nathan spoke softly, "The battle is over, and our time as guardians has come to an end. It's time for us to return home to Ember Bay." With those words, they prepared to embark on the journey back to the haven they valiantly defended, the bond forged in battle forever etched in their hearts.

THE END.

About the Author.

Dear Reader,
Born in the vibrant city of London in 1962, my journey has been one of constant movement and growth. From my first job at the tender age of 17, I've embraced the twists and turns of life with open arms. In 2021, I crossed the Atlantic to start a new chapter in the United States, bringing with me a lifetime of experiences and stories.

It was amidst this backdrop of change that inspiration struck, and the seeds of my book were sown. This book is more than just words on paper—it's a piece of my soul, a narrative tapestry woven from the threads of my life's adventures.
As you turn each page, I invite you to embark on this journey with me. May the story within resonate with you, as it has with me.

Warm regards,
George London.